[illegible]**berts** is the *New York Times* bes[illegible] of more than one hundred and ninety novels. A born storyteller, she creates a blend of warmth, humour and poignancy that speaks directly to her readers and has earned her almost every award for excellence in her field. The youngest of five children, Nora Roberts lives in western Maryland. She has two sons.

Visit her website at www.noraroberts.com

Also available by Nora Roberts

THE MACKADE BROTHERS
The Return of Rafe MacKade
The Pride of Jared MacKade
The Heart of Devin MacKade
The Fall of Shane MacKade

NIGHT TALES
Night Shift
Night Shadow
Nightshade
Night Smoke
Night Shield

THE O'HURLEYS
The Last Honest Woman
Dance to the Piper
Skin Deep
Without a Trace

THE STANISLASKIS
Taming Natasha
Falling for Rachel
Luring a Lady
Convincing Alex
Waiting for Nick
Considering Kate

THE CALHOUN WOMEN
The Calhoun Sisters
For the Love of Lilah
Suzanna's Surrender
Megan's Mate

CORDINA'S ROYAL FAMILY
Affaire Royale
Command Performance
The Playboy Prince
Cordina's Crown Jewel

THE MacGREGORS
Playing the Odds
Tempting Fate
All the Possibilities
One Man's Art
The MacGregors: Daniel & Ian
The MacGregor Brides: Christmas Fairytales
The MacGregor Grooms
The Perfect Neighbour
Rebellion

THE STARS OF MITHRA
Stars
Treasures

THE DONOVAN LEGACY
Captivated
Entranced
Charmed

Time and Again
Reflections
Night Moves
Dance of Dreams
Boundary Lines
Dream Makers
Risky Business
The Welcoming
The Right Path
Partners
The Art of Deception
The Winning Hand
Irish Rebel
The Law is a Lady
Summer Pleasures
Under Summer Skies
California Summer
Hazy Summer Nights
Summer Dreams
The Magic of Home
Catching Snowflakes
Christmas Magic
Mistletoe and Snow
Dual Image
Unfinished Business
Mind Over Matter
Best Laid Plans
Lessons Learned
Summer With You
Snow is Falling
Summer in the Sun
Loving Jack

Nora Roberts

Summer in the Sun

MILLS & BOON

First Published in Great Britain 2016
By Mills & Boon, an imprint of HarperCollins*Publishers*
1 London Bridge Street, London, SE1 9GF

ISBN: 978-0-263-92218-9

29-0616

Our policy is to use papers that are natural, renewable and recyclable products and made from wood grown in sustainable forests. The logging and manufacturing processes conform to the legal environmental regulations of the country of origin.

Printed and bound
by CPI Group (UK) Ltd, Croydon, CRO 4YY

Impulse

Chapter 1

She knew it was crazy. That was what she liked best about it. It was crazy, ridiculous, impractical and totally out of character. And she was having the time of her life. From the balcony of her hotel suite Rebecca could see the sweep of the beach, the glorious blue of the Ionian Sea, blushed now with streaks of rose from the setting sun.

Corfu. Even the name sounded mysterious, exciting, glamorous. And she was here, really here. Practical, steady-as-a-rock Rebecca Malone, who had never traveled more than five hundred miles from Philadelphia, was in Greece. Not just in Greece, she thought with a grin, but on the exotic island of Corfu, in one of the most exclusive resorts in Europe.

First-class, she thought as she leaned out to let the sweet breeze ruffle over her face. As long as it lasted, she was going first-class.

Her boss had thought she was suffering from temporary insanity. Edwin McDowell of McDowell, Jableki and Kline was never going to understand why a promising young CPA would resign from her position with one of the top accounting firms in Philadelphia. She'd made a good salary, she'd enjoyed excellent benefits, and she'd even had a small window in her office.

Friends and associates had wondered if she'd suffered a breakdown. After all, it wasn't normal, and it certainly wasn't Rebecca's style to quit a solid, well-paying job without the promise of a better one.

But she'd given her two weeks' notice, cleared out her desk and had cheerfully walked out into the world of the unemployed.

When she'd sold her condo and then in one frantic week, auctioned off every possession she owned—every stick of furniture, every pot and pan and appliance—they'd been certain she'd gone over the edge.

Rebecca had never felt saner.

She owned nothing that didn't fit in a suitcase. She no longer had any tax-deferred investments or retirement plans. She'd cashed in her certificates of deposit, and the home entertainment center she'd thought she couldn't live without was now gracing someone else's home.

It had been more than six weeks since she'd even looked at an adding machine.

For the first—and perhaps the only—time in her life, she was totally free. There were no responsibilities, no pressures, no hurried gulps of cold coffee. She hadn't packed an alarm clock. She no longer owned one. Crazy? No. Rebecca shook her head and laughed into the breeze. For as long as it lasted, she was going to grab life with both hands and see what it had to offer.

Aunt Jeannie's death had been her turning point. It had

come so suddenly, so unexpectedly, leaving Rebecca without any family. Aunt Jeannie had worked hard for most of her sixty-five years, always punctual, always responsible. Her position as head librarian had been her whole life. She'd never missed a day, never failed to do her duty. Her bills had been paid on time. Her promises had always been kept.

More than once Rebecca had been told she took after her mother's older sister. She was twenty-four, but she was—had been—as solid and sturdy as her maiden aunt. Two months into retirement, two months after dear Aunt Jeannie began to make plans to travel, to enjoy the rewards she'd worked so hard to earn, she was gone.

After Rebecca's grief had come the anger, then the frustration, then slowly, the realization that she was traveling the same straight road. She worked, she slept, she fixed well-balanced meals that she ate alone. She had a small circle of friends who knew she could be counted on in a crisis. Rebecca would always find the best and most practical answer. Rebecca would never drop her own problems in your lap—because she didn't have any. Rebecca, bless her, was a port in any storm.

She hated it, and she'd begun to hate herself. She had to do something.

And she was doing it.

It wasn't running away as much as it was breaking free. All her life she'd done what was expected of her and tried to make as few waves as possible while doing it. All through school a crushing shyness had kept her more comfortable with her books than with other teenagers. In college a need to succeed and justify her aunt's faith had locked her tightly into her studies.

She had always been good with figures—logical, thorough, patient. It had been easy, perhaps too easy, to pour herself into that one area, because there, and really only there, had she felt confident.

Now she was going to discover Rebecca Malone. In the weeks or months of freedom she had, she wanted to learn everything there was to know about the woman within. Perhaps there wasn't a butterfly inside the cocoon she'd wrapped herself in so comfortably, but whatever she found—whoever she found—Rebecca hoped she would enjoy her, like her, perhaps even respect her.

When the money ran out, she'd get another job and go back to being plain, practical Rebecca. Until that time she was rich, rootless and ready for surprises.

She was also hungry.

Stephen saw her the moment she entered the restaurant. It wasn't that she was particularly striking. Beautiful women passed through the world every day and they usually warranted a glance. But there was something about the way this one walked, as if she were ready for anything, even looking forward to it. He stopped, and because business was slow at this hour he took a second, longer look.

She was tall for a woman, and more angular than slender. Her skin was pale, and that made him think she had only just arrived at the resort or was shy of the sun. The white sundress that left her shoulders and back bare accented the lack of color and gave dramatic contrast to her short cap of raven hair.

She paused, then seemed to take a deep breath. Stephen could almost hear her satisfied sigh. Then she smiled at the headwaiter, and followed him to her table, tossing her head back, so that her hair, which she wore arrow-straight, swung away from her chin.

A nice face, Stephen concluded. Bright, intelligent, eager. Especially the eyes. They were pale, an almost translucent gray. But there was nothing pale in their expression. She smiled at the waiter again, then laughed and looked around the restaurant. She looked as if she'd never been happier in her life.

She saw him. When Rebecca's gaze first skimmed over the man leaning against the bar, her automatic shyness kicked in and had her looking away. Attractive men had stared at her before—though it wasn't exactly a daily event. She'd never been able to handle it with the aplomb—or even cynicism—of most of her contemporaries. To cover her momentary embarrassment, she lifted her menu.

He hadn't meant to linger more than a few moments longer, but the impulse came suddenly. Stephen flicked a hand at the waiter and had him scurrying over, nodding quickly at Stephen's murmured request and hurrying off. When he returned it was to deliver a bottle of champagne to Rebecca's table.

"Compliments of Mr. Nickodemus."

"Oh." Rebecca followed the waiter's gaze over to the man by the bar. "Well, I—" She brought herself up short before she could stammer. A sophisticated woman wouldn't stutter over a gift of champagne, she reminded herself. She'd accept it graciously, with dignity. And maybe—if she wasn't a complete fool—she'd relax enough to flirt with the man who offered it.

Stephen watched the expressions pass across her face. Fascinating, he mused, and realized that the vague boredom he'd been feeling had vanished. When she lifted her head and smiled at him, he had no idea that her heart was pounding. He saw only a casual invitation, and he answered it.

He wasn't just attractive, Rebecca realized as he crossed to her table. He was gorgeous. Eye-popping, mouth-dropping gorgeous. She had an image of Apollo and ancient Greek warriors. Thick blond hair streaked by the sun fell over the collar of his shirt. Smooth, bronzed skin was marred—and somehow enhanced—by a faint scar under his jawline. A strong jaw, she thought. A strong face, with the darkest, deepest blue eyes she'd ever seen.

"Good evening, I'm Stephen Nickodemus." His voice wasn't accented, it was rounded, rich. He might have come from anywhere. Perhaps it was that, more than anything else, that intrigued her.

Lecturing herself on poise and image, she lifted her hand. "Hello. I'm Rebecca, Rebecca Malone." She felt a quick flutter when he brushed his lips over her knuckles. Feeling foolish, she drew her hand away and balled it in her lap. "Thank you for the champagne."

"It seemed to suit your mood." He studied her, wondering why he was getting such a mix of signals. "You are by yourself?"

"Yes." Perhaps it was a mistake to admit it, but if she was going to live life to the fullest she had to take some risks. The restaurant wasn't crowded, but they were hardly alone. Take the plunge, she told herself, and tried another smile. "The least I can do is offer you a glass."

Stephen took the seat across from her, brushing the waiter aside to pour the wine himself. "You are American?"

"It shows."

"No. Actually, I thought you were French until you spoke."

"Did you?" That pleased her. "I've just come from Paris." She had to force herself not to touch her hair. She'd had it cut, with trepidation and delight, in a French salon.

Stephen touched his glass to hers. Her eyes bubbled with life as cheerfully as the wine. "Business?"

"No, just pleasure." What a marvelous word, she thought. *Pleasure.* "It's a wonderful city."

"Yes. Do you go often?"

Rebecca smiled into her glass. "Not often enough. Do you?"

"From time to time."

She nearly sighed at that. Imagine anyone speaking of going to Paris "from time to time." "I nearly stayed longer, but I'd promised myself Greece."

So she was alone, restless, and on the move. Perhaps that was why she had appealed to him, because he was, too. "Is Corfu your first stop?"

"Yes." She sipped at her drink. A part of her still believed it was all a dream. Greece, champagne, the man. "It's beautiful. Much more beautiful than I imagined it could be."

"It's your first trip, then?" He couldn't have said why that pleased him. "How long do you stay?"

"As long as I like." She grinned, savoring the feeling of freedom. "And you?"

He lifted his glass. "Longer, I think, than I had planned." When the waiter appeared at his side, Stephen handed over the menu, then spoke to him in soft, quick Greek. "If you don't object, I'd like to guide you through your first meal on the island."

The old Rebecca would have been too nervous to sit through a meal with a stranger. The new Rebecca took a second, deeper sip of champagne. "I'd love it. Thank you."

It was easy. Easy to sit, to laugh, to sample new and exotic tastes. She forgot that he was a stranger, forgot that the world she was living in now was only temporary. They didn't speak of anything important—only of Paris, and the weather, and the wine. Still, she was sure it was the most interesting conversation of her life. He looked at her when he spoke to her, looked at her as though he were delighted to spend an hour talking of nothing. The last man she'd had dinner with had wanted her to give him a discount when she did his taxes.

Stephen wasn't asking her for anything more than her company for dinner. When he looked at her it seemed unlikely that he'd care if she knew how to fill out Schedule C.

When he suggested a walk along the beach, she agreed without a qualm. What better way to end an evening than a walk in the moonlight?

"I was looking out at this from my window just before dinner." Rebecca stepped out of her shoes, then dangled them from her fingers as she walked. "I didn't think it could look more beautiful than it did at sunset."

"The sea changes, like a woman, in the light." He paused to touch a flame to the end of a slim cigar. "So men are drawn to her."

"Are you? Drawn to the sea?"

"I've spent my time on her. I fished in these waters as a boy."

She'd learned at dinner that he'd grown up traveling the islands with his father. "It must have been exciting, moving from place to place, seeing new things almost every day."

He shrugged. He'd never been sure whether the restlessness had been born in him or had been a product of his upbringing. "It had its moments."

"I love to travel." Laughing, she tossed her shoes aside, then stepped into the surf. The champagne was making her head swim and the moonlight felt as soft as rain. "I adore it." She laughed again when the spray washed up to dampen her skirts. The Ionian Sea. She was standing in it. "On a night like this I think I'll never go home."

She looked so vibrant, so alive, standing in the surf with her white skirts billowing. "Where's home?"

She glanced over her shoulder. The flirtatious look was totally unplanned and completely devastating. "I haven't decided. I want to swim." On impulse, she dived into the surf.

Stephen's heart stopped when she disappeared. He'd already kicked off his shoes and started forward when she rose up again. For a second time, his heart stopped.

She was laughing, her face lifted to the moonlight. Water cascaded from her hair, from her skin. The drops that clung to her were the only jewels she wore. Beautiful? No, she wasn't beautiful. She was electric.

"It's wonderful. Cool and soft and wonderful."

With a shake of his head, he stepped in far enough to take her hand and pull her toward shore. She was a little mad, perhaps, but engagingly so. "Are you always so impulsive?"

"I'm working on it. Aren't you?" She combed her hand through her dripping hair. "Or do you always send champagne to strange women?"

"Either way I answer that could be trouble. Here." He shrugged out of his jacket and draped it over her shoulders.

Unframed, washed clean, her face glowed in the moonlight. There was a graceful kind of strength in it, to the sweep of cheekbone, the slightly pointed chin. Delicate—except for the eyes. One look there showed power, a power that was still. "You're irresistible, Rebecca."

She stared at him, confused all over again, as he gathered the neck of the jacket close around her throat. "I'm wet," she managed.

"And beautiful." With his hands still on the jacket, he brought her toward him. "And fascinating."

That made her laugh again. "I don't think so, but thanks. I'm glad you sent me the champagne and guided me through my first meal." Her nerves began to jangle. His eyes stayed on hers, journeying only once to her mouth, which was still damp from the sea. Their bodies were close, close enough to brush. Rebecca began to shiver, and she knew it had nothing to do with wet clothes and the breeze.

"I should go in…change my dress."

There was something about her. The impulsiveness, the easy flirtatiousness, hid an unmistakable innocence that baffled and attracted him. Whatever it was, he wanted more.

"I'll see you again."

"Yes." She prayed for her heartbeat to slow. "It's not a very big island."

He smiled at that, slowly. She felt, with a mixture of relief and regret, the relaxation of his hands. "Tomorrow. I have business early. I'll be done by eleven, if that suits you. I'll show you Corfu."

"All right." Better judgment and nerves be damned. She wanted to go with him. "I'll meet you in the lobby." Carefully, because she suddenly wasn't sure she could manage it, she stepped back. Moonlight silhouetted him against the sea. “Good night, Stephen.”

She forgot to be sophisticated and dashed toward the hotel.

He watched her go. She puzzled him, puzzled him as no woman had since he’d been a boy and too young to understand that a woman was not meant to be understood. And he wanted her. That wasn’t new, but the desire had come with surprising speed and surprising force.

Rebecca Malone might have started out as an impulse, but she was now a mystery. One he intended to solve. With a little laugh, he bent to scoop up the shoes she’d forgotten. He hadn’t felt quite so alive in months.

Chapter 2

Stephen wasn't the kind of man who rearranged his schedule to spend the day with a woman. Especially a woman he barely knew. He was a wealthy man, but he was also a busy man, driven by both pride and ambition to maintain a high level of involvement in all his projects. He shouldered responsibility well and had learned to enjoy the benefits of hard work and dedication.

His time on Corfu wasn't free—or rather hadn't been planned as free. Mixing business and pleasure wasn't his style. He pursued both, separately, with utter concentration. Yet he found himself juggling appointments, meetings, conference calls, in order to have the afternoon open for Rebecca.

He supposed any man would want to get to know a woman who flirted easily over a champagne flute one moment and dived fully dressed into the sea the next.

"I've postponed your meeting with Theoharis until five-thirty this evening." Stephen's secretary scribbled on a notepad she had resting on her lap. "He will meet you for early cocktails in the suite. I've arranged for hors d'oeuvres and a bottle of ouzo."

"Always efficient, Elana."

She smiled and tucked a fall of dark hair behind her ear. "I try."

When Stephen rose to pace to the window, she folded her hands and waited. She had worked for him for five years, she admired his energy and his business acumen, and—fortunately for both of them—had long since gotten over an early crush. There was often speculation about their personal relationship, but though he could be friendly—even kind when it suited him—with Stephen, business was business.

"Contact Mithos in Athens. Have him telex that report by the end of the day. And I want to hear from Lereau by five, Paris time."

"Shall I call and give him a nudge?"

"If you think it's necessary." Restless, he dug his hands in his pockets. Where had this sudden discontent come from? he wondered. He was wealthy, successful, and free, as always, to move from place to place. As he stared out at the sea, he remembered the scent of Rebecca's skin. "Send flowers to Rebecca Malone's suite. Wildflowers, nothing formal. This afternoon."

Elana made a note, hoping she'd get a look at this Rebecca Malone before long. She had already heard through the grapevine that Stephen had had dinner with an American woman. "And the card?"

He wasn't a man for poetry. "Just my name."

"Anything else?"

"Yes." He turned and offered her a half smile. "Take some time off. Go to the beach."

Pad in hand, she rose. "I'll be sure to work it in. Enjoy your afternoon, Stephen."

He intended to. As she left him, Stephen glanced at his watch. It was fifteen minutes before eleven. There was work he could do to fill in the time, a quick call that could be made. Instead, he picked up Rebecca's shoes.

After three tries, Rebecca settled on an outfit. She didn't have an abundance of clothes, because she'd preferred to spend her funds on travel. But she had splurged here and there on her route through Europe. No tidy CPA suits, she thought as she tied a vivid fuchsia sash at the waist of her sapphire-colored cotton pants. No sensible shoes or pastel blouses. The last shock of color came from a primrose-hued blouse cut generously to layer over a skinny tank top in the same shade as the slacks.

The combination delighted her, if only because her firm had preferred quiet colors and clean lines.

She had no idea where she was going, and she didn't care.

It was a beautiful day, even though she'd awoken with a dull headache from the champagne, and the disorientation that went with it. A light, early breakfast on her terrace and a quick dip in the sea had cleared both away. She still had trouble believing that she could lounge through a morning as she pleased—and that she'd spent the evening with a man she'd just met.

Aunt Jeannie would have tut-tutted and reminded her of the dangers of being a woman alone. Some of her friends would have been shocked, others envious. But they would all have been astonished that steady Rebecca had strolled in the moonlight with a gorgeous man with a scar on his jawline and eyes like velvet.

If she hadn't had his jacket as proof, she might have thought she'd dreamed it. There had never been anything wrong with her imagination—just the application of it. Often she'd pictured herself in an exotic place with an exotic man, with moonlight and music. Imagined herself, she remembered. And then she'd turned on her calculator and gotten down to business.

But she hadn't dreamed this. She could still remember the giddy, half-terrified feeling that had swarmed through her when he'd gathered her close. When his mouth had been only an inch from hers and the sea and the champagne had roared in her head.

What if he had kissed her? What tastes would she have found? Rich, strong ones, she mused, almost able to savor them as she traced a fingertip over her lips. After just one evening she was absolutely certain there would be nothing lukewarm about Stephen Nickodemus. She wasn't nearly so certain about Rebecca.

She probably would have fumbled and blushed and stammered. With a shake of her head, she pulled a brush through her hair. Exciting men didn't tumble all over themselves to kiss neat, practical-minded women.

But he'd asked to see her again.

Rebecca wasn't certain whether she was disappointed or relieved that he hadn't pressed his advantage and kissed her. She'd been kissed before, held before, of course. But she had a feeling—a very definite feeling—that it wouldn't be the same with Stephen. He might make her want more, offer more, than she had with any other man.

Crossing bridges too soon, she decided as she checked the contents of her big straw bag. She wasn't going to have an affair with him, or with anyone. Even the new, improved Rebecca Malone wasn't the type for a casual affair. But maybe— She caught her lower lip between her teeth. If the time was right she might have a romance she'd remember long after she left Greece.

For now, she was ready, but it was much too early to go down. It would hardly make her look like a well-traveled woman of the world if she popped down to the lobby and paced for ten minutes. This was her fantasy, after all. She didn't want him to think she was inexperienced and overeager.

Only the knock on the door prevented her from changing her mind about her outfit one more time.

"Hello." Stephen studied her for a moment, unsmiling. He'd nearly been certain he'd exaggerated, but she was just as vibrant, just as exciting, in the morning as she had been in the moonlight. He held out her shoes. "I thought you might need these."

She laughed, remembering her impulsive dunk in the sea. "I didn't realize I'd left them on the beach. Come in a minute." With a neatness ingrained in her from childhood, she turned to take them to the bedroom closet. "I'm ready to go if you are."

Stephen lifted a brow. He preferred promptness, but he never expected it in anyone but a business associate. "I've got a Jeep waiting. Some of the roads are rough."

"Sounds great." Rebecca came out again, carrying her bag and a flat-brimmed straw hat. She handed Stephen his jacket, neatly folded. "I forgot to give this back to you last night." Should she offer to have it cleaned? she wondered when he only continued to look at her. Fiddling with the strap of her bag, she decided against it. "Does taking pictures bother you?"

"No, why?"

"Good, because I take lots of them. I can't seem to stop myself."

She wasn't kidding. As Stephen drove up into the hills, she took shots of everything. Sheep, tomato plants, olive groves and straggly sage. He stopped so that she could walk out near the edge of a cliff and look down at a small village huddled near the sea.

She wouldn't be able to capture it on film; she wasn't clever enough. But she knew she'd never forget that light, so pure, so clear, or the contrast between the orange tiled roofs and the low white-washed walls and the deep, dangerous blue of the water that flung itself against the weathered rock that rose into harsh crags. A stork, legs tucked, glided over the water, where fishing boats bobbed.

There were nets drying on the beach and children playing. Flowers bloomed and tangled where the wind had planted them, more spectacular than any planned arrangement could ever be.

"It's beautiful." Her throat tightened with emotion, and with a longing she couldn't have defined. "So calm. You imagine women baking black bread and the men coming home smelling of fish and the sea. It looks as though it hasn't changed in a hundred years."

"Very little." He glanced down himself, surprised and more than a little pleased that she would be touched by something so simple. "We cling to antiquity."

"I haven't seen the Acropolis yet, but I don't think it could be any more spectacular than this." She lifted her face, delighted by the way the wind whipped at it. Here, high above the sea, she absorbed everything—the salty, rough-edged bite of the wind, the clarity of color and sound, and the man beside her. Letting her camera dangle from its strap, she turned to him. "I haven't thanked you for taking the time to show me all of this."

He took her hand, not to raise it to his lips, just to hold it. It was a link he hadn't known he wanted. "I'm enjoying seeing the familiar through someone else's eyes. Your eyes."

Suddenly the edge of the cliff seemed too close, the sun too hot. Could he do that just by touching her? With an effort, Rebecca smiled, keeping her voice light. "If you ever come to Philadelphia, I'll do the same for you."

It was odd. She'd looked almost frightened for a moment. Fragile and frightened. Stephen had always carefully avoided women who were easily bruised. "I'll consider that a promise."

They continued to drive, over roads that jarred and climbed and twisted. She saw her first of the *agrimi*, the wild goat of Greece, and the rocky pastures dotted with sturdy sheep. And everywhere, rich and defiant, was the intense color of flowers.

He didn't complain when she asked him to stop so that she could snap pictures of tiny blue star blossoms that pushed their way through cracks in the rock. He listened to her delight as she framed a thick, thorny stem topped with a ragged yellow flower. It made him realize, and regret, that it had been years since he'd taken the time to look closely at the small, vital things that grew around him.

He looked now at Rebecca standing in the sunlight,

her hat fluttering around her face and her laugh dancing on the air.

Often the road clung to cliffs that plunged dizzily into the sea. Rebecca, who was too timid to fight rush-hour traffic, found it exhilarating.

She felt almost like another person. She *was* another person, she thought, laughing as she held on to her hat to keep the wind from snatching it away.

"I love it!" she shouted over the wind and the noise of the engine. "It's wild and old and incredible. Like no place I've ever been."

Still laughing, she lifted her camera and snapped his picture as he drove. He wore sunglasses with amber lenses and had a cigar clamped between his teeth. The wind blew through his hair and chased the smoke behind them. He stopped the Jeep, took the camera and snapped a picture of her in turn.

"Hungry?"

She dragged her tousled hair back from her face. "Starving."

He leaned over to open her door. A current passed through her, sharp and electric, strong enough to make him pause with his arm across her body and his face close to hers. It was there again, he thought as he waited and watched. The awareness, ripe and seductive. And the innocence, as alluring as it was contradictory. In a test—a test for both of them—he lifted a hand to stroke her cheek. It was as soft as her scent.

"Are you afraid of me, Rebecca?"

"No." That was true; she was nearly sure of it. "Should I be?"

He didn't smile. Through the amber lenses she saw that

his eyes were very intense. "I'm not entirely sure." When he pulled away he heard her release an unsteady breath. He wasn't feeling completely steady himself. "We'll have to walk a little first."

Confused, her mind churning, she stepped out onto the dirt path. A woman on a simple date didn't tremble every time a man got close, Rebecca told herself as Stephen lifted the picnic basket out of the back. She was behaving like a teenager, not a grown woman.

Troubled by his own thoughts, Stephen stopped beside her. He hesitated, then held out a hand. It felt good, simply good, when she put hers in it.

They walked through an olive grove in a companionable silence while the sun streamed down on dusty leaves and rocky ground. There was no sound of the sea here, but when the wind was right she could hear the screech of a gull far away. The island was small, but here it seemed uninhabited.

"I haven't had a picnic in years." Rebecca spread the cloth. "And never in an olive grove." She glanced around, wanting to remember every leaf and pebble. "Are we trespassing?"

"No." Stephen took a bottle of white wine from the basket. Rebecca left him to it and started rummaging in search of food.

"Do you know the owner?"

"I'm the owner." He drew the cork with a gentle pop.

"Oh." She looked around again. It should have occurred to her that he would own something impressive, different, exciting. "It sounds romantic. Owning an olive grove."

He lifted a brow. He owned a number of them, but he had never thought of them as romantic. They were simply profitable. He offered her a glass, then tapped it with his own. “To romance, then.”

She swept down her lashes, battling shyness. To Stephen, the gesture was only provocative. “I hope you’re hungry,” she began, knowing she was talking too fast. “It all looks wonderful.” She took a quick sip of wine to ease her dry throat, then set it aside to finish unpacking the basket.

There were sweet black olives as big as a man’s thumb, and there was a huge slab of sharp cheese. There were cold lamb and hunks of bread, and fruit so fresh it could have been just plucked from the stem.

Gradually she began to relax again.

“You’ve told me very little about yourself.” Stephen topped off her wine and watched her bite into a ripe red plum. “I know little more than that you come from Philadelphia and enjoy traveling.”

What could she tell him? A man like him was bound to be bored with the life story of the painfully ordinary Rebecca Malone. Lies had never come easily to her, so she skirted between fact and fiction. “There’s little more. I grew up in Philadelphia. I lost both of my parents when I was a teenager, and I lived with my aunt Jeannie. She was very dear, and she made the loss bearable.”

“It’s painful.” He flicked his lighter at the end of a cigar, remembering not only the pain, but also the fury he had felt when his father had died and left him orphaned at sixteen. “It steals childhood.”

“Yes.” So he understood that. It made her feel close to him, close and comfortable. “Maybe that’s why I like to travel. Every time you see a new place you can be a child again.”

“So you don’t look for roots?”

She glanced at him then. He was leaning back against the trunk of a tree, smoking lazily, watching carefully. "I don't know what I'm looking for."

"Is there a man?"

She moved her shoulders, determined not to be embarrassed. "No."

He took her hand, drawing her closer. "No one?"

"No, I…" She wasn't certain what she would have said, but could say nothing at all when he turned her palm upward and pressed his lips to its center. She felt the fire burst there, in her hand, then race everywhere.

"You're very responsive, Rebecca." He lowered her hand but kept it in his. He could feel the heat, but he wasn't sure whether it had sprung to her skin or to his own. "If there's no one, the men in your Philadelphia must be very slow."

"I've been too…busy."

His lips curved at that. There was a tremor in her voice, and there was passion in her eyes. "Busy?"

"Yes." Afraid she'd make a fool of herself, she drew her hand back. "This was wonderful." Trying to calm herself, she pushed a hand through her hair. "You know what I need?"

"No. Tell me."

"Another picture." She sprang to her feet and, steadier, grinned. "A memento of my first picnic in an olive grove. Let's see…you can stand right over there. The sun's good in front of that tree, and I should be able to frame in that section of the grove."

Amused, Stephen tapped out his cigar. "How much more film do you have?"

"This is the last roll—but I have scads back at the hotel." She flicked him a quick laughing glance. "I warned you."

"So you did." Competent hands, he thought as he watched her focus and adjust. He hadn't realized he could be as attracted to competence as he was to beauty. She mumbled to herself, tossing her head back so that her hair swung, then settled. His stomach tightened without warning.

Good God, he wanted her. She'd done nothing to make him burn and strain this way. He couldn't accuse her of taunting or teasing, and yet…he felt taunted. He felt teased. For the first time in his life he felt totally seduced by a woman who had done nothing more than give him a few smiles and a little companionship.

Even now she was chattering away as she secured her camera to the limb of a tree. Talking easily, as though they were just friends, as though she felt nothing more than a light, unimportant affection. But he'd seen it. Stephen felt his blood heat as he remembered the quick flash of arousal he'd seen on her face. He'd see it again. And more.

"I'm going to set the timer," Rebecca went on, blissfully unaware of Stephen's thoughts. "All you have to do is stand there. Once I get this damn thing set, I'm going to run over so it'll take one of both—There." She interrupted herself, crossed her fingers and ran to Stephen's side in a dash. "Unless I messed up, it'll snap all by itself in—"

The rest of the words slid down her throat as he crushed her against him and captured her mouth.

Chapter 3

Heat. Light. Speed. Rebecca felt them, felt each separate, distinct sensation. Urgency. Demand. Impatience. She tasted them, as clearly as wild honey, on his lips. Though she'd never experienced it, she had known exactly what it would be like to be with him, mouth to mouth and need to need.

In an instant the world had narrowed from what could be seen and understood to a pure, seamless blanket of emotion. It cloaked her, not softly, not in comfort, but tightly, hotly, irresistibly. Caught between fear and delight, she lifted a hand to his cheek.

God, she was sweet. Even as he dragged her closer, aroused by the simplicity of her acceptance, he was struck by—disarmed by—her sweetness. There had been a hesitation, almost too brief to be measured, before her lips had parted beneath his. Parted, invited, accepted.

There was a sigh, so soft it could barely be heard, as she stroked her hands up his back to his shoulders. Curious, simple, generous. A man could drown in such sweetness, fall prisoner to such pliancy. And be saved by it. Beneath the patterned shade of the olive tree, she gave him more than passion. She gave him hope.

Charmed, he murmured some careless Greek phrase lovers might exchange. The words meant nothing to her, but the sound of them on the still air, the feel of them stroking across her lips…seduction. Glorious seduction.

Pleasure burst in her blood, in her head, in her heart, thousands of tiny bubbles of it, until she was straining against him.

The quiet explosion rocked him. It tightened his chest, fuddled his mind. She fitted into his arms as if she'd been born for him. As if, somehow, they had known each other before, loved before, hungered before. Something seemed to erupt between them, something molten, powerful, dangerous. But it wasn't new. It was ancient, a whispering echo of ageless passions.

She began to tremble. How could this be so right, so familiar? It wasn't possible to feel safe and threatened at the same time. But she did. She clung to him while a dim, floating image danced through her head. She had kissed him before. Just like this. As her mind spun, she heard her own mindless murmurs answer his. As freely, as inescapably as the sun poured light, response flowed from her. She couldn't stop it. Frightened by her sudden loss of control, she struggled against him, against herself.

He slipped his hands up to her shoulders, but not to free her, to look at her. To look at how their coming together had changed her. It had changed him. Passion had made her eyes heavy, seductive. Fear had clouded them. Her lips were full, softened and parted by his. Her breath shivered through them. Under his hands he could feel the heat of her skin and the quick, involuntary trembling of her muscles.

No pretense here, he decided as he studied her. He was holding both innocence and delight in his hands.

"Stephen, I—"

"Again."

Then his face filled her vision and she was lost.

Differently. Should she have known that one man could hold one woman in so many different ways? That one man could kiss one woman with such stunning variety? There was gentleness now, as familiar and as novel as the urgency. His lips persuaded rather than demanded. They savored instead of devouring. Her surrender came as quietly, and as unmistakably, as her earlier passion. The trembling stopped; the fear vanished. With a complete trust that surprised them both, she leaned against him, giving.

More aroused by her serenity than by the storm that had come before, Stephen pulled back. He had to, or what had begun would finish without either of them saying a word. As he swore and pulled out a cigar, Rebecca placed a hand on the olive tree for support.

Moments, she thought. It had been only moments, and yet she felt as though years had passed, racing backward or forward, perhaps spinning in circles. In a place like this, with a man like this, what difference did it make what year it was? What century?

Half-terrified, she lifted a hand to her lips. Despite her fear, they curved under her touch. She could still taste him. Still feel him. And nothing, nothing, would ever be quite the same again.

He stared out at the rough and dusty land he'd known

as a boy, and beyond, to the stark, tumbling rocks where he and other wild things had climbed.

What was he doing with her? Furious with himself, he drew on the cigar. What was he feeling? It was new, and far from comfortable. And it was comfort he preferred, he reminded himself. Comfort and freedom. Bringing himself under control, he turned to her again, determined to treat what had happened as a man should—lightly.

She just stood there, with the sun and the shade falling over her. There was neither recrimination nor invitation in her eyes. She didn't flinch or step forward, but merely stood, watching him with the faintest of smiles, as if… As if, Stephen realized, she knew what questions he was asking himself—and the answers.

"It grows late."

She felt the ache and fought not to let it show on her face. "I guess you're right." She dragged a hand through her hair—it was the first sign of her agitation—then walked over to pick up her camera. "I should have a picture to remember all this by," she said, forcing brightness into her voice. Her breath caught when his fingers closed over her arm and whirled her around.

"Who are you?" he demanded. "What are you?"

"I don't know what you mean." The emotion burst out before she could stop it. "I don't know what you want."

With one jerk he had her tumbling against him. "You know what I want."

Her heart was in her throat, beating wildly. She found it strange that it was not fear but desire that she felt. She hadn't known she was capable of feeling a need that was so unreasonable, so reckless. It was almost purifying to experience it, and to see it mirrored in his eyes.

"It takes more than one afternoon." Didn't it? Her voice rose as she tried to convince herself. "It takes more than a picnic and a walk in the moonlight for me."

"One moment the temptress, the next the outraged innocent. Do you do it to intrigue me, Rebecca?" She shook her head, and his fingers tightened. "It works," he murmured. "You've hardly been out of my mind since I first saw you. I want to make love with you, here, in the sun."

Color flooded her face, not because she was embarrassed, but because she could imagine it, perfectly. And then what? Carefully she leveled her breathing. Whatever impulses she had followed, whatever bridges she had burned, she still needed answers.

"No." It cost her to go against her own needs and say it. "Not when I'm unsure and you're angry." She took a deep breath and kept her eyes on him. "You're hurting me, Stephen. I don't think you mean to."

Slowly he released her arm. He was angry, furious, but not at her refusal. The anger stemmed from the need she pulled from him, a need that had come too fast and too strong for him to channel. "We'll go back."

Rebecca merely nodded, then knelt to gather the remains of the picnic.

He was a busy man, much too busy to brood about a woman he barely knew and didn't understand at all. That was what Stephen told himself. He had reports to read, calls to make and paperwork—which he had both a talent and a distaste for—to deal with. A couple of simple kisses weren't enough to take a man's mind off his work.

But there hadn't been anything simple about them. Disgusted, Stephen pushed away from his desk and wandered to the terrace doors. He'd left them open because the breeze, and the fragrances it brought, helped him forget he was obligated to be inside.

For days he'd worked his way through his responsibilities, trying to ignore the nagging itch at the back of his mind—the itch that was Rebecca. There was no reason for him to stay on Corfu. He could have handled his business in Athens, or Crete, or in London, for that matter. Still, he'd made no plans to leave, though he'd also made no attempt to approach her.

She…concerned him, he decided. To be drawn to an attractive woman was as natural as breathing. To have the attraction cause discomfort, confusion, even annoyance was anything but natural. A taste of her hadn't been enough. Yet he hesitated.

She was…mysterious. Perhaps that was why he couldn't push her from his mind. On the surface she appeared to be an attractive, free-spirited woman who grabbed life with both hands. Yet there were undercurrents. The hints of innocence, of shyness. The sweetness. The complexity of her kept him wondering, thinking, imagining.

Perhaps that was her trick. Women had them…were entitled to them. It was a waste of time to begrudge them their illusions and their feminine magic. More than a waste of time, it was foolish, when a man could enjoy the benefits. But there was more, and somehow less, to Rebecca than innate feminine magic.

When he had kissed her, though it had been the first time, it had been like coming back to a lover, to a love, after a painful separation. When his lips had found hers, something had filled him. A heat, an impatience, a knowledge.

He knew her, knew more than her name and her background and the color of her eyes. He knew all of her. Yet he knew nothing.

Fantasies, he told himself. He didn't have time for them. Leaning a hip against the railing, he lit a cigar and watched the sea.

As always, it pulled at him, bringing back memories of a childhood that had been careless and too short. There were times, rare times, when he allowed himself to regret. Times when the sun was a white flash of heat and the water was blue and endless. His father had taught him a great deal. How to fish, how to see both beauty and excitement in new places, how to drink like a man.

Fifteen years, Stephen thought, a smile ghosting around his mouth. He still missed him, missed the companionship, the robust laughter. They had been friends, as well as parent and child, with a bond as easy, and as strong, as any Stephen had ever known. But his father had died as he would have wanted to, at sea and in his prime.

He would have taken one look at Rebecca, rolled his eyes, kissed his fingers and urged his son to enjoy. But Stephen wasn't the boy he had once been. He was more cautious, more aware of consequences. If a man dived into the sea, he should know the depth and the currents.

Then he saw her, coming from the sea. Water ran down her body, glistening in the strong sun, sparkling against skin that had warmed in the last few days to a dusky gold. As he looked, as he wanted, he felt his muscles clench, one by one, shoulders, stomach, thighs. Without his being aware, his fingers tightened, snapping the cigar in two. He hadn't known that desire could arouse a reaction so akin to anger.

She stopped, and though he knew she was unaware of

him, she might easily have been posing. To taunt, to tease, to invite. As drops of water slid down her, she stretched, lifting her face skyward. Her skimpy suit rested low over her boyish hips, shifted enticingly over the subtle curve of her breasts. At that moment, she was totally absorbed in her own pleasure and as unselfconscious as any young animal standing in the sun. Nothing had ever been so alluring.

Then, slowly, seductively, she combed her fingers through her hair, smiling, as if she enjoyed the wet, silky feel of it. Watching her, he felt the air back up and clog in his lungs. He could have murdered her for it, for making him want so unreasonably what he did not yet understand.

She plucked a long, mannish T-shirt from a straw bag and, after tugging it on, strolled barefoot into the hotel.

He stood there, waiting for the need to pass. But it built, layered with an ache that infuriated him and a longing that baffled him.

He should ignore her. Instinct warned him that if he didn't his life would never be the same. She was nothing more than a distraction, a momentary impulse he should resist. He should turn away, go back to work. He had commitments, obligations, and no time to waste on fantasies. With an oath, he tossed the broken cigar over the rail.

There were times, he thought, when a man had to trust in fate and dive in.

Chapter 4

Rebecca had hardly shut the door behind her before she turned back to answer the knock. The sun and the water had left her pleasantly tired, but all thoughts of a lazy catnap vanished when she saw Stephen.

He looked wonderful. Cool, a little windblown, intense. For days she'd wondered about him, wondered and wished. She felt her pulse skip and her lips curve just at the sight of him. With an effort, she kept her voice breezy.

"Hello. I wasn't sure you were still on the island."

It wasn't really a lie, she told herself. An offhand inquiry had assured her that Mr. Nickodemus hadn't checked out, but she hadn't actually seen him.

"I saw you come up from the beach."

"Oh." Unconsciously she tugged at the hem of her cover-up. To Stephen the small gesture was one more contradictory signal. "I can't seem to get enough of the sun and the sea. Would you like to come in?"

By way of an answer he stepped through and shut the

door behind him. It made a very quiet, a very final sound. Rebecca's carefully built poise began to crumble. "I never thanked you for the flowers." She made a gesture indicating the vase near the window, then brought her hands back together and linked them in front of her. "They're still beautiful. I…I thought I might run into you, in the dining room, on the beach, or…" Her words trailed off when he lifted a hand to her hair.

"I've been busy." He watched her eyes, eyes that were as clear as rainwater, blur at the slight touch. "Business."

It was ridiculous, she knew, but she wasn't at all sure she could speak. "If you have to work, I doubt you could pick a more beautiful place."

He stepped closer. She smelled of the water and the sun. "You're enjoying the resort, and the island."

Her hand was in his now, caught lightly. It took only that to make her knees weak. "Yes, very much."

"Perhaps you'd like to see it from a different perspective." Deliberately, wanting to test them both, he lifted her hand to his lips. He grazed her knuckles—it was barely a whisper of contact—and felt the jolt. She felt it, and he could see that she did, so it couldn't just be his imagination. "Spend the day with me tomorrow on my boat."

"What?"

He smiled, delighted with her response. "Will you come with me?"

Anywhere. Astonished, she stepped back. "I haven't any plans."

"Good." He closed the distance between them again. Her hands fluttered up in flustered defense, then settled again when he made no attempt to touch her. "Then I'll make them for you. I'll come for you in the morning. Nine?"

A boat. He'd said something about a boat. Rebecca drew in a deep breath and tried to pull herself together. This wasn't like her—going off into daydreams, feeling weak-kneed, being flooded with waves of desire. And it felt wonderful.

"I'd like that." She gave him what she hoped was an easy woman-of-the-world smile.

"Until tomorrow, then." He started for the door, then turned, a hand on the knob. "Rebecca, don't forget your camera."

She waited until he'd closed the door before she spun in three quick circles.

When Stephen had said "boat," Rebecca had pictured a trim little cabin cruiser. Instead, she stepped onto the glossy mahogany deck of a streamlined hundred-foot yacht.

"You could live on this," Rebecca said, then wished she'd bitten her tongue. But he only laughed.

"I often do."

"Welcome aboard, sir," a white-uniformed man with a British accent said.

"Grady. This is my guest, Miss Malone."

"Ma'am." Grady's cool British reserve didn't flicker for an instant, but Rebecca felt herself being summed up.

"Cast off when you're ready." Stephen took Rebecca's arm. "Would you like a tour?"

"Yes." A yacht. She was on a yacht. It took all her willpower to keep her camera in the bag. "I'd love to see it all."

He took her below, through four elegantly appointed cabins. Her comment about living on board had been said impulsively, but she could see now that it could be done easily, even luxuriously.

Above there was a large glassed-in cabin in which one could stretch out comfortably, out of the sun, and watch the sea, whatever the weather. She had known that there were people who lived like this. Part of her job had been to research and calculate so that those who did paid the government as little as possible. But to be there, to see it, to be surrounded by it, was entirely different from adding figures on paper.

There was a masculine feel to the cabin, to the entire boat—leather, wood, muted colors. There were shelves filled with books and a fully stocked bar, as well as a stereo system.

"All the comforts of home," Rebecca murmured, but she'd noted that there were doors and panels that could be secured in case of rough weather. What would it be like to ride out a storm at sea, to watch the rain lash the windows and feel the deck heave?

She gave a quick gasp when she felt the floor move. Stephen took her arm again to steady her.

"We're under way." Curious, he turned her to face him. "Are you afraid of boats?"

"No." She could hardly admit that the biggest one she'd been on before this had been a two-passenger canoe at summer camp. "It just startled me." Under way, she thought as she prayed that her system would settle. It was such an exciting, adventurous word. "Can we go out on deck? I'd like to watch."

It was exciting. She felt it the moment the wind hit her face and rushed through her hair. At the rail, she leaned out, delighted to see the island shrink and the sea spread. Because she couldn't resist and he didn't laugh at her, she took half a dozen pictures as the boat sped away from land.

"It's better than flying," she decided. "You feel a part of it. Look." With a laugh, she pointed. "The birds are chasing us."

Stephen didn't bother to glance at the gulls that wheeled and called above the boat's wake. He preferred to watch the delight and excitement bloom on her face. "Do you always enjoy so completely?"

"Yes." She tossed her hair away from her face, only to have the wind rush it back again. With another laugh, she stretched back from the railing, her face lifted to the sun. "Oh, yes."

Irresistible. With his hands at her waist, he spun her toward him. It was like holding a live wire. The shock rippled from her to him, then back again. "Everything?" His fingers spread over her back and, with the slightest pressure, moved her forward until their thighs met.

"I don't know." Instinctively she braced her hands on his shoulders. "I haven't tried everything." But she wanted to. Held close, with the sound of the water and the wind, she wanted to. Without giving a thought to self-preservation, she leaned toward him.

He swore, lightly, under his breath. Rebecca jolted back as if he had shouted at her. Stephen caught her hand as he nodded to the steward, who had just approached with drinks. "Thank you, Victor. Just leave everything." His voice was smooth enough, but Rebecca felt the tension in his hand as he led her to a chair.

He probably thought she was a fool, she decided. All but tumbling into his arms every time he touched her. He was obviously a man of the world—and a kind man, she added as she sipped her mimosa. Not all powerful men spoke kindly to those who worked for them. Her lips curved, a little wryly, as she sipped again. She knew that firsthand.

His body was in turmoil. Stephen couldn't remember, even in his youth, having had a woman affect him so irrationally. He knew how to persuade, how to seduce—and always with finesse. But whenever he was around this woman for more than five minutes he felt like a stallion being spurred and curbed at the same time.

And he was fascinated. Fascinated by the ease with which she went into his arms, by the trust he saw when he looked down into her eyes. As he had in the olive grove, he found himself believing he'd looked into those eyes, those rainwater-clear eyes, a hundred times before.

Still churning, he took out a cigar. The thought was fanciful, but his desire was very real. If there couldn't be finesse, perhaps there could be candor.

"I want you, Rebecca."

She felt her heart stop, then start up again with slow, dull throbs. Carefully she took another sip, then cleared her throat. "I know." It amazed her, flattered her, terrified her.

She seemed so cool. He envied her. "Will you come with me, to my cabin?"

She looked at him then. Her heart and her head were giving very different answers. It sounded so easy, so…natural. If there was a man she could give herself to, wholly, he was with her now. Complications, what complications there were, were her own.

But no matter how far she had run from Philadelphia and her own strict upbringing, there were still lines she couldn't cross.

"I can't."

"Can't?" He lit his cigar, astonished that they were discussing making love as though it were as casual a choice as what dinner entrée to chose. "Or won't?"

She drew a breath. Her palms were damp on the glass, and she set it down. "Can't. I want to." Her eyes, huge and lake-pale, clung to his. "I very much want to, but…"

"But?"

"I know so little about you." She picked up her glass again because her empty hands tended to twist together. "Hardly more than your name, that you own an olive grove and like the sea. It's not enough."

"Then I'll tell you more."

She relaxed enough to smile. "I don't know what to ask."

He leaned back in his chair, the tension dissolving as quickly as it had built. She could do that to him with nothing more than a smile. He knew no one who could excite and solace with so little effort.

"Do you believe in fate, Rebecca? In something unexpected, even unlooked-for, often a small thing that completely and irrevocably changes one's life?"

She thought of her aunt's death and her own uncharacteristic decisions. "Yes. Yes, I do."

"Good." His gaze skimmed over her face, quickly, then more leisurely. "I'd nearly forgotten that I believe it, too. Then I saw you, sitting alone."

There were ways and ways to seduce, she was discovering. A look, a tone, could be every bit as devastating as a caress. She wanted him more in that moment than she had ever known she could want anything. To give herself time, and distance, she rose and walked to the rail.

Even her silence aroused him. She had said she knew too little about him. He knew even less of her. And he didn't care. It was dangerous, possibly even destructive, but he didn't care. As he watched her with the wind billowing her shirt and her hair he realized that he didn't give a damn about where she had come from, where she had been, what she had done.

When lightning strikes, it destroys, though it blazes with power. Rising, he went to her and stood, as she did, facing the sea.

"When I was young, very young," he began, "there was another moment that changed things. My father was a man for the water. He lived for it. Died for it." When he went on it was almost as if he were speaking to himself now, remembering. Rebecca turned her head to look at him. "I was ten or eleven. Everything was going well, the nets were full. My father and I were walking along the beach. He stopped, dipped his hand into the water, made a fist and opened it. 'You can't hold it,' he said to me. 'No matter how you try or how you love or how you sweat.' Then he dug into the sand. It was wet and clung together in his hand. 'But this,' he said, 'a man can hold.' We never spoke of it again. When my time came, I turned my back on the sea and held the land."

"It was right for you."

"Yes." He lifted a hand to catch at the ends of her hair. "It was right. Such big, quiet eyes you have, Rebecca," he murmured. "Have they seen enough, I wonder, to know what's right for you?"

"I guess I've been a little slow in starting to look." Her blood was pounding thickly. She would have stepped back, but he shifted so that she was trapped between him and the rail.

"You tremble when I touch you." He slid his hands up

her arms, then down until their hands locked. "Have you any idea how exciting that is?"

Her chest tightened, diminishing her air even as the muscles in her legs went limp. "Stephen, I meant it when I said…" He brushed his lips gently over her temple. "I can't. I need to…" He feathered a kiss along her jawline, softly. "To think."

He felt her fingers go lax in his. She was suddenly fragile, outrageously vulnerable, irresistibly tempting. "When I kissed you the first time I gave you no choice." His lips trailed over her face, light as a whisper, circling, teasing, avoiding her mouth. "You have one now."

He was hardly touching her. A breath, a whisper, a mere promise of a touch. The slow, subtle passage of his lips over her skin couldn't have been called a kiss, could never have been called a demand. She had only to push away to end the torment. And the glory.

A choice? Had he told her she had a choice? "No, I don't," she murmured as she turned to find his lips with hers.

No choice, no past, no future. Only now. She felt the present, with all its needs and hungers, well up inside her. The kiss was instantly hot, instantly desperate. His heart pounded fast and hard against hers, thunderous now, as he twisted a hand in her hair to pull her head back. To plunder. No one had ever taken her like this. No one had ever warned her that a touch of violence could be so exciting. Her gasp of surprise turned into a moan of pleasure as his tongue skimmed over hers.

He thought of lightning bolts again, thought of that flash of power and light. She was electric in his arms, sparking, sizzling. Her scent, as soft, as seductive, as a whisper, clouded his mind, even as the taste of her heightened his appetite.

She was all woman, she was every woman, and yet she was like no other. He could hear each quick catch of her breath above the roar of the motor. With her name on his lips, he pressed them to the vulnerable line of her throat, where the skin was heated from the sun and as delicate as water.

She might have slid bonelessly to the deck if his body hadn't pressed hers so firmly against the rail. In wonder, in panic, she felt his muscles turn to iron wherever they touched her. Never before had she felt so fragile, so at the mercy of her own desires. The sea was as calm as glass, but she felt herself tossed, tumbled, wrecked. With a sigh that was almost a sob, she wrapped her arms around him.

It was the defenselessness of the gesture that pulled him back from the edge. He must have been mad. For a moment he'd been close, much too close, to dragging her down to the deck without a thought to her wishes or to the consequences. With his eyes closed, he held her, feeling the erratic beat of her heart, hearing her shallow, shuddering breath.

Perhaps he was still mad, Stephen thought. Even as the ragged edges of desire eased, something deeper and far more dangerous bloomed.

He wanted her, in a way no man could safely want a woman. Forever.

Fate, he thought again as he stroked her hair. It seemed he was falling in love whether he wished it or not. A few hours with her and he felt more than he had ever imagined he could feel.

There had been a few times in his life when he had seen

and desired on instinct alone. What he had seen and desired, he had taken. Just as he would take her. But when he took, he meant to keep.

Carefully he stepped back. “Maybe neither of us has a choice.” He dipped his hands into his pockets. “And if I touch you again, here, now, I won’t give you one.”

Unable to pretend, knowing they were shaking, she pushed her hands through her hair. She didn’t bother to disguise the tremor in her voice. She wouldn’t have known how. “I won’t want one.” She saw his eyes darken quickly, dangerously, but she didn’t know his hands were balled into fists, straining.

“You make it difficult for me.”

A long, shuddering breath escaped her. No one had ever wanted her this way. Probably no one ever would again. “I’m sorry. I don’t mean to.”

“No.” Deliberately he relaxed his hands. “I don’t think you do. That’s one of the things about you I find most intriguing. I will have you, Rebecca.” He saw something flicker in her eyes.... Excitement? Panic? A combination of the two, perhaps. “Because I’m sure of it, because I know you’re sure of it, I’ll do my best to give you a little more time.”

Her natural humor worked through the sliver of unease she felt. “I’m not sure whether I should thank you politely or run like hell.”

He grinned, surprising himself, then flicked a finger down her cheek. “I wouldn’t advise running, *matia mou.* I’d only catch you.”

She was sure of that, too. One look at his face, even with the smile that softened it, and she knew. Kind, yes, but with a steely underlying ruthlessness. "Then I'll go with the thank-you."

"You're welcome." Patience, he realized, would have to be developed. And quickly. "Would you like to swim? There's a bay. We're nearly there."

The water might, just might, cool her off. "I'd love it."

Chapter 5

The water was cool and mirror-clear. Rebecca lowered herself into it with a sigh of pure pleasure. Back in Philadelphia she would have been at her desk, calculator clicking, the jacket of her neat business suit carefully smoothed over the back of her chair. Her figures would always tally, her forms would always be properly filed.

The dependable, efficient Miss Malone.

Instead, she was swimming in a crystal-clear bay, letting the water cool and the sun heat. Ledgers and accounts were worlds away. Here, as close as a handspan, was a man who was teaching her everything she would ever want to know about needs, desires, and the fragility of the heart.

He couldn't know it, she thought. She doubted she'd ever have the courage to tell him that he was the only one who had ever made her tremble and burn. A man as physically aware as he would only be uncomfortable knowing he held an inexperienced woman in his arms.

The water lapped around her with a sound as quiet as

her own sigh. But he didn't know, because when she was in his arms she didn't feel awkward and inexperienced. She felt beautiful, desirable and reckless.

With a laugh, Rebecca dipped under the surface to let the water, and the freedom, surround her. Who would have believed it?

"Does it always take so little to make you laugh?"

Rebecca ran a hand over her slicked-back hair. Stephen was treading water beside her, smoothly, hardly making a ripple. His skin was dark gold, glistening-wet. His hair was streaked by the sun and dampened by the water, which was almost exactly the color of his eyes. She had to suppress an urge to just reach out and touch.

"A secluded inlet, a beautiful sky, an interesting man." With another sigh, she kicked her legs up so that she could float. "It doesn't seem like so little to me." She studied the vague outline of the mountains, far out of reach. "I promised myself that no matter where I went, what I did, I'd never take anything for granted again."

There was something in the way she said it, some hint of sadness, that pulled at him. The urge to comfort wasn't completely foreign in him, but he hadn't had much practice at it. "Was there a man who hurt you?"

Her lips curved at that, but he couldn't know that she was laughing at herself. Naturally, she'd dated. They had been polite, cautious evenings, usually with little interest on either side. She'd been dull, or at least she had never worked up the nerve to spread her wings. Once or twice, when she'd felt a tug, she'd been too shy, too much the efficient Rebecca Malone, to do anything about it.

With him, everything was different. Because she loved him. She didn't know how, she didn't know why, but she loved him as much as any woman could love any man.

"No. There's no one." She closed her eyes, trusting the water to carry her. "When my parents died, it hurt. It hurt so badly that I suppose I pulled back from life. I thought it was important that I be a responsible adult, even though I wasn't nearly an adult yet."

Strange that she hadn't thought of it quite that way until she'd stopped being obsessively responsible. Stranger still was how easy it was to tell him what she'd never even acknowledged herself.

"My aunt Jeannie was kind and considerate and loving, but she'd forgotten what it was like to be a young girl. Suddenly I realized I'd missed being young, lazy, foolish, all the things everyone's entitled to be at least once. I decided to make up for it."

Her hair was spread out and drifting on the water. Her eyes were closed, and her face was sheened with water. Not beautiful, Stephen told himself. She was too angular for real beauty. But she was fascinating…in looks, in philosophy…more, in the open-armed way she embraced whatever crossed her path.

He found himself looking around the inlet as he hadn't bothered to look at anything in years. He could see the sun dancing on the surface, could see the ripples spreading and growing from the quiet motion of their bodies. Farther away was the narrow curving strip of white beach, deserted now, but for a few birds fluttering over the sand. It was quiet, almost unnaturally quiet, the only sound the soft, monotonous slap of water against sand. And he was relaxed, totally, mind and body. Perhaps he, too, had forgotten what it was like to be young and foolish.

On impulse he put a hand on her shoulder and pushed her under.

She came up sputtering, dragging wet hair out of her eyes. He grinned at her and calmly continued to tread water. "It was too easy."

She tilted her head, considering him and the distance between them. Challenge leaped into her eyes, sparked with amusement. "It won't be the next time."

His grin only widened. When he moved, he moved fast, streaking under and across the water like an eel. Rebecca had time for a quick squeal. Dragging in a deep breath, she kicked out. He caught her ankle, but she was ready. Unresisting, she let him pull her under. Then, instead of fighting her way back to the surface, she wrapped her arms around him and sent them both rolling in an underwater wrestling match. They were still tangled, her arms around him, her hands hooked over his shoulders, when they surfaced.

"We're even." She gasped for air and shook the water out of her eyes.

"How do you figure?"

"If we'd had a mat I'd have pinned you. Want to go for two out of three?"

"I might." He felt her legs tangle with his as she kicked out lazily. "But for now I prefer this."

He was going to kiss her again. She saw it in his eyes, felt it in the slight tensing of the arm that locked them torso to torso. She wasn't sure she was ready. More, she was afraid she was much too ready.

"Stephen?"

"Hmm?" His lips were a breath away from hers. Then he found himself underwater again, his arms empty. He should have been furious. He nearly was when he pushed to surface. She was shoulder-deep in the water, a few feet away. Her laughter rolled over him, young, delighted, unapologetic.

"It was too easy." She managed a startled "whoops" when he struck out after her. She might have made it—she had enough of a lead—but he swam as though he'd been born in the water. Still, she was agile, and she almost managed to dodge him, but her laughter betrayed her. She gulped in water, choked, then found herself hauled up into his arms in thigh-deep water.

"I like to win." Deciding it was useless to struggle, she pressed a hand to her heart and gasped for air. "It's a personality flaw. Sometimes I cheat at canasta."

"Canasta?" The last thing he could picture the slim, sexy bundle in his arms doing was spending a quiet evening playing cards.

"I can't help myself." Still breathless, she laid her head on his shoulder. "No willpower."

"I find myself having the same problem." With a careless toss, he sent her flying through the air. She hit the water bottom first.

"I guess I deserved that." She struggled to her feet, water raining off her. "I have to sit." Wading through the water, she headed for the gentle slope of beach. She lay, half in and half out of the water, not caring that the sand would cling to her hair and skin. When he dropped down beside her, she reached out a hand for his. "I don't know when I've had a nicer day."

He looked down to where her fingers linked with his. The gesture had been so easy, so natural. He wondered how it could both comfort and arouse. "It's hardly over."

"It seems like it could last forever." She wanted it to go on and on. Blue skies and easy laughter. Cool water and endless hours. There had been a time, not so long before, when the days had dragged into nights and the nights into days. "Did you ever want to run away?"

With her hand still in his, he lay back to watch a few scattered rags of clouds drift. How long had it been, he wondered, since he'd really watched the sky? "To where?"

"Anywhere. Away from the way things are, away from what you're afraid they'll always be." She closed her eyes and could see herself brewing that first cup of coffee at exactly 7:15, opening the first file at precisely 9:01. "To drop out of sight," she murmured, "and pop up somewhere else, anywhere else, as someone completely different."

"You can't change who you are."

"Oh, but you can." Her tone suddenly urgent, she rose on her elbow. "Sometimes you have to."

He reached up to touch the ends of her hair. "What are you running from?"

"Everything. I'm a coward."

He looked into her eyes. They were so clear, so full of enthusiasm. "I don't think so."

"But you don't know me." A flicker of regret, then uncertainty, ran across her face. "I'm not sure I want you to."

"Don't I?" His fingers tightened on her hair, keeping her still. "There are people and circumstances that don't take months or years before they're understood. I look at you and something fits into place, Rebecca. I don't know why, but it is. I know you." He tugged her down for the lightest, the briefest, of kisses. "And I like what I see."

"Do you?" She smiled. "Really?"

"Do you imagine I spend the day with a woman only because I want to sleep with her?" She shrugged, and though her blush was very faint, he noticed it and was amused by it. How many women, he wondered, could kiss a man into oblivion, then blush? "Being with you, Rebecca, is a difficult pleasure."

She chuckled and began to draw circles in the wet sand. What would he say, what would he think, if he knew what she was? Or, more accurately, what she wasn't? It didn't matter, she told herself. She couldn't let it spoil what there was between them.

"I think that's the most wonderful compliment I've ever had."

"Where have you been?" he murmured.

When she moved restlessly, he held her still. "Don't. I'm not going to touch you. Not yet."

"That's not the problem." With her eyes closed, she tilted her chin up and let the sun beat down on her face. "The problem is, I want you to touch me, so much it frightens me." Taking her time, she sat up, gathering her courage. She wanted to be honest, and she hoped she wouldn't sound like a fool. "Stephen, I don't sleep around. I need you to understand, because this is all happening so quickly. But it's not casual."

He lifted a hand to her chin and turned her to face him. His eyes were as blue as the water, and, to her, as unfathomable. "No, it's not." He made the decision quickly, though he had been turning the idea over in his mind all day. "I have to go to Athens tomorrow. Come with me, Rebecca."

"Athens?" she managed, staring at him.

"Business. A day, two at the most. I'd like you with me." And he was afraid, more than he cared to admit, that when he returned she might be gone.

"I…" What should she say? What was right?

"You told me you'd planned to go." He'd push if necessary. Now that the idea had taken root, Stephen had no intention of going anywhere without her.

"Yes, but I wouldn't want to be in the way while you're working."

"You'll be in my way whether you're here or there."

Her head came up at that, and the look she gave him was both shy and stunning. He stifled the need to take her again, to roll until she was beneath him on the sand. He'd said he'd give her time. Perhaps what he'd really meant was that he needed time himself.

"You'll have your own suite. No strings, Rebecca. Just your company."

"A day or two," she murmured.

"It's a simple matter to have your room held for you here for your return."

Her return. Not his. If he left Corfu tomorrow she would probably never see him again. He was offering her another day, perhaps two. Never take anything for granted, she remembered. Never again.

Athens, she thought. It was true that she had planned to see it before she left Greece. But she would have gone alone. A few days before, that had been what she thought she wanted. The adventure of seeing new places, new people, on her own. Now the thought of going with him, of having him beside her when she first caught sight of the Acropolis, of having him want her with him, changed everything.

"I'd love to go with you." She rose quickly and dived into the water. She was in over her head.

Chapter 6

Athens was neither East nor West. It was spitted meat and spices roasting. It was tall buildings and modern shops. It was narrow, unpaved streets and clamorous bazaars. It had been the scene of revolution and brutality. It was ancient and civilized and passionate.

Rebecca quite simply fell in love at first sight.

She'd been seduced by Paris and charmed by London, but in Athens she lost her heart. She wanted to see everything at once, from sunrise to moonlight, and the heat-drenched afternoon between.

All that first morning, while Stephen was immersed in business meetings, she wandered. The hotel he'd chosen was lovely, but she was drawn to the streets and the people. Somehow she didn't feel like a visitor here. She felt like someone who had returned home after a long, long journey. Athens was waiting for her, ready to welcome her back.

Incredible. All her life she had accepted the parameters set for her. Now she was touring Old Athens, with its clicking worry beads and its open-fronted shops, where she could buy cheap plaster copies of monuments or elegant antiques.

She passed tavernas, but she was too excited to be tempted by the rich smells of coffee and baking. She heard the clear notes of a flute as she looked up and saw the Acropolis.

There was only one approach. Though it was still early, other tourists were making their way toward the ruins in twos and in groups. Rebecca let her camera hang by its strap. Despite the chattering around her, she felt alone, but beautifully so.

She would never be able to explain what it felt like to stand in the morning sun and look at something that had been built for the gods—something that had endured war and weather and time. It had been a place of worship. Even now, after centuries had passed, Rebecca felt the spiritual pull. Perhaps the goddess Athena, with her gleaming helmet and spear, still visited there.

Rebecca had been disappointed that Stephen couldn't join her on her first morning in Athens. Now she was glad to be alone—to sit and absorb and imagine without having to explain her thoughts.

How could she, after having seen so much, go back to so little? Sighing, she wandered through the temples. It wasn't just the awe she felt here, or the excitement she had felt in London and Paris, that had changed her. It was Stephen and everything she'd felt, everything she'd wanted, since she'd met him.

Perhaps she would go back to Philadelphia, but she would never be the same person. Once you fell in love, completely, totally in love, nothing was ever the same.

She wished it could be simple, the way she imagined it was simple for so many other women. An attractive man, a physical tug. But with Stephen, as with Athens, she'd lost her heart. However implausible it seemed, she had recognized the man, as well as the city, as being part of her, as being for her. Desire, when tangled up with love, could never be simple.

But how could you be sure you were in love when it had never happened to you before? If she were home, at least she would have a friend to talk to. With a little laugh, Rebecca walked out into the sunlight. How many times had she been on the receiving end of a long, scattered conversation from a friend who had fallen in love—or thought she had. The excitement, the unhappiness, the thrills. Sometimes she'd been envious, and sometimes she'd been grateful not to have the complication in her own life. But always, always, she'd offered calm, practical, even soothing advice.

Oddly enough, she didn't seem to be able to do the same for herself.

All she could think of was the way her heart pounded when he touched her, how excitement, panic and anticipation fluttered through her every time he looked at her. When she was with him, her feelings and fantasies seemed reasonable. When she was with him, she could believe in fate, in the matching of soul to soul.

It wasn't enough. At least that was what she would have told another woman. Attraction and passion weren't enough. Yet there was no explaining, even to herself, the sense of rightness she experienced whenever she was with him. If she were a fanciful person she would say it was as though she'd been waiting for him, waiting for the time and the place for him to come to her.

It sounded simple—if fate could be considered simple. Yet beneath all the pleasure and that sense of reunion was guilt. She couldn't shake it, and she knew she wouldn't be able to ignore it much longer. She wasn't the woman she had let him believe her to be. She wasn't the well-traveled at-loose-ends free spirit she pretended to be. No matter how many ties she'd cut, she was still Rebecca Malone. How would he feel about her once he knew how limited and dull her life had been?

How and when was she going to tell him?

A few more days, she promised herself as she began the walk back. It was selfish, perhaps it was even dangerous, but she wanted just a few more days.

It was midafternoon before she returned to the hotel. Ignoring the fact that she might be considered overeager, she went straight to Stephen's suite. She couldn't wait to see him, to tell him everything she'd seen, to show him everything she'd bought. Her easy smile faded a bit when his secretary Elana opened the door.

"Miss Malone." Gracious and self-confident, Elana waved her in. "Please sit down. I'll let Stephen know you're here."

"I don't want to interrupt." Rebecca shifted her bags, feeling gauche and foolish.

"Not at all. Have you just come in?"

"Yes, I…" For the first time, Rebecca noticed that her skin was damp and her hair tousled. In contrast, Elana was cool and perfectly groomed. "I really should go."

"Please." Elana urged Rebecca to a chair. "Let me get you a drink." With a half smile, Elana began to pour a tall glass of iced juice. She had expected Stephen's mystery lady to be smooth, controlled and stunning. It pleased her a great deal to find Rebecca wide-eyed, a little unsure, and clearly a great deal in love.

"Did you enjoy your morning?"

"Yes, very much." She accepted the glass and tried to relax. Jealousy, she realized, feeling herself flush at the realization. She couldn't remember ever having experienced the sensation before. Who wouldn't be jealous? she asked herself as she watched Elana walk to the phone. The Greek woman was gorgeous, self-contained, coolly efficient. Above all, she had a relationship with Stephen that Rebecca knew nothing about. How long has she known him? Rebecca wondered. And how well?

"Stephen's just finishing up some business," Elana said as she hung up the phone. With easy, economical moves, she poured herself a drink, then walked to the chair facing Rebecca. "What do you think of Athens?"

"I love it." Rebecca wished she'd taken the time to brush her hair and freshen her makeup. Lecturing herself, she sipped at her juice. "I'm not sure what I expected, but it's everything and more."

"Europeans see it as the East, Orientals see it as the West." Elana crossed her legs and settled back. It surprised her to realize that she was prepared to like Rebecca Malone. "What Athens is is Greek—and, more particularly, Athenian." She paused, studying Rebecca over the rim of her glass. "People often view Stephen in much the same way, and what he is is Stephen."

"How long have you worked for him?"

"Five years."

"You must know him well."

"Better than some. He's a demanding and generous employer and an interesting man. Fortunately, I like to travel and I enjoy my work."

Rebecca rubbed at a spot of dust on her slacks. "It never occurred to me that farming required so much traveling. I never realized how much was involved in growing olives."

Elana's brows rose in obvious surprise, but she continued smoothly when Rebecca glanced back at her. "Whatever Stephen does, he does thoroughly." She smiled to herself, satisfied. She hadn't been certain until now whether the American woman was attracted to Stephen or to his position. "Has Stephen explained to you about the dinner party this evening?"

"He said something about a small party here at the hotel. A business dinner."

"Men take these things more lightly than women." Feeling friendlier, Elena offered her first genuine smile. "It will be small, but quite extravagant." She watched as Rebecca automatically lifted a hand to her hair. "If you need anything—a dress, a salon—the hotel can accommodate you."

Rebecca thought of the casual sportswear she'd tossed into her bag before the impulsive trip to Athens. "I need everything."

With a quick, understanding laugh, Elana rose. "I'll make some calls for you."

"Thank you, but I don't want to interfere with your work."

"Seeing that you're comfortable is part of my work." They both glanced over when the door opened. "Stephen. You see, she hasn't run away." Taking her glass and her pad, she left them alone.

"You were gone a long time." He hated the fact that he'd begun to watch the clock and worry. He'd imagined her hurt or abducted. He'd begun to wonder if she would disappear from his life as quickly as she'd appeared in it. Now she was here, her eyes alive with pleasure, her clothes rumpled and her hair windblown.

"I guess I got caught up exploring." She started to rise, but before she could gain her feet he was pulling her out of the chair, seeking, finding her mouth with his.

His desperation whipped through her. His hunger incited her own. Without thought, without hesitation, she clung to him, answering, accepting. Already seduced, she murmured something, an incoherent sound that caught in her throat.

Good God, he thought, it wasn't possible, it wasn't sane, to want like this. Throughout the morning while all the facts and figures and demands of business had been hammering at him, he'd thought of her, of holding her, of tasting her, of being with her. When she had stayed away for so long he'd begun to imagine, then to fear, what his life would be like without her.

It wasn't going to happen. He scraped his teeth over her bottom lip, and she gasped and opened for him. He wouldn't let it happen. Where she came from, where she intended to go, no longer mattered. She belonged to him now. And, though he'd only begun to deal with it, he belonged to her.

But he needed some sanity, some logic. Fighting himself, Stephen drew her away from him. Her eyes remained closed, and her lips remained parted. A soft, sultry sound escaped them as her lashes fluttered upward.

"I…" She took a deep breath and let it out slowly. "I should go sightseeing more often."

Gradually he realized how hard his fingers were pressing into her arms. As if he were afraid she would slip away. Cursing himself, he relaxed. "I would have preferred to go with you."

"I understand you're busy. I'd have bored you silly, poking into every shop and staring at every column."

"No." If there was one thing he was certain of, it was that she would never bore him. "I'd like to have seen your first impression of Athens."

"It was like coming home," she told him, then hurried on because it sounded foolish. "I couldn't get enough." Laughing at herself, she gestured toward her bags. "Obviously. It's so different from anywhere I've ever been. At the Acropolis I couldn't even take any pictures, because I knew they couldn't capture the feeling. Then I walked along the streets and saw old men with *kom—konbou—*" She fumbled over the Greek and finally made a helpless gesture.

"Kombouloi," he murmured. "Worry beads."

"Yes, and I imagined how they might sit in those shadowy doorways watching the tourists go by, day after day, year after year." She sat, pleased to share her impressions with him. "I saw a shop with all these costumes, lots of tinsel, and some really dreadful plaster copies of the monuments."

He grinned and sat beside her. "How many did you buy?"

"Three or four." She bent down to rattle through her bags. "I bought you a present."

"A plaster statue of Athena?"

She glanced up, eyes laughing. "Almost. Then I found this tiny antique shop in the old section. It was all dim and dusty and irresistible. The owner had a handful of English phrases, and I had my phrase book. After we'd confused each other completely, I bought this."

She drew out an S-shaped porcelain pipe decorated with paintings of the wild mountain goats of Greece. Attached to it was a long wooden stem, as smooth as glass, tipped by a tarnished brass mouthpiece.

"I remembered the goats we'd seen on Corfu," she explained as Stephen examined it. "I thought you might like it, though I've never seen you smoke a pipe."

With a quiet laugh, he looked back at her, balancing the gift in both hands. "No, I don't—at least not of this nature."

"Well, it's more ornamental than functional, I suppose. The man couldn't tell me much about it—at least not that I could understand." She reached out to run a finger along the edge of the bowl. "I've never seen anything like it."

"I'm relieved to hear it." When she sent him a puzzled look, he leaned over to brush her lips with his. "*Matia mou,* this is a hashish pipe."

"A hashish pipe?" She stared, first in shock, then in fascination. "Really? I mean, did people actually use it?"

"Undoubtedly. Quite a number, I'd say, since it's at least a hundred and fifty years old."

"Imagine that." She pouted, imagining dark, smoky dens. "I guess it's not a very appropriate souvenir."

"On the contrary, whenever I see it I'll think of you."

She glanced up quickly, unsure, but the amusement in his eyes had her smiling again. "I should have bought you the plaster statue of Athena."

Taking her hands, he drew her to her feet. "I'm flattered that you bought me anything." She felt the subtle change as his fingers tightened on hers. "I want time with you, Rebecca. Hours of it. Days. There's too much I need to know." When she lowered her gaze, he caught her chin. "What are those secrets of yours?"

"Nothing that would interest you."

"You're wrong. Tomorrow I intend to find out all there is to know." He saw the quick flicker of unease in her eyes. Other men, he thought with an uncomfortable surge of jealousy. The hell with them. "No more evasions. I want you, all of you. Do you understand?"

"Yes, but—"

"Tomorrow." He cut her off, suddenly, completely, frustratingly Greek. "I have business that can't be avoided now. I'll come for you at seven."

"All right."

Tomorrow was years away, she told herself. She had time to decide what she would say, how she would say it. Before tomorrow came tonight. She would be everything she'd ever wanted to be, everything he wanted her to be.

"I'd better go." Before he could touch her again, she bent to gather her bags. "Stephen..." She paused at the door and turned to look at him as he stood in the middle of the room, comfortable with the wealth that surrounded him, confident with who and what he was. "You might be disappointed when you find out."

She left quickly, leaving him frowning after her.

Chapter 7

She was as nervous as a cat. Every time she looked in the mirror Rebecca wondered who the woman was who was staring back at her. It wasn't a stranger, but it was a very, very different Rebecca Malone.

Was it just the different hairstyle, poufed and frizzed and swept around her face? Could it be the dress, the glittery spill of aquamarine that left her arms and shoulders bare? No, it was more than that. More than makeup and clever stylists and glamorous clothes. It was in her eyes. How could she help but see it? How could anyone? The woman who looked back from the mirror was a woman in love.

What was she going to do about it? What could she do? she asked herself. She was still practical enough to accept that some things could never be changed. But was she bold enough, or strong enough, to take what she wanted and live with the consequences?

When she heard the knock on the door, Rebecca took a deep breath and picked up the useless compact-size evening bag she'd bought just that afternoon. It was all happening so fast. When she'd come back from Stephen's suite there had been a detailed message from Elana listing appointments—for a massage, a facial, hairstyling—along with the name of the manager of the hotel's most exclusive boutique. She hadn't had time to think, even for a minute, about her evening with Stephen. Or about any tomorrows.

Perhaps that was best, she decided as she pulled open the door. It was best not to think, not to analyze. It was best to accept and to act.

She looked like a siren, some disciple of Circe, with her windswept hair and a dress the color of seductive seas. Had he told himself she wasn't beautiful? Had he believed it? At that moment he was certain he'd never seen, never would see, a more exciting woman.

"You're amazing, Rebecca." He took her hand and drew her to him so that they stood in the doorway together. On the threshold.

"Why? Because I'm on time?"

"Because you're never what I expect." He brought her hand to his lips. "And always what I want."

Because she was speechless, she was glad when he closed the door at her back and led her to the elevators. He looked different from the man she had first met, the one who dressed with such casual elegance. Tonight there was a formality about him, and the sophistication she had sensed earlier was abundantly apparent in the ease with which he wore the black dinner jacket.

"The way you look," he told her, "it seems a shame to waste the evening on a business dinner."

"I'm looking forward to meeting some of your friends."

"Associates," he said with an odd smile. "When you've

been poor—and don't intend to be poor again—you rarely make friends in business."

She frowned. This was a side of him, the business side, that she didn't know. Would he be ruthless? She looked at him, saw it, and accepted it. Yes, a man like Stephen would always be ruthless with what belonged to him. "But enemies?"

"The same rule, in business, applies to friends and enemies. My father taught me more than fishing, Rebecca. He also taught me that to succeed, to attain, you must learn not only how to trust, but how far."

"I've never been poor, but I imagine it's frightening."

"Strengthening." He took her hand again when the elevator doors opened. "We have different backgrounds, Rebecca, but, fortunately, we've come to the same place."

He had no idea *how* different. Trust. He had spoken of trust. She discovered she wanted to tell him, tell him everything. Tell him that she knew nothing of elegant parties and glamorous lifestyles. She was a fraud, and when he found out he might laugh at her and brush her aside. But she wanted him to know.

"Stephen, I want to—"

"Stephen. Once more you outdo us all in your choice of women."

"Dimitri."

Rebecca stopped, caught on the brink of confession. The man who faced her was classically handsome. His silver mane contrasted with bronzed skin lined by a half century of sun. He wore a mustache that swept majestically over gleaming teeth.

"It was kind of you to invite us here this evening, but

it would be kinder still to introduce me to your lovely companion."

"Rebecca Malone, Dimitri Petropolis."

A diamond glittered on the hand he lifted to clasp Rebecca's. The hand itself was hard as rock. "A pleasure. Athens is already abuzz with talk of the woman who arrived with Stephen."

Certain he was joking, she smiled. "Then Athens must be in desperate need of news."

His eyes widened for a moment, then creased at the corners when he laughed. "I have no doubt you will provide an abundance of it."

Stephen slipped a hand under Rebecca's elbow. The look he sent Dimitri was very quick and very clear. They had competed over land, but there would be no competition over Rebecca.

"If you'll excuse us a moment, Dimitri, I'd like to get Rebecca some champagne."

"Of course." Amused—and challenged—Dimitri brushed at his mustache as he watched them walk away.

Rebecca had no way of knowing that to Stephen a small dinner party meant a hundred people. She sipped her first glass of wine, hoping she wouldn't embarrass them both by being foolishly shy and tongue-tied. In the past, whenever she had found herself in a crowd, she had always looked for the nearest corner to fade into. Not tonight, she promised herself, straightening her shoulders.

There were dozens of names to remember, but she filed them away as easily as she had always filed numbers. In the hour before dinner, while the guests mixed and mingled, she found herself at ease. The stomach flutters and hot blushes she'd often experienced at parties and functions simply didn't happen.

Perhaps she was the new Rebecca Malone after all.

She heard business discussed here and there. Most of it seemed to be hotel and resort business—talk of remodeling and expansions, mergers and takeovers. She found it odd that so many of the guests were in that trade, rather than prosperous farmers or olive growers.

Stephen came up behind her and murmured in her ear, "You look pleased with yourself."

"I am." He couldn't know that she was pleased to find herself at ease and comfortable in a party of strangers. "So many interesting people."

"Interesting." He brushed a finger over her wispy bangs. "I thought you might find it dull."

"Not at all." She took a last sip of champagne, then set the glass aside. Instantly a waiter was at her side, offering another. Stephen watched her smile her thanks.

"So you enjoy parties?"

"Sometimes. I'm enjoying this one, and having a chance to meet your associates."

Stephen glanced over her shoulder, summing up the looks and quiet murmurs. "They'll be talking about you for weeks to come."

She only laughed, turning in a slow circle. Around her was the flash of jewels and the gleam of gold. The sleek and the prosperous, the rich and the successful. It pleased her that she'd found more to talk about than tax shelters.

"I can't imagine they have so little on their minds. This is such a gorgeous room."

She looked around the huge ballroom, with its cream-and-rose walls, its glittering chandeliers and its gleaming floors. There were alcoves for cozy love seats and tall, thriving ornamental trees in huge copper pots. The tables, arranged to give a sense of intimacy, were already set with ivory cloths and slender tapers.

"It's really a beautiful hotel," she continued. "Everything about it runs so smoothly." She smiled up at him. "I'm torn between the resort in Corfu and this."

"Thank you." When she gave him a blank look, he tipped up her chin with his finger. "They're mine."

"Your what?"

"My hotels," he said simply, then led her to a table.

She spoke all through dinner, though for the first fifteen minutes she had no idea what she said. There were eight at Stephen's table, including Dimitri, who had shifted name cards so that he could sit beside her. She toyed with her seafood appetizer, chatted and wondered if she could have made a bigger fool out of herself.

He wasn't simply prosperous. He wasn't simply well-off. There was enough accountant left in Rebecca to understand that when a man owned what Stephen owned he was far, far more than comfortable.

What would he think of her when he found out what she was? Trust? How could she ever expect him to trust her now? She swallowed without tasting and managed to smile. Would he think she was a gold digger, that she had set herself up to run into him?

No, that was ridiculous.

She forced herself to look over and saw that Stephen was watching her steadily. She picked up her fork with one hand and balled up the napkin in her lap with the other.

Why couldn't he be ordinary? she wondered. Someone

vacationing, someone working at the resort? Why had she fallen in love with someone so far out of her reach?

"Have you left us?"

Rebecca jerked herself back to see Dimitri smiling at her. Flushing, she noticed that the next course had been served while she'd been daydreaming. "I'm sorry." With an effort she began to toy with the *salata Athenas.*

"A beautiful woman need never apologize for being lost in her own thoughts." He patted her hand, then let his fingers linger. He caught Stephen's dark look and smiled. If he didn't like the boy so much, he thought, he wouldn't get nearly so much pleasure from irritating him. "Tell me, how did you meet Stephen?"

"We met in Corfu." She thought of that first meal they had shared…quiet, relaxed, alone.

"Ah, soft nights and sunny days. You are vacationing?"

"Yes." Rebecca put more effort into her smile. If she stared into her salad she would only embarrass herself, and Stephen. "He was kind enough to show me some of the island."

"He knows it well, and many of the other islands of our country. There's something of the gypsy in him."

She had sensed that. Hadn't that been part of the attraction? Hadn't Rebecca just discovered the gypsy in herself? "Have you know him long?"

"We have a long-standing business relationship. Friendly rivals, you might say. When Stephen was hardly more than a boy he accumulated an impressive amount of land." He gestured expansively. "As you can see, he used it wisely. I believe he has two hotels in your country."

"Two? More?" Rebecca picked up her glass and took a long swallow of wine.

"So you see, I had wondered if you had met in America and were old friends."

"No." Rebecca nodded weakly as the waiter removed the salad and replaced it with moussaka. "We only just met a few days ago."

"As always, Stephen moves quickly and stylishly." Dimitri took her hand again, more than a little amused by the frown he saw deepening in Stephen's eyes. "Where is it in America you are from?"

"Philadelphia." Relax, she ordered herself. Relax and enjoy. "That's in the Northeast."

It infuriated Stephen to watch her flirting so easily, so effectively, with another man. She sat through course after course, barely eating, all the while gifting Dimitri with her shy smiles. Not once did she draw away when the older man touched her hand or leaned close. From where he sat, Stephen could catch a trace of her scent, soft, subtle, maddening. He could hear her quiet laugh when Dimitri murmured something in her ear.

Then she was standing with him, her hand caught in his, as he led her to the dance floor.

Stephen sat there, battling back a jealousy he despised, and watched them move together to music made for lovers. Under the lights her dress clung, then swayed, then shifted. Her face was close, too damn close, to Dimitri's. He knew what it was like to hold her like that, to breathe in the scent of her skin and her hair. He knew what it was to feel her body brush against his, to feel the life, the passion, bubbling. He knew what it was to see her eyes blur, her lips part, to hear that quiet sigh.

He had often put his stamp on land, but never on a woman. He didn't believe in it. But only a fool sat idly by and allowed another man to enjoy what was his. With a muttered oath, Stephen rose, strode out onto the dance floor and laid a hand on Dimitri's shoulder.

"Ah, well." The older man gave a regretful sigh and stepped aside. "Until later."

Before she could respond, Rebecca was caught against Stephen. With a sigh of her own, she relaxed and matched her steps to his. Maybe it was like a dream, she told herself as she closed her eyes and let the music fill her head. But she was going to enjoy every moment until it was time to wake up.

She seemed to melt against him. Her fingers moved lightly through his hair as she rested her cheek against his. Was this the way she'd danced with Dimitri? Stephen wondered, then cursed himself. He was being a fool, but he couldn't seem to stop himself. Then again, he'd had to fight for everything else in his life. Why should his woman be any different?

He wanted to drag her off then and there, away from everyone, and find some dark, quiet place to love her.

"You're enjoying yourself?"

"Yes." She wouldn't think about what he was, not now. Soon enough the night would be over and tomorrow would have to be faced. While the music played and he held her, she would only think of what he meant to her. "Very much."

The dreamy tone of her voice almost undid him. "Apparently Dimitri entertained you well."

"Mmm. He's a very nice man."

"You moved easily from his arms to mine."

Something in his tone pried through the pleasure she felt. Carefully she drew back so that she could see his face. "I don't think I know what you mean."

"I believe you do."

She was tempted to laugh, but there was no humor in Stephen's eyes. Rebecca felt her stomach knot as it always did when she was faced with a confrontation. "If I do, then I'd have to think you ridiculous. Maybe we'd better go back to the table."

"So you can be with him?" Even as the words came out he realized the unfairness, even the foolishness, of them.

She stiffened, retreating as far as she could from anger. "I don't think this is the place for this kind of discussion."

"You're quite right." As furious with himself as he was with her, he pulled her from the dance floor.

Chapter 8

"Stop it." By the time he'd dragged her to the elevators, Rebecca had gotten over her first shock. "What's gotten into you?"

"I'm simply taking you to a more suitable place for our discussion." He pulled her into the elevator, then punched the button for their floor.

"You have guests," she began, but he sent her a look than made her feel like a fool. Falling back on dignity, she straightened her shoulders. "I prefer to be asked if I want to leave, not dragged around as though I were a pack mule."

Though her heart was pounding, she sailed past him when the doors opened, intending to breeze into her own rooms and slam the door in his face. In two steps he had her arm again. Rebecca found herself guided, none too gently, into Stephen's suite.

"I don't want to talk to you," she said, because she was certain her teeth would begin to chatter at any moment. She didn't argue well in the best of circumstances. Faced with Stephen's anger, she was certain she would lose.

He said nothing as he loosened his tie and the first two buttons of his shirt. He went to the bar and poured two brandies. He was being irrational and he knew it, but he seemed unable to control it. That was new, he decided. But there had been many new emotions in him since Rebecca.

Walking back to Rebecca, he set one snifter by her elbow. When he looked at her…he wanted to shout, to beg, to demand, to plead. As a result, his voice was clipped and hard.

"You came to Athens with me, not with Dimitri or any other man."

She didn't touch the snifter. She was certain her hands would shake so hard that it would slip out of her grip. "Is that a Greek custom?" It amazed her—and bolstered her confidence—to hear how calm her voice was. "Forbidding a woman to speak to another man?"

"Speak?" He could still see the way Dimitri had bent his head close to hers. Dimitri, who was smooth and practiced. Dimitri, whose background would very likely mirror Rebecca's. Old money, privileged childhoods, quiet society. "Do you allow every man who speaks to you to hold you, to touch you?"

She didn't blush. Instead, the color faded from her cheeks. She shook, not with fear but with fury. "What I do, and with whom I do it, is my business. Mine."

Very deliberately he lifted his snifter and drank. "No."

"If you think that because I came here with you you have the right to dictate to me you're wrong. I'm my own person, Stephen." It struck her even as she said it that it was true. She was her own person. Each decision she made was her own. Filled with a new sense of power, she stepped forward. "No one owns me, not you, not anyone. I won't be ordered, I won't be forced, I won't be pressured." With a flick of her skirts, she turned. He had her again quickly, his hands on both of her arms, his face close.

"You won't go back to him."

"You couldn't stop me if that was what I wanted." She tossed her head back challengingly. "But I have no intention of going back downstairs to Dimitri, or anyone else." She jerked her arms free. "You idiot. Why should I want to be with him when I'm in love with you?"

She stopped, her eyes wide with shock, her lips parted in surprise. Overwhelmed by a combination of humiliation and fury, she spun around. Then she was struggling against him. "Leave me alone! Oh, God, just leave me alone!"

"Do you think I could let you go now?" He caught her hair in his hand, dragging it back until her eyes met his. In them she saw triumph and desire. "I feel as though I've waited all my life to hear you say those words." He rained kisses over her face until her struggles ceased. "You drive me mad," he murmured. "Being with you, being without you."

"Please." Colors, shapes, lights were whirling in her head. "I need to think."

"No. Ask me for anything else, but not more time." Gathering her close, he buried his face in her hair. "Do you think I make a fool of myself over every woman?"

"I don't know." She moaned when his lips trailed down her throat. Something wild and terrifying was happening inside her body. "I don't know you. You don't know me."

"Yes, I do." He pulled away just far enough to look down at her. "From the first moment I saw you, I knew you. Needed you. Wanted you."

It was true. She knew it, felt it, but she shook her head in denial. "It's not possible."

"I've loved you before, Rebecca, almost as much as I do now." He felt her go still. The color fled from her face again, but her eyes stayed steady on his.

"I don't want you to say what isn't real, what you're not sure of."

"Didn't you feel it, the first time I kissed you?" When he saw the acknowledgment in her eyes, his grip tightened. He could feel her heart thundering, racing to match the rhythm of his own. "Somehow you've come back to me, and I to you. No more questions," he said, before she could speak. "I need you tonight."

It was real. She felt the truth and the knowledge when his mouth found hers. If it was wrong to go blindly into need, then she would pay whatever price was asked. She could no longer deny him…or herself.

There was no gentleness in the embrace. It was as it had been the first time, lovers reunited, a hunger finally quenched. All heat and light. She gave more than she'd known she had. Her mouth was as avid as his, as seeking. Her murmurs were as desperate. Her hands didn't shake as they moved over him. They pressed, gripped, demanded. Greedy, she tugged the jacket from his shoulders.

Yes, he'd come back to her. If it was madness to believe it, then for tonight she'd be mad.

The taste of her, just the taste of her, was making his head swim and his blood boil. He nipped at her lip, then sucked until he heard her helpless whimper. He wanted her helpless. Something fierce and uncivilized inside him wanted her weak and pliant and defenseless. When she went limp in his arms he dived into her mouth and plundered. Her response tore at him, so sweet, so vulnerable, then suddenly so ardent.

Her hands, which had fluttered helplessly to her side, rose up again to pull at his shirt, to race under it to warmed flesh. She could only think of how right it felt to touch him, to press against him and wait for him to light new fires inside her.

With an oath, he swept her up into his arms and carried her to the bedroom.

The moon was waning and offered only the most delicate light. It fell in slants and shadows on the bed, dreamlike. But the vibrating of Rebecca's pulse told her this was no dream. There was the scent of jasmine from the sprigs in the vase beside the bed. It was a scent she would always remember, just as she would remember how dark and deep were the color of his eyes.

Needful, desperate, they tumbled onto the bed.

He wanted to take care with her. She seemed so small, so fragile. He wanted to show her how completely she filled his heart. But his body was on fire, and she was already moving like a whirlwind beneath him.

His mouth was everywhere, making her shudder and arch and ache. Desires she'd never known sprang to life inside her and took control. Delirious, she obeyed them, reveled in them, then searched for more.

They rolled across the bed in a passionate war that would have two victors, touching, taking, discovering. Impatient, he peeled the dress from her, moaning as he found her breasts with his hands, his lips, his teeth. Unreasoning desire catapulted through him when he felt her soar.

Her body felt like a furnace, impossibly hot, impossibly strong. Sensations rammed into her, stealing her breath.

Mindless and moaning, she writhed under him, open for any demand he might make, pulsing for any new knowledge he might offer.

Finally, finally, she knew what it was to love, to be loved, to be wanted beyond reason. Naked, she clung to him, awash in the power and the weakness, the glory and the terror.

He raced over her as if he already knew what would make her tremble, what would make her yearn. Never before had she been so aware, so in tune with another.

She made him feel like a god. He touched, and her skin vibrated under his hand. He tasted, and her flavor was like no other. She was moist, heated, and utterly willing. She seemed to explode beneath him, lost in pleasure, drugged by passion. No other woman had ever driven him so close to madness. Her head was thrown back, and one hand was flung out as her fingers dug into the sheets. Wanton, waiting, wild.

With her name on his lips, he drove into her. His breath caught. His mind spun. Her cry of pain and release echoed in his head, bringing him both triumph and guilt. His body went rigid as he fought to claw his way back. Then she seemed to close around him, body, heart, soul. As helpless as she, he crossed the line into madness and took her with him.

Chapter 9

Aftershocks of passion racked her. Stunned and confused, she lay in the shadowed light. Nothing had prepared her for this. No one had ever warned her that pleasure could be so huge or that need could be so jagged. If she had known… Rebecca closed her eyes and nearly laughed out loud. If she had known, she would have left everything behind years ago and searched the world for him.

Only him. She let out a quiet, calming sigh. Only him.

He was cursing himself, slowly, steadily, viciously. Innocent. Dear God. She'd been innocent, as fresh and untouched as spring, and he'd used her, hurt her, taken her.

Disgusted with himself, he sat up and reached for a cigar. He needed more than tobacco. He needed a drink, but he didn't trust his legs to carry him.

The flick of his lighter sounded like a gunshot. For an instant his face, hardened by anger and self-loathing, was illuminated.

"Why didn't you tell me?"

Still floating on an ocean of pleasure, she blinked her eyes open. "What?"

"Damn it, Rebecca, why didn't you tell me you hadn't been with a man before? That this—that I was your first?"

There was an edge of accusation in his voice. For the first time, she realized she was naked. Her cheeks grew hot as she fumbled for the sheet. One moment there was glory; the next, shame. "I didn't think of it."

"Didn't think of it?" His head whipped around. "Don't you think I had a right to know? Do you think this would have happened if I had known?"

She shook her head. It was true that she hadn't thought of it. It hadn't mattered. He was the first, the last, the only. But now it occurred to her that a man like him might not want to make love with an inexperienced woman. "I'm sorry." Her heart seemed to shrivel in her breast. "You said that you loved me, that you wanted me. The rest didn't seem to matter."

She'd cried out. He'd heard the shock and pain in her voice. And he hadn't been able to stop himself. Yes, he needed a drink. "It mattered," he tossed back as he rose and strode into the other room.

Alone, she let out a shuddering breath. Of course it mattered. Only a fool would have thought otherwise. He'd thought he was dealing with an experienced, emotionally mature woman who knew how to play the game. Words like *love* and *need* and *want* were interchangeable. Yes, he'd said he loved her, but to many love was physical and physical only.

She'd made a fool of herself and she'd infuriated him, and all because she'd begun a relationship built on illusions.

She'd knowingly taken the risk, Rebecca reminded herself as she climbed out of bed. Now she'd pay the price.

He was calmer when he started back to the bedroom. Calmer, though anger still bubbled inside him. First he would show her how it should have been, how it could be. Then they had to talk, rationally, coherently.

"Rebecca…" But when he looked at the bed it was empty.

She was wrapped in a robe and was hurling clothing into her suitcase when she heard him knock. With a shake of her head, she rubbed the tears from her cheeks and continued her frenzied packing. She wouldn't answer…. She wouldn't answer and be humiliated again.

"Rebecca." The moment of calm he'd achieved had vanished. Swearing through gritted teeth, he pounded on the door. "Rebecca, this is ridiculous. Open this door."

Ignoring him, she swept bottles and tubes of toiletries off the bureau and into her bag. He'd go away, she told herself, hardly aware that she'd begun to sob. He'd go away and then she'd leave, take a cab to the airport and catch the first plane to anywhere.

The sound of splintering wood had her rushing into the parlor in time to see the door give way.

She'd thought she'd seen fury before, but she'd been wrong. She saw it now as she stared into Stephen's face. Speechless, she looked from him to the broken door and back again.

Elana, tying the belt of her robe, rushed down the hall. "Stephen, what's happened? Is there a—"

He turned on her, hurling one short sentence in clipped Greek at her. Her eyes widened and she backed away, sending Rebecca a look that combined sympathy and envy.

"Do you think you have only to walk away from me?" He pushed the door back until it scraped against the battered jamb.

"I want—" Rebecca lifted a hand to her throat as if to push the words out. "I want to be alone."

"The hell with what you want." He started toward her, only to stop dead when she cringed and turned away. He'd forgotten what it was like to hurt, truly hurt, until that moment. "I asked you once if you were afraid of me. Now I see that you are." Searching for control, he dipped his hands into the pockets of the slacks he'd thrown on. She looked defenseless, terrified, and tears still streaked her cheeks. "I won't hurt you again. Will you sit?" When she shook her head, he bit off an oath. "I will."

"I know you're angry with me," she began when he'd settled into a chair. "I'll apologize if it'll do any good, but I do want to be alone."

His eyes had narrowed and focused. "You'll apologize? For what?"

"For…" What did he expect her to say? Humiliated, she crossed her arms and hugged her elbows. "For what happened…for not…explaining," she finished lamely. "For whatever you like," she continued as the tears started again. "Just leave me alone."

"Sweet God." He rubbed a weary hand over his face. "I can think of nothing in my life I've handled as badly as this." He rose, but stopped again when she automatically retreated. "You don't want me to touch you." His voice had roughened. He had to swallow to clear his throat. "I won't, but I hope you'll listen."

"There's nothing more to say. I understand how you feel and why you feel it. I'd rather we just left it at that."

"I treated you inexcusably."

"I don't want an apology."

"Rebecca—"

"I don't." Her voice rose, stopping his words, stopping her tears. "It's my fault. It's been my fault all along. No, no, no!" she shouted when he took another step. "I don't want you to touch me. I couldn't bear it."

He sucked in his breath, then let it out slowly. "You twist the knife well."

But she was shaking her head and pacing the room now. "It didn't matter at first—at least I didn't think it would matter. I didn't know who you were or that I would fall in love with you. Now I've waited too long and ruined everything."

"What are you talking about?"

Perhaps it was best, best for both of them, to lay out the truth. "You said you knew me, but you don't, because I've done nothing but lie to you, right from the first moment."

Slowly, carefully, he lowered himself to the arm of a chair. "What have you lied to me about?"

"Everything." Her eyes were drenched with regret when she looked at him. "Then, tonight… First I found out that you own hotels. *Own* them."

"It was hardly a secret. Why should it matter?"

"It wouldn't." She dropped her hands to her sides. "If I was what I'd pretended to be. After we'd made love and you—I realized that by pretending I'd let you have feelings for someone who didn't even exist."

"You're standing in front of me, Rebecca. You exist."

"No. Not the way you think, not the way I've let you think."

He prepared himself for the worst. "What have you done? Were you running away from America?"

"No. Yes." She had to laugh at that. "Yes, I was running." She gathered what composure she had left and folded her hands. "I did come from Philadelphia, as I told you. I've lived there all my life. Lived there, went to school there, worked there." She found a tissue in the pocket of her robe. "I'm an accountant."

He stared at her, one brow lifting, as she blew her nose. "I beg your pardon?"

"I said, I'm an accountant." She hurled the words at him, then whirled away to face the window. Stephen started to rise, then thought better of it.

"I find it difficult to imagine you tallying ledgers, Rebecca. If you'd sit down, maybe we could talk this through."

"Damn it, I said I'm an accountant. A CPA, specializing in corporate taxes. Up until a few weeks ago I worked for McDowell, Jableki and Kline in Philadelphia."

He spread his hands, taking it all in. "All right. What did you do? Embezzle?"

She tossed back her head and nearly exploded with laughter. If she said yes he'd probably be intrigued. But the time for intrigue was over. The time for the truth was now. "No. I've never done anything illegal in my life. I've never even had a parking ticket. I've never done anything at all out of the ordinary until a few weeks ago."

She began to pace again, too agitated to keep still. "I'd never traveled, never had a man send a bottle of champagne to my table, never walked along the beach in the moonlight, never had a lover."

He said nothing, not because he was angry or bored but because he was fascinated.

"I had a good job, my car was paid for, I had good, conservative investments that would have ensured me a comfortable retirement. In my circle of friends I'm known as dependable. If someone needs a sitter they know they can call Rebecca. If they need advice or someone to feed their fish while they're on vacation they don't have to worry. I was never late for work, never took five minutes extra for lunch."

"Commendable," he said, and earned a glare.

"Just the type of employee I imagine you'd like to hire."

He swallowed a chuckle. He'd been prepared for her to confess she had a husband, five husbands, a prison record. Instead she was telling him she was an accountant with an excellent work record. "I have no desire to hire you, Rebecca."

"Just as well." She turned away and started to prowl the room again. "You'd undoubtedly change your mind after I tell you the rest."

Stephen crossed his ankles and settled back. God, what a woman she was. "I'm anxious to hear it."

"My aunt died about three months ago, suddenly."

"I'm sorry." He would have gone to her then, but he could see she was far from ready. "I know how difficult it is to lose family."

"She was all I had left." Because she needed something to do, she pushed open the balcony doors. Warm, fragrant night air rushed in. "I couldn't believe she was gone. Just like that. No warning. Of course, I handled the funeral arrangements. No fuss, no frills. Just the way Aunt Jeannie would have wanted. She was a very economical woman, not only in finances but in dress, in speech, in manner. As long as I can remember, people compared me to her."

Stephen's brow lifted again as he studied the woman being buffeted by the breeze—the short red silk robe, the tousled hair.

"Soon after her death—I don't know if it was days or a week—something just snapped. I looked at myself, at my life, and I hated it." She dragged her hair back, only to have the wind catch it again. "I was a good employee, just like my aunt, a good credit risk, a dependable friend. Law-abiding, conservative and boring. Suddenly I could see myself ten, twenty, thirty years down the road, with nothing more than I had at that moment. I couldn't stand it."

She turned around. The breeze caught at the hem of her robe and sent it dancing around her legs. "I quit my job, and I sold everything."

"Sold?"

"Everything I owned—car, apartment, furniture, books, absolutely everything. I turned all the cash into traveler's checks, even the small inheritance from my aunt. Thousands of dollars. I know it might not sound like a lot to you, but it was more than I'd ever imagined having at once."

"Wait." He held up a hand, wanting to be certain he understood everything. "You're telling me that you sold your possessions, *all* your possessions?"

She couldn't remember ever having felt more foolish, and she straightened her shoulders defensively. "Right down to my coffeepot."

"Amazing," he murmured.

"I bought new clothes, new luggage, and flew to London. First-class. I'd never been on a plane before in my life."

"You'd never flown, but took your first trip across the Atlantic."

She didn't hear the admiration in his voice, only the amusement. "I wanted to see something different. To *be* something different. I stayed at the Ritz and took pictures of the changing of the guard. I flew to Paris and had my hair cut." Self-consciously she lifted a hand to it.

Because he could see that she was overwrought, he was careful not to smile. "You flew to Paris for a haircut."

"I'd heard some women discussing this stylist, and I—Never mind." It was no use trying to explain that she'd gone to the same hairdresser, to the same shops, for years. The same everything. "Right after Paris, I came here," she went on. "I met you. Things happened. I let them happen." Tears threatened. She could only pray he didn't see them. "You were exciting, and attracted to me. Or attracted to who you thought I was. I'd never had a romance. No one had ever looked at me the way you did."

Once more he chose his words carefully. "Are you saying that being with me was different? An adventure, like flying to a Paris salon?"

She would never be able to explain what being with him had meant to her. "Apologies and explanations really don't make any difference now. But I am sorry, Stephen. I'm sorry for everything."

He didn't see the tears, but he heard the regret in her voice. His eyes narrowed. His muscles tensed. "Are you apologizing for making love with me, Rebecca?"

"I'm apologizing for whatever you like. I'd make it up to you if I could, but I don't know how, unless I jump out the window."

He paused, as if he were considering it. "I don't think this requires anything quite that drastic. Perhaps if you'd sit down calmly?"

She shook her head and stayed where she was. “I can’t handle any more of this tonight, Stephen. I’m sorry. You’ve every right to be angry.”

He rose, the familiar impatience building. But she was so pale, looked so fragile, sounded so weary. He hadn’t treated her gently before. At least he could do so now.

“All right. Tomorrow, then, after you’ve rested.” He started to go to her, then checked himself. It would take time to show her that there were other ways to love. Time to convince her that love was more, much more than an adventure. “I want you to know that I regret what happened tonight. But that, too, will wait until tomorrow.” Though he wanted to touch a hand to her cheek, he kept it fisted in his pocket. “Get some rest.”

She had thought her heart was already broken. Now it shattered. Not trusting her voice, she nodded.

He left her alone. The door scraped against the splintered jamb as he secured it. She supposed there might have been a woman somewhere who’d made a bigger fool of herself. At the moment, it didn’t seem to matter.

At least there was something she could do for both of them. Disappear.

Chapter 10

It was her own fault, she supposed. There were at least half a dozen promising accounting positions in the want ads. Not one of them interested her. Rebecca circled them moodily. How could she be interested in dental plans and profit sharing? All she could think about, all she'd been able to think about for two weeks, was Stephen.

What had he thought when he'd found her gone? Relief? Perhaps a vague annoyance at business left unfinished? Pen in hand, Rebecca stared out of the window of the garden apartment she'd rented. In her fantasies she imagined him searching furiously for her, determined to find her, whatever the cost. Reality, she thought with a sigh, wasn't quite so romantic. He would have been relieved. Perhaps she wasn't sophisticated, but at least she'd stepped out of his life with no fuss.

Now it was time to get her own life in order.

First things first. She had an apartment, and the little square of lawn outside the glass doors was going to make her happy. That in itself was a challenge. Her old condo had been centrally located on the fifth floor of a fully maintained modern building.

This charming and older development was a good thirty miles from downtown, but she could hear the birds in the morning. She would be able to look out at old oaks and sweeping maples and flowers she would plant herself. Perhaps it wasn't as big a change as a flight to Paris, but for Rebecca it was a statement.

She'd bought some furniture. *Some* was the operative word. Thus far she'd picked out a bed, one antique table and a single chair.

Not logical, Rebecca thought with a faint smile. No proper and economical living room suite, no tidy curtains. Even the single set of towels she'd bought was frivolous. And exactly what she'd wanted. She would do what she'd secretly wanted to do for years—buy a piece here, a piece there. Not because it was a good buy or durable, but because she wanted it.

She wondered how many people would really understand the satisfaction of making decisions not because they were sensible but because they were desirable. She'd done it with her home, her wardrobe. Even with her hair, she thought, running a hand through it. Outward changes had led to inner changes. Or vice versa. Either way, she would never again be the woman she'd been before.

Or perhaps she would be the woman she'd always been but had refused to acknowledge.

Then why was she circling ads in the classifieds? Rebecca asked herself. Why was she sitting here on a beautiful morning planning a future she had no interest in? Perhaps it was true that she would never have the one thing, the one person, she really wanted. There would be no more picnics or walks in the moonlight or frantic nights in bed. Still, she had the memories, she had the moments, she had the dreams. There would be no regrets where Stephen was concerned. Not now, and not ever. And if she was now more the woman she had been with him, it had taken more than a change in hairstyle.

She was stronger. She was surer. She was freer. And she'd done it herself.

She could think of nothing she wanted less than to go back into someone else's firm, tallying figures, calculating profit and loss. So she wouldn't. Rebecca sank into the chair as the thought struck home.

She wouldn't. She wouldn't go job hunting, carrying her résumé, rinsing sweaty palms in the rest room, putting her career and life in someone else's hands again. She'd open her own firm. A small one, certainly. Personalized. Exclusive, she decided, savoring the word. Why not? She had the skill, the experience, and—finally—she had the courage.

It wouldn't be easy. In fact, it would be risky. The money she had left would have to go toward renting office space, equipment, a phone system, advertising. With a bubbling laugh, she sprang up and searched for a legal pad and a pencil. She had to make lists—not only of things to do but of people to call. She had enough contacts from her McDowell, Jableki and Kline days. Maybe, just maybe, she could persuade some of her former clients to give her a try.

"Just a minute," she called out when she heard the knock on the door. She scribbled a reminder to look for file cabinets as she went to answer. She'd much rather have some good solid oak file cabinets than a living room sofa.

She knew better than to open the door without checking the security peephole, but she was much too involved with her plans to think about such things. When she opened the door, she found herself face-to-face with Stephen.

Even if she could have spoken, he wasn't in the mood to let her. "What in the hell do you think you're doing?" he demanded as he slammed the door behind him. "Do you deliberately try to drive me mad, or does it come naturally to you?"

"I—I don't—" But he was already yanking her against him. Whatever words she might have spoken dissolved into a moan against his lips. Her pad fell to the floor with a slap. Even as her arms came up around him he was thrusting her away.

"What kind of game are you playing, Rebecca?" When she just shook her head, he dug his hands into his pockets and paced the wide, nearly empty room. He was unshaven, disheveled and absolutely gorgeous. "It's taken me two weeks and a great deal of trouble to find you. I believe we'd agreed to talk again. I was surprised to discover you'd not only left Athens, but Europe." He swung back and pinned her with a look. "Why?"

Still reeling from his entrance, she struggled not to babble. "I thought it best that I leave."

"You thought?" He took a step toward her, his fury so palatable that she braced herself. "You thought it best," he repeated. "For whom?"

"For you. For both of us." She caught herself fiddling with the lapels of her robe and dropped her hands. "I knew you were angry with me for lying to you and that you regretted what had happened between us. I felt it would be better for both of us if I—"

"Ran away?"

Her chin came up fractionally. "Went away."

"You said you loved me."

She swallowed. "I know."

"Was that another lie?"

"Please don't." She turned away, but there was nowhere to go. "Stephen, I never expected to see you again. I'm trying to make some sense out of my life, to do things in a way that's not only right but makes me happy. In Greece, I guess, I did what made me happy, but I didn't think about what was right. The time with you was…"

"Was what?"

Dragging both hands through her hair, she turned to him again. It was as if the two weeks had never been. She was facing him again, trying to explain what she feared she could never explain. "It was the best thing that ever happened to me, the most important, the most unforgettable, the most precious. I'll always be grateful for those few days."

"Grateful." He wasn't sure whether to laugh or murder her. Stepping forward, he surprised them both by slipping his hands lightly around her throat. "For what? For my giving you your first fling? A fast, anonymous romance with no consequences?"

"No." She lifted a hand to his wrist but made no attempt to struggle. "Did you come all this way to make me feel more guilty?"

"I came all this way because I finish what I begin. We'd far from finished, Rebecca."

"All right." Be calm, she told herself. When a man was this close to the edge, a woman's best defense was serenity. "If you'll let me go, we'll talk. Would you like some coffee?"

His fingers tightened reflexively, then slowly relaxed. "You've bought a new pot."

"Yes." Was that humor in his eyes? she wondered. "There's only one chair. Why don't you use it while I go into the kitchen?"

He took her arm. "I don't want coffee, or a chair, or a pleasant conversation."

It seemed serenity wouldn't work. "All right, Stephen. What do you want?"

"You. I'd thought I'd made that fairly obvious." When she frowned, he glanced around the apartment. "Now tell me, Rebecca, is this what you want? A handful of rooms to be alone in?"

"I want to make the best of the rest of my life. I've already apologized for deceiving you. I realize that—"

"Deceiving me." He held up a finger to stop her. "I've wanted to clear that point up myself. How did you deceive me?"

"By letting you think that I was something I'm not."

"You're not a beautiful, interesting woman? A passionate woman?" He lifted a brow as he studied her. "Rebecca, I have too much pride to ever believe you could deceive me that completely."

He was confusing her—deliberately, she was sure. "I told you what I'd done."

"What you'd done," he agreed. "And how you'd done it." He brought his hand to her throat again, this time in a caress. His anger hadn't made her knees weak. She felt them tremble now at his tenderness. "Selling your possessions and flying to Paris for a new hairstyle. Quitting your job and grabbing life with both hands. You fascinate me." Her eyes stayed open wide when he brushed his lips over hers.

"I think the time is nearly over when you'll be so easily flattered. It's almost a pity." He drew her closer, slowly, while his mouth touched hers. Relief coursed through him as he felt her melt and give. "Do you think it was your background that attracted me?"

"You were angry," she managed.

"Yes, angry at the idea that I had been part of your experiment. Furious," he added before he deepened the kiss. "Furious that I had been of only passing interest." She was heating in his arms, just as he remembered, just as he needed, softening, strengthening. "Shall I tell you how angry? Shall I tell you that for two weeks I couldn't work, couldn't think, couldn't function, because you were everywhere I looked and nowhere to be found?"

"I had to go." She was already tugging at his shirt to find the flesh beneath. To touch him again, just for a moment. To be touched by him. "When you said you regretted making love…" Her own words brought her back. Quickly she dropped her hands and stepped away.

He stared at her for a moment, then abruptly swore and began to pace. "I've never thought myself this big a fool. I hurt you that night in a much different way than I'd believed. Then I handled it with less finesse than I might the most unimportant business transaction." He paused, sighing. For the first time she saw clearly how incredibly weary he was.

"You're tired. Please, sit down. Let me fix you something."

He took a moment to press his fingers to his eyes. Again he wanted to laugh—while he strangled her. She was exactly what he needed, what he understood. Yet at the same time she baffled him.

"You weaken me, Rebecca, and bring out the fool I'd forgotten I could be. I'm surprised you allowed me to set foot into your home. You should have—" As quickly as the anger had come, it faded. As quickly as the tension had formed, it eased. Everything he'd needed to see was in her eyes. Carefully now, he drew a deep breath. A man wasn't always handed so many chances at happiness.

"Rebecca, I never regretted making love with you." He stopped her from turning with the lightest of touches on her shoulder. "I regretted only the way it happened. Too much need and too little care. I regret, I'll always regret, that for your first time there was fire but no warmth." He took her hands in his and brought them to his lips.

"It was beautiful."

"In its way." His fingers tightened on hers. Still so innocent, he thought. Still so generous. "It was not kind or patient or tender, as love should be the first time."

She felt hope rise in her heart again. "None of that mattered."

"It mattered, more than I can ever tell you. After, when you told me everything, it only mattered more. If I had done what my instincts told me to do that night you would never have left me. But I thought you needed time before you could bear to have me touch you again." Slowly, gently, he drew the tip of her finger into his mouth and watched her eyes cloud over. "Let me show you what I should have shown you then." With her hands locked in his, he looked into her eyes. "Do you want me?"

It was time for the truth. "Yes."

He lifted her into his arms and heard her breath catch. "Do you trust me?"

"Yes."

When he smiled, her heart turned over. "Rebecca, I must ask you one more thing."

"What is it?"

"Do you have a bed?"

She felt her cheeks heat even as she laughed. "In there."

She was trembling. It reminded him how careful he had to be, how precious this moment was to both of them. The sun washed over the bed, over them, as he lay beside her. And kissed her—only kissed her, softly, deeply, thoroughly, until her arms slipped from around him to fall bonelessly to her sides. She trembled still as he murmured to her, as his lips brushed over her cheeks, her throat.

He had shown her the desperation love could cause, the sharp-edged pleasure, the speed and the fury. Now he showed her that love could mean serenity and sweetness.

And she showed him.

He had thought to teach her, not to learn, to reassure her but not to be comforted. But he learned, and he was comforted. The need was there, as strong as it had been the first time. But strength was tempered with patience. As he slipped his hands down her robe to part it, to slide it away from her skin, he felt no need to hurry. He could delight in the way the sun slanted across her body, in the way her flesh warmed to his touch.

Her breath was as unsteady as her hands as she undressed him. But not from nerves. She understood that now. She felt strong and capable and certain. Anticipation made her tremble. Pleasure made her shudder. She gave a sigh that purred out of her lips as she arched against his seeking hands. Then he nipped lightly at her breast and she bounded from serenity to passion in one breathless leap.

Still he moved slowly, guiding her into a kind of heated

torment she'd never experienced. Desire boiled in her, and his name sprang to her lips and her body coiled like a spring. Chaining down his own need, he set hers free and watched as she flew over the first peak.

"Only for me," he murmured as she went limp in his arms. "Only for me, Rebecca." With his own passions strapped, he slipped into her, determined to watch her build again. "Tell me you love me. Look at me and tell me."

She opened her eyes. She could barely breathe. Somehow the strength was pouring back into her, but so fast, so powerfully. Sensation rolled over sensation, impossibly. She moved with him, pressed center to center, heart to heart, but all she could see were his eyes, so dark, so blue, so intense. Perhaps she was drowning in them.

"I love you, Stephen."

Then she was falling, fathoms deep, into his eyes, into the sea. With her arms locked around him, she dragged him under with her.

He pulled her against him so that he could stroke her hair and wait for his pulse to level. She'd been innocent. But the surprise, the one he'd been dealing with for weeks, was that until Rebecca he'd been just as innocent. He'd known passion, but he'd never known intimacy, not the kind that reached the heart as fully as the body. And yet…

"We've been here before," he murmured. "Do you feel it, too?"

She linked her fingers with his. "I never believed in things like that until you. When I'm with you it's like remembering." She lifted her head to look at him. "I can't explain it."

"I love you, Rebecca, only more knowing who you are, why you are."

She touched a hand to his cheek. "I don't want you to say anything you don't really feel."

"How can a woman be so intelligent and still so stupid?" With a shake of his head, Stephen rolled on top of her. "A man doesn't travel thousands of miles for this, however delightful it may be. I love you, and though it annoyed me for quite some time I'm accustomed to it now."

"Annoyed you."

"Infuriated." He kissed her to cut off whatever retort she might make. "I'd seen myself remaining free for years to come. Then I met a woman who sold her coffeepot so she could take pictures of goats."

"I certainly have no intention of interfering with your plans."

"You already have." He smiled, holding her still when she tried to struggle away. "Marriage blocks off certain freedoms and opens others."

"Marriage?" She stopped struggling but turned her head to avoid another kiss.

"Soon." He nuzzled her neck. "Immediately."

"I never said I'd marry you."

"No, but you will." With his fingertips only, he began to arouse her. "I'm a very persuasive man."

"I need to think." But she was trembling again. "Stephen, marriage is very serious."

"Deadly. And I should warn you that I've already decided to murder any man you look at for more than twenty seconds."

"Really?" She turned her head back, prepared to be angry. But he was smiling. No one else had ever smiled at her in quite that way. "Really?"

"I can't let you go, Rebecca. Can't and won't. Come back with me. Marry me. Have children with me."

"Stephen—"

He laid a finger to her lips. "I know what I'm asking you. You've already started a new life, made new plans. We've had only days together, but I can make you happy. I can promise to love you for a lifetime, or however many lifetimes we have. You once dived into the sea on impulse. Dive with me now, Rebecca. I swear you won't regret it."

Gently she pressed her lips to his fingertip, then drew his hand away. "All my life I've wondered what I might find if I had the courage to look. I found you, Stephen." With a laugh she threw her arms around him. "When do you want to leave?"

* * * * *

Second Nature

To Deb Horm, for the mutual memories.

Prologue

. . .With the moon full and white and cold. He saw the shadows shift and shiver like living things over the ice-crusted snow. Black on white. Black sky, white moon, black shadows, white snow. As far as he could see there was nothing else. There was such emptiness, an absence of color, the only sound the whistling moan of wind through naked trees. But he knew he wasn't alone, that there was no safety in the black or the white. Through his frozen heart moved a trickle of hot fear. His breath, labored, almost spent, puffed out in small white clouds. Over the frosted ground fell a black shadow. There was no place left to run.

Hunter drew on his cigarette, then stared at the words on the terminal through a haze of smoke. Michael Trent was dead. Hunter had created him, molded him exclusively for that cold, pitiful death under a full moon. He felt a sense of accomplishment rather than remorse for destroying the man he knew more intimately than he knew himself.

He'd end the chapter there, however, leaving the details

of Michael's murder to the readers' imagination. The mood was set, secrets hinted at, doom tangible but unexplained. He knew his habit of doing just that both frustrated and fascinated his following. Since that was precisely his purpose, he was pleased. He often wasn't.

He created the terrifying, the breathtaking, the unspeakable. Hunter explored the darkest nightmares of the human mind and, with cool precision, made them tangible. He made the impossible plausible and the uncanny commonplace. The commonplace he would often turn into something chilling. He used words the way an artist used a palette and he fabricated stories of such color and simplicity a reader was drawn in from the first page.

His business was horror, and he was phenomenally successful.

For five years he'd been considered the master of his particular game. He'd had six runaway bestsellers, four of which he'd transposed into screenplays for feature films. The critics raved, sales soared, letters poured in from fans all over the world. Hunter couldn't have cared less. He wrote for himself first, because the telling of a story was what he did best. If he entertained with his writing, he was satisfied. But whatever reaction the critics and the readers had, he'd still have written. He had his work; he had his privacy. These were the two vital things in his life.

He didn't consider himself a recluse; he didn't consider himself unsociable. He simply lived his life exactly as he chose. He'd done the same thing six years before...before the fame, success and large advances.

If someone had asked him if having a string of bestsellers had changed his life, he'd have answered, why should it? He'd been a writer before *The Devil's Due* had shot to number one on the *New York Times* list. He was a writer now. If he'd wanted his life to change, he'd have become a plumber.

Some said his life-style was calculated—that he created the image of an eccentric for effect. Good promotion. Some said he raised wolves. Some said he didn't exist at all but was a clever product of a publisher's imagination. But Hunter Brown had a fine disregard for what anyone said. Invariably, he listened only to what he wanted to hear, saw only what he chose to see and remembered everything.

After pressing a series of buttons on his word processor, he set up for the next chapter. The next chapter, the next word, the next book, was of much more importance to him than any speculative article he might read.

He'd worked for six hours that day, and he thought he was good for at least two more. The story was flowing out of him like ice water: cold and clear.

The hands that played the keys of the machine were beautiful—tanned, lean, long-fingered and wide-palmed. One might have looked at them and thought they would compose concertos or epic poems. What they composed were dark dreams and monsters—not the dripping-fanged, scaly-skinned variety, but monsters real enough to make the flesh crawl. He always included enough realism, enough of the everyday, in his stories to make the horror commonplace and all too plausible. There was a creature lurking in the dark closet of his work, and that creature was the private fear of every man. He found it, always. Then, inch by inch, he opened the closet door.

Half forgotten, the cigarette smoldered in the overflowing ashtray at his elbow. He smoked too much. It was perhaps the only outward sign of the pressure he put on himself, a pressure he'd have tolerated from no one else. He wanted this book finished by the end of the month, his self-imposed deadline. In one of his rare impulses, he'd agreed to speak at a writers' conference in Flagstaff the first week of June.

It wasn't often he agreed to public appearances, and when he did it was never at a large, publicized event. This particular conference would boast no more than two hundred published and aspiring writers. He'd give his workshop, answer questions, then go home. There would be no speaker's fee.

That year alone, Hunter had summarily turned down offers from some of the most prestigious organizations in the publishing business. Prestige didn't interest him, but he considered, in his odd way, the contribution to the Central Arizona Writers' Guild a matter of paying his dues. Hunter had always understood that nothing was free.

It was late afternoon when the dog lying at his feet lifted his head. The dog was lean, with a shining gray coat and the narrow, intelligent look of a wolf.

"Is it time, Santanas?" With a gentleness the hand appeared made for, Hunter reached down to stroke the dog's head. Satisfied, but already deciding that he'd work late that evening, he turned off his word processor.

Hunter stepped out of the chaos of his office into the tidy living room with its tall, many-paned windows and lofted ceiling. It smelled of vanilla and daisies. Large and sleek, the dog padded alongside him.

After pushing open the doors that led to a terra-cotta patio, he looked into the thick surrounding woods. They shut him in, shut others out. Hunter had never considered which, only knew that he needed them. He needed the peace, the mystery and the beauty, just as he needed the rich red walls of the canyon that rose up around him. Through the quiet he could hear the trickle of water from the creek and smell the heady freshness of the air. These he never took for granted; he hadn't had them forever.

Then he saw her, walking leisurely down the winding path toward the house. The dog's tail began to swish back and forth.

Sometimes, when he watched her like this, Hunter would think it impossible that anything so lovely belonged to him. She was dark and delicately formed, moving with a careless confidence that made him grin even as it made him ache. She was Sarah. His work and his privacy were the two vital things in his life. Sarah was his life. She'd been worth the struggles, the frustration, the fears and the pain. She was worth everything.

Looking over, she broke into a smile that flashed with braces. *"Hi, Dad!"*

Chapter 1

The week a magazine like *Celebrity* went to bed was utter chaos. Every department head was in a frenzy. Desks were littered, phones were tied up and lunches were skipped. The air was tinged with a sense of panic that built with every hour. Tempers grew short, demands outrageous. In most offices the lights burned late into the night. The rich scent of coffee and the sting of tobacco smoke were never absent. Rolls of antacids were consumed and bottles of eye drops constantly changed hands. After five years on staff, Lee took the monthly panic as a matter of course.

Celebrity was a slick, respected publication whose sales generated millions of dollars a year. In addition to stories on the rich and famous, it ran articles by eminent psychologists and journalists, interviews with both statesmen and rock stars. Its photography was first-class, just as its text was thoroughly researched and concisely written. Some of its detractors might have termed it quality gossip, but the word *quality* wasn't forgotten.

An ad in *Celebrity* was a sure bet for generating sales and interest and was priced accordingly. *Celebrity* was, in a tough competitive business, one of the leading monthly publications in the country. Lee Radcliffe wouldn't have settled for less.

"How'd the piece on the sculptures turn out?"

Lee glanced up at Bryan Mitchell, one of the top photographers on the West Coast. Grateful, she accepted the cup of coffee Bryan passed her. In the past four days, she'd had a total of twenty hours sleep. "Good," she said simply.

"I've seen better art scrawled in alleys."

Though she privately agreed, Lee only shrugged. "Some people like the clunky and obscure."

With a laugh, Bryan shook her head. "When they told me to photograph that red and black tangle of wire to its best advantage, I nearly asked them to shut off the lights."

"You made it look almost mystical."

"I can make a junkyard look mystical with the right lighting." She shot Lee a grin. "The same way you can make it sound fascinating."

A smile touched Lee's mouth but her mind was veering off in a dozen other directions. "All in a day's work, right?"

"Speaking of which—" Bryan rested one slim jean-clad hip on Lee's organized desk, drinking her own coffee black. "Still trying to dig something up on Hunter Brown?"

A frown drew Lee's elegant brows together. Hunter Brown was becoming her personal quest and almost an obsession. Perhaps because he was so completely inaccessible, she'd become determined to be the first to break through the cloud of mystery. It had taken her nearly five years to earn her title as staff reporter, and she had a reputation for being tenacious, thorough and cool. Lee knew she'd earned those adjectives. Three months of hitting blank walls in researching Hunter Brown didn't deter her. One way or the other, she was going to get the story.

"So far I haven't gotten beyond his agent's name and his editor's phone number." There might've been a hint of frustration in her tone, but her expression was determined. "I've never known people so closemouthed."

"His latest book hit the stands last week." Absently, Bryan picked up the top sheet from one of the tidy piles of papers Lee was systematically dealing with. "Have you read it?"

"I picked it up, but I haven't had a chance to start it yet."

Bryan tossed back the long honey-colored braid that fell over her shoulder. "Don't start it on a dark night." She sipped at her coffee, then gave a laugh. "God, I ended up sleeping with every light in the apartment burning. I don't know how he does it."

Lee glanced up again, her eyes calm and confident. "That's one of the things I'm going to find out."

Bryan nodded. She'd known Lee for three years, and she didn't doubt Lee would. "Why?" Her frank, almond-shaped eyes rested on Lee's.

"Because—" Lee finished off her coffee and tossed the empty cup into her overflowing wastebasket "—no one else has."

"The Mount Everest syndrome," Bryan commented, and earned a rare, spontaneous grin.

A quick glance would have shown two attractive women in casual conversation in a modern, attractively decorated office. A closer look would have uncovered the contrasts. Bryan, in jeans and a snug T-shirt, was completely relaxed. Everything about her was casual and not quite tidy, from her smudged sneakers to the loose braid. Her sharp-featured, arresting face was touched only with a hasty dab of mascara. She'd probably meant to add lipstick or blusher and then forgotten.

Lee, on the other hand, wore a very elegant ice-blue suit, and the nerves that gave her her drive were evident in the hands that were never quite still. Her hair was expertly cut in a short swinging style that took very little care—which was every bit as important to her as having it look good. Its shade fell somewhere between copper and gold. Her skin was the delicate, milky white some redheads bless and others curse. Her makeup had been meticulously applied that morning, down to the dusky blue shadow that matched her eyes. She had delicate, elegant features offset by a full and obviously stubborn mouth.

The two women had entirely different styles and entirely different tastes but oddly enough, their friendship had begun the moment they'd met. Though Bryan didn't always like Lee's aggressive tactics and Lee didn't always approve of Bryan's laid-back approach, their closeness hadn't wavered in three years.

"So." Bryan found the candy bar she'd stuck in her jeans pocket and proceeded to unwrap it. "What's your master plan?"

"To keep digging," Lee returned almost grimly. "I do have a couple of connections at Horizon, his publishing house. Maybe one of them'll come through with something." Without being fully aware of it, she drummed her fingers on the desk. "Damn it, Bryan, he's like the man who wasn't there. I can't even find out what state he lives in."

"I'm half inclined to believe some of the rumors," Bryan

said thoughtfully. Outside Lee's office someone was having hysterics over the final editing of an article. "I'd say the guy lives in a cave somewhere, full of bats with a couple of stray wolves thrown in. He probably writes the original manuscript in sheep's blood."

"And sacrifices virgins every new moon."

"I wouldn't be surprised." Bryan swung her feet lazily while she munched on her chocolate bar. "I tell you the man's weird."

"*Silent Scream*'s already on the bestseller list."

"I didn't say he wasn't brilliant," Bryan countered, "I said he was weird. What kind of a mind does he have?" She shook her head with a half-sheepish smile. "I can tell you I wished I'd never heard of Hunter Brown last night while I was trying to sleep with my eyes open."

"That's just it." Impatient, Lee rose and paced to the tiny window on the east wall. She wasn't looking out; the view of Los Angeles didn't interest her. She just had to move around. "What kind of mind *does* he have? What kind of life does he live? Is he married? Is he sixty-five or twenty-five? Why does he write novels about the supernatural?" She turned, her impatience and her annoyance showing beneath the surface of the sophisticated grooming. "Why did you read his book?"

"Because it was fascinating," Bryan answered immediately. "Because by the time I was on page 3, I was so into it you couldn't have gotten the book away from me with a crowbar."

"And you're an intelligent woman."

"Damn right," Bryan agreed and grinned. "So?"

"Why do intelligent people buy and read something that's going to terrify them?" Lee demanded. "When you pick up a Hunter Brown, you know what it's going to do to you, yet his books consistently spring to the top of the bestseller list and stay there. Why does an obviously intelligent man write books like that?" She began, in a habit Bryan recognized, to fiddle with whatever was at hand—the leaves of a philodendron, the stub of a pencil, the left earring she'd removed during a phone conversation.

"Do I hear a hint of disapproval?"

"Yeah, maybe." Frowning, Lee looked up again. "The man is probably the best colorist in the country. If he's describing a room in an old house, you can smell the dust. His characterizations are so real you'd swear you'd met the people in his books. And he uses that talent to write about things that go bump in the night. I want to find out why."

Bryan crumpled her candy wrapper into a ball. "I know a woman who has one of the sharpest, most analytical minds I've ever come across. She has a talent for digging up obscure facts, some of them impossibly dry, and turning them into intriguing stories. She's ambitious, has a remarkable talent for words, but works on a magazine and lets a half-finished novel sit abandoned in a drawer. She's lovely, but she rarely dates for any purpose other than business. And she has a habit of twisting paper clips into ungodly shapes while she's talking."

Lee glanced down at the small mangled piece of metal in her hands, then met Bryan's eyes coolly. "Do you know why?"

There was a hint of humor in Bryan's eyes, but her tone was serious enough. "I've tried to figure it out for three years, but I can't precisely put my finger on it."

With a smile, Lee tossed the bent paper clip into the trash. "But then, you're not a reporter."

* * *

Because she wasn't very good at taking advice, Lee switched on her bedside lamp, stretched out and opened Hunter Brown's latest novel. She would read a chapter or two, she decided, then make it an early night. An early night was an almost sinful luxury after the week she'd put in at *Celebrity.*

Her bedroom was done in creamy ivories and shades of blue from the palest aqua to indigo. She'd indulged herself here, with dozens of plump throw pillows, a huge Turkish rug and a Queen Anne stand that held an urn filled with peacock feathers and eucalyptus. Her latest acquisition, a large ficus tree, sat by the window and thrived.

She considered this room the only truly private spot in her life. As a reporter, Lee accepted that she was public property as much as the people she sought out. Privacy wasn't something she could cling to when she constantly dug into other people's lives. But in this little corner of the world, she could relax completely, forget there was work to do, ladders to climb. She could pretend L.A. wasn't bustling outside, as long as she had this oasis of peace. Without it, without the hours she spent sleeping and unwinding there, she knew she'd overload.

Knowing herself well, Lee understood that she had a tendency to push too hard, run too fast. In the quiet of her bedroom she could recharge herself each night so that she'd be ready for the race again the following day.

Relaxed, she opened Hunter Brown's latest effort.

Within a half hour, Lee was disturbed, uncomfortable and completely engrossed. She'd have been angry with the author for drawing her in if she hadn't been so busy turning pages. He'd put an ordinary man in an extraordinary situation and done it with such skill that Lee was already relating to the teacher who'd found himself caught up in a small town with a dark secret.

The prose flowed and the dialogue was so natural she could hear the voices. He filled the town with so many recognizable things, she could have sworn she'd been there herself. She knew the story was going to give her more than one bad moment in the dark, but she had to go on. That was the magic of a major storyteller. Cursing him, she read on, so tense that when the phone rang beside her, the book flew out of her hands. Lee swore again, at herself, and lifted the receiver.

Her annoyance at being disturbed didn't last. Grabbing a pencil, she began to scrawl on the pad beside the phone. With her tongue caught between her teeth, she set down the pencil and smiled. She owed the contact in New York an enormous favor, but she'd pay off when the time came, as she always did. For now, Lee thought, running her hand over Hunter's book, she had to make arrangements to attend a small writers' conference in Flagstaff, Arizona.

She had to admit the country was impressive. As was her habit, Lee had spent the time during the flight from L.A. to Phoenix working, but once she'd changed to the small commuter plane for the trip to Flagstaff, her work had been forgotten. She'd flown through thin clouds over a vastness almost impossible to conceive after the skyscrapers and traffic of Los Angeles. She'd looked down on the peaks and dips and castlelike rocks of Oak Creek Canyon, feeling a drumming excitement that was rare in a woman who wasn't easily impressed. If she'd had more time…

Lee sighed as she stepped off the plane. There was never time enough.

The tiny airport boasted a one-room lobby with a choice of concession stand or soda and candy machines. No loudspeaker announced incoming and outgoing flights. No skycap bustled up to her to relieve her of her bags. There wasn't a line of cabs waiting outside to compete for the handful of people who'd disembarked. With her garment bag slung over her shoulder, she frowned at the inconvenience. Patience wasn't one of her virtues.

Tired, hungry and inwardly a little frazzled by the shaky commuter flight, she stepped up to one of the counters. "I need to arrange for a car to take me to town."

The man in shirtsleeves and loosened tie stopped pushing buttons on his computer. His first polite glance sharpened when he saw her face. She reminded him of a cameo his grandmother had worn at her neck on special occasions. Automatically he straightened his shoulders. "Did you want to rent a car?"

Lee considered that a moment, then rejected it. She hadn't come to do any sight-seeing, so a car would hardly be worthwhile. "No, just transportation into Flagstaff." Shifting her bag, she gave him the name of her hotel. "Do they have a courtesy car?"

"Sure do. You go on over to that phone by the wall there. Number's listed. Just give 'em a call and they'll send someone out."

"Thank you."

He watched her walk to the phone and thought he was the one who should have said thank-you.

Lee caught the scent of grilling hot dogs as she crossed the room. Since she'd turned down the dubious tray offered on the flight, the scent had her stomach juices swimming. Quickly and efficiently, she dialed the hotel, gave her name and was assured a car would be there within twenty minutes. Satisfied, she bought a hot dog and settled in one of the black plastic chairs to wait.

She was going to get what she'd come for, Lee told herself almost fiercely as she looked out at the distant mountains. The time wasn't going to be wasted. After three months of frustration, she was finally going to get a firsthand look at Hunter Brown.

It had taken skill and determination to persuade her editor-in-chief to spring for the trip, but it would pay off. It had to. Leaning back, she reviewed the questions she'd ask Hunter Brown once she'd cornered him.

All she needed, Lee decided, was an hour with him. Sixty minutes. In that time, she could pull out enough information for a concise, and very exclusive, article. She'd done precisely that with this year's Oscar winner, though he'd been reluctant, and a presidential candidate, though he'd been hostile. Hunter Brown would probably be both, she decided with a half smile. It would only add spice. If she'd wanted a bland, simple life, she'd have bent under the pressure and married Jonathan. Right now she'd be planning her next garden party rather than calculating how to ambush an award-winning writer.

Lee nearly laughed aloud. Garden parties, bridge parties and the yacht club. That might have been perfect for her family, but she'd wanted more. More what? her mother had demanded, and Lee could only reply, Just more.

Checking her watch, she left her luggage neatly stacked by the chair and went into the ladies' room. The door had hardly closed behind her when the object of all her planning strolled into the lobby.

He didn't often do good deeds, and then only for people he had a genuine affection for. Because he'd gotten into town with time to spare, Hunter had driven to the airport with the intention of picking up his editor. With barely a glance around, he walked over to the same counter Lee had approached ten minutes before.

"Flight 471 on time?"

"Yes, sir, got in ten minutes ago."

"Did a woman get off?" Hunter glanced at the nearly empty lobby again. "Attractive, mid-twenties—"

"Yes, sir," the clerk interrupted. "She just stepped into the rest room. That's her luggage over there."

"Thanks." Satisfied, Hunter walked over to Lee's neat stack of luggage. Doesn't believe in traveling light, he noticed, scanning the garment bag, small Pullman and briefcase. Then, what woman did? Hadn't his Sarah taken two suitcases for the brief three-day stay with his sister in Phoenix? Strange that his little girl should be two parts woman already. Perhaps not so strange, Hunter reflected. Females were born two parts woman, while males took years to grow out of boyhood—if they ever did. Perhaps that's why he trusted men a great deal more.

Lee saw him when she came back into the lobby. His back was to her, so that she had only the impression of a tall, leanly built man with black hair curling carelessly down to the neck of his T-shirt. Right on time, she thought with satisfaction, and approached him.

"I'm Lee Radcliffe."

When he turned, she went stone-still, the impersonal smile freezing on her face. In the first instant, she couldn't have said why. He was attractive—perhaps too attractive. His face was narrow but not scholarly, raw-boned but not rugged. It was too much a combination of both to be either. His nose was straight and aristocratic, while his mouth was sculpted like a poet's. His hair was dark and full and unruly, as though he'd been driving fast for hours with the wind blowing free. But it wasn't these things that caused her to lose her voice. It was his eyes.

She'd never seen eyes darker than his, more direct, more…disturbing. It was as though they looked through her. No, not through, Lee corrected numbly. Into. In ten seconds, they had looked into her and seen everything.

He saw a stunning, milk-pale face with dusky eyes gone wide in astonishment. He saw a soft, feminine mouth, lightly tinted. He saw nerves. He saw a stubborn chin and molten copper hair that would feel like silk between the fingers. What he saw was an outwardly poised, inwardly tense woman who smelled like spring evenings and looked like a *Vogue* cover. If it hadn't been for that inner tension, he might have dismissed her, but what lay beneath people's surfaces always intrigued him.

He skimmed her neat traveling suit so quickly his eyes might never have left hers. "Yes?"

"Well, I…" Forced to swallow, she trailed off. That alone infuriated her. She wasn't about to be set off into stammers by a driver for the hotel. "If you've come to pick me up," Lee said curtly, "you'll need to get my bags."

Lifting a brow, he said nothing. Her mistake was simple and obvious. It would have taken only a sentence from him to correct it. Then again, it was her mistake, not his. Hunter had always believed more in impulses than explanations. Bending down, he picked up the Pullman, then slung the strap of the garment bag over his shoulder. "The car's out here."

She felt a great deal more secure with the briefcase in her hand and his back to her. The oddness, Lee told herself, had come from excitement and a long flight. Men never surprised her; they certainly never made her stare and stammer. What she needed was a bath and something a bit more substantial to eat than that hot dog.

The car he'd referred to wasn't a car, she noted, but a Jeep. Supposing this made sense, with the steep roads and hard winters, Lee climbed in.

Moves well, he thought, and dresses flawlessly. He noted too that she bit her nails. "Are you from the area?" Hunter asked conversationally when he'd stowed her bags in the back.

"No. I'm here for the writers' conference."

Hunter climbed in beside her and shut the door. Now he knew where to take her. "You're a writer?"

She thought of the two chapters of her manuscript she'd brought along in case she needed a cover. "Yes."

Hunter swung through the parking lot, taking the back road that led to the highway. "What do you write?"

Settling back, Lee decided she might as well try her routine out on him before she was in the middle of two hundred published and aspiring writers. "I've done articles and some short stories," she told him truthfully enough. Then she added what she'd rarely told anyone. "I've started a novel."

With a speed that surprised but didn't unsettle her, he burst onto the highway. "Are you going to finish it?" he asked, showing an insight that disturbed her.

"I suppose that depends on a lot of things."

He took another careful look at her profile. "Such as?"

She wanted to shift in her seat but forced herself to be still. This was just the sort of question she might have to answer over the weekend. "Such as if what I've done so far is any good."

He found both her answer and her discomfort reasonable. "Do you go to many of these conferences?"

"No, this is my first."

Which might account for the nerves, Hunter mused, but he didn't think he'd found the entire answer.

"I'm hoping to learn something," Lee said with a small smile. "I registered at the last minute, but when I learned Hunter Brown would be here, I couldn't resist."

The frown in his eyes came and went too quickly to be noticed. He'd agreed to do the workshop only because it wouldn't be publicized. Even the registrants wouldn't know he'd be there, until the following morning. Just how, he wondered, had the little redhead with the Italian shoes and midnight eyes found out? He passed a truck. "Who?"

"Hunter Brown," Lee repeated. "The novelist."

Impulse took over again. "Is he any good?"

Surprised, Lee turned to study his profile. It was infinitely easier to look at him, she discovered, when those eyes weren't focused on her. "You've never read any of his work?"

"Should I have?"

"I suppose that depends on whether you like to read with all the lights on and the doors locked. He writes horror fiction."

If she'd looked more closely, she wouldn't have missed the quick humor in his eyes. "Ghouls and fangs?"

"Not exactly," she said after a moment. "Not that simple. If there's something you're afraid of, he'll put it into words and make you wish him to the devil."

Hunter laughed, greatly pleased. "So, you like to be scared?"

"No," Lee said definitely.

"Then why do you read him?"

"I've asked myself that when I'm up at 3:00 A.M. finishing one of his books." Lee shrugged as the Jeep slowed for the turn-off. "It's irresistible. I think he must be a very odd man," she murmured, half to herself. "Not quite, well, not quite like the rest of us."

"Do you?" After a quick, sharp turn, he pulled up in front of the hotel, more interested in her than he'd planned to be. "But isn't writing just words and imagination?"

"And sweat and blood," she added, moving her shoulders again. "I just don't see how it could be very comfortable to live with an imagination like Brown's. I'd like to know how he feels about it."

Amused, Hunter jumped out of the Jeep to retrieve her bags. "You're going to ask him."

"Yes." Lee stepped down. "I am."

For a moment, they stood on the sidewalk, silently. He looked at her with what might have been mild interest, but she sensed something more—something she shouldn't have felt from a hotel driver after a ten-minute acquaintance. For the second time she wanted to shift and made herself stand still. Wasting no more words, Hunter turned toward the hotel, her bags in hand.

It didn't occur to Lee until she was following him inside that she'd had a nonstop conversation with a hotel driver, a conversation that hadn't dwelt on the usual pleasantries or tourist plugs. As she watched him walk to the desk, she felt an aura of cool confidence from him and traces, very subtle traces, of arrogance. Why was a man like this driving back and forth and getting nowhere? she wondered. Stepping up to the desk, she told herself it wasn't her concern. She had bigger fish to fry.

"Lenore Radcliffe," she told the clerk.

"Yes, Ms. Radcliffe." He handed her a form and imprinted her credit card before he passed her a key. Before she could take it, Hunter slipped it into his own hand. It was then she noticed the odd ring on his pinky, four thin bands of gold and silver twisted into one.

"I'll take you around," he said simply, then crossed through the lobby with her again in his wake. He wound through a corridor, turned left, then stopped. Lee waited while he unlocked the door and gestured her inside.

The room was on the garden level with its own patio, she was pleased to note. As she scanned the room, Hunter carelessly switched on the TV and flipped through the channels before he checked the air conditioner. "Just call the desk if you need anything else," he advised, stowing her garment bag in the closet.

"Yes, I will." Lee hunted through her purse and came up with a five. "Thank you," she said, holding it out.

His eyes met hers again, giving her that same frozen jolt they had in the airport. She felt something stir deep within but wasn't sure if it was trying to reach out to him or struggling to hide. The fingers holding the bill nearly trembled. Then he smiled, so quickly, so charmingly, she was speechless.

"Thank you, Ms. Radcliffe." Without a blink, Hunter pocketed the five dollars and strolled out.

Chapter 2

If writers were often considered odd, writers' conferences, Lee was to discover, were oddities in themselves. They certainly couldn't be considered quiet or organized or stuffy.

Like nearly every other of the two hundred or so participants, she stood in one of the dozen lines at 8:00 A.M. for registration. From the laughing and calling and embracing, it was obvious that many of the writers and would-be writers knew one another. There was an air of congeniality, shared knowledge and camaraderie. Overlaying it all was excitement.

Still, more than one member stood in the noisy lobby like a child lost in a shipwreck, clinging to a folder or briefcase as though it were a life preserver and staring about with awe or simple confusion. Lee could appreciate the feeling, though she looked calm and poised as she accepted her packet and pinned her badge to the mint-green lapel of her blazer.

Concentrating on the business at hand, she found a chair

in a corner and skimmed the schedule for Hunter Brown's workshop. With a dawning smile, she took out a pen and underlined.

CREATING HORROR THROUGH
ATMOSPHERE AND EMOTION
Speaker to be announced.

Bingo, Lee thought, capping her pen. She'd make certain she had a front-row seat. A glance at her watch showed her that she had three hours before Brown began to speak. Never one to take chances, she took out her notebook to skim over the questions she'd listed, while people filed by her or merely loitered, chatting.

"If I get rejected again, I'm going to put my head in the oven."

"Your oven's electric, Judy."

"It's the thought that counts."

Amused, Lee began to listen to the passing comments with half an ear while she added a few more questions.

"And when they brought in my breakfast this morning, there was a five-hundred-page manuscript under my plate. I completely lost my appetite."

"That's nothing. I got one in my office last week written in calligraphy. One hundred and fifty thousand words of flowing script."

Editors, she mused. She could tell them a few stories about some of the submissions that found their way to *Celebrity.*

"He said his editor hacked his first chapter to pieces so he's going into mourning before the rewrites."

"I always go into mourning before rewrites. It's after a

rejection that I seriously consider taking up basket weaving as a profession."

"Did you hear Jeffries is here again trying to peddle that manuscript about the virgin with acrophobia and telekinesis? I can't believe he won't let it die a quiet death. When's your next murder coming out?"

"In August. It's poison."

"Darling, that's no way to talk about your work."

As they passed by her, Lee caught the variety of tones, some muted, some sophisticated, some flamboyant. Gestures and conversations followed the same wide range. Amazed, she watched one man swoop by in a long, dramatic black cape.

Definitely an odd group, Lee thought, but she warmed to them. It was true she confined her skill to articles and profiles, but at heart she was a storyteller. Her position on the magazine had been hard-earned, and she'd built her world around it. For all her ambition, she had a firm fear of rejection that kept her own manuscript unfinished, buried in a drawer for weeks and sometimes months at a time. At the magazine, she had prestige, security and room for advancement. The weekly paycheck put the roof over her head, the clothes on her back and the food on her table.

If it hadn't been so important that she prove she could do all this for herself, she might have taken the chance of sending those first hundred pages to a publishing house. But then… Shaking her head, Lee watched the people mill through the registration area, all types, all sizes, all ages. Clothes varied from trim professional suits to jeans to flamboyant caftans and smocks. Apparently style was a matter of taste and taste a matter of individuality. She wondered if she'd see quite the same variety anywhere else. Absently, she glanced at the partial manuscript she'd tucked into her briefcase. Just for cover, she reminded herself. That was all.

No, she didn't believe she had it in her to be a great writer, but she knew she had the skill for great reporting. She'd never, never settle for being second-rate at anything.

Still, while she was here, it wouldn't hurt to sit in on one or two of the seminars. She might pick up some pointers. More important, she told herself as she rose, she might be able to stretch this trip into another story on the ins and outs of a writers' conference. Who attended, why, what they did, what they hoped for. Yes, it could make quite an interesting little piece. The job, after all, came first.

An hour later, a bit more enthusiastic than she wanted to be after her first workshop, she wandered into the coffee shop. She'd take a short break, assimilate the notes she'd written, then go back and make certain she had the best seat in the house for Hunter Brown's lecture.

Hunter glanced up from his paper and watched her enter the coffee shop. Lee Radcliffe, he mused, finding her of more interest than the local news he'd been scanning. He'd enjoyed his conversation with her the day before, and as often as not, he found conversations tedious. She had a quality about her—an innate frankness glossed with sophistication—that he found intriguing enough to hold his interest. An obsessive writer who believed that the characters themselves were the plot of any book, Hunter always looked for the unique and the individual. Instinct told him Lee Radcliffe was quite an individual.

Unobserved, he watched her. From the way she looked absently around the room it was obvious she was preoccupied. The suit she wore was very simple but showed both style and taste in the color and cut. She was a woman who could wear the simple, he decided, because she was a woman who'd been born with style. If he wasn't very much mistaken, she'd been born into wealth as well. There was always a subtle difference between those who were accustomed to money and those who'd spent years earning it.

So where did the nerves come from? he wondered. Curious, he decided it would be worth an hour of his time to try to find out.

Setting his paper aside, Hunter lit a cigarette and continued to stare at her, knowing there was no quicker way to catch someone's eye.

Lee, thinking more about the story she was going to write than the coffee she'd come for, felt an odd tingle run up her spine. It was real enough to give her an urge to turn around and walk out again when she glanced over and found herself staring back at the man she'd met at the airport.

It was his eyes, she decided, at first not thinking of him as a man or the hotel driver from the previous day. It was his eyes. Dark, almost the color of jet, they'd draw you in and draw you in until you were caught, and every secret you'd ever had would be secret no longer. It was frightening. It was…irresistible.

Amazed that such a fanciful thought had crept into her own practical, organized mind, Lee approached him. He was just a man, she told herself, a man who worked for his living like any other man. There was certainly nothing to be frightened of.

"Ms. Radcliffe." With the same unsmiling stare, he gestured to the chair across from him. "Buy you a cup of coffee?"

Normally she would've refused, politely enough. But now, for some intangible reason, Lee felt as though she had a point to prove. For the same intangible reason, she felt she had to prove it to him as much as to herself. "Thank you." The moment she sat down, a waitress was there, pouring coffee.

"Enjoying the conference?"

"Yes." Lee poured cream into the cup, stirring it around and around until a tiny whirlpool formed in the center. "As disorganized as everything seems to be, there was an amazing amount of information generated at the workshop I went to this morning."

A smile touched his lips, so lightly that it was barely there at all. "You prefer organization?"

"It's more productive." Though he was dressed more formally than he'd been the day before, the pleated slacks and open-necked shirt were still casual. She wondered why he wasn't required to wear a uniform. But then, she thought, you could put him in one of those nifty white jackets and neat ties and his eyes would simply defy them.

"A lot of fascinating things can come out of chaos, don't you think?"

"Perhaps." She frowned down at the whirlpool in her cup. Why did she feel as though she was being sucked in, in just that way? And why, she thought with a sudden flash of impatience, was she sitting here having a philosophical discussion with a stranger when she should be outlining the two stories she planned to write?

"Did you find Hunter Brown?" he asked her as he studied her over the rim of his cup. Annoyed with herself, he guessed accurately, and anxious to be off doing.

"What?" Distracted, Lee looked back up to find those strange eyes still on her.

"I asked if you'd run into Hunter Brown." The whisper of a smile was on his lips again, and this time it touched his eyes as well. It didn't make them any less intense.

"No." Defensive without knowing why, Lee sipped at her cooling coffee. "Why?"

"After the things you said yesterday, I was curious what you'd think of him once you met him." He took a drag from his cigarette and blew smoke out in a haze. "People usually have a preconceived image of someone but it rarely holds up in the flesh."

"It's difficult to have any kind of an image of someone who hides away from the world."

His brow went up, but his voice remained mild. "Hides?"

"It's the word that comes to my mind," Lee returned, again finding that she was speaking her thoughts aloud to him. "There's no picture of him on the back of any of his books, no bio. He never grants interviews, never denies or substantiates anything written about him. Any awards he's received have been accepted by his agent or his editor." She ran her fingers up and down the handle of her spoon. "I've heard he occasionally attends affairs like this, but only if it's a very small conference and there's no publicity about his appearance."

All during her speech, Hunter kept his eyes on her, watching every nuance of expression. There were traces of frustration, he was certain, and of eagerness. The lovely cameo face was calm while her fingers moved restlessly. She'd be in his next book, he decided on the spot. He'd never met anyone with more potential for being a central character.

Because his direct, unblinking stare made her want to stammer, Lee gave him back the hard, uncompromising look. "Why do you stare at me like that?"

He continued to do so without any show of discomfort. "Because you're an interesting woman."

Another man might have said beautiful, still another might have said fascinating. Lee could have tossed off either one with light scorn. She picked up her spoon again, then set it down. "Why?"

"You have a tidy mind, innate style, and you're a bundle of nerves." He liked the way the faint line appeared between her brows when she frowned. It meant stubbornness to him, and tenacity. He respected both. "I've always been intrigued by pockets," Hunter went on. "The deeper the better. I find myself wondering just what's in your pockets, Ms. Radcliffe."

She felt the tremor again, up her spine, then down. It wasn't comfortable to sit near a man who could do that. She had a moment's sympathy for every person she'd ever interviewed. "You have an odd way of putting things," she muttered.

"So I've been told."

She instructed herself to get up and leave. It didn't make sense to sit there being disturbed by a man she could dismiss with a five-dollar tip. "What are you doing in Flagstaff?" she demanded. "You don't strike me as someone who'd be content to drive back and forth to an airport day after day, shuttling passengers and hauling luggage."

"Impressions make fascinating little paintings, don't they?" He smiled at her fully, as he had the day before when she'd tipped him. Lee wasn't sure why she'd felt he'd been laughing at her then, any more than why she felt he was laughing at her now. Despite herself, her lips curved in response. He found the smile a pleasant and very alluring surprise.

"You're a very odd man."

"I've been told that, too." His smile faded and his eyes became intense again. "Have dinner with me tonight."

The question didn't surprise her as much as the fact that she wanted to accept, and nearly had. "No," she said, cautiously retreating. "I don't think so."

"Let me know if you change your mind."

She was surprised again. Most men would've pressed a bit. It was, well, expected, Lee reflected, wishing she could figure him out. "I have to get back." She reached for her briefcase. "Do you know where the Canyon Room is?"

With an inward chuckle, he dropped bills on the table. "Yes, I'll show you."

"That's not necessary," Lee began, rising.

"I've got time." He walked with her out of the coffee shop and into the wide, carpeted lobby. "Do you plan to do any sight-seeing while you're here?"

"There won't be time." She glanced out one of the wide windows at the towering peak of Humphrey Peak. "As soon as the conference is over I have to get back."

"To where?"

"Los Angeles."

"Too many people," Hunter said automatically. "Don't you ever feel as though they're using up your air?"

She wouldn't have put it that way, would never have thought of it, but there were times she felt a twinge of what might be called claustrophobia. Still, her home was there, and more important, her work. "No. There's enough air, such as it is, for everyone."

"You've never stood at the south rim of the canyon and looked out, and breathed in."

Again, Lee shot him a look. He had a way of saying things that gave you an immediate picture. For the second time, she regretted that she wouldn't be able to take a day or two to explore some of the vastness of Arizona. "Maybe some other time." Shrugging, she turned with him as he headed down a corridor to the right.

"Time's fickle," he commented. "When you need it, there's too little of it. Then you wake up at three o'clock in the morning, and there's too much of it. It's usually better to take it than to anticipate it. You might try that," he said, looking down at her again. "It might help your nerves."

Her brows drew together. "There's nothing wrong with my nerves."

"Some people can thrive on nervous energy for weeks at a time, then they have to find that little valve that lets the steam escape." For the first time, he touched her, just fingertips to the ends of her hair. But she felt it, experienced it, as hard and strong as if his hand had closed firmly over hers. "What do you do to let the steam escape, Lenore?"

She didn't stiffen, or casually nudge his hand away as she would have done at any other time. Instead, she stood still, toying with a sensation she couldn't remember ever experiencing before. Thunder and lightning, she thought. There was thunder and lightning in this man, deep under the strangely aloof, oddly open exterior. She wasn't about to be caught in the storm.

"I work," she said easily, but her fingers had tightened on the handle of her briefcase. "I don't need any other escape valve." She didn't step back, but let the haughtiness that had always protected her enter her tone. "No one calls me Lenore."

"No?" He nearly smiled. It was this look, she realized, the secret amusement the onlooker could only guess at rather than see, that most intrigued. She thought he probably knew that. "But it suits you. Feminine, elegant, a little distant. *And the only word there spoken was the whispered word, 'Lenore'!* Yes." He let his fingertips linger a moment longer on her hair. "I think Poe would've found you very apt."

Before she could prevent it, before she could anticipate it, her knees were weak. She'd felt the sound of her own name feather over her skin. "Who are you?" Lee found herself demanding. Was it possible to be so deeply affected by someone without even knowing his name? She stepped forward in what seemed to be a challenge. "Just who are you?"

He smiled again, with the oddly gentle charm that shouldn't have suited his eyes yet somehow did. "Strange, you never asked before. You'd better go in," he told her as people began to gravitate toward the open doors of the Canyon Room. "You'll want a good seat."

"Yes." She drew back, a bit shaken by the ferocity of the desire she felt to learn more about him. With a last look over her shoulder, Lee walked in and settled in the front row. It was time to get her mind back on the business she'd come for, and the business was Hunter Brown. Distractions like incomprehensible men who drove Jeeps for a living would have to be put aside.

From her briefcase, Lee took a fresh notebook and two pencils, slipping one behind her ear. Within a few moments, she'd be able to see and study the mysterious Hunter

Brown. She'd be able to listen and take notes with perfect freedom. After his lecture, she'd be able to question him, and if she had her way, she'd arrange some kind of one-on-one for later.

Lee had given the ethics of the situation careful thought. She didn't feel it would be necessary to tell Brown she was a reporter. She was there as an aspiring writer and had the fledgling manuscript to prove it. Anyone there was free to try to write and sell an article on the conference and its participants. Only if Brown used the words *off the record* would she be bound to silence. Without that, anything he said was public property.

This story could be her next step up the ladder. Would be, Lee corrected. The first documented, authentically researched story on Hunter Brown could push her beyond *Celebrity*'s scope. It would be controversial, colorful and, most important, exclusive. With this under her belt, even her quietly critical family would be impressed. With this under her belt, Lee thought, she'd be that much closer to the top rung, where her sights were always set.

Once she was there, all the hard work, the long hours, the obsessive dedication, would be worth it. Because once she was there, she was there to stay. At the top, Lee thought almost fiercely. As high as she could reach.

On the other side of the doors, on the other side of the corridor, Hunter stood with his editor, half listening to her comments on an interview she'd had with an aspiring writer. He caught the gist, that she was excited about the writer's potential. It was a talent of his to be able to conduct a perfectly lucid conversation when his mind was on something entirely different. It was something he roused himself to do only when the mood was on him. So he spoke to his editor and thought of Lee Radcliffe.

Yes, he was definitely going to use her in his next book. True, the plot was only a vague notion in his head, but he already knew she'd be the core of it. He needed to dig a bit deeper before he'd be satisfied, but he didn't foresee any problem there. If he'd gauged her correctly, she'd be confused when he walked to the podium, then stunned, then furious. If she wanted to talk to him as badly as she'd indicated, she'd swallow her temper.

A strong woman, Hunter decided. A will of iron and skin like cream. Vulnerable eyes and a damn-the-devil chin. A character was nothing without contrasts, strengths and weaknesses. And secrets, he thought, already certain he'd discover hers. He had another day and a half to explore Lenore Radcliffe. Hunter figured that was enough.

The corridor was full of laughter and complaints and enthusiasm as people loitered or filed through into the adjoining room. He knew what it was to feel enthusiastic about being a writer. If the pleasure went out of it, he'd still write. He was compelled to. But it would show in his work. Emotions always showed. He never *allowed* his feeling and thoughts to pour into his work—they would have done so regardless of his permission.

Hunter considered it a fair trade-off. His emotions, his thoughts, were there for anyone who cared to read them. His life was completely and without exception his own.

The woman beside him had his affection and his respect. He'd argued with her over motivation and sentence structure, losing as often as winning. He'd shouted at her, laughed with her and given her emotional support through her recent divorce. He knew her age, her favorite drink and her weakness for cashews. She'd been his editor for three years, which is as close to a marriage as many people come. Yet she had no idea he had a ten-year-old daughter named Sarah who liked to bake cookies and play soccer.

Hunter took a last drag on his cigarette as the president of the small writers' group approached. The man was a slick, imaginative science fiction writer whom Hunter had read and enjoyed. Otherwise, he wouldn't be there, about to make one of his rare appearances in the writing community.

"Mr. Brown, I don't need to tell you again how honored we are to have you here."

"No—" Hunter gave him the easy half smile "—you don't."

"There's liable to be quite a commotion when I announce you. After your lecture, I'll do everything I can to keep the thundering horde back."

"Don't worry about it. I'll manage."

The man nodded, never doubting it. "I'm having a small reception in my suite this evening, if you'd like to join us."

"I appreciate it, but I have a dinner engagement."

Though he didn't know quite what to make of the smile, the organization's president was too intelligent to press his luck when he was about to pull off a coup. "If you're ready then, I'll announce you."

"Any time."

Hunter followed him into the Canyon Room, then loitered just inside the doors. The room was already buzzing with anticipation and curiosity. The podium was set on a small stage in front of two hundred chairs that were nearly all filled. Talk died down when the president approached the stage, but continued in pockets of murmurs even after he'd begun to speak. Hunter heard one of the men nearest him whisper to a companion that he had three publishing houses competing for his manuscript. Hunter skimmed over the crowd, barely listening to the beginning of his introduction. Then his gaze rested again on Lee.

She was watching the speaker with a small, polite smile on her lips, but her eyes gave her away. They were dark and eager. Hunter let his gaze roam down until it rested in her lap. There, her hand opened and closed on the pencil. A bundle of nerves and energy wrapped in a very thin layer of confidence, he thought.

For the second time Lee felt his eyes on her, and for the second time she turned so that their gazes locked. The faint line marred her brow again as she wondered what he was doing inside the conference room. Unperturbed, leaning easily against the wall, Hunter stared back at her.

"His career's risen steadily since the publication of his first book, only five years ago. Since the first, *The Devil's Due*, he's given us the pleasure of being scared out of our socks every time we pick up his work." At the mention of the title, the murmurs increased and heads began to swivel. Hunter continued to stare at Lee, and she back at him, frowning. "His latest, *Silent Scream*, is already solid in the number-one spot on the bestseller list. We're honored and privileged to welcome to Flagstaff—Hunter Brown."

The effusive applause competed with the growing murmurs of two hundred people in a closed room. Casually, Hunter straightened from the wall and walked to the stage. He saw the pencil fall out of Lee's hand and roll to the floor. Without breaking rhythm, he stooped and picked it up.

"Better hold on to this," he advised, looking into her

astonished eyes. As he handed it back, he watched astonishment flare into fury.

"You're a—"

"Yes, but you'd better tell me later." Walking the rest of the way to the stage, Hunter stepped behind the podium and waited for the applause to fade. Again he skimmed the crowd, but this time with such a quiet intensity that all sound died. For ten seconds there wasn't even the sound of breathing. "Terror," Hunter said into the microphone.

From the first word he had them spellbound, and held them captive for forty minutes. No one moved, no one yawned, no one slipped out for a cigarette. With her teeth clenched tight, Lee knew she despised him.

Simmering, struggling against the urge to spring up and stalk out, Lee sat stiffly and took meticulous notes. In the margin of the book she drew a perfectly recognizable caricature of Hunter with a dagger through his heart. It gave her enormous satisfaction.

When he agreed to field questions for ten minutes, Lee's was the first hand up. Hunter looked directly at her, smiled and called on someone three rows back.

He answered professional questions professionally and evaded any personal references. She had to admire his skill, particularly since she was well aware he so seldom spoke in public. He showed no nerves, no hesitation and absolutely no inclination to call on her, though her hand was up and her eyes shot fiery little darts at him. But she was a reporter, Lee reminded herself. Reporters got nowhere if they stood on ceremony.

"Mr. Brown," Lee began, and rose.

"Sorry." With his slow smile, he held up a hand. "I'm afraid we're already overtime. Best of luck to all of you."

He left the podium and the room, under a hail of applause. By the time Lee could work her way to the doors, she'd heard enough praise of Hunter Brown to turn her simmering temper to boil.

The nerve, she thought as she finally made it into the corridor. The unspeakable nerve. She didn't mind being bested in a game of chess; she could handle having her work criticized and her opinion questioned. All in all, Lee considered herself a reasonable, low-key person with no more than her fair share of conceit. The one thing she couldn't, wouldn't, tolerate was being made a fool of.

Revenge sprang into her mind, nasty, petty revenge. Oh, yes, she thought as she tried to work her way through the thick crowd of Hunter Brown fans, she'd have her revenge, somehow, some way. And when she did, it would be perfect.

She turned off at the elevators, knowing she was too full of fury to deal successfully with Hunter at that moment. She needed an hour to cool off and to plan. The pencil she still held snapped between her fingers. If it was the last thing she did, she was going to make Hunter Brown squirm.

Just as she started to push the button for her floor, Hunter slipped inside the elevator. "Going up?" he asked easily, and pushed the number himself.

Lee felt the fury rise to her throat and burn. With an effort, she clamped her lips tight on the venom and stared straight ahead.

"Broke your pencil," Hunter observed, finding himself more amused than he'd been in days. He glanced at her open notebook, spotting the meticulously drawn caricature. An appreciative grin appeared. "Well done," he told her. "How'd you enjoy the workshop?"

Lee gave him one scathing look as the elevator doors opened. "You're a fount of trivial information, Mr. Brown."

"You've got murder in your eyes, Lenore." He stepped into the hall with her. "It suits your hair. Your drawing makes it clear enough what you'd like to do. Why don't you stab me while you have the chance?"

As she continued to walk, Lee told herself she wouldn't give him the satisfaction of speaking to him. She wouldn't speak to him at all. Her head jerked up. "You've had a good laugh at my expense," she grated, and dug in her briefcase for her room key.

"A quiet chuckle or two," he corrected while she continued to simmer and search. "Lose your key?"

"No, I haven't lost my key." Frustrated, Lee looked up until fury met amusement. "Why don't you go away and sit on your laurels?"

"I've always found that uncomfortable. Why don't you vent your spleen, Lenore; you'd feel better."

"Don't call me Lenore!" she exploded as her control slipped. "You had no right to use me as the brunt of a joke. You had no right to pretend you worked for the hotel."

"You assumed," he corrected. "As I recall, I never pretended anything. You asked for a ride yesterday; I simply gave you one."

"You knew I thought you were the hotel driver. You were standing there beside my luggage—"

"A classic case of mistaken identity." He noted that her skin tinted with pale rose when she was angry. An attractive side effect, Hunter decided. "I'd come to pick up my editor, who'd missed her Phoenix connection, as it turned out. I thought the luggage was hers."

"All you had to do was say that at the time."

"You never asked," he pointed out. "And you did tell me to get the luggage."

"Oh, you're infuriating." Clamping her teeth shut, she began to fumble in her briefcase again.

"But brilliant. You mentioned that yourself."

"Being able to string words together is an admirable talent, Mr. Brown." Hauteur was one of her most practiced skills. Lee used it to the fullest. "It doesn't make you an admirable person."

"No, I wouldn't say I was, particularly." While he waited for her to find her key, Hunter leaned comfortably against the wall.

"You carried my luggage to my room," she continued, infuriated. "I gave you a five-dollar tip."

"Very generous."

She let out a huff of breath, grateful that her hands were busy. She didn't know how else she could have prevented herself from slapping his calm, self-satisfied face. "You've had your joke," she said, finding her key at last. "Now I'd like you to do me the courtesy of never speaking to me again."

"I don't know where you got the impression I was courteous." Before she could unlock the door, he'd put his hand over hers on the key. She felt the little tingle of power and cursed him for it even as she met his calmly amused look. "You did mention, however, that you'd like to speak to me. We can talk over dinner tonight."

She stared at him. Why should she have thought he

wouldn't be able to surprise her again? "You have the most incredible nerve."

"You mentioned that already. Seven o'clock?"

She wanted to tell him she wouldn't have dinner with him even if he groveled. She wanted to tell him that and all manner of other unpleasant things. Temper fought with practicality. There was a job she'd come to do, one she'd been working on unsuccessfully for three months. Success was more important than pride. He was offering her the perfect way to do what she'd come to do, and to do it more extensively than she could've hoped for. And perhaps, just perhaps, he was opening the door himself for her revenge. It would make it all the sweeter.

Though it was a large lump, Lee swallowed her pride.

"That's fine," she agreed, but he noticed she didn't look too pleased. "Where should I meet you?"

He never trusted easy agreement. But then Hunter trusted very little. She was going to be a challenge, he felt. "I'll pick you up here." His fingers ran casually up to her wrist before he released her. "You might bring your manuscript along. I'm curious to see your work."

She smiled and thought of the article she was going to write. "I very much want you to see my work." Lee stepped into her room and gave herself the small satisfaction of slamming the door in his face.

Chapter 3

Midnight-blue silk. Lee took a great deal of time and gave a great deal of thought to choosing the right dress for her evening with Hunter. It was business.

The deep-blue silk shot through with thin silver threads appealed to her because of its clean, elegant lines and lack of ornamentation. Lee would, on the occasions when she shopped, spend as much time choosing the right scarf as she would researching a subject. It was all business.

Now, after a thorough debate, she slipped into the silk. It coolly skimmed her skin; it draped subtly over curves. Her own reflection satisfied her. The unsmiling woman who looked back at her presented precisely the sort of image she wanted to project—elegant, sophisticated and a bit remote. If nothing else, this soothed her bruised ego.

As Lee looked back over her life, concentrating on her career, she could remember no incident where she'd found herself bested. Her mouth became grim as she ran a brush through her hair. It wasn't going to happen now.

Hunter Brown was going to get back some of his own, if for no other reason than that half-amused smile of his. No one laughed at her and got away with it, Lee told herself as she slapped the brush back on the dresser smartly enough to make the bottles jump. Whatever game she had to play to get what she wanted, she'd play. When the article on Hunter Brown hit the stands, she'd have won. She'd have the satisfaction of knowing he'd helped her. In the final analysis, Lee mused, there was no substitute for winning.

When the knock sounded at her door, she glanced at her watch. Prompt. She'd have to make a note of it. Her mood was smug as, after picking up her slim evening bag, she went to answer.

Inherently casual in dress, but not sloppy, she noted, filing the information away as she glanced at the open-collared shirt under his dark jacket. Some men could wear black tie and not look as elegant as Hunter Brown looked in jeans. That was something that might interest her readers. By the end of the evening, Lee reminded herself, she'd know all she possibly could about him.

"Good evening." She started to step across the threshold, but he took her hand, holding her motionless as he studied her.

"Very lovely," Hunter declared. Her hand was very soft and very cool, though her eyes were still hot with annoyance. He liked the contrast. "You wear silk and a very alluring scent but manage to maintain that aura of untouchability. It's quite a talent."

"I'm not interested in being analyzed."

"The curse or blessing of the writer," he countered. "Depending on your viewpoint. Being one yourself, you should understand. Where's your manuscript?"

She'd thought he'd forget—she'd hoped he would. Now, she was back to the disadvantage of stammering. "It, ah, it isn't…"

"Bring it along," Hunter ordered. "I want to take a look at it."

"I don't see why."

"Every writer wants his words read."

She didn't. It wasn't polished. It wasn't perfect. Without a doubt, the last person she wanted to allow a glimpse of her inner thoughts was Hunter. But he was standing, watching, with those dark eyes already seeing beyond the outer layers. Trapped, Lee turned back into the room and slipped the folder from her briefcase. If she could keep him busy enough, she thought, there wouldn't be time for him to look at it anyway.

"It'll be difficult for you to read anything in a restaurant," she pointed out as she closed the door behind her.

"That's why we're having dinner in my suite."

When she stopped, he simply took her hand and continued on to the elevators as if he hadn't noticed. "Perhaps I've given you the wrong impression," she began coldly.

"I don't think so." He turned, still holding her hand. His palm wasn't as smooth as she'd expected a writer's to be. The palm was as wide as a concert pianist's, but it was ridged with calluses. It made, Lee discovered, a very intriguing and uncomfortable combination. "My imagination hasn't gone very deeply into the prospect of seducing you, Lenore." Though he felt her stiffen in outrage, he drew her into the elevator. "The point is, I don't care for restaurants and I care less for crowds and interruptions." The elevator hummed quietly on the short ascent. "Have you found the conference worthwhile?"

"I'm going to get what I came for." She stepped through the doors as they slid open.

"And what's that?"

"What did you come for?" she countered. "You don't exactly make it a habit to attend conferences, and this one is certainly small and off the beaten path."

"Occasionally I enjoy the contact with other writers." Unlocking the door, he gestured her inside.

"This conference certainly isn't bulging with authors who've attained your degree of success."

"Success has nothing to do with writing."

She set her purse and folder aside and faced him straight on. "Easy to say when you have it."

"Is it?" As if amused, he shrugged, then gestured toward the window. "You should drink in as much of the view as you can. You won't see anything like this through any window in Los Angeles."

"You don't care for L.A." If she was careful and clever, she should be able to pin him down on where he lived and why he lived there.

"L.A. has its points. Would you like some wine?"

"Yes." She wandered over to the window. The vastness still had the power to stun her and almost…almost frighten. Once you were beyond the city limits, you might wander for miles without seeing another face, hearing another voice. The isolation, she thought, or perhaps just the space itself, would overwhelm. "Have you been there often?" she asked, deliberately turning her back to the window.

"Hmm?"

"To Los Angeles?"

"No." He crossed to her and offered a glass of pale-gold wine.

"You prefer the East to the West?"

He smiled and lifted his glass. "I make it a point to prefer where I am."

He was very adept at evasions, she thought, and turned away to wander the room. It seemed he was also very adept at making her uneasy. Unless she missed her guess, he did both on purpose. "Do you travel often?"

"Only when it's necessary."

Tipping back her glass, Lee decided to try a more direct approach. "Why are you so secretive about yourself? Most people in your position would make the most of the promotion and publicity that's available."

"I don't consider myself secretive, nor do I consider myself most people."

"You don't even have a bio or a photo on your book covers."

"My face and my background have nothing to do with the stories I tell. Does the wine suit you?"

"It's very good." Though she'd barely tasted it. "Don't you feel it's part of your profession to satisfy the readers' curiosity when it comes to the person who creates a story that interests them?"

"No. My profession is words—putting words together so that someone who reads them is entertained, intrigued and satisfied with a tale. And tales spring from imagination rather than hard fact." He sipped wine himself and approved it. "The teller of the tale is nothing compared to the tale itself."

"Modesty?" Lee asked with a trace of scorn she couldn't prevent.

The scorn seemed to amuse him. "Not at all. It's a matter of priorities, not humility. If you knew me better, you'd understand I have very few virtues." He smiled, but Lee told herself she'd imagined that brief predatory flash in his eyes. Imagined, she told herself again and shuddered. Annoyed at her own reaction, she held out her wineglass for a refill.

"Have you any virtues?"

He liked the fact that she struck back even when her nerves were racing. "Some say vices are more interesting and certainly more entertaining than virtues." He filled her glass to just under the rim. "Would you agree?"

"More interesting, perhaps more entertaining." She refused to let her eyes falter from his as she drank. "Certainly more demanding."

He mulled this over, enjoying her quick response and her clean, direct thought-patterns. "You have an interesting mind, Lenore; you keep it exercised."

"A woman who doesn't finds herself watching other people climb to the top while she fills water glasses and makes the coffee." She could have cursed in frustration the moment she'd spoken. It wasn't her habit to speak that freely. The point was, she was here to interview him, Lee reminded herself, not the other way around.

"An interesting analogy," Hunter murmured. Ambition. Yes, he'd sensed that about her from the beginning. But what was it she wanted to achieve? Whatever it was, he mused, she wouldn't be above stepping over a few people to get it. He found he could respect that, could almost admire it. "Tell me, do you ever relax?"

"I beg your pardon?"

"Your hands are rarely still, though you appear to have a great deal of control otherwise." He noted that at his words her fingers stopped toying with the stem of her glass.

"Since you've come into this room, you haven't stayed in one spot more than a few seconds. Do I make you nervous?"

Sending him a cool look, she sat on the plush sofa and crossed her legs. "No." But her pulse thudded a bit when he sat down beside her.

"What does?"

"Small loud dogs."

He laughed, pleased with the moment and with her. "You're a very entertaining woman." He took her hand lightly in his. "I should tell you that's my highest compliment."

"You set a great store by entertainment."

"The world's a grim place—worse, often tedious." Her hand was delicate, and delicacy drew him. Her eyes held secrets, and there was little that intrigued him more. "If we can't be entertained, there're only two places to go. Back to the cave, or on to oblivion."

"So you entertain with terror." She wanted to shift farther away from him, but his fingers had tightened almost imperceptibly on her hand. And his eyes were searching for her thoughts.

"If you're worried about the unspeakable terror lurking outside your bedroom window, would you worry about your next dentist appointment or the fact that your washer overflowed?"

"Escape?"

He reached up to touch her hair. It seemed a very casual, very natural gesture to him. Lee's eyes flew open as if she'd been pinched. "I don't care for the word *escape*."

She was a difficult combination to resist, Hunter thought, as he let his fingertips skim down the side of her throat. The fiery hair, the vulnerable eyes, the cool gloss of breeding, the bubbling nerves. She'd make a fascinating character and, he realized, a fascinating lover. He'd already decided to have her for the first; now, as he toyed with the ends of her hair, he decided to have her for the second.

She sensed something when his gaze locked on hers again. Decision, determination, desire. Her mouth went dry. It wasn't often that she felt she could be outmatched by another. It was rarer still when anyone or anything truly frightened her. Though he said nothing, though he moved no closer, she found herself fighting back fear—and the knowledge that whatever game she challenged him to, she would lose because he would look into her eyes and know each move before she made it.

A knock sounded at the door, but he continued to look at her for long silent seconds before he rose. "I took the liberty of ordering dinner," he said, so calmly that Lee wondered if she'd imagined the flare of passion she'd seen in his eyes. While he went to the door, she sat where she was, struggling to sort her own thoughts. She was imagining things, Lee told herself. He couldn't see into her and read her thoughts. He was just a man. Since the game was hers, and only she knew the rules, she wouldn't lose. Settled again, she rose to walk to the table.

The salmon was tender and pink. Pleased with the choice, Lee sat down at the table as the waiter closed the door behind him. So far, Lee reflected, she'd answered more questions than Hunter. It was time to change that.

"The advice you gave earlier to struggling writers about blocking out time to write every day no matter how discouraged they get—did that come from personal experience?"

Hunter sampled the salmon. "All writers face discouragement from time to time. Just as they face criticism and rejection."

"Did you face many rejections before the sale of *The Devil's Due*?"

"I suspect anything that comes too easily." He lifted the wine bottle to fill her glass again. She had a face made for candlelight, he mused as he watched the shadow and light flicker over the cream-soft skin and delicate features. He was determined to find out what lay beneath, before the evening ended.

He never considered he was using her, though he fully intended to pick her brain for everything he could learn about her. It was a writer's privilege.

"What made you become a writer?"

He lifted a brow as he continued to eat. "I was born a writer."

Lee ate slowly, planning her next line of questions. She had to move carefully, avoid putting him on the defensive, maneuver around any suspicions. She never considered she was using him, though she fully intended to pick his brain for everything she could learn about him. It was a reporter's privilege.

"Born a writer," she repeated, flaking off another bite of salmon. "Do you think it's that simple? Weren't there elements in your background, circumstances, early experiences, that led you toward your career?"

"I didn't say it was simple," Hunter corrected. "We're all born with a certain set of choices to make. The matter of making the right ones is anything but simple. Every novel written has to do with choices. Writing novels is what I was meant to do."

He interested her enough that she forgot the unofficial interview and asked for herself, "So you always wanted to be a writer?"

"You're very literal-minded," Hunter observed. Comfortable, he leaned back and swirled the wine in his glass. "No, I didn't. I wanted to play professional soccer."

"Soccer?"

Her astonished disbelief made him smile. "Soccer," he repeated. "I wanted to make a career of it and might have been successful at it, but I had to write."

Lee was silent a moment, then decided he was telling her precisely the truth. "So you became a writer without really wanting to."

"I made a choice," Hunter corrected, intrigued by the orderly logic of her mind. "I believe a great many people are born writer or artist, and die without ever realizing it. Books go unwritten, paintings unpainted. The fortunate ones are those who discover what they were meant to do. I might have been an excellent soccer player; I might have been an excellent writer. If I'd tried to do both, I'd have been no more than mediocre. I chose not to be mediocre."

"There're several million readers who'd agree you made the right choice." Forgetting the cool facade, she propped her elbows on the table and leaned forward. "Why horror fiction, Hunter? Someone with your skill and your imagination could write anything. Why did you turn your talents toward that particular genre?"

He lit a cigarette so that the scent of tobacco stung the air. "Why do you read it?"

She frowned; he hadn't turned one of her questions back on her for some time. "I don't as a rule, except yours."

"I'm flattered. Why mine?"

"Your first was recommended to me, and then..." She hesitated, not wanting to say she'd been hooked from the first page. Instead, she ran her fingertip around the rim of her glass and sorted through her answer. "You have a way of creating atmosphere and drawing characters that make the impossibility of your stories perfectly believable."

He blew out a stream of smoke. "Do you think they're impossible?"

She gave a quick laugh, a laugh he recognized as genuine from the humor that lit her eyes. It did something very special to her beauty. It made it accessible. "I hardly believe in people being possessed by demons or a house being inherently evil."

"No?" He smiled. "No superstitions, Lenore?"

She met his gaze levelly. "None."

"Strange, most of us have a few."

"Do you?"

"Of course, and even the ones I don't have fascinate me." He took her hand, linking fingers firmly. "It's said some people are able to sense another's aura, or personality if the word suits you better, by a simple clasp of hands." His palm was warm and hard as he kept his eyes fixed on hers. She could feel, cool against her hand, the twisted metal of his ring.

"I don't believe that." But she wasn't so sure, not with him.

"You believe only in what you see or feel. Only in what can be touched with one of the five senses that you understand." He rose, drawing her to her feet. "Everything that is can't be understood. Everything that's understood can't be explained."

"Everything has an explanation." But she found the words, like her pulse, a bit unsteady.

She might have drawn her hand away, and he might have let her, but her statement seemed to be a direct challenge. "Can you explain why your heart beats faster when I step closer?" His face looked mysterious, his eyes like jet in the candlelight. "You said you weren't afraid of me."

"I'm not."

"But your pulse throbs." His fingertip lightly touched the hollow of her throat. "Can you explain why when we've yet to spend even one full day together, I want to touch you, like this?" Gently, incredibly gently, he ran the back of his hand up the side of her face.

"Don't." It was only a whisper.

"Can you explain this kind of attraction between two strangers?" He traced a finger over her lips, felt them tremble, wondered about their taste.

Something soft, something flowing, moved through her. "Physical attraction's no more than chemistry."

"Science?" He brought her hand up, pressing his lips to the center of her palm. She felt the muscles in her thighs turn to liquid. "Is there an equation for this?" Still watching her, he brushed his lips over her wrist. Her skin chilled, then heated. Her pulse jolted and scrambled. He smiled. "Does this—" he whispered a kiss at the corner of her mouth "—have to do with logic?"

"I don't want you to touch me like this."

"You want me to touch you," Hunter corrected. "But you can't explain it." In an expected move, he thrust his hands into her hair. "Try the unexplainable," he challenged before his lips closed over hers.

Power. It sped through her. Desire was a rush of heat.

She could feel need sing through her as she stood motionless in his arms. She should have refused him. Lee was experienced in the art of refusals. There was suddenly no wit to evade, no strength to refuse.

For all his intensity, for all the force of his personality, the kiss was meltingly soft. Though his fingers were strong and firm in her hair, so firm if she'd tried to move away she'd have found herself trapped, his lips were as gentle and warm as the light that flickered on the table beside them. She didn't know when she reached for him, but her arms were around him, bodies merging, silk rustling. The quiet, intoxicating taste of wine was on his tongue. Lee drank it in. She could smell the candle wax and her own perfume. Her ordered, disciplined mind swam first with confusion, then with sensation after alluring sensation.

Her lips were cool but warmed quickly. Her body was tense but slowly relaxed. He enjoyed both changes. She wasn't a woman who gave herself freely or easily. He knew that just as he knew she wasn't a woman often taken by surprise.

She seemed very small against him, very fragile. He'd always treated fragility with great care. Even as the kiss grew deeper, even as his own need grew surprisingly greater, his mouth remained gentle on hers, teasing, requesting. He believed that lovemaking, from first touch to fulfillment, was an art. He believed that art could never be rushed. So, slowly, patiently, he showed her what might be, while his hands stayed only in her hair and his mouth stayed softly on her.

He was draining her. Lee could feel her will, her strength, her thoughts, seeping out of her. And as they drained away, a flood of sensation replenished what she lost. There was no dealing with it, no…explaining. It could only be experienced.

Pleasure this fluid couldn't be contained. Desire this strong couldn't be guided. It was the lack of control more than the flood of feeling that frightened her most. If she lost her control, she'd lose her purpose. Then she would flounder. With a murmured protest, she pulled away but found that while he freed her lips, he still held her.

Later, he thought, at some lonely, dark hour, he'd explore his own reaction. Now he was much more interested in hers. She looked at him as though she'd been struck—face pale, eyes dark. Though her lips parted, she said nothing. Under his fingers he could feel the light tremor that coursed through her—once, then twice.

"Some things can't be explained, even when they're understood." He said it softly, so softly she might have thought it a threat.

"I don't understand you at all." She put her hands on his forearms as if to draw him away. "I don't think I want to anymore."

He didn't smile as he let his hands slide down to her shoulders. "Perhaps not. You'll have a choice to make."

"No." Shaken, she stepped away and snatched up her purse. "The conference ends tomorrow and I go back to L.A." Suddenly angry, she turned to face him. "You'll go back to whatever hole it is you hide in."

He inclined his head. "Perhaps." It was best she'd put some distance between them. Very abruptly, he realized that if he'd held her a moment longer, he wouldn't have let her go. "We'll talk tomorrow."

She didn't question her own illogic, but shook her head. "No, we won't talk anymore."

He didn't correct her when she walked to the door, and he stood where he was when the door closed behind her. There was no need to contradict her; he knew they'd talk again. Lifting his glass of wine, Hunter gathered up the manuscript she'd forgotten and settled himself in a chair.

Chapter 4

Anger. Perhaps what Lee felt was simple anger, without other eddies and currents of emotion, but she wasn't certain whom she felt angry with.

What had happened the evening before could have been avoided—should have been, she corrected as she stepped out of the shower. Because she'd allowed Hunter to set the pace and the tone, she'd put herself in a vulnerable position *and* she'd wasted a valuable opportunity. If Lee had learned anything in her years as a reporter, it was that a wasted opportunity was the most destructive mistake in the business.

How much did she know of Hunter Brown that could be used in a concise, informative article? Enough for a paragraph, Lee thought in disgust. A very short paragraph.

She might have only one chance to make up for lost time. Time lost because she'd let herself feel like a woman instead of thinking like a reporter. He'd led her along on a leash, she admitted bitterly, rubbing a towel over her dripping hair while the heat lamp in the ceiling warmed her skin. Instead of balking, she'd gone obediently where he'd taken her. And had missed the most important interview of her career. Lee tossed down the towel and stalked out of the steamy bathroom.

Telling herself she felt nothing but annoyance for him and for herself, Lee pulled on a robe before she sat down at the small writing desk. She still had some time before room service would deliver her first cup of coffee, but there wasn't any more time to waste. Business first…and last. She pulled out a pad and pencil.

HUNTER BROWN. Lee headed the top of the pad in bold letters and underlined the name. The problem had been, she admitted, that she hadn't approached Hunter—the assignment—logically, systematically. She could correct that now with a basic outline. She had, after all, seen him, spoken to him, asked him a few elementary questions. As far as she knew, no other reporter could make such a claim. It was time to stop berating herself for not tying everything up neatly in a matter of hours and make the slim advantage she still had work for her. She began to write in a decisive hand.

APPEARANCE. Not typical. Now there was a positive statement, she thought with a frown. In three bold strokes, she crossed out the words. Dark; lean, rangy build, she wrote. Like a long-distance runner, a cross-country skier. Her eyes narrowed as she brought his face to the foreground of her memory. Rugged face, offset by an air of intelligence. Most outstanding feature—eyes. Very dark, very direct, very…unnerving.

Was that editorializing? she asked herself. Would those long, quiet stares disturb everyone? Shrugging the question away, Lee continued to write. Tall, perhaps six-one, approximately a hundred sixty pounds. Very confident. Musician's hands, poet's mouth.

A bit surprised by her own description, Lee went on to her next category.

PERSONALITY. Enigmatic. Not enough, she decided, huffing slightly. Arrogant, self-absorbed, rude. Definitely editorializing. She set down her pen and took a deep breath, then picked it up again. A skilled, mesmerizing speaker, she admitted in print. Perceptive, cool, taciturn and open by turns, physical.

The last word had been a mistake, Lee discovered, as it brought back the memory of that long, soft, draining kiss, the gentleness of the mouth, the firmness of his hands. No, that wasn't for publication, nor would she need notes to bring back all the details, all the sensations. She would, however, be wise to remember that he was a man who moved quickly when he chose, a man who apparently took precisely what he wanted.

Humor? Yes, under the intensity there was humor in him. She didn't like recalling how he'd laughed at her, but when she had such a dearth of material, she needed every detail, uncomfortable or not.

She remembered every word he'd said on his philosophy of writing. But how could she translate something so intangible into a few clean, pragmatic sentences? She could say he thought of his work as an obligation. A vocation. It just wasn't enough, she thought in frustration. She needed his own words here, not a translation of his meaning. The simple truth was, she had to speak to him again.

Dragging a hand through her hair, she read over her orderly notes. She should have held the reins of the conversation from the very beginning. If she was an expert on anything, it was on channeling and steering talk along the lines she wanted. She'd interviewed subjects more close-mouthed than Hunter, more hostile, but she couldn't remember any more frustrating.

Absently, she began to tap the end of her pencil against the table. It wasn't her job to be frustrated, but to be productive. It wasn't her job, she added, to allow herself to be so utterly seduced by an assignment.

She could have prevented the kiss. It still wasn't clear to Lee why she hadn't. She could have controlled her response to it. She didn't want to dwell on why she hadn't. It was much too easy to remember that long, strangely intense moment and in remembering, to feel it all again. If she was going to prevent herself from doing that, and remember instead all the reasons she'd come to Flagstaff, she had to put Hunter Brown firmly in the category of assignment and keep him there. For now, her biggest problem was how she was going to manage to see him again.

Professionally, she warned herself. But she couldn't sit still thinking of it, or him. Pacing, she tried to block out the incredibly gentle feel of his mouth on hers. And failed.

A flood of feeling; she'd never experienced anything like it. The weakness, the power—it was beyond her to understand it. The longing, the need—how could she know the way to control it?

If she understood him better perhaps… No. Lee lifted her hairbrush, then set it down again. No, understanding Hunter would have nothing to do with fighting her desire for him. She'd wanted to be touched by him, and though she had no logical reason for it, she'd wanted to be touched more than she'd wanted to do her job. It was unprecedented, Lee admitted as she absently pushed bottles and jars around on her dresser. When something was unprecedented, you had to make up your own guidelines.

Uneasy, she glanced up and saw a pale woman with sleepy eyes and unruly hair reflected in the glass. She looked too young, too…fragile. No one ever saw her without the defensive shield of grooming, but she knew what was beneath the fastidiousness and gloss. Fear. Fear of failure.

She'd built her confidence stone by meticulous stone, until most of the time she believed in it herself. But at moments like this, when she was alone, a little weary, a little discouraged, the woman inside crept out, and with her, all the tiny doubts and fears behind that laboriously built wall.

She'd been trained from birth to be little more than an intelligent, attractive ornament. Well-spoken, well-groomed, well-disciplined. It was all her family expected of her. No, Lee corrected. It was *what* had been expected of her. In that respect, she'd already failed.

What trick of fate had made it so impossible for her to fit the mold she'd been fashioned for? Since childhood she'd known she needed more, yet it had taken her until after college to store up enough courage to break away from the road that would have led her from proper debutante to proper matron.

When she'd told her parents she wasn't going to be Mrs. Jonathan T. Willoby, but was leaving Palm Springs to live and work in Los Angeles, she'd been quaking inside. Not until later did she realize it had been their training that had seen her through the very difficult meeting. She'd been taught to remain cool and composed, never to raise her voice, never to show any vulgar signs of temper. When she'd spoken to them, she'd seemed perfectly sure of her own mind, while in truth she'd been terrified of leaving that comfortable gilt cage they'd been fashioning for her since before she was born.

Five years later, the fear had dulled, but it remained. Part of her drive to reach the top in her profession came from the very basic need to prove herself to her parents.

Foolish, she told herself, turning away from the vulnerability of the woman in the glass. She had nothing to prove to anyone, unless it was to herself. She'd come for a story, and that was her first, her only priority. The story was going to gel for her if she had to dog Hunter Brown's footsteps like a bloodhound.

Lee looked down at her notebook again, and at the notes that filled less than a page. She'd have more before the day was over, she promised herself. Much more. He wouldn't get the upper hand again, nor would he distract her from her purpose. As soon as she'd dressed and had her morning coffee, she'd look for Hunter. This time, she'd stay firmly behind the wheel.

When she heard the knock, Lee glanced at the clock beside her bed and gave a little sigh of frustration. She was running behind schedule, something she never permitted herself to do. She'd deliberately requested coffee and rolls for nine o'clock so that she could be dressed and ready to go when they were delivered. Now she'd have to rush to make certain she had a couple of solid hours with Hunter before check-out time. She wasn't going to miss an opportunity twice.

Impatient with herself, she went to the door, drew off the chain and pulled it open.

"You might as well eat nothing if you think you can subsist on a couple of pieces of bread and some jam." Before she could recover, Hunter swooped by her, carrying her breakfast tray. "And an intelligent woman never answers the door without asking who's on the other side." Setting the tray on the table, he turned to pin her with one of his long, intrusive stares.

She looked younger without the gloss of makeup and careful style. The traces of fragility he'd already sensed had no patina of sophistication over them now, though her robe was silk and the sapphire color flattering. He felt a flare of desire and a simultaneous protective twinge. Neither could completely deaden his anger.

She wasn't about to let him know how stunned she was to see him, or how disturbed she was that he was here alone with her when she was all but naked. "First a chauffeur, now a waiter," she said coolly, unsmiling. "You're a man of many talents, Hunter."

"I could return the compliment." Because he knew just how volatile his temper could be, he poured a cup of coffee. "Since one of the first requirements of a fiction writer is that he be a good liar, you're well on your way." He gestured to a chair, putting Lee uncomfortably in the position of visitor. As though she weren't the least concerned, she crossed the room and seated herself at the table.

"I'd ask you to join me, but there's only one cup." She broke a croissant in two and nibbled on it, unbuttered. "You're welcome to a roll." With a steady hand, she added cream to the coffee. "Perhaps you'd like to explain what you mean about my being a good liar."

"I suppose it's a requirement of a reporter as well." Hunter saw her fingers tense on the flaky bit of bread then relax, one by one.

"No." Lee took another bite of her roll as if her stomach hadn't just sunk to her knees. "Reporters deal in fact, not fiction." He said nothing, but the silent look demanded more of her than a dozen words would have. Taking her time, determined not to fumble again, she sipped at her coffee. "I don't remember mentioning that I was a reporter."

"No, you didn't mention it." He caught her wrist as she set down the cup. The grip of his fingers told her immediately just how angry he was. "You quite deliberately didn't mention it."

With a jerk of her head, she tossed the hair out of her eyes. If she'd lost, she wouldn't go down groveling. "It wasn't required that I tell you." Ignoring the fact that he held one of her hands prisoner, Lee picked up her croissant with the other and took a bite. "I paid my registration fee."

"And pretended to be something you're not."

She met his gaze without flinching. "Apparently, we both pretended to be something we weren't, right from the start."

He tilted his head at her reference to their initial meeting. "I didn't want anything from you. You, on the other hand, went beyond the harmless in your deception."

She didn't like the way it sounded when he said it—so petty, so dirty. And so true. If his fingers hadn't been biting into her wrist, she might have found herself apologizing. Instead, Lee held her ground. "I have a perfect right to be here and a perfect right to try to sell an article on any facet of this conference."

"And I," he said, so mildly her flesh chilled, "have a perfect right to my privacy, to the choice of speaking to a reporter or refusing to speak to one."

"If I'd told you that I was on staff at *Celebrity*," she

threw back, making her first attempt to free her arm, "would you have spoken to me at all?"

He still held her wrist; he still held her eyes. For several long seconds, he said nothing. "That's something neither of us will ever know now." He released her wrist so abruptly, her arm dropped to the table, clattering the cup. Lee found that she'd squeezed the flaky pastry into an unpalatable ball.

He frightened her. There was no use denying it even to herself. The force of his anger, so finely restrained, had tiny shocks of cold moving up and down her back. She didn't know him or understand him, nor did she have any way of being certain of what he might do. There was violence in his books; therefore, there was violence in his mind. Clinging to her composure, she lifted her coffee again, drank and tasted absolutely nothing.

"I'm curious to know how you found out." Good, her voice was calm, unhurried. She took the cup in both hands to cover the one quick tremor she couldn't control.

She looked like a kitten backed into a corner, Hunter observed. Ready to spit and scratch, even though her heart was pounding hard enough to be almost audible. He didn't want to respect her for it when he'd rather strangle her. He didn't want to feel a strong urge to touch the pale skin of her cheek. Being deceived by a woman was perhaps the only thing that still had the power to bring him to this degree of rage.

"Oddly enough, I took an interest in you, Lenore. Last night—" He saw her stiffen and felt a certain satisfaction. No, he wasn't going to let her forget that, any more than he could forget it himself. "Last night," he repeated slowly, waiting until her gaze lifted to his again, "I wanted to make love with you. I wanted to get beneath the careful layer of polish and discover you. When I had, you'd have looked as you do now. Soft, fragile, with your mouth naked and your eyes clouded."

Her bones were already melting, her skin already heating, and it was only words. He didn't touch her, didn't attempt to, but the sound of his voice flowed over her skin like the gentlest of caresses. "I don't—I had no intention of letting you make love to me."

"I don't believe in making love to a woman, only with." His eyes never left hers. She could feel her head begin to swim with passion, her breath tremble with it. "Only with," Hunter repeated. "When you left, I turned to the next best way of discovering you."

Lee gripped her hands together in her lap, knowing she had to control the shudders. How could a man have such power? And how could she fight it? Why did she feel as though they were already lovers—was it just the sense of inevitability that they would be, no matter what her choice? "I don't know what you mean." Her voice was no longer calm.

"Your manuscript."

Uncomprehending, she stared. She'd completely forgotten it the night before in her fear of him, and of herself. Anger and frustration had prevented her from remembering it that morning. Now, on top of a dazed desire, she felt the helplessness of a novice confronted by the master. "I never intended for you to read it," she began. Without thinking, she was shredding her napkin in her lap. "I don't have any aspirations toward being a novelist."

"Then you're a fool as well as a liar."

All sense of helplessness fled. No one, no one in all of

her memory, had ever spoken to her like that. "I'm neither a fool nor a liar, Hunter. What I am is an excellent reporter. I want to write an exclusive, in-depth and accurate article on you for our readers."

"Why do you waste your time writing gossip when you've got a novel to finish?"

She went rigid. The eyes that had been clouded with confused desire became frosty. "I don't write gossip."

"You can gloss over it, you can write it with style and intelligence, but it's still gossip." Before Lee could retort, he rose up so quickly, so furiously, her own words were swallowed. "You've no right working forty hours a week on anything but the novel you have inside you. Talent's a two-headed coin, Lenore, and the other side's obligation."

"I don't know what you're talking about." She rose, too, and found she could shout just as effectively as he. "I know my obligations, and one of them's to write a story on you for my magazine."

"And what about the novel?"

Flinging up her hands, she whirled away from him. "What about it?"

"When do you intend to finish it?"

Finish it? She should never have started it. Hadn't she told herself that a dozen times? "Damn it, Hunter, it's a pipe dream."

"It's good."

She turned back, her brows still drawn together with anger but the eyes beneath them suddenly wary. "What?"

"If it hadn't been, your camouflage would have worked very well." He drew out a cigarette while she stared at him. How could he be so patient, move so slowly, when she was ready to jump at every word? "I nearly called you last night to see if you had any more with you, but decided it would keep. I called my editor instead." Still calm, he blew out smoke. "When I gave the chapters to her to read, she recognized your name. Apparently she's quite a fan of *Celebrity*."

"You gave her..." Astonished, Lee dropped into the chair again. "You had no right to show anyone."

"At the time, I fully believed you were precisely what you'd led me to believe you were."

She stood again, then gripped the back of her chair. "I'm a reporter, not a novelist. I'd like you to get the manuscript from her and return it to me."

He tapped his cigarette in an ashtray, only then noticing her neatly written notes. As he skimmed them, Hunter felt twin surges of amusement and annoyance. So, she was trying to put him into a few tidy little slots. She'd find it more difficult than she'd imagined. "Why should I do that?"

"Because it belongs to me. You had no right to give it to anyone else."

"What are you afraid of?" he demanded.

Of failure. The words were almost out before Lee managed to bite them back. "I'm not afraid of anything. I do what I'm best at, and I intend to continue doing it. What are you afraid of?" she retorted. "What are you hiding from?"

She didn't like the look in his eyes when he turned his head toward her again. It wasn't anger she saw there, nor was it arrogance, but something beyond both. "I do what I do best, Lenore." When he'd come into the room, he hadn't planned to do any more than rake her to the bone for her deception and berate her for wasting her talent. Now, as he watched her, Hunter began to think there was a better way to do that and at the same time learn more about her for his own purposes. He was a long way from finished with Lenore Radcliffe. "Just how important is doing a story on me to you?"

Alerted by the change in tone, Lee studied him cautiously. She'd tried everything else, she decided abruptly, perhaps she could appeal to his ego. "It's very important. I've been trying to learn something about you for over three months. You're one of the most popular and critically acclaimed writers of the decade. If you—"

He cut her off by merely lifting a hand. "If I decided to give you an interview, we'd have to spend a great deal of time together, and under my terms."

Lee heard the little warning bell, but ignored it. She could almost taste success. "We can hash out the terms beforehand. I keep my word, Hunter."

"I don't doubt that, once it's given." Crushing out his cigarette, Hunter considered the angles. Perhaps he was asking for trouble. Then again, he hadn't asked for any in quite some time. He was due. "How much more of the manuscript do you have completed?"

"That has nothing to do with this." When he merely lifted a brow and stared, she clenched her teeth. Humor him, Lee told herself. You're too close now. "About two hundred pages."

"Send the rest to my editor." He gave her a mild look. "I'm sure you have her name by now."

"What does that have to do with the interview?"

"It's one of the terms," Hunter told her easily. "I've plans for the week after next," he continued. "You can join me—with another copy of your manuscript."

"Join you? Where?"

"For two weeks I'll be camping in Oak Creek Canyon. You'd better buy some sturdy shoes."

"Camping?" She had visions of tents and mosquitoes. "If you're not leaving for your vacation right away, why can't we set up the interview a day or two before?"

"Terms," he reminded her. "My terms."

"You're trying to make this difficult."

"Yes." He smiled then, just a hint of amusement around his sculpted mouth. "You'll work for your exclusive, Lenore."

"All right." Her chin came up. "Where should I meet you and when?"

Now he smiled fully, appreciating determination when he saw it. "In Sedona. I'll contact you when I'm certain of the date—and when my editor's let me know she's received the rest of your manuscript."

"I hardly see why you're using that to blackmail me."

He crossed to her then, unexpectedly combing his fingers through her hair. It was casual, friendly and uncannily intimate. "Perhaps one of the first things you should know about me is I'm eccentric. If people accept their own eccentricities, they can justify anything they do. Anything at all." He ended the words by closing his mouth over hers.

He heard her suck in her breath, felt her stiffen. But she didn't struggle away. Perhaps she was testing herself, though he didn't think she could know she tested him, too. He wanted to carry her to the rumpled bed, slip off that thin swirl of silk and fit his body to hers. It would fit; somehow he already knew. She'd move with him, for him, as if they'd always been lovers. He knew, though he couldn't explain.

He could feel her melting into him, her lips growing

warm and moist from his. They were alone and the need was like iron. Yet he knew, without understanding, that if they made love now, sated that need, he'd never see her again. They both had fears to face before they became lovers, and after.

Hunter gave himself the pleasure of one long, last kiss, drawing her taste into him, allowing himself to be overwhelmed, just for a moment, by the feel of her against him. Then he forced himself to level, forced himself to remember that they each wanted something from the other—secrets and an intimacy both would put into words in their own ways.

Drawing back, he let his hands linger only a moment on the curve of her cheek, the softness of her hair, while she said nothing. "If you can get through two weeks in the canyon, you'll have your story."

Leaving her with that, he turned and strolled out the door.

"If I can make it through two weeks," Lee muttered, pulling a heavy sweater out of her drawer. "I tell you, Bryan, I've never met anyone who says as little who can irritate me as much." Ten days back in L.A. hadn't dulled her fury.

Bryan fingered the soft wool of the sweater. "Lee, don't you have *any* grub-around clothes?"

"I bought some sweatshirts," she said under her breath. "I haven't spent a great deal of my time in a tent."

"Advice." Before another pair of the trim slacks could be packed into the knapsack Lee had borrowed from her, Bryan took her hand.

Lee lifted one thin coppery brow. "You know I detest advice."

Grinning, Bryan dropped down on the bed. "I know. That's why I can never resist dishing it out. Lee, really, I know you have a pair of jeans. I've *seen* you wear them." She brushed at the hair that escaped her braid. "Designer or not, take jeans, not seventy-five-dollar slacks. Invest in another pair or two," she went on while Lee frowned down at the clothes still in her free hand. "Put that gorgeous wool sweater back in your drawer and pick up a couple of flannel shirts. That'll take care of the nights if it turns cool. Now…"

Because Lee was listening with a frown of concentration, she continued. "Put in some T-shirts; blouses are for the office, not for hiking. Take at least one pair of shorts and invest in some good thick socks. If you had more time, I'd tell you to break in those new hiking boots, because they're going to make you suffer."

"The salesman said—"

"There's nothing wrong with them, Lee, except they've never been out of the box. Face it—" She stretched back among Lee's collection of pillows. "You've been too concerned about packing enough paper and pencils to worry about gear. If you don't want to make an ass of yourself, listen to momma."

With a quick hiss of breath, Lee replaced the sweater. "I've already made an ass of myself, several times." She slammed one of her dresser drawers. "He's not going to get the best of me during these next two weeks, Bryan. If I have to sleep out in a tent and climb rocks to get this story, then I'll do it."

"If you tried real hard, you could have fun at the same time."

"I'm not looking for fun. I'm looking for an exclusive."

"We're friends."

Though it was a statement, not a question, Lee glanced over. "Yes." For the first time since she'd begun packing, she smiled. "We're friends."

"Then tell me what it is that bothers you about this guy. You've been ready to chew your nails for over a week." Though she spoke lightly, the concern leaked through. "You wanted to interview Hunter Brown, and you're going to interview Hunter Brown. How come you look like you're preparing for war?"

"Because that's how I feel." With anyone else, Lee would have evaded the question or turned cold. Because it was Bryan, she sat on the edge of the bed, twisting a newly purchased sweatshirt in her hands. "He makes me want what I don't want to want, feel what I don't want to feel. Bryan, I don't have room in my life for complications."

"Who does?"

"I know exactly where I'm going," Lee insisted, a bit too vehemently. "I know exactly how to get there. Somehow I have a feeling that Hunter's a detour."

"Sometimes a detour is more interesting than a planned route, and you get to the same place eventually."

"He looks at me as though he knows what I'm thinking. More, as if he knows what I thought yesterday, or last year. It's not comfortable."

"You've never looked for the comfortable," Bryan stated, pillowing her head on her folded arms. "You've always looked for a challenge. You've just never found one in a man before."

"I don't want one in a man." Violently, Lee stuffed the sweatshirt into the knapsack. "I want them in my work."

"You don't have to go."

Lee lifted her head. "I'm going."

"Then don't go with your teeth gritted." Crossing her legs under her, Bryan sat up. She was as rumpled as Lee was tidy but seemed oddly suited to the luxurious pile of pillows around her. "This is a tremendous opportunity for you, professionally and personally. Oak Creek's one of the most beautiful canyons in the country. You'll have two weeks to be part of it. There's a man who doesn't bore or cater to you." She grinned at Lee's arch look. "You know damn well they do one or the other and you can't abide it. Enjoy the change of scene."

"I'm going to work," Lee reminded her. "Not to pick wildflowers."

"Pick a few anyway; you'll still get your story."

"And make Hunter Brown squirm."

Bryan gave her throaty laugh, tossing a pillow into the air. "If that's what you're set on doing, you'll do it. I'd feel sorry for the guy if he hadn't given me nightmares." After a quick grimace, her look softened into one of affection. "And Lee…" She laid her hand over her friend's. "If he makes you want something, take it. Life isn't crowded with offers. Give yourself a present."

Lee sat silently for a moment, then sighed. "I'm not sure if I'd be giving myself a present or a curse." Rising, she went to her dresser. "How many pairs of socks?"

"But is she pretty?" Sarah sat in the middle of the rug, one leg bent toward her while she tried valiantly to hook the other behind her neck. "*Really* pretty?"

Hunter dug into the basket of laundry. Sarah had scrupulously reminded him it was his turn to sort and fold. "I wouldn't use the word *pretty.* A carefully arranged basket of fruit's pretty."

Sarah giggled, then rolled and arched into a back bend. She liked nothing better than talking with her father, because no one else talked like him. "What word would you use then?"

Hunter folded a T-shirt with the name of a popular rock band glittered across it. "She has a rare, classic beauty that a lot of women wouldn't know precisely what to do with."

"But she does?"

He remembered. He wanted. "She does."

Sarah laid down on her back to snuggle with the dog that stretched out beside her. She liked the soft, warm feel of Santanas's fur, in much the same way she liked to close her eyes and listen to her father's voice. "She tried to fool you," Sarah reminded him. "You don't like it when people try to fool you."

"To her way of thinking, she was doing her job."

With one hand on the dog's neck, Sarah looked up at her father with big, dark eyes so much like his own. "You never talk to reporters."

"They don't interest me." Hunter came upon a pair of jeans with a widening hole in the knee. "Aren't these new?"

"Sort of. So why are you taking her camping with you?"

"Sort of new shouldn't have holes already, and I'm not taking her; she's coming with me."

Digging in her pocket, she came up with a stick of gum. She wasn't supposed to chew any because of her braces, so she fondled the wrapped piece instead. In six months, Sarah thought, she was going to chew a dozen pieces, all at once. "Because she's a reporter or because she has a rare, classic beauty?"

Hunter glanced down to see his daughter's eyes laughing at him. She was entirely too clever, he decided, and threw a pair of rolled socks at her. "Both, but mostly because I find her interesting and talented. I want to see how much I can find out about her, while she's trying to find out about me."

"You'll find out more," Sarah declared, idly tossing the socks up in the air. "You always do. I think it's a good idea," she added after a moment. "Aunt Bonnie says you don't see enough women, especially women who challenge your mind."

"Aunt Bonnie thinks in couples."

"Maybe she'll incite your simmering passion."

Hunter's hand paused on its way to the basket. "What?"

"I read it in a book." Expertly, she rolled so that her feet touched the floor behind her head. "This man met this woman, and they didn't like each other at first, but there was this strong physical attraction and this growing desire, and—"

"I get the picture." Hunter looked down at the slim, dark-haired girl on the floor. She was his daughter, he thought. She was ten. How in God's name had they gotten involved in the subject of passion? "You of all people should know that things don't often happen in real life the way they do in books."

"Fiction's based on reality." Sarah grinned, pleased to throw one of his own quotes back at him. "But before you do fall in love with her, or have too much simmering passion, I want to meet her."

"I'll keep that in mind." Still watching her, Hunter held

up three unmatched socks. "Just how does this happen every week?"

Sarah considered the socks a moment, then sat up. "I think there's a parallel universe in the dryer. On the other side of the door, at this very minute, someone else is holding up three unmatched socks."

"An interesting theory." Reaching down, Hunter grabbed her. As Sarah's laughter bounced off the lofted ceiling, he dropped her, bottom first, into the basket.

Chapter 5

It was like every western she'd ever seen. With the sun bright in her eyes, Lee could almost see outlaws outrunning posses and Indians hiding in wait behind rocks and buttes. If she let her imagination go, she could almost hear the hoofbeats ring against the rock-hard ground. Because she was alone in the car, she could let her imagination go.

The rich red mountains rose up into a painfully blue sky. There was a vastness that was almost outrageous in scope, with no lushness, with no need for any, with no patience for any. It made her throat dry and her heart thud.

There was green—the silvery green of sage clinging to the red, rocky soil and the deeper hue of junipers, which would give way to a sudden, seemingly planned sparseness. Yet the sparseness was rich in itself. The space, the overwhelming space, left her stunned and humble and oddly hungry for more. Everywhere there were more rocky ridges, more color, more… Lee shook her head. Just more.

Even when she came closer to town, the houses and

buildings couldn't compete with the openness. Stop signs, streetlights, flower gardens, were inconsequential. Her car joined more cars, but five times the number would still have been insignificant. It was a view you drank in, she thought, but its taste was hot and packed a punch.

She liked Sedona immediately. Its tidy western flavor suited the fabulous backdrop instead of marring it. She hadn't been sure anything could.

The main street was lined with shops with neat signs and clean plate glass. She noticed lots of wood, lots of bargains and absolutely no sense of urgency. Sedona clung to the aura of town rather than city. It seemed comfortable with itself and with the spectacular spread of sky. Perhaps, Lee mused as she followed the directions to the rental-car drop-off, just perhaps, she'd enjoy the next two weeks after all.

Since she was early for her arranged meeting time with Hunter even after dealing with the paperwork on her rental car, Lee decided she could afford to indulge herself playing tourist. She had nearly an hour to vacation before work began again.

The liquid silver necklaces and turquoise earrings in the shop windows tempted her, but she moved past them. There'd be plenty of opportunities after this little adventure for something frivolous—as a reward for success. For now, she was only passing time.

But the scent of fudge drew her. Slipping inside the little shop that claimed to sell the world's best, Lee bought a half pound. For energy, she told herself as the sample melted in her mouth. There was no telling what kind of food she'd get over the next two weeks. Hunter had very specifically told her when he contacted her by phone that he'd handle the supplies. The fudge, Lee told herself, would be emergency rations.

Besides, some of Bryan's advice had been valid enough. There was no use going into this thing thinking she'd be miserable and uncomfortable. There wasn't any harm getting into the spirit a bit, Lee decided as she strolled into a western-wear shop. If she viewed the next two weeks as a working vacation, she'd be much better off.

Though she toyed with conch belts for a few minutes, Lee rejected them. They wouldn't suit her, any more than the fringed or sequined shirts would. Perhaps she'd pick one up for Bryan before heading back to L.A. Anything Bryan put on suited her, Lee mused with something closer to a sigh than to envy. Bryan never had to feel restricted to the tailored, the simple or the proper.

Was it a matter of suitability, Lee wondered, or a matter of image? With a shrug, she ran a fingertip down the shoulder of a short suede jacket. Image or not, she'd locked herself into it for too long to change now. She didn't want to change, in any case, Lee reminded herself as she wandered through rows and rows of hats. She understood Lee Radcliffe just as she was.

Telling herself she'd stay only another minute, she set her knapsack at her feet. She wasn't particularly athletic. Lee tried on a khaki-colored Stetson with a curved brim. She wasn't flighty. She exchanged the first hat for a smaller one with a spray of feathers in the band. What she was, was businesslike and down-to-earth. She dropped a black flat-brimmed hat on her head and studied the result. Sedate, she decided, smiling a little. Practical. Yes, if she were in the market for—

"You're wearing it all wrong."

Before Lee could react, two strong hands were tilting the hat farther down on her head. Critically, Hunter angled it slightly, then stepped away. "Yes, it's the perfect choice for you. The contrast with your hair and skin, that practical sort of dash." Taking her shoulders, he turned her toward the mirror, where both his image and hers looked back at her.

She saw the way his fingers held her shoulders, long and confident. She could see how small she looked pressing against him. In no more than an instant, Lee could feel the pleasure she wanted to ignore and the annoyance she had to concentrate on.

"I've no intention of buying it." Embarrassed, she drew the hat off and returned it to the shelf.

"Why not?"

"I've no need for it."

"A woman who buys only what she needs?" Amusement crossed his face even as anger crossed hers. "A sexist remark if I've ever heard one," Hunter continued before she could speak. "Still, it's a pity you won't buy it. It gives you a breezy air of confidence."

Ignoring that, Lee bent down and picked up her knapsack again. "I hope I haven't kept you waiting long. I got into town early and decided to kill some time."

"I saw you wander in here when I drove in. Even in jeans you walk as though you were wearing a three-piece suit." While she tried to work out if that had been a compliment, he smiled. "What kind did you buy?"

"What?" She was still frowning over his comment.

"Fudge." He glanced down at the bag. "What kind did you buy?"

Caught again, Lee thought, nearly resigned to it. "Some milk chocolate and some rocky road."

"Good choice." Taking her arm, he led her through the shop. "If you're determined to resist the hat, we may as well get started."

She noted the Jeep parked at the curb and narrowed her eyes. This was certainly the same one he'd had in Flagstaff. "Have you been staying in Arizona?"

He circled the hood, leaving her to climb in on her own. "I've had some business to take care of."

Her reporter's sense sharpened. "Research?"

He gave her that odd ghost of a smile. "A writer's always researching." He wouldn't tell her—yet—that his research on Lenore Radcliffe had led him to some intriguing conclusions. "You brought a copy of the rest of your manuscript?"

Unable to prevent herself, Lee shot him a look of intense dislike. "That was one of the conditions."

"So it was." Easily he backed up, then pulled into the thin stream of traffic. "What's your impression of Sedona?"

"I can see that the weather and the atmosphere would draw the tourist trade." She found it necessary to sit very erect and to look straight ahead.

"The same might be said of Maui or the South of France."

She couldn't stop her lips from curving, but turned to look out the side window. "It has the air of having been here forever, with very little change. The sense of space is fierce, not at all soothing, but it pulls you in. I suppose it makes me think of the people who first saw it from horseback or the seat of a wagon. I imagine some of them would have been compelled to build right away, to set up a community so that the vastness didn't overwhelm them."

"And others would have been drawn to the desert or the mountains so that the buildings wouldn't close them in."

As she nodded, it occurred to her that she might fit into the first group, and he into the second.

The road he took narrowed and twisted down. He didn't drive sedately, but with the air of a man who knew he could negotiate whatever curve was thrown at him. Lee gripped the door handle, determined not to comment on his speed. It was like taking the downhill rush of a roller coaster without having had the preparatory uphill climb. They whooshed down, a rock wall on one side, a spiraling drop on the other.

"Do you camp often?" Her knuckles were whitening on the handle, but though she had to shout to be heard she was satisfied that her voice was calm enough.

"Now and again."

"I'm curious…" She stopped and cleared her throat as Hunter whipped around a snaking turn. "Why camping?" Did the rocks in the sheer wall beside them ever loosen and tumble onto the road? She decided it was best not to think about it. "A man in your position could go anywhere and do anything he chose."

"This is what I chose," he pointed out.

"All right. Why?"

"There are times when everyone needs simplicity."

Her foot pressed down on the floorboard as if it were a brake pedal. "Isn't this just one more way you have of avoiding people?"

"Yes." His easy agreement had her turning her head to stare at him. He was amused to note that her hand loosened on the handle and that her concentration was on him now rather than the road. "It's also a way of getting away from my work. You never get away from writing, but there are times you need to get away from the trappings of writing."

Her gaze sharpened. Though her fingers itched for her notebook, Lee had faith in her own powers of retention. "You don't like trappings."

"We don't always like what's necessary."

Oblivious to the speed and the curves now, Lee tucked one leg under her and turned toward him. That attracted him, Hunter reflected. The way she'd unconsciously drop that careful shield whenever something challenged her mind. That attracted him every bit as much as her cool, nineteenth-century beauty.

"What do you consider trappings as regards your profession?"

"The confinement of an office, the hum of a machine, the paperwork that's unavoidable but interferes with the story flow."

Odd, but that was precisely what she needed in order to maintain discipline. "If you could change it, what would you do?"

He smiled again. Hunter had never known anyone who thought in more basic terms or straighter lines. "I'd go back a few centuries to when I could simply travel and tell the story."

She believed him. Though he had wealth and fame and critical acclaim, Lee believed him. "None of the rest means anything to you, does it? The glory, the admiration?"

"Whose admiration?"

"Your readers and the critics."

He pulled off the road next to a small wooden building that served as a trading post. "I'm not indifferent to my readership, Lenore."

"But to the critics."

"I admire the orderliness of your mind," he said and stepped from the Jeep.

It was a good beginning, Lee thought, pleased, as she climbed out the passenger side. He'd already told her more than anyone else knew, and the two weeks had barely begun. If she could just keep him talking, learn enough generalities, then she could pin him down on specifics. But she'd have to pace herself. When you were dealing with a master of evasion, you had to tread carefully. She couldn't afford to relax.

"Do we have to check in?"

From behind her back Hunter grinned, while Lee struggled to pull out her knapsack. "I've already taken care of the paperwork."

"I see." Her pack was heavy, but she told herself she'd refuse any offer of assistance and carry it herself. A moment later, she saw it wouldn't be an issue. Hunter merely stood aside, watching as she wriggled into the shoulder straps. So much for chivalry, she thought, annoyed that he hadn't given her the opportunity to assert her independence. She caught the gleam in his eye. He read her mind much too easily.

"Want me to carry the fudge?"

She closed her fingers firmly over the bag. "I'll manage."

With his own gear on his back, Hunter started down a path, leaving her no choice but to follow. He moved as though he'd been walking dirt paths all his life—as if perhaps he'd cut a few of his own. Though she felt out of place in her hiking boots, Lee was determined to keep up and to make it look easy.

"You've camped here before?"

"Mmm-hmm."

"Why?"

He stopped, turning to fix her with that dark, intense stare that always took her breath away. "You only have to look."

She did and saw that the walls and peaks of the canyon rose up as if they'd never stop. They were a color and texture unique to themselves, enhanced by the snatches of green from rough, hardy trees and shrubs that seemed to grow out of the rock. As she had from the air, Lee thought of castles and fortresses, but without the distance the plane had given her, she couldn't be sure whether she was storming the walls or being enveloped by them.

She was warm. The sun was strong, even with the shade of trees that grew thickly at this elevation. Though she saw other people—children, adults, babies carried papoose-style—she felt no sense of crowding.

It's like a painting, she realized all at once. It's as though we're walking into a canvas. The feeling it gave her was both eerie and irresistible. She shifted the pack on her back as she kept pace with Hunter.

"I noticed some houses," she began. "I didn't realize people actually lived in the canyon."

"Apparently."

Sensing his mind was elsewhere, Lee lapsed into silence. She'd done too well to start pushing. For now, she'd follow Hunter, since he obviously knew where he was going.

It surprised her that she found the walk pleasant. For years her life had been directed by deadlines, rush and self-imposed demands. If someone had asked her where she'd choose to spend two weeks relaxing, her mind would have gone blank. But when ideas had begun to come, roughing it in a canyon in Arizona wouldn't have made the top ten. She'd never have considered that the purity of air and the unimpeded arch of sky would be so appealing to her.

She heard a quiet, musical tinkle that took her several moments to identify. The creek, Lee realized. She could smell the water. The new sensation gave her a quick thrill. Her guide, and her project, continued to move at a steady pace in front of her. Lee banked down the urge to share her discovery with him. He'd only think her foolish.

Did she realize how totally out of her element she looked? Hunter wondered. It had taken him only one glance to see that the jeans and the boots she wore were straight out of the box. Even the T-shirt that fit softly over her torso was obviously boutiqueware rather than a department-store purchase. She looked like a model posing as a camper. She smelled expensive, exclusive. Wonderful. What kind of woman carried a worn knapsack and wore sapphire studs in her ears?

As her scent wafted toward him again, carried on the breeze, Hunter reminded himself that he had two weeks to find out. Whatever notes she would make on him, he'd be making an equal number on her. Perhaps both of them would have what they wanted before the time was up. Perhaps both of them would have cause to regret it.

He wanted her. It had been a long time since he'd wanted anything, anyone, that he didn't already have. Over the past days he'd thought often of her response to that long, lingering kiss. He'd thought of his own response. They'd learn about each other over the next two weeks, though they each had their own purposes. But nothing was free. They'd both pay for it.

The quiet soothed him. The towering walls of the canyon soothed him. Lee saw their ferocity, he their tranquillity. Perhaps they both saw what they needed to see.

"For a woman, and a reporter, you have an amazing capacity for silence."

The weight of her pack was beginning to take precedence over the novelty of the scenery. Not once had he asked if she wanted to stop and rest, not once had he even bothered to look back to see if she was still behind him. She wondered why he didn't feel the hole her eyes were boring into his back.

"You have an amazing capacity for the insulting compliment."

Hunter turned to look at her for the first time since they'd started out. There was a thin sheen of perspiration on her brow and her breath came quickly. It didn't detract an iota from her cool, innate beauty. "Sorry," he said, but didn't appear to be. "Have I been walking too fast? You don't look out of shape."

Despite the ache that ran down the length of her back, Lee straightened. "I'm *not* out of shape." Her feet were killing her.

"The site's not much farther." Reaching down to his hip, he lifted the canteen and unscrewed the top. "It's perfect weather for hiking," he said mildly. "Mid-seventies, and there's a breeze."

Lee managed to suppress a scowl as she eyed the canteen. "Don't you have a cup?"

It took Hunter a moment to realize she was perfectly serious. Wisely, he decided to swallow the chuckle. "Packed away with the china," he told her soberly enough.

"I'll wait." She hooked her hands in the front straps of her knapsack to ease some of the weight.

"Suit yourself." While Lee looked on, Hunter drank deeply. If he sensed her resentment, he gave no sign as he capped the canteen again and resumed the walk.

Her throat was all the drier at the thought of water. He'd done it on purpose, she thought while she gritted her teeth. Did he think she'd missed that quick flash of humor in his eyes? It was just one more thing to pay him back for when the time came. Oh, she couldn't wait to write the article and expose Hunter Brown for the arrogant, coldhearted demigod he'd set himself up to be.

She wouldn't be surprised if he was walking her in circles, just to make her suffer. Bryan had been all too right about the boots. Lee had lost count of the number of campsites they'd passed, some occupied and some empty. If this was his way of punishing her for not revealing from the start that she worked for *Celebrity*, he was certainly doing an elaborate job.

Disgusted, exhausted, with her legs feeling less like flesh and more like rubber, she reached out and grabbed his arm. "Just why, when you obviously have a dislike for women and for reporters, did you agree to spend two weeks with me?"

"Dislike women?" His brows arched. "My likes and dislikes aren't as generalized as that, Lenore." Her skin was warm and slightly damp when he curled his fingers around the back of her neck. "Have I given you the impression I dislike you?"

She had to fight the urge to stretch like a cat under his hand. "I don't care what your personal feelings are toward me. This is business."

"For you." His fingers squeezed gently, bringing her an inch closer. "I'm on vacation. Do you know, your mouth's every bit as appealing now as it was the first time I saw it."

"I don't want to appeal to you." But her voice was breathy. "I want you to think of me only as a reporter."

The smile hovered at the edges of his mouth, around the corners of his eyes. "All right," he agreed. "In a minute."

Then he touched his lips to hers, as gently as he had the first time, and as devastatingly. She stood still, amazed to feel as intense a swirl of sensation as she had before. When he touched her, hardly touching her, it was as if she'd never been kissed before. A new discovery, a fresh beginning—how could it be?

The weight on her back seemed to vanish. The ache in her muscles turned into a deeper, richer ache that penetrated to the bone. Her lips parted, though she knew what she invited. Then his tongue joined with hers, slipping into the moistness, drinking up her flavor.

Lee felt the urgency scream through her body, but he was patient. So patient, she couldn't know what the patience cost him. He hadn't expected pain. No woman had ever brought him pain with desire. He hadn't expected the need to flame through him like brushfire, fast and out of control. Hunter had a vision, with perfect clarity, of what it would be like to take her there, on the ground, under the blazing sun with the canyon circling like castle walls around them and the sky like a cathedral dome.

But there was too much fear in her. He could sense it. Perhaps there was too much fear in him. When they came together, it might have the power to topple both their worlds.

"Your lips melt against mine, Lenore," he whispered. "It's all but impossible to resist."

She drew back, aroused, alarmed and all too aware of how helpless she'd been. "I don't want to repeat myself, Hunter," she managed. "And I don't want to amuse you with clichés, but this is business. I'm a reporter on assignment. If we're to make it through the next two weeks peacefully, it'd be wise to remember that."

"I don't know about the peace," he countered, "but we'll try your rules first."

Suspicious, but finding no room to argue, Lee followed him again. They walked out of the sunlight into the dim coolness of a stand of trees. The creek was distant but still audible. From somewhere to the left came the tinny sound of music from a portable radio. Closer at hand was the rustling of small animals. With a nervous look around, Lee convinced herself they were nothing more than squirrels and rabbits.

With the trees closing around them, they might have been anywhere. The sun filtered through, but softly, on the rough, uneven ground. There was a clearing, small and snug, with a circle of stones surrounding a long-dead campfire. Lee glanced around, fighting off the uneasiness. Somehow, she hadn't thought it would be this remote, this quiet, this…alone.

"There're shower and bathroom facilities a few hundred yards east," Hunter began as he slipped off his pack. "Primitive but adequate. The metal can's for trash. Be sure the lid's tightly closed or it'll attract animals. How's your sense of direction?"

Gratefully, she slipped out of her own pack and let it

drop. "It's fine." Now, if she could just take off the boots and rest her feet.

"Good. Then you can gather some firewood while I set up the tent."

Annoyed with the order, she opened her mouth, then firmly shut it again with only a slight hiss. He wouldn't have any cause to complain about her. But as she started to stalk off, the rest of his sentence hit home.

"What do you mean *the* tent?"

He was already unfastening the straps of his pack. "I prefer sleeping in something in case it rains."

"*The* tent," Lee repeated, closing in on him. "As in singular?"

He didn't even spare her a look. "One tent, two sleeping bags."

She wasn't going to explode; she wasn't going to make a scene. After taking a deep breath, she spoke precisely. "I don't consider those adequate arrangements."

He didn't speak for a minute, not because he was choosing his words but because the unpacking occupied him more than the conversation. "If you want to sleep in the open, it's up to you." Hunter drew out a slim, folded piece of material that looked more like a bedsheet than a tent. "But when we decide to become lovers, the arrangements won't make any difference."

"We didn't come here to be lovers," Lee snapped back furiously.

"A reporter and an assignment," Hunter replied mildly. "Two sexless terms. They shouldn't have any problem sharing a tent."

Caught in her own logic, Lee turned and stalked away.

She wouldn't give him the satisfaction of seeing her behave like a woman.

Hunter lifted his head and watched her storm off through the trees. She'd make the first move, he promised himself, suddenly angry. By God, he wouldn't touch her until she came to him.

While he set up camp, he tried to convince himself it was as easy as it sounded.

Chapter 6

Two sexless terms, Lee repeated silently as she scooped up some twigs. Bastard, she thought with grim satisfaction, was also a sexless term. It suited Hunter Brown to perfection. He had no business treating her like a fool just because she'd made a fool of herself already.

She wasn't going to give an inch. She'd sleep in the damn sleeping bag in the damn tent for the next thirteen nights without saying another word about it.

Thirteen, she thought, sending a malicious look over her shoulder. He'd probably planned that, too. If he thought she was going to make a scene, or curl up outside the tent to sleep in the open to spite him, he'd be disappointed. She'd be scrupulously professional, unspeakably cooperative and utterly sexless. Before it was over, he'd think he'd been sharing his tent with a robot.

But she'd know better. Lee let out one long, frustrated breath as she scouted for more sticks. She'd know there was a man beside her in the night. A powerfully sexy, impossibly attractive man who could make her blood swim with no more than a look.

It wouldn't be easy to forget she was a woman over the next two weeks, when she'd be spending every night with a man who already had her nerves jumping.

Her job wasn't to make herself forget, Lee reminded herself, but to make certain *he* forgot. A challenge. That was the best way to look at it. It was a challenge she promised herself she'd succeed at.

With her arms full of sticks and twigs, Lee lifted her chin. She felt hot, dirty and tired. It wasn't an auspicious way to begin a war. Ignoring the ache, she squared her shoulders. She might have to sacrifice a round or two, but she'd win the battle. With a dangerous light in her eyes, she headed toward camp.

She had to be grateful his back was to her when she walked into the clearing. The tent was smaller, much, much smaller, than she'd imagined. It was fashioned from tough, lightweight material that looked nearly transparent. It arched, rounded rather than pointed at the peak, and low to the ground. So low, Lee noted, that she'd have to crawl to get inside. Once in, they'd be forced to sleep nearly elbow to elbow. Then and there, she determined to sleep like a rock. Unmoving.

The size of the tent preoccupied her, so that she didn't notice what Hunter was doing until she was almost beside him. Fresh rage broke out as she dropped her load of wood on the ground. "Just what the hell do you think you're doing?"

Unperturbed by the fury in her voice, Hunter glanced up. In one hand he held a large clear-plastic bag filled with makeup, in the other a flimsy piece of peach-colored material trimmed with ivory lace. "You did know we were going camping," he said mildly, "not to the Beverly Wilshire?"

The color she considered the curse of fair skin flooded her cheeks. "You have no right to go digging around in my things." She snatched the teddy out of his hand, then balled it in her fist.

"I was unpacking." Idly, he turned the makeup bag over to study it from both sides. "I thought you knew to bring only necessities. While I'll admit you have a very subtle, experienced way with this sort of thing—" he gestured with the bag "—eye shadow and lip gloss are excess baggage around a campfire." His voice was infuriatingly friendly, his eyes were only lightly amused. "I've seen you without any of it and had no cause to complain. You certainly don't have to bother with this on my account."

"You conceited jerk." Lee snatched the bag out of his hand. "I don't care if I look like a hag on your account." Taking the knapsack, she stuffed her belongings back inside. "It's *my* baggage, and I'll carry it."

"You certainly will."

"You officious sonofa—" She broke off, barely. "Just don't tell me how to run my life."

"Now, now, name-calling's no way to promote goodwill." Rising, Hunter held out a friendly hand. "Truce?"

Lee eyed him warily. "On what terms?"

He grinned. "That's what I like about you, Lenore, no easy capitulations. A truce with as little interference as possible on both sides. An amiable business arrangement." He saw her relax slightly and couldn't resist the temptation to ruffle her feathers again. "You won't complain about my coffee, and I won't complain when you wear that little scrap of lace to bed."

She gave him a cool smile as she took his hand. "I'm sleeping in my clothes."

"Fair enough." He gave her hand a quick squeeze. "I'm not. Let's see about that coffee."

As he often did, he left her torn between frustration and amusement.

When he put his mind to it, Lee was to discover, Hunter could make things easier. Without fuss, he had the campfire burning and the coffee brewing. Its scent alone was enough to soothe her temper. The economical way he went about it made her think more kindly of him.

There was no point in being at each other's throats for the next two weeks, she decided as she found a convenient rock to sit on. Relaxing might be out of the question, she mused, watching him take clever, compact cooking utensils out of the pack, but animosity wouldn't help, not with a man like Hunter. He was playing games with her. As long as she knew that and avoided the pitfalls, she'd get what she'd come for. So far, she'd allowed him to set the rules and change them at his whim. That would have to change. Lee hooked her hands around a raised knee.

"Do you go camping to get away from the pressure?"

Hunter didn't look back at her, but checked the lantern. So, they were going to start playing word games already. "What pressure?"

Lee might have sighed if she weren't so determined to be pleasantly professional. "There must be pressures from all sides in your line of work. Demands from your publisher, disagreements with your editor, a story that just won't gel the way you want it to, deadlines."

"I don't believe in deadlines."

There was something, Lee thought, and reached for her

notepad. "But doesn't every writer face deadlines from time to time? And can't they be an enormous pressure when the story isn't flowing or you're blocked?"

"Writer's block?" Hunter poured coffee into a metal cup. "There's no such thing."

She glanced over for only a second, brow raised. "Oh, come on, Hunter, some very successful writers have suffered from it, even sought professional help. There must have been a time in your career when you found yourself up against a wall."

"You push the wall out of the way."

Frowning, she accepted the cup he handed her. "How?"

"By working through it." He had a jar of powdered milk, which she refused. "If you don't believe in something, refuse to believe it exists, it doesn't, not for you."

"But you write about things that couldn't possibly exist."

"Why not?"

She stared at him, a dark, attractive man sitting on the ground drinking coffee from a metal cup. He looked so at ease with himself, so relaxed, that for a moment she found it difficult to connect him to the man who created stark terror out of words. "Because there aren't monsters under the bed or demons in the closet."

"There's demons in every closet," he disagreed mildly, "some better hidden than others."

"You're saying you believe in what you write about."

"Every writer believes in what he writes. There'd be no purpose in it otherwise."

"You think some—" She didn't want to use the word *demon* again, and her hand moved in frustration as she sought the right phrase. "Some evil force," Lee chose, "can actually manipulate people?"

"It's more accurate to say I don't believe in anything. Possibilities." Did his eyes become darker, or was it her imagination? "There's no limit to possibilities, Lenore."

His eyes were too dark to read. If he was playing with her, baiting her, she couldn't tell. Uncomfortable, she shifted the topic. "When you sit down to write a story, you craft it, spending hours, days, on the angles and the edges, the same way a carpenter builds a cabinet."

He liked her analogy. Hunter sipped at the strong black coffee, enjoying the taste, enjoying the mingled scents of burning wood, summer and Lee's quiet perfume. "Telling a story's an art, writing's a craft."

Lee felt a quick kick of excitement. That was exactly what she was after, those concise little quotes that gave an insight into his character. "Do you consider yourself an artist, then, or a craftsman?"

He drank without hurry, noting that Lee had barely touched her coffee. The eagerness was with her again, her pen poised, her eyes fixed on his. He found he wanted her more when she was like this. He wanted to see that eager look on her face for him, for the man, not the writer. He wanted to sense the ripe anticipation, lover to lover, arms reaching, mouth softening.

If he were writing the script, he'd keep these two people from fulfilling each other's needs for some time yet. It was necessary to flesh them out a bit first, but the ache told him what he needed. Carefully he arranged another piece of wood on the fire.

"An artist by birth," he said at length, "a craftsman by choice."

"I know it's a standard question," she began, with a brisk

professionalism that made him smile, "but where do you get your ideas?"

"From life."

She looked over again as he lit a cigarette. "Hunter, you can't convince me that the plot for *Devil's Due* came out of the everyday."

"If you take the everyday, twist it, add a few maybes, you can come up with anything."

"So you take the ordinary, twist it and come up with the extraordinary." Understanding this a bit better, she nodded, satisfied. "How much of yourself goes into your characters?"

"As much as they need."

Again it was so simply, so easily, said, she knew he meant it exactly. "Do you ever base one of your characters on someone you know?"

"From time to time." He smiled at her, a smile she neither trusted nor understood. "When I find someone intriguing enough. Do you ever get tired of writing about other people when you've got a world of characters in your own head?"

"It's my job."

"That's not an answer."

"I'm not here to answer questions."

"Why are you here?"

He was closer. Lee hadn't realized he'd moved. He was sitting just below her, obviously relaxed, slightly curious, in charge. "To do an interview with a successful, award-winning author."

"An award-winning author wouldn't make you nervous."

The pencil was growing damp in her hand. She could have cursed in frustration. "You don't."

"You lie too quickly, and not easily at all." His hands

rested loosely on his knees as he watched her. The odd ring he wore glinted dully, gold and silver. "If I were to touch you, just touch you, right now, you'd tremble."

"You think too much of yourself," she told him, but rose.

"I think of you," he said, so quietly the pad slipped out of her hand, unnoticed. "You make me want, I make you nervous." He was looking into her again; she could almost feel it. "It should be an interesting combination over the next couple of weeks."

He wasn't going to intimidate her. He *wasn't* going to make her tremble. "The sooner you remember I'm going to be working for the next two weeks, the simpler things will be." Trying to sound haughty nearly worked. Lee wondered if he heard the slight catch in her voice.

"Since you're resigned to working," he said easily, "you can give me a hand starting dinner. After tonight, we'll take turns making meals."

She wasn't going to give him the satisfaction of telling him she knew nothing about cooking over a fire. He already knew. Neither would she give the satisfaction of being confused by his mercurial mood changes. Instead, Lee brushed at her bangs. "I'm going to wash up first."

Hunter watched her start off in the wrong direction, but said nothing. She'd find the shower facilities sooner or later, he figured. Things would be more interesting if neither of them gave the other an inch.

He wasn't sure, but Hunter thought he heard Lee swear from somewhere behind him. Smiling a little, he leaned back against the rock and finished his cigarette.

Groggy, stiff and sniffing the scent of coffee in the air, Lee woke. She knew exactly where she was—as far over on her side of the tent as she could get, deep into the sleeping bag Hunter had provided for her. And alone. It took her only seconds to sense that Hunter no longer shared the tent with her. Just as it had taken her hours the night before to convince herself it didn't matter that he was only inches away.

Dinner had been surprisingly easy. Easy, Lee realized as she stared at the ceiling of the tent, because Hunter's mood had shifted again when she'd returned to help him fix it. Amiable? No, she decided, cautiously stretching her cramped muscles. *Amiable* was too free a word when applied to Hunter. *Moderately friendly* was more suitable. Cooperative he hadn't been at all. He'd spent the evening hours reading by the light of his lamp, while she'd taken out a fresh notepad and begun what would be a journal on her two weeks in Oak Creek Canyon.

She found it helpful to write down her feelings. Lee had often used her manuscript in much the same fashion. She could say what she wanted, feel what she wanted, without ever taking the risk that anyone would read her words. Perhaps it hadn't worked out precisely that way with her book, since Hunter had read more of her neat double-spaced typing under the steady lamplight, but the journal would be for no one's eyes but her own.

In any case, she thought, it was to her advantage that he'd been occupied with her manuscript. She hadn't had to talk to him as the night had grown later, the darkness deeper. While he'd still been reading, she'd been able to crawl into the tent and squeeze herself into a corner. When he'd joined her, much later, it hadn't been necessary to exchange words in the intimacy of the tent. She'd made certain he'd thought her asleep—though sleep hadn't come for hours.

In the quiet, she'd listened to him breathe beside her. Quiet, steady. That was the kind of man he was. Lee had lain still, telling herself the closeness meant nothing. But this morning, she saw that her nails, which had begun to grow again, had been gnawed down.

The first night was bound to be the hardest, she told herself and sat up, dragging a hand through her hair. She'd survived it. Her problem now was how to get by him and to the showers, where she could change out of the clothes she'd slept in and fix her hair and face. Cautiously, she crept forward to peek through the tent flap.

He knew she was awake. Hunter had sensed it almost the moment she'd opened her eyes. He'd gotten up early to start coffee, knowing that if he'd had trouble sleeping beside her, he'd never have been able to handle waking with her.

He'd seen little more than the coppery mass of hair above the sleeping bag in the dim morning light of the tent. Because he'd wanted to touch it, draw her to him, wake her, he'd given himself some distance. Today he'd walk for miles and fish for hours. Lee could stick to her role of reporter, and by answering her questions he'd learn as much about her as she believed she was learning about him. That was his plan, Hunter reminded himself, and poured a second cup of coffee. He was better off remembering it.

"Coffee's hot," Hunter commented without turning around. Though she'd taken great care to be quiet, he'd heard Lee push the tent flap aside.

Biting back an oath, Lee scooped up her pack. The man had ears like a wolf. "I want to shower first," she mumbled.

"I told you that you didn't have to fix up your face for me." He began to arrange strips of bacon in a skillet. "I like it fine the way it is."

Infuriated, Lee scrambled to her feet. "I'm not fixing anything for you. Sleeping all night in my clothes tends to make me feel dirty."

"Probably sleep better without them." Hunter agreed mildly. "Breakfast's in fifteen minutes, so I'd move along if I wanted to eat."

Clutching her bag and her dignity, Lee strode off through the trees.

He wouldn't get to her so easily if she wasn't stiff and grubby and half-starved, she thought, making her way along the path to the showers. God knows how he could be so cheerful after spending the night sleeping on the ground. Maybe Bryan had been right all along. The man was weird. Lee took her shampoo and her plastic case of French-milled soap and stepped into a shower stall.

The spot he'd chosen might be magnificent, the air might smell clean and pure, but a sleeping bag wasn't a feather bed. Lee stripped and hung her clothes over the door. She heard the water running in the stall next to hers and sighed. For the next two weeks she'd be sharing bathroom facilities. She might as well get used to it.

The water came out in a steady gush, lukewarm. Gritting her teeth, she stepped under. Today, she was going to begin to dig out a few more personal facts on Hunter Brown.

Was he married? She frowned, then deliberately relaxed her features. The question was for the article, not for herself. His marital status meant nothing to her.

He probably wasn't. She soaped her hair vigorously. What woman would put up with him? Besides, wouldn't a wife come along on camping trips even if she detested them? Would that kind of man marry anyone who didn't like precisely what he did?

What did he do for relaxation? Besides playing Daniel Boone in the woods, she added with a grim smile. Where did he live? Where had he grown up? What sort of childhood had he had?

The water streamed over her, sluicing away soap and shampoo. The curiosity she felt was purely professional. Lee found she had to remind herself of that a bit too often. She needed the whole man to do an incisive article. She needed the whole man…

Alarmed at her own thoughts, she opened her eyes wide, then swore when shampoo stung them. Damn the whole man! she thought fiercely. She'd take whatever pieces of him she could get and write an article that would pay him back, in spades, for all the trouble he'd caused her.

Clean, fragrant and shivering, she turned off the water. It wasn't until that moment that Lee remembered she hadn't brought a towel. Campground showers didn't lay in their own linen supply. Damn it, how was she supposed to remember everything?

Dripping, her chilled skin covered with gooseflesh, she stood in the middle of the stall and swore silently and pungently. For as long as she could stand it, Lee let the air dry her while she squeezed water out of her hair. Revenge, she thought, placing the blame squarely on Hunter's shoulders. Sooner or later, she'd have it.

She reached under the stall door for her pack and pulled out a fresh sweatshirt. Resigned, she dabbed at her wet face with the soft outside. Once she'd dragged it over her damp shoulders, she hunted up underwear. Though her clothes clung to her, her skin warmed. In front of the line of sinks and mirrors, she plugged in her blow-dryer and set to work on her hair.

In spite of him, Lee thought, not because of him, she spent more than her usual time perfecting her makeup. Satisfied, she repacked her portable hairdryer and left the showers, smelling lightly of jasmine.

Her scent was the first thing he sensed when she stepped back into the clearing. Hunter's stomach muscles tightened. As if he were unaffected, he finished off another cup of coffee, but he didn't taste it.

Calmer and much more at ease now, Lee stowed her pack before she walked toward the low-burning campfire. On a small shelf of rocks beside it sat the skillet with the remainder of the bacon and eggs. She didn't have to taste them to know they were cold.

"Feel better?" Hunter asked conversationally.

"I feel fine." She wouldn't say one word about the food being cold and, Lee told herself as she scooped her breakfast onto a plate, she'd eat every bite. She'd give him no more cause to smirk at her.

While she nibbled on the bacon, Lee glanced over at him. He'd obviously showered earlier. His hair glinted in the sun and he smelled cleanly of soap without the interference of cologne or after-shave. A man didn't use after-shave if he didn't bother with a razor, Lee concluded, studying the shadow of stubble over his chin. It should've made him look unkempt, but somehow he managed to look oddly dashing. She concentrated on her cold eggs.

"Sleep well?"

"I slept fine," she lied, and gratefully washed down her breakfast with strong, hot coffee. "You?"

"Very well," he lied, and lit a cigarette. She was getting on nerves he hadn't known he had.

"Have you been up long?"

Since dawn, Hunter thought. "Long enough." He glanced down at her barely scuffed hiking boots and wondered how long it would take before her feet just gave out. "I plan to do some hiking today."

She wanted to groan but put on a bright smile. "Fine, I'd like to see some of the canyon while I'm here." Preferably in a Jeep, she thought, swallowing the last crumb of bacon. If there was one cliché she could now attest to, it was that the open air increased the appetite.

It took Lee perhaps half again as long to wash up the breakfast dishes with the plastic water container as it would've taken Hunter, but she already understood the unstated rule. One cooks, the other cleans.

By the time she was finished, he was standing impatiently, binocular and canteen straps crisscrossed over his chest and a light pack in one hand. This he shoved at her. Lee resisted the urge to shove it back at him.

"I want my camera." Without giving him a chance to complain, she dug it out of her own gear and slipped the small rectangle into the back pocket of her jeans. "What's in here?" she asked, adjusting the strap of the pack over her shoulder.

"Lunch."

Lee lengthened her stride to keep up with Hunter as he headed out of the clearing. If he'd packed a lunch, she'd have to resign herself to a very long day on her feet. "How do you know where you're going and how to get back?"

For the first time since she'd returned to camp smelling like fragility and flowers, Hunter smiled. "Landmarks, the sun."

"Do you mean moss growing on one side of a tree?" She looked around, hoping to find some point of reference for herself. "I've never trusted that sort of thing."

She wouldn't know east from west, either, he mused, unless they were discussing L.A. and New York. "I've got a compass, if that makes you feel better."

It did—a little. When you hadn't the faintest idea how something worked, you had to take it on faith. Lee was far from comfortable putting her faith in Hunter.

But as they walked, she forgot to worry about losing her way. The sun was a white flash of light, and though it was still shy of 9:00 A.M., the air was warm. She liked the way the light hit the red walls of the canyon and deepened the colors. The path inclined upward, narrow, pebbled with loose stones. She heard people laugh, and the sound carried so cleanly over the air, they might have been standing beside her.

Green became sparser as they climbed. What she saw now was scrubby bushes, dusty and faded, that forced their way out of thin ribbons of dirt in the rock. Curious, she broke off a spray of leaves. Their scent was strong, tangy and fresh. Then she found she had to dash to catch up with Hunter. It had been his idea to hike, but he didn't appear to be enjoying it. More, he looked like a man who had some urgent, unpleasant appointment to keep.

It might be a good time, Lee considered, to start a casual conversation that could lead to the kind of personal information she was shooting for. As the path became steadily steeper, she decided she'd better talk while she had the breath to do it. The sweatshirt had been a mistake, too. Her back was damp again, this time from sweat.

"Have you always preferred the outdoors?"

"For hiking."

Undaunted, she scowled at his back. "I suppose you were a Boy Scout."

"No."

"Your interest in camping and hiking is fairly new, then."

"No."

She had to grit her teeth to hold back a groan. "Did you go off and pitch a tent in the woods with your father when you were a boy?"

She'd have been interested in the amused expression on his face if she could have seen it. "No."

"You lived in the city, then."

She was clever, Hunter reflected. And persistent. He shrugged. "Yes."

At last, Lee thought. "What city?"

"L.A."

She tripped over a rock and nearly stumbled headlong into his back. Hunter never slackened his pace. "L.A.?" she repeated. "You live in Los Angeles and still manage to bury yourself so that no one knows you're there?"

"I grew up in L.A.," he said mildly. "In a part of the city you'd have little occasion for visiting. Socially, Lenore Radcliffe, formerly of Palm Springs, wouldn't even know such neighborhoods existed."

That pulled her up short. Again, she had to dash to catch him, but this time she grabbed his arm and made him stop. "How do you know I came from Palm Springs?"

He watched her with the tolerant amusement she found

both infuriating and irresistible. "I did my research. You graduated from U.C.L.A. with honors, after three years in a very classy Swiss boarding school. Your engagement to Jonathan Willoby, up-and-coming plastic surgeon, was broken when you accepted a position in *Celebrity*'s Los Angeles office."

"I was never engaged to Jonathan," she began furiously, then decisively bit her tongue. "You have no business probing into my life, Hunter. I'm doing the article, not you."

"I make it a habit to find out everything I can about anyone I do business with. We do have a business arrangement, don't we, Lenore?"

He was clever with words, she thought grimly. But so was she. "Yes, and it consists of my interviewing you, not the other way around."

"On my terms," Hunter reminded her. "I don't talk to anyone unless I know who they are." He reached out, touching the ends of her hair as he'd done once before. "I think I know who you are."

"You don't," she corrected, struggling against the need to back away from a touch that was barely a touch. "And you don't have to. But the more honest and open you are with me, the more honest the article I write will be."

He uncapped the canteen. When she refused his offer with a shake of her head, Hunter drank. "I am being honest with you." He secured the cap. "If I made it easier for you, you wouldn't get a true picture of who I am." His eyes were suddenly dark, intense and piercing. Without warning, he reached out. The power in his eyes made her believe he could quite easily sweep her off the path. Yet his hand skimmed down her cheek, light as rain. "You wouldn't understand what I am," he said quietly. "Perhaps, for my own reasons, I want you to."

She'd have been less frightened if he'd shouted at her, raged at her, grabbed at her. The sound of her own heartbeat vibrated in her head. Instinctively, she stepped back, escape her first and only thought. Her foot met empty space.

In an instant, she was caught against him, pressed body to body, so that the warmth from his seeped right into hers. The fear tripled so that she arched back, raising both hands to his chest.

"Idiot," he said, with an edge to his voice that made her head snap up. "Take a look behind you before you tell me to let you go."

Automatically, she turned her head to look over her shoulder. Her stomach rose up to her throat, then plummeted. The hands that had been poised to push him away grabbed his shoulders until the fingers dug into his flesh. The view behind her was magnificent, sweeping and straight down.

"We—we walked farther up than I'd thought," she managed. And if she didn't sit down, very, very soon, she was going to disgrace herself.

"The trick is to watch where you're going." Hunter didn't move her away from the edge, but took her chin in his hand until their eyes met and held. "Always watch exactly where you're going, then you'll know how to fall."

He kissed her, just as unexpectedly as before, but not so gently. Not nearly so gently. This time, she felt the full force of the strength that had been only an undercurrent each other time his mouth had touched hers. If she'd pitched back and taken that dizzying fall, she'd have been no more helpless than she was at this moment, molded to him, supported by him, wrapped around him. The edge was close—inside her, behind her. Lee couldn't tell which would be more fatal. But she knew, helplessly, that either could break her.

He hadn't meant to touch her just then, but the demanding climb up the path hadn't deadened the need he'd woken with. He'd take this much, her taste, her softness, and make it last until she willingly turned to him. He wanted the sweetness she tried to gloss over, the fragility she tried to deny. And he wanted the strength that kept her pushing for more. Yes, he thought he knew her and was very close to understanding her. He knew he wanted her.

Slowly, very slowly, for lingering mouth-to-mouth both soothed and excited him, Hunter drew her away. Her eyes were as clouded as his thoughts, her pulse as rapid as his. He shifted her until she was close to the cliff wall and away from the drop.

"Never step back unless you've looked over your shoulder first," he said quietly. "And don't step forward until you've tested the ground."

Turning, he continued up the path, leaving her to wonder if he'd been speaking of hiking or something entirely different.

Chapter 7

Lee wrote in her journal:

On the eighth day of this odd on-again off-again interview, I know more about Hunter and understand less. By turns, he's friendly, then distant. There's an aloof streak in him, bound so tightly around his private life that I've found no way through it. When I ask about his preference in books, he can go on indefinitely—apparently he has no real preference except for the written word itself. When I ask about his family, he just smiles and changes the subject or gives me one of those intense stares and says nothing. In either case, he keeps a cloak of mystery around his privacy.

He's possibly the most efficient man I've ever met. There's no waste of time, no extra movements and, infuriating to me, never a mistake, when it comes to starting a campfire or cooking a meal—such as they are. Yet, he's content to do absolutely nothing for hours at a time.

He's fastidious—the camp looks as if we've been here no more than a half hour rather than a week—yet he hasn't shaved in that amount of time. The beard should look scruffy, but somehow it looks so natural I find myself wondering if he didn't always have one.

Always, I've been able to find a category to slip an assignment into. An acquaintance into. Not with Hunter. In all this time, I've found no easy file for him.

Last night we had a heated discussion on Sylvia Plath, and this morning I found him paging through a comic book over coffee. When I questioned him on it, his answer was that he respected all forms of literature. I believed him. One of the problems I'm having on this assignment is that I find myself believing everything he says, no matter how contradictory the statement might be to another he makes. Can a total lack of consistency make someone consistent?

He's the most complex, frustrating, fascinating man I've ever known. I've yet to find a way of controlling the attraction he holds for me, or even the proper label for it. Is it physical? Hunter's very compelling physically. Is it intellectual? His mind has such odd twists and turns, it takes all my effort to follow them.

Either of these I believe I could handle successfully enough. Over the years, I've had to deal professionally with attractive, intelligent, charismatic men. It's a challenge, certainly, but here I have the uncomfortable feeling that I'm caught in the middle of a silent chess game and have already lost my queen.

My greatest fear at this moment is that I'm going to find myself emotionally involved.

Since the first day we walked up the canyon, he hasn't touched me. I can still remember exactly how I felt, exactly what the air smelled like at that moment. It's foolish, overly romantic and absolutely true.

Each night we sleep together in the same tent, so close I can feel his breath. Each morning I wake alone. I should be grateful that he isn't making this assignment any more difficult than it already is, and yet I find myself waiting to be held by him.

For over a week I've thought of little else but him. The more I learn, the more I want to know—for myself. Too much for myself.

Twice, I've woken in the middle of the night, aching, and nearly turned to him. Now, I wonder what would happen if I did. If I believed in the spells and forces Hunter writes of, I'd think one was on me. No one's ever made me want so much, feel so much. Fear so much. Every night, I wonder.

Sometimes Lee wrote of the scenery and her feelings about it. Sometimes, she wrote a play-by-play description of the day. But most of the time, more of the time, she wrote of Hunter. What she put down in her journal had nothing to do with her organized, precisely written notes for the article. She wouldn't permit it. What she didn't understand, and what she wouldn't write down in either space, was that she was losing sleep. And she was having fun.

Though he was cannily evasive on personal details, she was gathering information. Even now, barely halfway through the allotted time, Lee had enough for a solid, successful article—more, she knew, than she'd expected to gather. But she wanted even more, for her readers and, undeniably, for herself.

"I don't see how any self-respecting fish could be fooled by something like this." Lee fiddled with the small rubbery fly Hunter attached to her line.

"Myopic," Hunter countered, bending to choose his own lure. "Fish are notoriously nearsighted."

"I don't believe you." Clumsily, she cast off. "But this time *I'm* going to catch one."

"You'll need to get your fly in the water first." He glanced down at the line tangled on the bank of the creek before expertly casting his own.

He wouldn't even offer to help. After a week in his company, Lee had learned not to expect it. She'd also learned that if she wanted to compete with him in this, or in a discussion of eighteenth-century English literature, she had to get into the spirit of things.

It wasn't simple and it wasn't quick, but kneeling, Lee worked on the tangles until she was back to square one. She shot a look at Hunter, who appeared much too engrossed with the surface of the creek to notice her progress. By now, Lee knew better. He saw everything that went on around him, whether he looked or not.

Standing a few feet away, Lee tried again. This time, her lure landed with a quiet plop.

Hunter saw the rare, quick grin break out, but said nothing. She was, he'd learned, a woman who generally took herself too seriously. Yet he saw the sweetness beneath, and the warmth Lee tried to be so frugal with.

She had a low, smoky laugh she didn't use often enough. It only made him want to urge it out of her.

The past week hadn't been easy for her. Hunter hadn't intended it to be. You learned more about people by observing them in difficult situations than at a catered cocktail party. He was adding to the layers of the first impression he'd had, at the airport in Flagstaff. But he had layers still to go.

She could, unlike most people he knew, be comfortable with long spells of silence. It appealed to him. The more careless he became in his attire and appearance, the more meticulous she became in hers. It amused him to see her go off every morning and return with her makeup perfected and her hair carefully groomed. Hunter made sure they'd been mussed a bit by the end of the day.

Hiking, fishing. Hunter had seen to it that her jeans and boots were thoroughly broken in. Often, in the evening, he'd caught her rubbing her tired feet. When she was back in Los Angeles, sitting in her cozy office, she wouldn't forget the two weeks she'd spent in Oak Creek Canyon.

Now, Lee stood near the edge of the creek, a fishing rod held in both hands, a look of smug concentration on her face. He liked her for it—for her innate need to compete and for the vulnerability beneath the confidence. She'd stand there, holding the rod, until he called a halt to the venture. Back in camp, he knew she'd rub her hands with cream and they would smell lightly of jasmine and stay temptingly soft.

Since it was her turn to cook, she'd do it, though she still fumbled a bit with the utensils and managed to singe almost anything she put on the fire. He liked her for that, too—for the fact that she never gave up on anything.

Her curiosity remained unflagging. She'd question him, and he'd evade or answer as he chose. Then she'd grant him silence to read, while she wrote. Comfortable. Hunter found that she was an unusually comfortable woman in the quiet light of a campfire. Whether she knew it or not, she relaxed then, writing in the journal, which intrigued him, or going over her daily notes for the article, which didn't.

He'd expected to learn about her during the two weeks

together, knowing he'd have to give some information on himself in return. That, he considered, was an even enough exchange. But he hadn't expected to enjoy her companionship.

The sun was strong, the air almost still, with an early-morning taste to it. But the sky wasn't clear. Hunter wondered if she'd noticed the bank of clouds to the east and if she realized there'd be a storm by nightfall. The clouds held lightning. He simply sat cross-legged on the ground. It'd be more interesting if Lee found out for herself.

The morning passed in silence, but for the occasional voice from around them or the rustle of leaves. Twice Hunter pulled a trout out of the creek, throwing the second back because of size. He said nothing. Lee said nothing, but barely prevented herself from grinding her teeth. On every jaunt, he'd gone back to camp with fish. She'd gone back with a sore neck.

"I begin to wonder," she said, at length, "if you've put something on that lure that chases fish away."

He'd been smoking lazily and now he stirred himself to crush out the cigarette. "Want to change rods?"

She slanted him a look, taking in the slight amusement in his arresting face. When her muscles quivered, Lee stiffened them. Would she never become completely accustomed to the way her body reacted when they looked at each other? "No," she said coolly. "I'll keep this one. You're rather good at this sort of thing, for a boy who didn't go fishing."

"I've always been a quick study."

"What did your father do in L.A.?" Lee asked, knowing he would either answer in the most offhand way or evade completely.

"He sold shoes."

It took a moment, as she'd been expecting the latter. "Sold shoes?"

"That's right. In the shoe department of a moderately successful department store downtown. My mother sold stationery on the third floor." He didn't have to look at her to know she was frowning, her brows drawn together. "Surprised?"

"Yes," she admitted. "A bit. I suppose I imagined you'd been influenced by your parents to some extent and that they'd had some unusual career or interests."

Hunter cast off again with an agile flick of his wrist. "Before my father sold shoes, he sold tickets at the local theater; before that, it was linoleum, I think." His shoulders moved slightly before he turned to her. "He was a man trapped by financial circumstances into working, when he'd been born to dream. If he'd been born into affluence, he might've been a painter or a poet. As it was, he sold things and regularly lost his job because he wasn't suited to selling anything, not even himself."

Though he spoke casually, Lee had to struggle to distance herself emotionally. "You speak as though he's not living."

"I've always believed my mother died from overwork, and my father from lack of interest in life without her."

Sympathy welled up in her throat. She couldn't swallow at all. "When did you lose them?"

"I was eighteen. They died within six months of each other."

"Too old for the state to care for you," she murmured, "too young to be alone."

Touched, Hunter studied her profile. “Don’t feel sorry for me, Lenore. I managed very well.”

“But you weren’t a man yet.” No, she mused, perhaps he had been. “You had college to face.”

“I had some help, and I waited tables for a while.”

Lee remembered the wallet full of credit cards she’d carried through college. Anything she’d wanted had always been at her fingertips. “It couldn’t have been easy.”

“It didn’t have to be.” He lit a cigarette, watching the clouds move slowly closer. “By the time I was finished with college, I knew I was a writer.”

“What happened from the time you graduated from college to when your first book was published?”

He smiled through the smoke that drifted between them. “I lived, I wrote, I went fishing when I could.”

She wasn’t about to be put off so easily. Hardly realizing she did it, Lee sat down on the ground beside him. “You must’ve worked.”

“Writing, though many disagree, is work.” He had a talent for making the sharpest sarcasm sound mildly droll.

Another time, she might have smiled. “You know that’s not what I mean. You had to have an income, and your first book wasn’t published until nearly six years ago.”

“I wasn’t starving in a garret, Lenore.” He ran a finger down the hand she held on the rod and felt a flash of pleasure at the quick skip of her pulse. “You’d just have been starting at *Celebrity* when *The Devil’s Due* hit the stands. One might say our stars were on the rise at the same time.”

“I suppose.” She turned from him to look back at the surface of the creek again.

“You’re happy there?”

Unconsciously, she lifted her chin. “I’ve worked my way up from gofer to staff reporter in five years.”

“That’s not an answer.”

“Neither are most of yours,” she mumbled.

“True enough. What’re you looking for there?”

“Success,” she said immediately. “Security.”

“One doesn’t always equal the other.”

Her voice was as defiant as the look she aimed at him. “You have both.”

“A writer’s never secure,” Hunter disagreed. “Only a foolish one expects to be. I’ve read all of the manuscript you brought.”

Lee said nothing. She’d known he’d bring it up before the two weeks were over, but she’d hoped to put it off a bit longer. The faintest of breezes played with the ends of her hair while she sat, staring at the moving waters of the creek. Some of the pebbles looked like gems. Such were illusions.

“You know you have to finish it,” he told her calmly. “You can’t make me believe you’re content to leave your characters in limbo, when you’ve drawn them so carefully. Your story’s two-thirds told, Lenore.”

“I don’t have time,” she began.

“Not good enough.”

Frustrated, she turned to him again. “Easy for you to say from your little pinnacle of fame. I have a demanding full-time job. If I give it my time and my talent, there’s no place I can go but up at *Celebrity*.”

“Your novel needs your time and talent.”

She didn’t like the way he said it—as if she had no real choice. “Hunter, I didn’t come here to discuss my work, but you and yours. I'm flattered that you think my novel has some merit, but I have a job to do."

"Flattered?" he countered. The deep, black gaze pinned her again, and his hand closed over hers. "No, you're not. You wish I'd never seen your novel and you don't want to discuss it. Even if you were convinced it was worthwhile, you'd still be afraid to put it all on the line."

The truth grated on her nerves and on her temper. "My job is my first priority. Whether that suits you or not doesn't matter. It's none of your business."

"No, perhaps not," he said slowly, watching her. "You've got a fish on your line."

"I don't want you to—" Eyes narrowing, she broke off. "What?"

"There's a fish on your line," he repeated. "You'd better reel it in."

"I've got one?" Stunned, Lee felt the rod jerk in her hands. "I've got one! Oh, God." She gripped the rod in both hands again and watched the line jiggle. "I've really caught one. What do I do now?"

"Reel it in," Hunter suggested again, leaning back on the grass.

"Aren't you going to help?" Her hands felt foolishly clumsy as she started to crank the reel. Hoping leverage would give her some advantage, she scrambled to her feet. "Hunter, I don't know what I'm doing. I might lose it."

"Your fish," he pointed out. Grinning, he watched her. Would she look any more exuberant if she'd been given an interview with the president? Somehow, Hunter didn't think so, though he was sure Lee would disagree. But then, she couldn't see herself at that moment, hair mussed, cheeks glowing, eyes wide and her tongue caught firmly between her teeth. The late-morning sunlight did exquisite things to her skin, and the quick laugh she gave when she pulled the struggling fish from the water ran over the back of his neck like soft fingers.

Desire moved lazily through him as he took his gaze up the long length of leg flattered by brief shorts, then over the subtle curves accented by the shifting of muscle under her shirt as she continued to fight with the fish, to her face, still flushed with surprise.

"Hunter!" She laughed as she held the still-wriggling fish high over the grass. "I did it."

It was nearly as big as the largest one he'd caught that week. He pursed his lips as he sized it up. It was tempting to compliment her, but he decided she looked smug enough already. "Gotta get it off the hook," he reminded her, shifting only slightly on his elbows.

"Off the hook?" Lee shot him an astonished look. "I don't want to touch it."

"You have to touch it to take it off the hook."

Lee lifted a brow. "I'll just toss it back in."

With a shrug, Hunter shut his eyes and enjoyed the faint breeze. The hell she would. "Your fish, not mine."

Torn between an abhorrence of touching the still-flopping fish and pride at having caught it, Lee stared down at Hunter. He wasn't going to help; that was painfully obvious. If she threw the fish back into the water, he'd smirk at her for the rest of the evening. Intolerable. And, she reasoned logically, wouldn't she still have to touch it to get rid of it? Setting her teeth, Lee reached out a hand for the catch of the day.

It was wet, slippery and cold. She pulled her hand back. Then, out of the corner of her eye, she saw Hunter grinning up at her. Holding her breath, Lee took the trout firmly in one hand and wiggled the hook out with the other. If he hadn't been looking at her, challenging her, she never would've managed it. With the haughtiest air at her disposal, she dropped the trout into the small cooler Hunter brought along on fishing trips.

"Very good." He closed the lid on the cooler before he reeled in his line. "That looks like enough for tonight's dinner. You caught a good-sized one, Lenore."

"Thank you." The words were icily polite and self-satisfied.

"It'll nearly be enough for both of us, even after you've cleaned it."

"It's as big as…" He was already walking back toward camp, so that she had to run to catch up with him and his statement. "*I* clean it?"

"Rule is, you catch, you clean."

She planted her feet, but he wasn't paying attention. "I'm not cleaning any fish."

"Then you don't eat any fish." His words were as offhand and careless as a shrug.

Abandoning pride, Lee caught at his arm. "Hunter, you'll have to change the rule." She sighed, but convinced herself she wouldn't choke on the word. At least not very much. "Please."

He stopped, considering. "If I clean it, you've got to balance the scales—" the smile flickered over his face "—no pun intended, by doing me a favor."

"I can cook two nights in a row."

"I said a favor."

Her head turned sharply, but one look at his face had her laughing. "All right, what's the deal?"

"Why don't we leave it open-ended?" he suggested. "I don't have anything in mind at the moment."

This time, she considered. "It'll be negotiable?"

"Naturally."

"Deal." Turning her palms up, Lee wrinkled her nose. "Now I'm going to wash my hands."

She hadn't realized she could get such a kick out of catching a fish or out of cooking it herself over an open fire. There were other things Lee hadn't realized. She hadn't looked at the trim gold watch on her wrist in days. If she hadn't kept a journal, she probably wouldn't know what day it was. It was true that her muscles still revolted after a night in the tent and the shower facilities were an inconvenience at best, purgatory at worst, but despite herself she was relaxing.

For the first time in her memory, her day wasn't regimented, by herself or by anyone else. She got up when she woke, slept when she was tired and ate when she was hungry. For the moment, the word *deadline* didn't exist. That was something she hadn't allowed herself since the day she'd walked out of her parents' home in Palm Springs.

No matter how rapid Hunter could make her pulse by one of those unexpected looks, or how much desire for him simmered under the surface, she found him comfortable to be with. Because it was so unlikely, Lee didn't try to find the reasons. On this late afternoon, in the hour before dusk, she was content to sit by the fire and tend supper.

"I never knew anything could smell so good."

Hunter continued to pour a cup of coffee before he glanced over at her. "We cooked fish two days ago."

"Your fish," Lee pointed out, carefully turning the trout. "This one's mine."

He grinned, wondering if she remembered just how horrified she'd been the first time he'd suggested she pick up a rod and reel. "Beginner's luck."

Lee opened her mouth, ready with a biting retort, then saw the way he smiled at her. Not only did her retort vanish, but so did much of her defensive wall. She let out a long, quiet breath as she turned back to the skillet. The man became only more dangerous with familiarity. "If fishing depends on luck," she managed, "you've had more than your share."

"Everything depends on luck." He held out two plates. Lee slipped the sizzling trout onto them, then sat back to enjoy.

"If you believe that, what about fate? You've said more than once that we can fight against our fate, but we can't win."

He lifted a brow. That consistently sharp, consistently logical mind of hers never failed to impress him. "One works with the other." He tasted a bit of trout, noting that she'd been careful enough not to singe her own catch. "It's your fate to be here, with me. You were lucky enough to catch a fish for dinner."

"It sounds to me as though you twist things to your own point of view."

"Yes. Doesn't everyone?"

"I suppose." Lee ate, thoughtfully studying the view over his shoulder. Had anything ever tasted this wonderful? Would anything ever again? "But not everyone makes it work as well as you." Reluctantly, she accepted some of the dried fruit he offered. He seemed to have an unending supply, but Lee had yet to grow used to the taste or texture.

"If you could change one thing about your life, what would it be?"

Perhaps because he'd asked without preamble, perhaps because she was so unexpectedly relaxed, Lee answered without thinking. "I'd have more."

He didn't, as her parents had done, ask more what. Hunter only nodded. "We could say it's your fate to want it, and your luck to have it or not."

Nibbling on an apricot, she studied him. The lowering light and flickering fire cast his face in shadows. They suited him. The short, rough beard surrounded the poet's mouth, making it all the more compelling. He was a man a woman would never be able to ignore, never be able to forget. Lee wondered if he knew it. Then she nearly laughed. Of course he did. He knew entirely too much.

"What about you?" She leaned forward a bit, as she did whenever the answer was important. "What would you change?"

He smiled in the way that made her blood heat. "I'd take more," he said quietly.

She felt the shiver race up her spine, was all but certain Hunter could see it. Lee found she was compelled to remind herself of her job. "You know," she began easily enough, "you've told me quite a bit over this week, more in some ways than I'd expected, but much less in others." Steady again, she took another bite of trout. "I might understand you quite a bit better if you'd give me a run-through of a typical day."

He ate, enjoying the tender, open-air flavor. The clouds

were rolling in, the breeze picking up. He wondered if she noticed. "There's no such thing as a typical day."

"You're evading again."

"Yeah."

"It's my job to pin you down."

He watched her over the rim of his coffee cup. "I like watching you do your job."

She laughed. It seemed he could always frustrate and amuse her at the same time. "Hunter, why do I have the feeling you're doing your best to make this difficult for me?"

"You're very perceptive." Setting his plate aside, he began to toy with the ends of her hair in a habit she could never take casually. "I have an image of a woman with a romantic kind of beauty and an orderly, logical mind."

"Hunter—"

"Wait, I'm just fleshing her out. She's ambitious, full of nerves, highly sensuous without being fully aware of it." He could see her eyes change, growing as dark as the sky above them. "She's caught in the middle of something she can't explain or understand. Things happen around her and she's finding it more and more difficult to distance herself from it. And there's a man, a man she desires but can't quite trust. He doesn't offer her the logical explanations she wants, but the illogic he offers seems terrifyingly close to the truth. If she puts her trust in him, she has to turn her back on most of what she believes is fact. If she doesn't, she'll be alone."

He was talking to her, about her, for her. Lee knew her throat was dry and her palms were damp, but she didn't know if it was from his words or the light touch on the ends of her hair. "You're trying to frighten me by weaving a plot around me."

"I'm weaving a plot around you," Hunter agreed. "Whether I frighten you or not depends on how successful I am with that plot. Shadows and storms are my business." As if on cue, lightning snaked out in the sky overhead. "But all writers need a foil. Smooth, pale skin—" He stroked the back of his hand up her cheek. "Soft hair with touches of gold and fire. Against that I have darkness, wind, voices that speak from shadows. Logic against the impossible. The unspeakable against cool, polished beauty."

She swallowed to relieve the dryness in her throat and tried to speak casually. "I suppose I should be flattered, but I'm not sure I want to see myself molded into a character in a horror story."

"That comes back to fate again, doesn't it?" Lightning ripped through the early dusk as their eyes met again. "I need you, Lenore," he murmured. "For the tale I have to tell—and more."

Nerves prickled along her skin, all the more frantically because of the relaxed hours. "It's going to rain." But her voice wasn't calm and even. Her senses were already swimming. When she started to rise, she found that her hand was caught in his and that he stood with her. The wind blew around her, stirring leaves, stirring desire. The light dimmed to shadow. Thunder rumbled.

What she saw in his eyes chilled her, then heated her blood so quickly she had no way to keep up with the change. The grip on her hand was light. Lee could've broken the hold if she'd had the will to do so. It was his look that drained the will from her. They stood there, hands touching, eyes locked, while the storm swirled like madness around them.

Perhaps life was made up of the choices Hunter had once spoken of. Perhaps luck swayed the balance. But at that moment, for hardly more than a heartbeat, Lee believed that fate ruled everything. She was meant to go to him, to give to him, with no more choice than one of the characters his imagination formed.

Then the sky opened. The rain poured out. The shock of the sudden drenching had Lee jolting back, breaking contact. Yet for several long seconds she stood still while water ran over her and lightning flashed in wicked bolts.

"Damn it!" But he knew she spoke to him, not the storm. "Now what am I supposed to do?"

Hunter smiled, barely resisting the urge to cup her face in his hands and kiss her until her legs gave way. "Head for drier land." He continued to smile despite the rain, the wind, the lightning.

Wet, edgy and angry, Lee crawled inside the tent. He's enjoying this, she thought, tugging on the sodden laces of her boots. There's nothing he likes better than to see me at my worst. It would probably take a week for the boots to dry out, she thought grimly as she managed to pry the first one off.

When Hunter slipped into the tent beside her, she said nothing. Concentrating on anger seemed the best solution. The pounding of the rain on the sides of the tent made the space inside seem to shrink. She'd never been more aware of him, or of herself. Water dripped uncomfortably down her neck as she leaned forward to pull off her socks.

"I don't suppose this'll last long."

Hunter pulled the sodden shirt over his head. "I wouldn't count on it stopping much before morning."

"Terrific." She shivered and wondered how the hell she was supposed to get out of the wet clothes and into dry ones.

Hunter turned the lantern he'd carried in with him down to a dim glow. "Relax and listen to it. It's different from rain in the city. There's no swish of tires on wet asphalt, no horns, no feet running on the sidewalk." He took a towel out of his pack and began to dry her hair.

"I can do it." She reached up, but his hands continued to massage.

"I like to do it. Wet fire," he murmured. "That's what your hair looks like now."

He was so close she could smell the rain on him. The heat from his body called subtly, temptingly, to hers. Was the rain suddenly louder, or were her senses more acute? For a moment, she thought she could hear each individual drop as it hit the tent. The light was dim, a smoky gray that held touches of unreality. Lee felt as though she'd been running away from this one isolated spot all her life. Or perhaps she'd been running toward it.

"You need to shave," she murmured, and found that her hand was already reaching out to touch the untrimmed growth of beard on his face. "This hides too much. You're already difficult to know."

"Am I?" He moved the towel over her hair, soothing and arousing by turns.

"You know you are." She didn't want to turn away now, from the look that could infuse such warmth through her chilled, damp skin. Lightning flashed, illuminating the tent brilliantly before plunging it back into gloom. Yet, through the gloom she could see all she needed to, perhaps more than she wanted to. “It’s my job to find out more, to find out everything.”

“And my right to tell you only what I want to.”

“We just don’t look at things the same way.”

“No.”

She took the towel and, half dreaming, began to dry his hair. “We have no business being together like this.”

He hadn’t known desire with claws. If he didn’t touch her soon, he’d be ripped through. “Why?”

“We’re too different. You look for the unexplainable, I look for the logical.” But his mouth was so near hers, and his eyes held such power. “Hunter…” She knew what was going to happen, recognized the impossibility of it and the pain that was bound to follow. “I don’t want this to happen.”

He didn’t touch her, though he was certain he’d soon be mad from the lack of it. “You have a choice.”

“No.” It was said quietly, almost on a sigh. “I don’t think I do.” She let the towel fall. She saw the flicker of lightning and waited, six long heartbeats, for the answering thunder. “Maybe neither one of us has a choice.”

Her breath was already unsteady as she let her hands curl over his bare shoulders. There was strength there. She wanted to feel it, but had been afraid to. His eyes never left hers as she touched him. Though the force of need curled tight in his stomach, he’d let her set the pace this first time, this most important time.

Her fingers were long and smooth on his skin, cool, not so much hesitant as cautious. They ran down his arms, moving slowly over his chest and back until desire was taut as a bow poised for firing. The sound of the rain drummed in his head. Her face was pale and elegant in the gloomy light. The tent was suddenly too big. He wanted her in a space that was too small to move in unless they moved together.

She could hardly believe she could touch him this way, freely, openly, so that his skin quivered under the trace of her fingers. All the while, he watched her with a passion so fierce it would have terrified her if she hadn't been so dazed with her own need. Carefully, afraid to make the wrong move and break the mood for both of them, she touched her mouth to his.

The rough brush of beard was a stunning contrast to the softness of his lips. He gave back to her such feelings, such warmth, with no pressure. She'd never known anyone who could give without taking. This generosity was, to her, the ultimate seduction. In that moment, any reserve she'd clung to was washed away. Her arms went around his neck, her cheek pressed to his.

"Make love to me, Hunter."

He drew her away, only far enough so that they could see each other again. Wet hair curled around her face. Her eyes were as the sky had been an hour before. Dusky and clouded. "With."

Her lips curved. Her heart opened. He poured inside. "Make love with me."

Then his hands were framing her face, and the kiss was so gentle it drugged every cell of her body. She felt him tug the wet shirt from her, and shivered once before he warmed her. His body felt so strong against hers, so solid, yet his hands played over her with the care of a jeweler polishing a rare gem. He sighed when she touched him, so she touched once again, wanting to give pleasure as it was given to her.

She'd thought the panic would return, or at least the need to rush. But they'd been given all the time in the world. The rain could fall, the thunder bellow. It didn't involve them. She tasted hunger on his lips, but he held it in check. He'd sup slowly. Pleasure bubbled up inside her and came softly through her lips.

His mouth on her breast had the need leaping up to the next plane. Yet he didn't hurry, even when she arched against him. His tongue flicked, his teeth nibbled, until he could feel the crazed desire vibrating through her. She thought only of him now, Hunter knew it even as he struggled to hold the reins of his own passion. She'd have more. She'd take all. And so, by God, would he.

When she struggled with the snap of his jeans, he let her have her way. He wanted to be flesh-to-flesh with her, body-to-body, without barriers. In his mind, he'd already had her bare, like this, a dozen times. Her hair was cool and wet, her skin smooth and fragrant. Spring flowers and summer rain. The scents raced through him as her hands became more urgent.

Her breathing was ragged as she tugged the wet denim down his legs. She recognized strength, power and control. It was only the last she needed to break so that she could have what she ached for.

Wherever she could reach, she touched, she tasted, wallowing in pleasure each time she heard his breath tremble. Her shorts were drawn slowly down her body by strong, clever hands, until she wore nothing but the lacy triangle riding low on her hips. With his lips, he journeyed down, down her body, slowly, so that the bristle of beard awakened every pore. His tongue slid under the lace, making her gasp. Then, as abruptly as the storm had broken, Lee was lost in a morass of sensation too dark, too deep, to understand.

He felt her explode, and the power sang through him. He heard her call his name, and the greed to hear it again almost overwhelmed him. Bracing himself over her, Hunter held back that final, desperate need until she opened her eyes. She'd look at him when they came together. He'd promised himself that.

Dazed, trembling, frenzied, Lee stared at him. He looked invincible. "What do you want from me?"

His mouth swooped down on hers, and for the first time the kiss was hard, urgent, almost brutal with the force of passion finally unleashed. "Everything." He plunged into her, catapulting them both closer to the crest. "Everything."

Chapter 8

Dawn was clear as glass. Lee woke to it slowly, naked, warm and, for the first time in over a week, comfortable. And for the first time in over a week, she woke not precisely sure where she was.

Her head was pillowed in the curve of Hunter's shoulder, her body turned toward his of its own volition and by the weight of the arm held firmly around her. There was a drowsy feeling that was a mix of security and excitement. In all of her memory, she couldn't recall experiencing anything quite like it.

Before she was fully awake, she smelled the lingering fragrance of rain on his skin and remembered. In remembering, she took a deep, drinking breath of the scent.

It was like a dream, like something in some subliminal fantasy, or a scene that had come straight from the imagination. She'd never offered herself to anyone so freely before, or so completely. Never. Lee knew there'd never been anyone who'd tempted her to.

She could still remember the sensation of her lips touching his, and all doubt, all fear, melting away with the gentle contact.

Should she feel so content now that the rain had stopped and dawn was breaking? Fantasies were for that private hour of the night, not for the daylight. After all, it hadn't been a dream, and there'd be no pretending it had been. Perhaps she should be appalled that she'd given him exactly what he'd demanded: everything.

She couldn't. No, it was more than that, she realized. She wouldn't. Nothing, no one, would spoil what had happened, not even she herself.

Still, it might be best if he didn't realize quite yet how completely victorious he'd been. Lee let her eyes close and wrapped the sensation of closeness around her. For the next few days, there was no desk, no typewriter, no phone ringing with more demands. There'd be no self-imposed schedule. For the next few days, she was alone with her lover. Maybe the time had come to pick those wildflowers.

She tilted her head, wanting to look at him, trying not to wake him. Over the week they'd spent in such intimate quarters, she'd never seen him sleep. Every other morning he'd been up, already making coffee. She wanted the luxury of absorbing him when he was unaware.

Lee knew that most people looked more vulnerable in sleep, more innocent, perhaps. Hunter looked just as dangerous, just as compelling, as ever. True, those dark, intense eyes were hidden, but knowing the lids could lift at any moment, and the eyes spear you with that peculiar power, didn't add innocence to his face, only more mystery.

Lee discovered she didn't want it to. She was glad he was more dangerous than the other men she'd known. In an odd way, she was glad he was more difficult. She hadn't fallen in love with the ordinary, the everyday, but with the unique.

Fallen in love. She ran the phrase around in her head, taking it apart and putting it back together again with the caution she was prone to. It triggered a trickle of unease. The phrase itself connoted bruises. Hadn't Hunter himself warned her to test the ground before she started forward? Even warned, she hadn't. Even seeing the pit, she hadn't checked her step. The tumble she'd taken had a soft fall. This time. Lee knew it was all too possible to stumble and be destroyed.

She wasn't going to think about it. Lee allowed herself the luxury of cuddling closer. She was going to find those wildflowers and enjoy each individual petal. The dream would end soon enough, and she'd be back to the reality of her life. It was, of course, what she wanted. For a while, she lay still, just listening to the silence.

The clever thing to do, she thought lazily, would be to hang their wet clothes out in the sun. Her boots certainly needed drying out, but in the meantime, she had her sneakers. She yawned, thinking she wanted a few moments to write in her journal as well. Hunter's breathing was slow and even. A smile curved her lips. She could do all that, then come back and wake him. Waking him, in whatever way she chose, was a lover's privilege.

Lover. Skimming her gaze over his face again, she wondered why she didn't feel any particular surprise at the word. Was it possible she'd recognized it from the beginning? Foolish, she told herself, and shook her head.

Slowly, she shifted away from him, then crawled to the front of the tent to peek out. Even as she reached for the flap, a hand closed around her ankle. Hunter pillowed his other hand under his head as he watched her.

"If you're going out like that, we won't keep everyone away from the campsite for long."

As she was naked, the haughty look she sent him lost something. "I was just looking out. I thought you were asleep."

He smiled, thinking she was the only woman who could make a viable stab at dignity while on her hands and knees in a tent, without a stitch on. The finger around her ankle stroked absently. "You're up early."

"I thought I'd hang these clothes out to dry."

"Very practical." Because he sensed she was feeling awkward, Hunter sat up and grabbed her arm, tugging until she tumbled back, sprawled over him. Content, he held her against him and sighed. "We'll do it later."

Unsure whether to laugh or complain, Lee blew the hair out of her eyes as she propped herself on one elbow. "I'm not tired."

"You don't have to be tired to lie down." Then he rolled on top of her. "It's called relaxing."

As the planes of his body fit against the curves of hers, Lee felt the warmth seep in. A hundred tiny pulse points began to drum. "I don't think this has a lot to do with relaxing."

"No?" He'd wanted to see her like this, in the thin light of dawn with her hair mussed from his hands, her skin flushed from sleep, her limbs heavy from a night of loving and alert for more. He ran a hand down her with a surge of possession that wasn't quite comfortable, wasn't quite expected. "Then we'll relax later, too." He saw her lips form a gentle smile just before he brushed his over them.

Hunter didn't question that he wanted her just as urgently now as he had all the days and nights before. He rarely questioned feelings, because he trusted them. Her arms went around him, her lips parted. The completeness of her giving shot a shaft of heat through him that turned to a unified warmth. Lifting his head, Hunter looked down at her.

Milkmaid skin over a duchess's cheekbones, eyes like the sky at dusk and hair like copper shot with gold. Hunter gave himself the pleasure of looking at all of her, slowly.

She was small and sleek and smooth. He ran a fingertip along the curve of her shoulder and studied the contrast of his skin against hers. Fragile, delicate—but he remembered how much strength there was inside her.

"You always look at me as if you know everything there is to know about me."

The intensity in his eyes remained, as he caught her hand in his. "Not enough. Not nearly enough." With the lightest of touches, he kissed her shoulder, her temple, then her lips.

"Hunter..." She wanted to tell him that no one had ever made her feel this way before. She wanted to tell him that no one had ever made her want so badly to believe in magic and fairy tales and the simplicity of love. But as she started to speak, courage deserted her. She was afraid to risk, afraid to fail. Instead she touched a hand to his cheek. "Kiss me again."

He understood there was something more, something he needed to know. But he understood, too, that when something fragile was handled clumsily, it broke. He did as she asked and savored the warm, dark taste of her mouth.

Soft...sweet...silky. It was how he could make her feel

with only a kiss. The ground was hard and unyielding under the thin tent mattress, but it might have been a luxurious pile of feathers. It was so easy to forget where she was, when he was with her this way, to forget a world existed outside that small space two bodies required. He could make her float, and she'd never known she'd wanted to. He could make her ache, and she'd never known there could be pleasure from it. He spoke against her mouth words she didn't need to understand. She wanted and was wanted, needed and was needed. She loved…

With an inarticulate murmur of acceptance for whatever he could give, Lee drew him closer. Closer. The moment was all that mattered.

Deep, intoxicating, tender, the kiss went on and on and on.

Even an imagination as fluid as his hadn't fantasized anything so sweet, anything so soft. It was as though she melted into him, giving everything before he could ask. Once, only once, only briefly, it sped through his mind that he was as vulnerable as she. The unease came, flicking at the corner of his mind. Then her hands ran over him, stroking, and he accepted the weakness.

Only one other person had ever had the power to reach inside him and hold his heart. Now there were two. The time to deal with it was tomorrow. Today was for them alone.

Without hurry, he whispered kisses over her face. Perhaps it was a homage to beauty, perhaps it was much, much more. He didn't question his motives as he traced the slope of her cheek. There was an immediacy he'd never experienced before, but it didn't carry the urgency he'd expected.

She was there for him as long as he needed. He understood that, without words.

"You smell of spring and rain," he murmured against her ear. "Why should that drive me mad?"

The words vibrated through her, as arousing as the most intimate caress. Heavy-lidded, clouded, her eyes met his. "Just show me. Show me again."

He loved her with such generosity. Each touch was a separate pleasure, each kiss a luxurious taste. Patience—there was more patience in him than in her. Her body was tossed between utter contentment and urgency, until reason was something too vague to grasp.

"Here—" He nibbled lightly at her breast, listening to and allured by her unsteady breaths. "You're small and soft. Here—" He took his hand over her hip to her thigh. "You're taut and lean. I can't seem to touch enough, taste enough." He drew the peak of her breast into his mouth, so that she arched against him, center to center.

"Hunter." His name was barely audible, but the sound of it was enough to bring him to desperation. "I need you."

God, had he wanted to hear that so badly? Struggling to understand what those three simple words had triggered, he buried his mouth against her skin. But he couldn't think, only feel. Only want. "You have me."

With his hands and lips alone, he took her spiraling over the first peak.

Her movements beneath him grew wild, her murmurs frenzied, but she was unaware. All Lee knew was that they were flesh-to-flesh. This was the storm he'd gentled the night before, the power unleashed, the demands unsoftened. The tenderness became passion so quickly, she could only ride with it, blind to her own power and her own demands. She was spinning too fast in the world they'd created to know how hungrily her mouth sought him, how sure were her own hands. She drew from him everything he drew from her. Again and again she took him to the edge, and again and again he clung, wanting more. And still more.

Greed. He'd never known this degree of greed. With the blood pounding in his head, singing in his veins, he molded his open mouth to hers. With his hands gripping her hips, he rolled until she lay over him. They were still mouth-to-mouth when they joined, and her gasp of pleasure rocketed through him.

Strength seemed to build, impossibly. She thought she could feel each individual muscle of her body coil and release as they moved together. Power called to power. Lee remembered the lightning, remembered the thunder, and lived it again. When the storm broke, she was clasped against him, as if the heat had fused them.

Minutes, hours, days. Lee couldn't have measured the time. Slowly, her body settled. Gradually, her heartbeat leveled. With her body pressed close to his, she could feel each breath he took and found a foolish satisfaction that the rhythm matched her own.

"A pity we wasted a week." Finding the effort to open his eyes too great, Hunter kept them closed as he combed his fingers through her hair.

She smiled a little, because he couldn't see. "Wasted?"

"If we'd started out this way, I'd've slept a lot better."

"Really?" Schooling her features, Lee lifted her head. "Have you had trouble sleeping?"

His eyelids opened lazily. "I've rarely found it necessary to get up at dawn, unless it's to write."

The surge of pleasure made her voice smug. She traced a fingertip over his shoulder. "Is that so?"

"You insisted on wearing that perfume to make me crazy."

"To make you crazy?" Folding her arms on his chest, she arched a brow. "It's a very subtle scent."

"Subtle." He ran a casual hand over her bottom. "Like a hammer in the solar plexus."

The laugh nearly escaped. "You were the one who insisted we share a tent."

"Insisted?" He gave her a mildly amused glance. "I told you I had no objection if you chose to sleep outside."

"Knowing I wouldn't."

"True, but I didn't expect you to resist me for so long."

Her head came up off her folded arms. "Resist you?" she repeated. "Are you saying you plotted this out like a scene in a book?"

Grinning, he pillowed his arms behind his head. God, he couldn't remember a time he'd felt so clean, so…complete. "It worked."

"Typical," she said, wishing she were insulted and trying her best to act as though she were. "I'm surprised there was room in here for the two of us and your inflated ego."

"And your stubbornness."

She sat up at the word, both brows disappearing under her tousled bangs. "I suppose you thought I'd just—" her hand gestured in a quick circle "—fall at your feet."

Hunter considered this a moment, while he gave himself the pleasure of memorizing every curve of her body.

"It might've been nice, but I'd figured a few detours into the scenario."

"Oh, had you?" She wondered if he realized he was steadily digging himself into a hole. "I bet we can come up with a great many more." Searching in her pack, Lee found a fresh T-shirt. "Starting now."

As she started to drag the shirt over her head, Hunter grabbed the hem and yanked. Lee tumbled down on top of him again, to find her mouth captured. When he let her surface, she narrowed her eyes. "You think you're pretty clever, don't you?"

"Yeah." He caught her chin in his hand and kissed her again. "Let's have breakfast."

She swallowed a laugh, but her eyes gave her away. "Bastard."

"Okay, but I'm still hungry." He tugged her shirt down her torso before he started to dress.

Lying back, Lee strugggled into a pair of jeans. "I don't suppose, now that the point's been made, we could finish out this week at a nice resort?"

Hunter dug out a fresh pair of socks. "A resort? Don't tell me you're having problems roughing it, Lenore."

"I wouldn't say problems." She stuck a hand in one boot and found the inside damp. Resigned, she hunted for her sneakers. "But there is the matter of having fantasies about a hot tub and a soft bed." She pressed a hand to her lower back. "Wonderful fantasies."

"Camping does take a certain amount of strength and endurance," he said easily. "I suppose if you've reached your limit and want to quit—"

"I didn't say anything about quitting," she retorted. She set her teeth, knowing whichever way she went, she lost.

"We'll finish out the damn two weeks," she mumbled, and crawled out of the tent.

Lee couldn't deny that the quality of the air was exquisite and the clarity of the sky more perfect than any she'd ever seen. Nor, if he'd asked, would she have told Hunter that she wanted to be back in Los Angeles. It was a matter of basic creature comforts, she thought. Like soaking in hot, fragrant water and stretching out on a firm, linen-covered mattress. Certainly, it wasn't more than most people wanted in their day-to-day lives. But then, she reflected, Hunter Brown wasn't most people.

"Fabulous, isn't it?" His arms came around her waist, drawing her back to his chest. He wanted her to see what he saw, feel what he felt. Perhaps he wanted it too much.

"It's a beautiful spot. It hardly seems real." Then she sighed, not entirely sure why. Would Los Angeles seem more real to her when this final week was up? At the very least, she understood the tall buildings and crowded streets. Here—here she seemed so small, and that top rung of the ladder seemed so vague and unimportant.

Abruptly, she turned and clung to him. "I hate to admit it, but I'm glad you brought me." She found she wanted to continue clinging, continue holding, so that there wouldn't be a time when she had to let go. Pushing away all thoughts of tomorrow, Lee told herself to remember the wildflowers. "I'm starving," she said, able to smile when she drew away. "It's your turn to cook."

"A small blessing."

Lee gave him a quick jab before they cleaned up the dishes they'd left out in the rain.

In his quick, efficient manner, Hunter had the campfire burning and bacon sizzling. Lee sat back, absorbing the scents while she watched him break eggs into the pan.

"We've been through a lot of eggs," she commented idly. "How do you manage to keep them fresh out here?"

Because she was watching his hands, she missed the quick smile. "Just one of the many mysteries of life. You'd better pass me a plate."

"Yes, but— Oh, look." The movement that had caught her eye turned out to be two rabbits, curious enough to bound to the edge of the clearing and watch. The mystery of the eggs was forgotten in the simple fascination of something she'd just begun to appreciate. "Every time I see one, I want to touch."

"If you managed to get close enough to touch, they'd show you they have very sharp teeth."

Shrugging, she dropped her chin to her knees and continued to stare back at the visitors. "The bunnies I think about don't bite."

Hunter reached for a plate himself. "Bunnies, fuzzy little squirrels and cute raccoons are nice to look at but foolish to handle. I remember having a long, heated argument with Sarah on the subject a couple of years ago."

"Sarah?" Lee accepted the plate he offered, but her attention was fully on him.

Until that moment, Hunter hadn't realized how completely he'd forgotten who she was and why she was there. To have mentioned Sarah so casually showed him he needed to keep personal feelings separate from professional agreements. "Someone very special," he told her as he scooped the remaining eggs onto his plate. He remembered his daughter's comment about simmering passion and falling in love. The smile couldn't be prevented. "I imagine she'd like to meet you."

Lee felt something cold squeeze her heart and fought to ignore it. They'd said nothing about commitment, nothing about exclusivity. They were adults. She was responsible for her own emotions and their consequences. "Would she?" Taking the first bite of eggs, she tasted nothing. Her eyes were drawn to the ring on his finger. It wasn't a wedding band, but… She had to ask, she had to know before things went any further.

"The ring you wear," she began, satisfied her voice was even. "It's very unusual. I've never seen another quite like it."

"You shouldn't." He ate with the ease of a man completely content. "My sister made it."

"Sister?" If her name was Sarah…

"Bonnie raises children and makes jewelry," Hunter went on. "I'm not sure which comes first."

"Bonnie." Nodding, she forced herself to continue eating. "Is she your only sister?"

"There were just the two of us. For some odd reason, we got along very well." He remembered those early years when he was struggling to learn how to be both father and mother to Sarah. He smiled. "We still do."

"How does she feel about what you do?"

"Bonnie's a firm believer that everyone should do exactly what suits them. As long as they're married, with a half-dozen children." He grinned, recognizing the unspoken question in Lee's eyes. "In that area, I've disappointed her." He paused for a moment, the grin fading. "Do you think I could make love with you if I had a wife waiting for me at home?"

She dropped her gaze to her plate. Why could he always read her when she couldn't read him? "I still don't know very much about you."

He didn't know if he consciously made the decision at that moment or if he'd been ready to make it all along. "Ask," he said simply.

Lee looked up at him. It no longer mattered if she needed to know for herself or for her job. She just needed to know. "You've never been married?"

"No."

"Is that an outgrowth of your need for privacy?"

"No, it's an outgrowth of not finding anyone who could deal with the way I live and my obligations."

Lee mulled this over, thinking it a rather odd way to phrase it. "Your writing?"

"Yes, there's that."

She started to press further, then decided to change directions. Personal questions could be reciprocated with personal questions. "You said you hadn't always wanted to be a writer, but were born to be one. What made you realize it?"

"I don't think it was a matter of realizing, but of accepting." Understanding that she wanted something specific, he drew out a cigarette, studying the tip. He was no more certain why he was answering than Lee was why she was asking. "It must've been in my first year of college. I'd written stories ever since I could remember, but I was dead set on a career as an athlete. Then I wrote something that seemed to trigger it. It was nothing fabulous," he added thoughtfully. "A very basic plot, simple background, but the characters pulled me in. I knew them as well as I knew anyone. There was nothing else for me to do."

"It must've been difficult. Publishing isn't an easy field. Even when you break in, it isn't particularly lucrative unless you write bestsellers. With your parents gone, you had to support yourself."

"I had experience waiting tables." He smiled, a bit more easily now. "And detested it. Sometimes you have to put it all on the line, Lenore. So I did."

"How did you support yourself from the time you graduated from college until you broke through with *The Devil's Due*?"

"I wrote."

Lee shook her head, forgetting the half-full plate on her lap. "The articles and short stories couldn't have brought in very much. And that was your first book."

"No, I'd had a dozen others before it." Blowing out a stream of smoke, he reached for the coffeepot. "Want some?"

She leaned forward a bit, her brows drawing together. "Look, Hunter, I've been researching you for months. I might not have gotten much, but I know every book, every article and every short story you've written, including the majority of your college work. There's no way I'd've missed a dozen books."

"You know everything Hunter Brown's written," he corrected and poured himself coffee.

"That's precisely what I said."

"You didn't research Laura Miles."

"Who?"

He sipped, enjoying the coffee and the conversation more than he'd anticipated. "A great many writers use pseudonyms. Laura Miles was mine."

"A woman's name?" Confused on one level, reporter's

instincts humming on another, she frowned at him. "You wrote a dozen books before *The Devil's Due* under a woman's name?"

"Yeah. One of the problems with writing is that the name alone can project a certain perception of the author." He offered her the last piece of bacon. "Hunter Brown wasn't right for what I was doing at the time."

Lee let out a frustrated breath. "What were you doing?"

"Writing romance novels." He flicked his cigarette into the fire.

"Writing… *You?*"

He studied her incredulous face before he leaned back. He was used to criticism of genre fiction and, more often than not, amused by it. "Do you object to the genre in general, or to my writing in it?"

"I don't—" Confused, she broke off to try to gather her thoughts. "I just can't picture you writing happy-ever-after love stories. Hunter, I just finished *Silent Scream*. I kept my bedroom door locked for a week." She dragged a hand through her hair as he quietly watched her. "Romances?"

"Most novels have some kind of relationship with them. A romance simply focuses on it, rather than using it as a subplot or a device."

"But didn't you feel you were wasting your talent?" Lee knew his skill in drawing the reader in from the first page, from the first sentence. "I understand there being a matter of putting food on the table, but—"

"No." He cut her off. "I never wrote for the money, Lenore, any more than the novel you're writing is done for financial gain. As far as wasting my talent, you shouldn't look down your nose at something you don't understand."

"I'm sorry, I don't mean to be condescending. I'm

just—" Helplessly, she shrugged. "I'm just surprised. No, I'm astonished. I see those colorful little paperbacks everywhere, but—"

"You never considered reading one," he finished. "You should, they're good for you."

"I suppose, for simple entertainment."

He liked the way she said it, as though it were something to be enjoyed in secret, like a child's lollipop. "If a novel doesn't entertain, it isn't a novel and it's wasted your time. I imagine you've read *Jane Eyre*, *Rebecca*, *Gone with the Wind*, *Ivanhoe*."

"Yes, of course."

"Romances. A lot of the same ingredients are in those colorful little paperbacks."

He was perfectly serious. At that moment, Lee would've given up half the books in her personal library for the chance to read one Laura Miles story. "Hunter, I want to print this."

"Go ahead."

Her mouth was already open for the argument she'd expected. "Go ahead?" she repeated. "You don't care?"

"Why should I? I'm not ashamed of the work I did as Laura Miles. In fact..." He smiled, thinking back. "I'm rather pleased with most of it."

"Then why—" She shook her head as she began to absently nibble on cold bacon. "Damn it, Hunter, why haven't you ever said so before? Laura Miles is as much a deep, dark secret as everything else about you."

"I never met a reporter I chose to tell before." He rose, stretching, and enjoyed the wide blue expanse of sky. Just as he'd never met a woman he'd have chosen to live with before. Hunter was beginning to wonder if one had very much to do with the other. "Don't complicate the simple, Lenore," he told her, thinking aloud. "It usually manages to complicate itself."

Setting her plate aside, she stood in front of him. "One more question, then."

He brought his gaze back down to hers. She hadn't bothered to fuss with her hair or makeup that morning, as she had from the first morning of the trip. For a moment, he wondered if the reporter was too anxious for the story or the woman was too involved with the man. He wished he knew. "All right," he agreed. "One more question."

"Why me?"

How did he answer what he didn't know? How did he answer what he was hesitant to ask himself? Framing her face, he brought his lips to hers. Long, lingering, and very, very new. "I see something in you," Hunter murmured, holding her face still so that he could study it. "I want something from you. I don't know what either one is yet, and maybe I never will. Is that answer enough?"

She put her hands on his wrists and felt his life pump through them. It was almost possible to believe hers pumped through them, too. "It has to be."

Chapter 9

Standing high on the bluff, Lee could see down the canyon, over the peaks and pinnacles, beyond the rich red buttes to the sheer-faced walls. There were pictures in them. People, creatures, stories. They pleased her all the more because she hadn't realized she could find them.

She hadn't known land could be so demanding, or so compelling. Not knowing that, how could she have known she would feel at home so far away from the world she knew or the life she'd made?

Perhaps it was the mystery, the awesomeness—the centuries of work nature had done to form beauty out of rock, the centuries it had yet to work. Weather had landscaped, carved and created without pampering. It might have been the quiet she'd learned to listen to, the quiet she'd learned to hear more than she'd ever heard sound before. Or it might have been the man she'd discovered in the canyon, who was slowly, inevitably dominating every aspect of her life in much the same way wind, water and sun dominated the shape of everything around her. He wouldn't pamper, either.

They'd been lovers only a matter of days, yet he seemed to know just where her strengths lay, and her weaknesses. She learned about him, step by gradual step, always amazed that each new discovery came so naturally, as though she'd always known. Perhaps the intensity came from the briefness. Lee could almost accept that theory, but for the timelessness of the hours they spent together.

In two days, she'd leave the canyon, and the man, and go back to being the Lee Radcliffe she'd molded herself into over the years. She'd step back into the rhythm, write her article and go on to the next stage of her career.

What choice was there? Lee asked herself as she stood with the afternoon sun beating down on her. In L.A., her life had direction, it had purpose. There, she had one goal: to succeed. That goal didn't seem so important here and now, where just being, just breathing, was enough, but this world wasn't the one she would live in day after day. Even if Hunter had asked, even if she'd wanted to, Lee couldn't go on indefinitely in this unscheduled, unplanned existence. Purpose, she wondered. What would her purpose be here? She couldn't dream by the campfire forever.

But two days. She closed her eyes, telling herself that everything she'd done and everything she'd seen would be forever implanted in her memory. Did the time left have to be so short? And the time ahead of her loomed so long.

"Here." Hunter came up alongside her, holding out a pair of binoculars. "You should always see as far as you can."

She took them, with a smile for the way he had of putting things. The canyon zoomed closer, abruptly becoming more personal. She could see the water rushing by in the creek, rushing with a sound too distant to be heard. Why had she never noticed how unique each leaf on a tree could be? She could see other campers loitering near their sites or mingling with the day tourists on paths. Lee let the binoculars drop. They brought intrusion too close.

"Will you come back next year?" She wanted to be able to picture him there, looking out over the endless space, remembering.

"If I can."

"It won't have changed," she murmured. If she came back, five, ten years from then, the creek would still snake by, the buttes would still stand. But she couldn't come back. With an effort, she shook off the mood and smiled at him. "It must be nearly lunchtime."

"It's too hot to eat up here." Hunter wiped at the sweat on his brow. "We'll go down and find some shade."

"All right." She could see the dust plume up from his boots as he walked. "Someplace near the creek." She glanced to the right. "Let's go this way, Hunter. We haven't walked down there yet."

He hesitated only a moment. "Fine." Holding her hand, he took the path she'd chosen.

The walk down was always easier than the walk up. That was another invaluable fact Lee had filed away during the last couple of weeks. And Hunter, though he held her hand, didn't guide or lead. He simply walked his own way. Just as he'd walk his own way in forty-eight hours, she mused, and stretched her stride to keep pace with him.

"Will you start on your next book as soon as you get back?"

Questions, he thought. He'd never known anyone with such an endless supply of questions. "Yes."

"Are you ever afraid you'll, well, dry up?"

"Always."

Interested, she stopped a moment. "Really?" She'd considered him a man without any fear at all. "I'd have thought that the more success you achieved, the more confident you'd become."

"Success is a deity that's never satisfied." She frowned, a bit uncomfortable with his description. "Every time I face that first blank page, I wonder how I'll ever get through a beginning, middle and end."

"How do you?"

He began to walk again, so that she had to keep up or be left behind. "I tell the story. It's as simple and as miserably complex as that."

So was he, she reflected, that simple, that complex. Lee thought over his words as she felt the temperature gradually change with the decrease in elevation.

It seemed tidier in this section of the canyon. Once she thought she heard the purr of a car's engine, a sound she hadn't heard in days. The trees grew thicker, the shade more generous. How strange, she reflected, to have those sheer, unforgiving walls at her back and a cozy little forest in front of her. More unreality? Then, glancing down, she saw a patch of small white flowers. Lee picked three, leaving the rest for someone else. She hadn't come for them, she remembered as she tucked them in her hair, but she was glad, so very glad, to have found them.

"How's this?" He turned to see her secure the last flower in her hair. The need for her, the complete her, rose inside of him so swiftly it took his breath away. Lenore. He had no trouble understanding why the man in Poe's verse had mourned the loss of her to the point of madness. "You grow lovelier. Impossible." Hunter touched a fingertip to her cheek. Would he, too, grow mad from mourning the loss of her?

Her face, lifted to the sun, needed nothing more than the luminescence of her skin to make it exquisite. But how long, he wondered, how long would she be content to shun the polish? How long would it be before she craved the life she'd begun to carve out for herself?

Lee didn't smile, because his eyes prevented her. He was looking into her again, for something… Something. She wasn't certain, even if she'd known what it was, that she could give him the answer he wanted. Instead, she did what he'd once done. Placing her hands on his shoulders, she touched her mouth to his. With her eyes squeezed shut, she dropped her head onto his chest.

How could she leave? How could she not? There seemed to be no direction she could go and not lose something essential. "I don't believe in magic," she murmured, "but if I did, I'd say this was a magic place. Now, in the day, it's quiet. Sleeping, perhaps. But at night, the air would be alive with spirits."

He held her closer as he rested his neck on top of her head. Did she realize how romantic she was? he wondered. Or just how hard she fought not to be? A week ago, she might have had such a thought, but she'd never have said it aloud. A week from now… Hunter bit back a sigh. A week from now, she'd give no more thought to magic.

"I want to make love with you here," he said quietly. "With the sunlight streaming through the leaves and onto your skin. In the evening, just before the dew falls. At dawn, when the light's caught somewhere between rose and gray."

Moved, ruled by love, she smiled up at him. "And at midnight, when the moon's high and anything's possible."

"Anything's always possible." He kissed one cheek, then the other. "You only have to believe it."

She laughed, a bit shakily. "You almost make me believe it. You make my knees weak."

His grin flashed as he swept her up in his arms. "Better?"

Would she ever feel this free again? Throwing her arms around his neck, Lee kissed him with all the feeling that welled inside her. "Yes. And if you don't put me down, I'll want you to carry me back to camp."

The half smile touched his lips. "Decided you aren't hungry after all?"

"Since I doubt you've got anything in that bag but dried fruit and sunflower seeds, I don't have any illusions about lunch."

"I've still got a couple pieces of fudge."

"Let's eat."

Hunter dropped her unceremoniously on the ground. "It shows the woman's basic lust centers around food."

"Just chocolate," Lee disagreed. "You can have my share of the sunflower seeds."

"They're good for you." Digging into the pack, he pulled out some small clear-plastic bags.

"I can handle the raisins," Lee said unenthusiastically. "But I can do without the seeds."

Shrugging, Hunter popped two in his mouth. "You'll be hungry before dinner."

"I've been hungry before dinner for two weeks," she tossed back, and began to root through the pack herself for the fudge. "No matter how good seeds and nuts and little dried pieces of apricot are for you, they don't take the place of red meat—" she found a small square of fudge "—or chocolate."

Hunter watched her close her eyes in pure pleasure as she chewed the candy. "Hedonist."

"Absolutely." Her eyes were laughing when she opened them. "I like silk blouses, French champagne and lobster with warm butter sauce." She sighed as she sat back, wondering if Hunter had any emotional attachment to the last piece of fudge. "I especially enjoy them after I've worked all week to justify having them."

He understood that, perhaps too well. She wasn't a woman who wanted to be taken care of, nor was he a man who believed anyone should have a free ride. But what future was there in a relationship when two people couldn't acclimate to each other's life-style? He'd never imposed his on anyone else, nor would he permit anyone to sway him from his own. And yet, now that he felt the clock ticking the hours away, the days away, he wondered if it would be as simple to go back, alone, as he'd once expected it to be.

"You enjoy living in the city?" he asked casually.

"Of course." It wasn't possible to tell him that she hated the thought of going back, alone, to what she'd always thought was perfect for her. "My apartment's twenty minutes from the magazine."

"Convenient." And practical, he mused. It seemed she would always choose the practical, even if she had a whim for the fanciful. He opened the canteen and drank. When he passed it to Lee, she accepted. She'd learned to make a number of adjustments.

"I suppose you work at home."

"Yes."

She touched a hand absently to one of the flowers in her hair. "That takes discipline. I think most people need the structure of an office away from their living space to accomplish anything."

"You wouldn't."

She looked over then, wishing they could talk about more personal things without bringing on that quiet sense of panic. Better that they talked of work or the weather, or of nothing at all. "No?"

"You'd drive yourself harder than any supervisor or time clock." He bit into an apple slice. "If you put your mind to it, you'd have that manuscript finished within a month."

Restlessly, she moved her shoulders. "If I worked eight hours a day, without any other obligations."

"The story's your only obligation."

She held back a sigh. She didn't want to argue or even debate, not when they had so little time left together. Yet if they didn't discuss her work, she might not be able to prevent herself from talking about her feelings. That was a circle without any meeting point.

"Hunter, as a writer, you can feel that way about a book. I suppose you have to. I have a job, a career that demands blocks of time and a great deal of my attention. I can't simply put that into hiatus while I speculate on my chances of getting a manuscript published."

"You're afraid to risk it."

It was a direct hit to her most sensitive area. Both of them knew her anger was a defense. "What if I am? I've worked hard for my position at *Celebrity*. Everything I've done there, and every benefit I've received, I've earned on my own. I've already taken enough risks."

"By not marrying Jonathan Willoby?"

The fury leaped into her eyes quickly, interesting him. So, it was still a sore point, Hunter realized. A very sore point.

"Do you find that amusing?" Lee demanded. "Does the fact that I reneged on an unspoken agreement appeal to your sense of humor?"

"Not particularly. But it intrigues me that you'd consider it possible to renege on something unspoken."

From the meticulous way she recapped the canteen, he gauged just how angry she was. Her voice was cool and detached, as he hadn't heard it for days. "My family and the Willobys have been personally and professionally involved for years. The marriage was expected of me and I knew it from the time I was sixteen."

Hunter leaned back against the trunk of a tree until he was comfortable. "And at sixteen you didn't consider that sort of expectation antiquated?"

"How could you possibly understand?" Fuming, she rose. The nerves that had been dormant for days began to jump again. Hunter could almost see them spring to life. "You said your father was a dreamer who made his living as a salesman. My father was a realist who made his living socializing and delegating. He socialized with the Willobys. He delegated me to complete the social and professional merger with them by marrying Jonathan." Even now, the tidy, unemotional plans gave her a twinge of distaste. "Jonathan was attractive, intelligent, already successful. My father never considered that I'd object."

"But you did," Hunter pointed out. "Why do you continue to insist on paying for something that was your right?"

Lee whirled to him. It was no longer possible for her

to answer coolly, to rebuff with aloofness. "Do you know what it cost me not to do what was expected of me? Everything I did, all my life, was ultimately for their approval."

"Then you did something for yourself." Without hurry, he rose to face her. "Is your career for yourself, Lenore, or are you still trying to win their approval?"

He had no right to ask, no right to make her search for the answer. Pale, she turned away from him. "I don't want to discuss this with you. It's none of your concern."

"Isn't it?" Abruptly as angry as she, Hunter spun her around again. "Isn't it?" he repeated.

Her hands curled around his arms—whether in protest or for support, she wasn't certain. Now, she thought, now perhaps she'd reached that edge where she had to make a stand, no matter how unsteady the ground under her feet. "My life and the way I live it are my business, Hunter."

"Not anymore."

"You're being ridiculous." She threw back her head, the better to meet his eyes. "This argument doesn't even have a point."

Something was building inside him so quickly he didn't have a chance to fight it or reason it through. "You're wrong."

She was beginning to tremble without knowing why. Along with the anger came the quick panic she recognized too well. "I don't know what you want."

"You." She was crushed against him before she understood her own reaction. "All of you."

His mouth closed over hers with none of the gentle patience he usually showed. Lee felt a lick of fear that was almost immediately swallowed by raging need.

He'd made her feel passion before, but not so swiftly.

Desire had burst inside her before, but not so painfully. Everything was as it always was whenever he touched her, and yet everything was so different.

Was it anger she felt from him? Frustration? Passion? She only knew that the control he mastered so finely was gone. Something strained inside him, something more primitive than he'd let free before. This time, they both knew it could break loose. Her blood swam with the panicked excitement of anticipation.

Then they were on the ground, with the scent of sun-warmed leaves and cool water. She felt his beard scrape over her cheek before he buried his mouth in her throat. Whatever drove him left her no choice but to race with him to the end that waited for both of them.

He didn't question his own desperation. He couldn't. If she held off sharing certain pieces of herself with him, she still shared her body willingly. He wanted more, all, though he told himself it wasn't reasonable. Even now, as he felt her body heat and melt for him, he knew he wouldn't be satisfied. When would she give her feelings to him as freely? For the first time in his life, he wanted too much.

He struggled back to the edge of reason, resisting the wave after wave of need that raged through him. This wasn't the time, the place or the way. In his mind, he knew it, but emotion battled to betray him. Still holding her close, he buried his face in her hair and waited for the madness to pass.

Stunned, as much by his outburst of passion as by her unquestioning response, Lee lay still. Instinctively, she stroked a hand down his back to soothe. She knew him well enough to understand that his temper was rarely unguarded. Now she knew why.

Hunter lifted his head to look at her, seeing on a surge of self-disgust that her eyes were wary again. The flowers had fallen from her hair. Taking one, he pressed it into her hand. "You're much too fragile to be handled so clumsily."

His eyes were so intense, so dark, it was impossible for her to relax again. Against his back, her fingers curled and uncurled. There was a warning somewhere in her brain that he wanted more than she'd expected him to want, more than she knew how to give. Play it light, Lee ordered herself, and deliberately stilled the movement of her fingers. She smiled, though her eyes remained cautious.

"I should've waited until we were back in the tent before I made you angry."

Understanding what she was trying to do, Hunter lifted a brow. Under his voice, and hers, was a strain both of them pretended not to hear. "We can go back now. I can toss you around a bit more."

As the panic subsided, she sent him a mild glance. "I'm stronger than I look."

"Yeah?" He sent her a smile of his own. He had the long hours of night to think about what had happened and what he was going to do about it. "Show me."

More confident than she should've been, Lee pushed against him, intent on rolling him off her. He didn't budge. The look of calm amusement on his face had her doubling her efforts. Breathless, unsuccessful, she lay back and frowned at him. "You're heavier than you look," she complained. "It must be all those sunflower seeds."

"Your muscles are full of chocolate," he corrected.

"I only had one piece," she began.

"Today. By my count, you've polished off—"

"Never mind." Her brow arched elegantly. The nerves

in her stomach hadn't completely subsided. "If you want to talk about unhealthy habits, you're the one who smokes too much."

He shrugged, accepting the truth. "Everyone's entitled to one vice."

Her grin became wicked, then sultry. "Is that your only one?"

If she'd planned to make her mouth irresistible, she'd succeeded. Hunter lowered his to nibble at the sweetness. "I've never been one to consider pleasures vices."

Sighing, she linked her arms around his neck. They didn't have enough time left to waste it arguing, or even thinking. "Why don't we go back to the tent so you can show me what you mean?"

He laughed softly and shifted to kiss the curve of her shoulder. Her laugh echoed his, then Lee's smile froze when she glanced down the length of his body to what stood at their feet.

Fear ripped through her. She couldn't have screamed. Her short, unpainted nails dug into Hunter's back.

"What—" He lifted his head. Her face was ice-white and still. Though her body was rigid beneath his, there was lively fear in the hands that dug into his back. Muscles tense, he turned to look in the direction she was staring. "Damn." The word was hardly out of his mouth before a hundred pounds of fur and muscle leaped on him. This time, Lee's scream tore free.

Adrenaline born of panic gave her the strength to send the three of them rolling to the edge of the bank. As she struck out blindly, Lee heard Hunter issue a sharp command. A whimper followed it.

"Lenore." Her shoulders were gripped before she could

spring to her feet. In her mind, the only thought was to find a weapon to defend them. "It's all right." Without giving her a choice, Hunter held her close. "It's all right, I promise. He won't hurt you."

"My God, Hunter, it's a wolf!" Every nightmare she'd ever read or heard about fangs and claws spun in her mind. With her arms wrapped around him to protect him, as much as for protection for herself, Lee turned her head. Silver eyes stared back at her from a silver coat.

"No." He felt the fresh fear jump through her and continued to soothe. "He's only half wolf."

"We've got to do something." Should they run? Should they sit perfectly still? "He attacked—"

"Greeted," Hunter corrected. "Trust me, Lenore. He's not vicious." Annoyed and resigned, Hunter held out a hand. "Here, Santanas."

A bit embarrassed at having lost control of himself, the dog crawled forward, head down. Speechless, Lee watched Hunter stroke the thick silver-gray fur.

"He's usually better behaved," Hunter said mildly. "But he hasn't seen me for nearly two weeks."

"Seen you?" She pressed herself closer to Hunter. "But…" Logic began to seep through her panic as she saw the dog lick Hunter's extended hand. "You called him by name," she said shakily. "What did you call him?"

Before Hunter could answer, there was a rustling in the trees behind them. Lee had nearly mustered the breath to scream again when another voice, young and high, shouted out. "Santanas! You come back here. I'm going to get in trouble."

"Damn right," Hunter mumbled under his breath.

Lee drew back far enough to look into Hunter's face. "Just what the hell's going on?"

"A reunion," he said simply.

Puzzled, with her heart still pounding in her ears, Lee watched the girl break through the trees. The dog's tail began to thump the ground.

"Santanas!" She stopped, her dark braids whipping back and forth. Smiling, she uninhibitedly showed her braces. "Whoops." The quick exclamation trailed off as Lee was treated to a long intense stare that was hauntingly familiar. The girl stuck her hands in the pockets of cutoff jeans, scuffing the ground with battered sneakers. "Well, hi." Her gaze shifted to Hunter briefly before it focused on Lee again. "I guess you wonder what I'm doing here."

"We'll get into that later," Hunter said in a tone both females recognized as basic male annoyance.

"Hunter—" Lee drew farther away, traces of anger and anxiety working their way through the confusion. She couldn't bring herself to look away from the dark, dark eyes of the girl who stared at her. "What's going on here?"

"Apparently a lesson in manners should be," he returned easily. "Lenore, the creature currently sniffing at your hand is Santanas, my dog." At the gesture of his hand, the large, lean animal sat and lifted a friendly paw. Dazed, Lee found herself taking it while she turned to watch the dog's master. She saw Hunter's gaze travel beyond her with a smile that held both irony and pride. "The girl rudely staring at you is Sarah. My daughter."

Chapter 10

Daughter…Sarah…

Lee turned her head to meet the dark, direct eyes that were a duplicate of Hunter's. Yes, they were a duplicate. It struck her like a blast of air. He had a child? This lovely, slender girl with a tender mouth and braids secured by mismatched rubber bands was Hunter's daughter? So many opposing emotions moved through her that she said nothing. Nothing at all.

"Sarah." Hunter spoke into the drumming silence. "This is Ms. Radcliffe."

"Sure, I know, the reporter. Hi."

Still sitting on the ground, with the dog now sniffing around her shoulder, Lee felt like a complete fool. "Hello." She hoped the word wasn't as ridiculously formal as it sounded to her.

"Dad said I shouldn't call you pretty because pretty was like a bowl of fruit." Sarah didn't tilt her head as one might to study from a new angle, but Lee had the impression she was being weighed and dissected like a still life. "I like your hair," Sarah declared. "Is it a real color?"

"A definite lesson in manners," Hunter put in, more amused than annoyed. "I'm afraid Sarah's a bit of a brat."

"He always says that." Sarah moved thin, expressive shoulders. "He doesn't mean it, though."

"Until today." He ruffled the dog's fur, wondering just how he would handle the situation. Lee was still silent, and Sarah's eyes were all curiosity. "Take Santanas back to the house. I assume Bonnie's there."

"Yeah. We came back yesterday because I remembered I had a soccer game and she had an inspiration and couldn't do anything with it in Phoenix with all the kids running around like monkeys."

"I see." And though he did, perfectly, Lee was left floundering in the dark. "Go ahead, then, we'll be right along."

"Okay. Come on, Santanas." Then she shot Lee a quick grin. "He looks pretty ferocious, but he doesn't bite." As the girl darted away, Lee wondered if she'd been speaking of the dog or her father. When she was once again alone with Hunter, Lee remained still and silent.

"I'll apologize for the rudeness of my family, if you'd like."

Family. The word struck her, a dose of reality that flung her out of the dream. Rising, Lee meticulously dusted off her jeans. "There's no need." Her voice was cool, almost chill. Her muscles were wire-taut. "Since the game's over, I'd like you to drive me into Sedona so I can arrange for transportation back to L.A."

"Game?" In one long, easy motion, he came to his feet, then took her hand, stopping its nervous movement. It was a gesture that had become so much of a habit, neither of them noticed. "There's no game, Lenore."

"Oh, you played it very well." The hurt she wouldn't permit in her voice showed clearly in her eyes. Her hand remained cold and rigid in his. "So well, in fact, I completely forgot we were playing."

Patience deserted him abruptly and without warning. Anger he could handle, with more anger or with amusement. But hurt left him with no defense, no attack. "Don't be an idiot. Whatever game there was ended a few nights ago in the tent."

"Ended." Tears sprang to her eyes, stunning her. Furiously she blinked them back, filled with self-disgust, but not before he'd seen them. "No, it never ended. You're an excellent strategist, Hunter. You seemed to be so open with me that I didn't think you were holding anything back." She jerked her hand from his, longing for the luxury of dissolving into those hot, cleansing tears. "How could you?" she demanded. "How could you touch me that way and lie?"

"I never lied to you." His voice was as calm as hers, his eyes were as full of passion.

"You have a child." Something snapped inside her, so that she had to grip her hands together to prevent herself from wringing them. "You have a half-grown daughter you never mentioned to me. You told me you'd never been married."

"I haven't been," he said simply, and waited for the inevitable questions.

They leaped into her mind, but Lee found she couldn't ask them. She didn't want to know. If she was to put him out of her life immediately and completely, she couldn't ask. "You said her name once, and when I asked, you avoided answering."

"Who asked?" he countered. "You or the reporter?"

She paled, and her step away from him said more than a dozen words.

"If that was an unfair question," he said, feeling his way carefully, "I'm sorry."

Lee stifled a bitter answer. He'd just said it all. "I want to go back to Sedona. Will you drive me, or do I have to arrange for a car?"

"Stop this." He gripped her shoulders before she could back farther away. "You've been a part of my life for a few days; Sarah's been my life for ten years. I take no risks with her." She saw the fury come and go in his eyes as he fought against it. "She's off the record, do you understand? She stays off the record. I won't have her childhood disturbed by photographers dogging her at soccer games or hanging from trees at school picnics. Sarah's not an item for the glossy pages of any magazine."

"Is that what you think of me?" she whispered. "We've come no further than that?" She swallowed a mixture of pain and betrayal. "Your daughter won't be mentioned in any article I write. You have my word. Now let me go."

She wasn't speaking only of the hands that held her there, and they both knew it. He felt a bubble of panic he'd never expected, a twist of guilt that left him baffled. Frustrated, he stared down at her. He'd never realized she could be a complication. "I can't." It was said with such simplicity her skin iced. "I want you to understand, and I need time for that."

"You've had nearly two weeks to make me understand, Hunter."

"Damn it, you came here as a reporter." He paused, as if waiting for her to confirm or deny, but she said nothing. "What happened between us wasn't planned or expected by either one of us. I want you to come back with me to my home."

Somehow she met his eyes levelly. "I'm still a reporter."

"We have two days left in our agreement." His voice softened, his hands gentled. "Lenore, spend those two days with me at home, with my daughter."

"You have no problem asking for everything, do you?"

"No." She was still holding herself away from him. No matter how badly he wanted to, Hunter knew better than to try to draw her closer. Not yet. "It's important to me that you understand. Give me two days."

She wanted to say no. She wanted to believe she could deny him even that and turn away, go away, without regrets. But there'd be regrets, Lee realized, if she went back to L.A. without taking whatever was left. "I can't promise to understand, but I'll stay two more days."

Though she was reluctant, he held her hand to his lips. "Thank you. It's important to me."

"Don't thank me," she murmured. The anger had slipped away so quietly, she couldn't recall it. "Things have changed."

"Things changed days ago." Still holding her hand, he drew her in the direction Sarah had gone. "I'll come back for the gear."

Now that the first shock had passed, the second occurred to her. "But you live here in the canyon."

"That's right."

"You mean to tell me you have a house, with hot and

cold running water and a normal bed, but you chose to spend two weeks in a tent?"

"It relaxes me."

"That's just dandy," she muttered. "You've had me showering with lukewarm water and waking up with aching muscles, when you knew I'd've given a week's pay for one tub bath."

"Builds character," he claimed, more comfortable with her annoyance.

"The hell it does. You did it deliberately." She stopped, turning to him as the sun dappled light through the trees. "You did it all deliberately to see just how much I could tolerate."

"You were very impressive." He smiled infuriatingly. "I admit I never expected you to last out a week, much less two."

"You sonofa—"

"Don't get cranky now," he said easily. "You can take as many baths as you like over the next couple of days." He swung a friendly arm over her shoulder before she could prevent it. And he'd have time, he thought, to explain to her about Sarah. Time, he hoped, to make her understand. "I'll even see to it that you have that red meat you've been craving."

Fury threatened. Control strained. "Don't you dare patronize me."

"I'm not; you're not a woman a man could patronize." Though she mistrusted his answer, his voice was bland with sincerity and he wasn't smiling. "I'm enjoying you and, I suppose, the foul-up of my own plans. Believe me, I hadn't intended for you to find out I lived a couple miles from the campsite in quite this way."

"Just how did you intend for me to find out?"

"By offering you a quiet candlelight dinner on our last night. I'd hoped you'd see the—ah—humor in the situation."

"You'd've been wrong," she said precisely, then caught sight of the house cocooned in the trees.

It was smaller than she'd expected, but with the large areas of glass in the wood, it seemed to extend into the land. It made her think of dolls' houses and fairy tales, though she didn't know why. Dolls' houses were tidy and formal and laced with gingerbread. Hunter's house was made up of odd angles and unexpected peaks. A porch ran across the front, where the roof arched to a high pitch. Plants spilled over the banister—bloodred geraniums in jade-green pots. The roof sloped down again, then ran flat over a parallelogram with floor-to-ceiling windows. On the patio that jutted out from it, a white wicker chair lay overturned next to a battered soccer ball.

The trees closed in around it. Closed it in, Lee thought. Protected, sheltered, hid. It was like a house out of a play, or… Stopping, she narrowed her eyes and studied it again. "This is Jonas Thorpe's house in *Silent Scream*."

Hunter smiled, rather pleased she'd seen it so quickly. "More or less. I wanted to put him in isolation, miles away from what would normally be considered civilized, but in reality, the only safe place left."

"Is that how you look at it?" she wondered aloud. "As the only safe place left?"

"Often." Then a shriek, which after a heart-stopping moment Lee identified as laughter, ripped through the silence. It was followed by an excited bout of barking and a woman's frazzled voice. "Then there're other times," Hunter murmured as he led Lee toward the front door.

Even as he opened it, Sarah came bounding out. Unsure of her own feelings, Lee watched the girl throw her arms around her father's waist. She saw Hunter stroke a hand over the dark hair at the crown of Sarah's head.

"Oh, Dad, it's so funny! Aunt Bonnie was making a bracelet out of glazed dough and Santanas ate it—or he chewed on it until he found out it tasted awful."

"I'm sure Bonnie thinks it's a riot."

Her eyes, so like her father's, lit with a wicked amusement that would've made a veteran fifth-grade teacher nervous. "She said she had to take that sort of thing from art critics, but not from half-breed wolves. She said she'd make some tea for Lenore, but there aren't any cookies because we ate them yesterday. And she said—"

"Never mind, we'll find out for ourselves." He stepped back so that Lee could walk into the house ahead of him. She hesitated for a moment, wondering just what she was walking into, and his eyes lit with the same wicked amusement as Sarah's. They were quite a pair, Lee decided, and stepped forward.

She hadn't expected anything so, well, normal in Hunter Brown's home. The living room was airy, sunny in the afternoon light. *Cheerful.* Yes, Lee realized, that was precisely the word that came to mind. No shadowy corners or locked doors. There were wildflowers in an enameled vase and plump pillows on the sofa.

"Were you expecting witches' brooms and a satin-lined coffin?" he murmured in her ear.

Annoyed, she stepped away from him. "Of course not.

I suppose I didn't expect you to have something quite so… domesticated."

He arched a brow at the word. "I am domesticated."

Lee looked at him, at the face that was half rugged, half aristocratic. On one level, perhaps, she mused. But only on one.

"I guess Aunt Bonnie's got the mess in the kitchen pretty well cleaned up." Sarah kept one arm around her father as she gave Lee another thorough going-over. "She'd like to meet you because Dad doesn't see nearly enough women and never talks to reporters. So maybe you're special because he decided to talk to you."

While she spoke, she watched Lee steadily. She was only ten, but already she'd sensed there was something between her father and this woman with the dark-blue eyes and nifty hair. What she didn't know was exactly how she felt about it yet. In the manner of her father, Sarah decided to wait and see.

Equally unsure of her own feelings, Lee went with them into the kitchen. She had an impression of sunny walls, white trim and confusion.

"Hunter, if you're going to keep a wolf in the house, you should at least teach him to appreciate art. Hi, I'm Bonnie."

Lee saw a tall, thin woman with dark-brown shoulder-length hair streaked liberally with blond. She wore a purple T-shirt with faded pink printing over cutoffs as ragged as her niece's. Her bare feet were tipped at the toes with hot-pink polish. Studying her thin model's face, Lee couldn't be sure if she was years older than Hunter or years younger. Automatically she held out her hand in response to Bonnie's out-stretched one.

"How do you do?"

"I'd be doing a lot better if Santanas hadn't tried to make a snack of my latest creation." She held up a golden-brown half circle with ragged ends. "Just lucky for him it was a dreadful idea. Anyway, sit." She gestured to a table piled with bowls and canisters and dusted the flour. "I'm making tea."

"You didn't turn the kettle on," Sarah pointed out, and did so herself.

"Hunter, the child's always picking on details. I worry about her."

With a shrug of acceptance, he picked up what looked like a small doughnut and might, with imagination, have been an earring. "You're finding gold and silver too traditional to work with these days?"

"I thought I might start a trend." When Bonnie smiled, she became abruptly and briefly stunning. "In any case, it was a small failure. Probably cost you less than three dollars in flour. Sit," she repeated as she began to transfer the mess from the table to the counter behind her. "So, how was the camping trip?"

"Enlightening. Wouldn't you say, Lenore?"

"Educational," she corrected, but thought the last half hour had been the most educational of all.

"So, you work for *Celebrity*." Bonnie's long, twisted gold earrings swung when she walked, much like Sarah's braids. "I'm a faithful reader."

"That's because she's had a couple of embarrassingly flattering write-ups."

"Write-ups?" Lee watched Bonnie dust her flour-covered hands on her cutoffs.

Hunter smiled as he watched his sister reach for a tin of

tea and send others clattering to the counter. "Professionally she's known as B. B. Smithers."

The name rang a bell. For years, B. B. Smithers had been considered the queen of avant-garde jewelry. The elite, the wealthy and the trendy flocked to her for personal designs. They paid, and paid well, for her talent, her creativity, and the tiny Bs etched into the finished product. Lee stared at the thin, somewhat clumsy woman with something close to wonder. "I've admired your work."

"But you wouldn't wear it," Bonnie put in with a smile as she shoved tumbled boxes and tins out of her way. "No, it's the classics for you. What a fabulous face. Do you want lemon in your tea? Do we have any lemons, Hunter?"

"Probably not."

Taking this in stride, Bonnie set the teapot on the table to let the tea steep. "Tell me, Lenore, how did you talk the hermit into coming out of his cave?"

"By making him furious, I believe."

"That might work." She sat down across from Lee as Sarah walked to her father's side. Her eyes were softer than her brother's, less intense, but not, Lee thought, less perceptive. "Did the two weeks playing pioneer in the canyon give you the insight to write an article on him?"

"Yes." Lee smiled, because there was humor in Bonnie's eyes. "Plus I gained a growing affection for box springs and mattresses."

The quick, stunning smile flashed again. "My husband takes the children camping once a year. That's when I go to Elizabeth Arden's for the works. When we come home, both of us feel we've accomplished several small miracles."

"Camping's not so bad," Sarah commented in her father's defense.

"Is that so?" He patted her bottom as he drew her closer. "Why is it that you always have this all-consuming desire to visit Bonnie in Phoenix whenever I start packing gear?"

She giggled, and her arm went easily around his shoulder. "Must be coincidence," she said in a dry tone that echoed his. "Did he make you go fishing?" Sarah wanted to know. "And sit around for just *hours*?"

Lee watched Hunter's brow lift before she answered. "Actually, he did, ah, suggest fishing several days running."

"Ugh" was Sarah's only comment.

"But I caught a bigger fish than he did."

Unimpressed, Sarah shook her head. "It's awfully boring." She sent her father an apologetic glance. "I guess somebody's got to do it." Leaning her head against her father's, she smiled at Lee. "Mostly he's never boring, he just likes some weird stuff. Like fishing and beer."

"Sarah doesn't consider Hunter's shrunken-head collection at all unusual." Bonnie picked up the teapot. "Are you having some?" she asked her brother.

"I'll pass. Sarah and I'll go and break camp."

"Take your wolf with you," Bonnie told him as she poured tea into Lee's cup. "He's still on my hit list. By the way, a couple of calls from New York came in for you yesterday."

"They'll keep." As he rose, he ran a careless hand down Lee's hair, a gesture not lost on either of the other females in the room. "I'll be back shortly."

She started to offer her help, but it was so comfortable in the sunny, cluttered kitchen, and the tea smelled like heaven. "All right." She saw the proprietary hand Sarah put on her father's arm and thought it just as well to stay where she was.

Together, father and daughter walked to the back door. Hunter whistled for the dog, then they were gone.

Bonnie stirred her tea. "Sarah adores her father."

"Yes." Lee thought of the way they'd looked, side by side.

"And so do you."

Lee had started to lift her cup; now it only rattled in the saucer. "I beg your pardon?"

"You're in love with Hunter," Bonnie said mildly. "I think it's marvelous."

She could've denied it—vehemently, icily, laughingly, but hearing it said aloud seemed to put her in some kind of trance. "I don't—that is, it doesn't..." Lee stopped, realizing she was running the spoon handle through her hands. "I'm not sure how I feel."

"A definite symptom. Does being in love worry you?"

"I didn't say I was." Again, Lee stopped. Could anyone make evasions with those soft doe eyes watching? "Yes, it worries me a lot."

"Only natural. I used to fall in and out of love like some people change clothes. Then I met Fred." Bonnie laughed into her tea before she sipped. "I went around with a queasy stomach for weeks."

Lee pressed a hand to her own before she rose. Tea wasn't going to help. She had to move. "I have no illusions about Hunter and myself," she said, more firmly than she'd expected to. "We have different priorities, different tastes." She looked through the kitchen window to the high red walls far beyond the clustering trees. "Different lives. I have to get back to L.A."

Bonnie calmly continued to drink tea. "Of course." If Lee heard the irony, she didn't respond to it. "There are people who have it fixed in their heads that in order to have a relationship, the two parties involved must be on the same wavelength. If one adores sixteenth-century French poetry and the other detests it, there's no hope." She noticed Lee's frown but continued, lightly. "Fred's an accountant who gets a primal thrill out of interest rates." She wiped absently at a smudge of flour on the table. "Statistically, I suppose we should've divorced years ago."

Lee turned back, unable to be angry, unable to smile. "You're a great deal like Hunter, aren't you?"

"I suppose. Is your mother Adreanne Radcliffe?"

Though she no longer wanted it, Lee came back to the table for her tea. "Yes."

"I met her at a party in Palm Springs two, no, must've been three years ago. Yes, three," Bonnie said decisively, "because I was still nursing Carter, my youngest, and he's currently terrorizing everyone at nursery school. Just last week he tried to cook a goldfish in a toy oven. You're not at all like your mother, are you?"

It took a moment for Lee to catch up. She set down her tea again, untasted. "Aren't I?"

"Do you think you are?" Bonnie tossed her tousled, streaked hair behind her shoulder. "I don't mean any offense, but she wouldn't know what to say to anyone not born to the blue, so to speak. I'd've considered her a very sheltered woman. She's very lovely; you certainly appear to've inherited her looks. But that seems to be all."

Lee stared down at her tea. How could she explain that, because of the strong physical resemblance between her and her mother, she'd always figured there were other resemblances. Hadn't she spent her childhood and adolescence trying to find them, and all of her adult life trying to repress them? A sheltered woman. She found it a terrifying phrase, and too close to what she herself could have become.

"My mother has standards," she answered, at length. "She never seems to have any trouble living up to them."

"Oh, well, everyone should do what they do best." Bonnie propped her elbows on the table, lacing her fingers so that the three rings on her right hand gleamed and winked. "According to Hunter, the thing you do best is write. He mentioned your novel to me."

The irritation came so quickly Lee hadn't the chance to mask it. "He's the kind of man who can't admit when he's made a mistake. I'm a reporter, not a novelist."

"I see." Still smiling blandly, Bonnie dropped her chin onto her laced fingers. "So, what are you going to report about Hunter?"

Was there a challenge under the smile? A trace of mockery? Whatever there was at the edges, Lee couldn't help but respond to it. Yes, she thought again, Bonnie Smithers was a great deal like her brother.

"That he's a man who considers writing both a sacred duty and a skilled profession. That he has a sense of humor that's often so subtle it takes you hours to catch up. That he believes in choices and luck with the same stubbornness that he believes in fate." Pausing, she lifted her cup. "He values the written word, whether it's in comic books or Chaucer, and he works desperately hard to do what he considers his job: to tell the story."

"I like you."

Cautiously, Lee smiled. "Thank you."

"I love my brother," Bonnie went on easily. "More than that, I admire him, for personal and professional reasons. You understand him. Not everyone would."

"Understand him?" Lee shook her head. "It seems to me that the more I find out about him, the less I understand. He's shown me more beauty in a pile of rocks than I'd ever have found for myself, yet he writes about horror and fears."

"And you consider that a contradiction?" Bonnie shrugged as she leaned back in her chair. "It's just that Hunter sees both sides of life very clearly. He writes about the dark side because it's the most intriguing."

"Yet he lives…" Lee gestured as she glanced around the kitchen.

"In a cozy little house nestled in the woods."

The laugh came naturally. "I wouldn't precisely call it cozy, but it's certainly not what you'd expect from the country's leading author of horror and occult fiction."

"The country's leading author of horror and occult fiction has a child to raise."

"Yes." Lee's smile faded. "Yes, Sarah. She's lovely."

"Will she be in your article?"

"No." Again, she lifted her gaze to Bonnie's. "No, Hunter made it clear he objected to that."

"She's the focal point of his life. If he seems a bit overprotective in certain ways, believe me, it's a completely unselfish act." When Lee merely nodded, Bonnie felt a stirring of sympathy. "He hasn't told you about her?"

"No, nothing."

There were times Bonnie's love and admiration for Hunter became clouded with frustration. A great many times. This woman was in love with him, was one step away from being irrevocably committed to him. Any fool could see it, Bonnie mused. Any fool except Hunter. "As I said, there are times he's overly protective. He has his reasons, Lenore."

"And will you tell me what they are?"

She was tempted. It was time Hunter opened that part of his life, and she was certain this was the woman he should open it to. "The story's Hunter's," Bonnie said at length. "You should hear it from him." She glanced around idly as she heard the Jeep pull up in the drive. "They're back."

"I guess I'm glad you brought her back," Sarah commented as they drove the last mile toward home.

"You guess?" Hunter turned his head, to see his daughter looking pensively through the windshield.

"She's beautiful, like a princess." For the first time in months, Sarah worried her braces with her tongue. "You like her a lot, I can tell."

"Yes, I like her a lot." He knew every nuance of his daughter's voice, every expression, every gesture. "That doesn't mean I like you any less."

Sarah gave him one long look. She needed no other words from him to reaffirm love. "I guess you have to like me," she decided, half teasing, "'cause we're stuck with each other. But I don't think she does."

"Why shouldn't Lenore like you?" Hunter countered, able to follow her winding statement without any trouble.

"She doesn't smile much."

Not enough, he silently agreed, but more each day. "When she relaxes, she does."

Sarah shrugged, unconvinced. "Well, she looked at me awful funny."

"Your grammar's deteriorating."

"She did."

Hunter frowned a bit as he turned into the dirt drive to their house. "It's only that she was surprised. I hadn't mentioned you to her."

Sarah stared at him a moment, then put her scuffed sneakers on the dash. "That wasn't very nice of you."

"Maybe not."

"You'd better apologize."

He sent his daughter a mild glance. "Really?"

She patted Santanas's head when he leaned over the back of her seat and dropped it on her shoulder. "Really. You always make me apologize when I'm rude."

"I didn't consider that you were any of her business." At first, Hunter amended silently. Things changed. Everything changed.

"You always make me apologize, even when I make up excuses," Sarah pointed out unmercifully. When they pulled up by the house, she grinned at him. "And even when I hate apologizing."

"Brat," he mumbled, setting the brake.

With a squeal of laughter, Sarah launched herself at him. "I'm glad you're home."

He held her close a moment, absorbing her scent—youthful sweat, grass and flowery shampoo. It seemed impossible that ten years had passed since he'd first held her. Then she'd smelled of powder and fragility and fresh linen. It seemed impossible that she was half-grown and the time had been so short.

"I love you, Sarah."

Content, she cuddled against him a moment, then, lifting her head, she grinned. "Enough to make pizza for dinner?"

He pinched her subtly pointed chin. "Maybe just enough for that."

Chapter 11

When Lee thought of family dinners, she thought of quiet meals at a glossy mahogany table laid with heavy Georgian silver, meals where conversation was subdued and polite. It had always been that way for her.

Not this dinner.

The already confused kitchen became chaotic while Sarah dashed around, half dancing, half bobbing, as she filled her father in on every detail of the past two weeks. Oblivious to the noise, Bonnie used the kitchen phone to call home and check in with her husband and children. Santanas, forgiven, lay sprawled on the floor, dozing. Hunter stood at the counter, preparing what Sarah claimed was the best pizza in the stratosphere. Somehow he managed to keep up with his daughter's disjointed conversation, answer the questions Bonnie tossed at him and cook at the same time.

Feeling like oil poured heedlessly on a tub of churning water, Lee began to clear the table. If she didn't do something, she decided, she'd end up standing in the middle of the room with her head swiveling back and forth, like a fan at a tennis match.

"I'm supposed to do that."

Awkwardly, Lee set down the teapot she'd just lifted and looked at Sarah. "Oh." Stupid, she berated herself. Haven't you any conversation for a child?

"You can help, I guess," Sarah said after a moment. "But if I don't do my chores, I don't get my allowance." Her gaze slid to her father, then back again. "There's this album I want to buy. You know, the Total Wrecks."

"I see." Lee searched her mind for even a wispy knowledge of the group but came up blank.

"They're actually not as bad as the name makes them sound," Bonnie commented on her way out to the kitchen. "Anyway, Hunter won't dock your pay if you take on an assistant, Sarah. It's considered good business sense."

Turning his head, Hunter caught his sister's quick grin before she waltzed out of the room. "I suppose Lee should earn her supper as well," he said easily. "Even if it isn't red meat."

The smile made it difficult for her to casually lift the teapot again.

"You'll like the pizza better," Sarah stated confidently. "He puts *everything* on it. Anytime I have friends over for dinner, they always want Dad's pizza." As she continued to clear the table, Lee tried to imagine Hunter competently preparing meals for several young, chattering girls. She simply couldn't. "I think he was a cook in another life."

Good Lord, Lee thought, did the child already have views on reincarnation?

"The same way you were a gladiator," Hunter said dryly.

Sarah laughed, childlike again. "Aunt Bonnie was a slave sold at an Arabian auction for thousands and thousands of drachmas."

"Bonnie has a very fluid ego."

With a clatter, Sarah set the cups in the sink. "I think Lenore must've been a princess."

With a damp cloth in her hands, Lee looked up, not certain if she should smile.

"A medieval princess," Sarah went on. "Like with King Arthur."

Hunter seemed to consider the idea a moment, while he studied his daughter and the woman under discussion. "It's a possibility. One of those delicate jeweled crowns and filmy veils would suit her."

"And dragons." Obviously enjoying the game, Sarah leaned back against the counter, the better to imagine Lee in a flowing pastel gown. "A knight would have to kill at least one full-grown male dragon before he could ask for her hand."

"True enough," Hunter murmured, thinking that dragons came in many forms.

"Dragons aren't easy to kill." Though she spoke lightly, Lee wondered why her stomach was quivering. It was entirely too easy to imagine herself in a great torchlit hall, with jewels winking from her hair and from the bodice of a rich silk gown.

"It's the best way to prove valor," Sarah told her, nibbling on a slice of green pepper she'd snitched from her father. "A princess can't marry just anyone, you know. The king would either give her to a worthy knight, or marry her off to a neighboring prince so he could have more land with peace and prosperity."

Incredibly, Lee pictured her father, staff in hand, decreeing that she would marry Jonathan of Willoby.

"I bet you never had to wear braces."

Cast from one century to another in the blink of an eye, Lee merely stared. Sarah was frowning at her with the absorbed, absorbing concentration she could have inherited only from Hunter. It was all so foolish, Lee thought. Knights, princesses, dragons. For the first time, she was able to smile naturally at the slim, dark girl who was a part of the man she loved.

"Two years."

"You did?" Interest sprang into Sarah's solemn face. She stepped forward, obviously to get a better look at Lee's teeth. "It worked good," she decided. "Did you hate them?"

"Every minute."

Sarah giggled, so that the silver flashed. "I don't mind too much, 'cept I can't chew gum." She sent a sulky look over her shoulder in Hunter's direction. "Not even one stick."

"Neither could I." Ever, she thought, but didn't add it. Gum chewing was not permitted in the Radcliffe household.

Sarah studied her another moment, then nodded. "I guess you can help me set the table, too."

Acceptance, Lee was to discover, was just that simple.

The sun was streaming into the kitchen while they ate. It was rich and golden, without those harsh, stunning flashes of white she remembered from the cliffs of the canyon. She found it peaceful, despite all the talk and laughter and arguments swimming around her.

Her fantasies had run to eating a thick, rare steak and a crisp chef's salad in a dimly lit, quiet restaurant where the hovering waiter saw that your glass of Bordeaux was never empty. She found herself in a bright, noisy kitchen, eating pizza stringy with cheese, chunky with slices of green pepper and mushroom, spiced with pepperoni and hot sausage. And while she did, she found herself agreeing with Sarah's accolade. The best in the stratosphere.

"If only Fred could learn how to make one of these." Bonnie cut into her second slice with the same dedication she'd cut into her first. "On a good day he makes a superior egg salad, but it's not the same."

"With a family the size of yours," Hunter commented, "you'd need to set up an assembly line. Five hungry children could keep a pizzeria hopping."

"And do," Bonnie agreed. "In a bit less than seven months, it'll be six."

She grinned as Hunter's knife paused. "Another?"

"Another." Bonnie winked across the table at her niece. "I always said I'd have half a dozen kids," she said casually to Lee. "People should do what they do best."

Hunter reached over to take her hand. Lee saw the fingers interlock. "Some might call it overachievement."

"Or sibling rivalry," she tossed back. "I'll have as many kids as you do best sellers." With a laugh, she squeezed her brother's hand. "It takes us about the same length of time to produce."

"When you bring the baby to visit, she should sleep in my room." Sarah bit off another mouthful of pizza.

"She?" Hunter ruffled her hair before he started to eat again.

"It'll be a girl." With the confidence of youth, Sarah nodded. "Aunt Bonnie already has three boys, so another girl makes it even."

"I'll see what I can do," Bonnie told her. "Anyway, I'll be heading back in the morning. Cassandra, she's my oldest," she put in for Lee's benefit, "has decided she wants a tattoo." She closed her eyes as she leaned back. "Ah, it's nice to be needed."

"A tattoo?" Sarah wrinkled her nose. "That's gross. Cassie's nuts."

"Fred and I are forced to agree."

Interested, Hunter lifted his wine. "Where does she want it?"

"On the curve of her right shoulder. She insists it'll be very tasteful."

"Dumb." Sarah handed out the decree with a shrug. "Cassie's thirteen," she added, rolling her eyes. "Boy, is she a case."

Lee choked back a laugh at both the facial and verbal expressions. "How will you handle it?"

Bonnie only smiled. "Oh, I think I'll take her to the tattoo parlor."

"But you wouldn't—" Lee broke off, seeing Bonnie's liberally streaked hair and shoulder-length earrings. Perhaps she would.

With a laugh, Bonnie patted Lee's hand. "No, I wouldn't. But it'll be a lot more effective if Cassie makes the decision herself—which she will, the minute she gets a good look at all those nasty little needles."

"Sneaky," Sarah approved with a grin.

"Clever," Bonnie corrected.

"Same thing." With her mouth half-full, she turned to Lee. "There's always a crisis at Aunt Bonnie's house," she said confidentially. "Did you have brothers and sisters?"

"No." Was that wistfulness she saw in the child's eyes? She'd often had the same wish herself. "There was only me."

"I think it's better to have them, even though it gets crowded." She slanted her father a guileless smile. "Can I have another piece?"

The rest of the evening passed, not quietly but, for all the noise, peacefully. Sarah dragged her father outside for soccer practice, which Bonnie declined, grinning. Her condition, she claimed, was too delicate. Lee, over her protests, found herself drafted. She learned, though her aim was never very accurate, to kick a ball with the side of her foot and bounce it off her head. She enjoyed it, which surprised her, and didn't feel like a fool, which surprised her more.

Dusk came quickly, then a dark that flickered with fireflies. Though her eyes were heavy, Sarah groaned about going to bed until Hunter agreed to carry her up on his back. Lee didn't have to be told it was a nightly ritual; she only had to see them together.

He'd said Sarah was his life, and though she'd only seen them together for a matter of hours, Lee believed it.

She'd never have expected the man whose books she'd read to be a devoted father, content to spend his time with a ten-year-old girl. She'd never have imagined him here, in a house so far away from the excitement of the city. Even the man she'd grown to know over the past two weeks didn't quite fit the structure of being parent, disciplinarian and mentor to a ten-year-old. Yet he was.

If she superimposed the image of Sarah's father over those of her lover and the author of *Silent Scream,* they all seemed to meld into one. The problem was dealing with it.

Righting the overturned chair on the patio, Lee sat. She could hear Sarah's sleepy laughter drift through the open window above her. Hunter's voice, low and indistinct, followed it. It was an odd way to spend her last hours with Hunter, here in his home, only a few miles from the campsite where they'd become lovers. And yes, she realized as she stared up at the stars, friends. She very much wanted to be his friend.

Now, when she wrote the article, she'd be able to do so with knowledge of both sides of him. It was what she'd come for. Lee closed her eyes because the stars were suddenly too bright. She was going back with much more and, because of it, much less.

"Tired?"

Opening her eyes, she looked up at Hunter. This was how she'd always remember him, cloaked in shadows, coming out of the darkness. "No. Is Sarah asleep?"

He nodded, coming around behind her to put his hands on her shoulders. This was where he wanted her. Here, when night was closing in. "Bonnie, too."

"You'd work now," she guessed. "When the house was quiet and the windows dark."

"Yes, most of the time. I finished my last book on a night like this." He hadn't been lonely then, but now… "Let's walk. The moon's full.

"Afraid? I'll give you a talisman." He slipped his ring off his pinky, sliding it onto her finger.

"I'm not superstitious," she said loftily, but curled her fingers into her palm to hold the ring in place.

"Of course you are." He drew her against his side as they walked. "I like the night sounds."

Lee listened to them—the faintest breeze through the trees, the murmur of water, the singsong of insects. "You've lived here a long time." As the day had passed, it had become less feasible to think of his living anywhere else.

"Yes. I moved here the year Sarah was born."

"It's a lovely spot."

He turned her into his arms. Moonlight spilled over her, silver, jewellike in her hair, marbling her skin, darkening her eyes. "It suits you," he murmured. He ran a hand through her hair, then watched it fall back into place. "The princess and the dragon."

Her heart had already begun to flutter. Like a teenager's, Lee thought. He made her feel like a girl on her first date. "These days women have to kill their own dragons."

"These days—" his mouth brushed over hers "—there's less romance. If these were the Dark Ages, and I came upon you in a moonlit wood, I'd take you because it was my right. I'd woo you because I'd have no choice." His voice darkened like the shadows in the trees surrounding them. "Let me love you now, Lenore, as if it were the first time."

Or the last, she thought dimly as his lips urged her to soften, to yield, to demand. With his arms around her, she could let her consciousness go. Imagine and feel. Lovemaking consisted of nothing more. Even as her head tilted back in submission, her arms strengthened around him, challenging him to take whatever he wanted, to give whatever she asked.

Then his hands were on her face, gently, as gently as they'd ever been, memorizing the slope and angle of her bones, the softness of her skin. His lips followed, tasting, drinking in each separate flavor. The pleasure that could come so quickly ran liquid through her. Bonelessly, she slid with him to the ground.

He'd wanted to love her like this, in the open, with the

moon silvering the trees and casting purple shadows. He'd wanted to feel her muscles coil and go fluid under the touch of his hand. What she gave to him now was something out of his own dreams and much, much more real than anything he'd ever had. Slowly, he undressed her, while his lips and the tips of his fingers both pleasured and revered her. This would be the night when he gave her all of him and when he asked for all of her.

Moonlight and shadows washed over her, making his heart pound in his ears. He heard the creek bubble nearby to mix with her quiet sighs. The woods smelled of night. And so, as she buried his face against her neck, did she.

She felt the surging excitement in him, the growing, straining need that swept her up. Willingly, she went into the whirlpool he created. There the air was soft to the touch and streaked with color. There she would stay, endlessly possessed.

His skin was warm against hers. She tasted, her head swimming from pleasure, power and newly awakened dizzying speed. Ravenous for more, she raced over him, acutely aware of every masculine tremble beneath her, every drawn breath, every murmur of her name.

Silver and shadows. Lee felt them every bit as tangibly as she saw them flickering around her. The silver streak of power. The dark shadow of desire. With them, she could take him to that trembling precipice.

When he swore, breathlessly, she laughed. Their needs were tangled together, twining tighter. She felt it. She celebrated it.

The air seemed to still, the breeze pause. The sounds that had grown to one long din around them seemed to hush. The fingers tangled in her hair tightened desperately. In the silence, their eyes met and held, moment after moment.

Her lips curved as she opened for him.

She could have slept there, effortlessly, with the bare ground beneath her, the sky overhead and his body pressed to hers. She might have slept there, endlessly, like a princess under a spell, if he hadn't drawn her up into his arms.

"You fall asleep like a child," he murmured. "You should be in bed. My bed."

Lee sighed, content to stay where she was. "Too far."

With a low laugh, he kissed the hollow between her neck and shoulder. "Should I carry you?"

"Mmm." She nestled against him. "'Kay."

"Not that I object, but you might be a bit disconcerted if Bonnie happened to walk downstairs while I was carrying you in, naked."

She opened her eyes, so that her irises were dusky blue slits under her lashes. Reality was returning. "I guess we have to get dressed."

"It might be advisable." His gaze skimmed over her, then back to her face. "Should I help you?"

She smiled. "I think that we might have the same result with you dressing me as we do with you undressing me."

"An interesting theory." Hunter reached over her for the brief strip of ivory lace.

"But this isn't the time to test it out." Lee plucked her panties out of his hand and wiggled into them. "How long have we been out here?"

"Centuries."

She shot him a look just before her head disappeared into her shirt. She wasn't completely certain he was exaggerating. "The least I deserve after these past two weeks is a real mattress."

He took her hand, pressing her palm to his lips. "You're welcome to share mine."

Lee curled her fingers around his briefly, then released them. "I don't think that's wise."

"You're worried about Sarah."

It wasn't a question. Lee took her time, making certain all the clouds of romance were out of her head before she spoke. "I don't know a great deal about children, but I imagine she's unprepared for someone sharing her father's bed."

Silence lay for a moment, like the eye of a storm. "I've never brought a woman to our home before."

The statement caused her to look at him quickly, then, just as quickly, look away. "All the more reason."

"All the more reason for many things." He dressed without speaking while Lee stared out into the trees. So beautiful, she thought. And more and more distant.

"You wanted to ask me about Sarah, but you didn't."

She moistened her lips. "It's not my business."

Her chin was captured quickly, not so gently. "Isn't it?" he demanded.

"Hunter—"

"This time you'll have the answer without asking." He dropped his hand, but his gaze never faltered. She needed nothing else to tell her the calm was over. "I met a woman, almost a dozen years ago. I was writing as Laura Miles by then, so that I could afford a few luxuries. Dinner out occasionally, the theater now and then. I was still living in L.A., alone, enjoying my work and the benefits it brought me. She was a student in her last year. Brains and ambition she had in abundance, money she didn't have at all. She was on scholarship and determined to be the hottest young attorney on the West Coast."

"Hunter, what happened between you and another woman all those years ago isn't my business."

"Not just another woman. Sarah's mother."

Lee began to pull at the tuft of grass by her side. "All right, if it's important for you to tell me, I'll listen."

"I cared about her," he continued. "She was bright, lovely and full of dreams. Neither of us had ever considered becoming too serious. She still had law school to finish, the bar to pass. I had stories to tell. But then, no matter how much we plan, fate has a way of taking over."

He drew out a cigarette, thinking back, remembering each detail. His tiny, cramped apartment with the leaky plumbing, the battered typewriter with its hiccuping carriage, the laughter from the couple next door that would often seep through the thin walls.

"She came by one afternoon. I knew something was wrong because she had afternoon classes. She was much too dedicated to skip classes. It was hot, one of those sultry, breathless days. The windows were up, and I had a little portable fan that stirred the air around without doing much to cool it. She'd come to tell me she was pregnant."

He could remember the way she'd looked if he concentrated. But he never chose to. But whether he chose to or not, he'd always be able to remember the tone of her voice when she'd told him. Despair, laced with fury and accusation.

"I said I cared about her, and that was true. I didn't love her. Still, our parents' values do trickle down. I offered to marry her." He laughed then, not humorously, but not, Lee reflected, bitterly. It was the laugh of a man who'd accepted the joke life had played on him. "She refused, almost as angry with the solution I'd offered as she was with the pregnancy. She had no intention of taking on a husband and a child when she had a career to carve out. It might be difficult to understand, but she wasn't being cold, simply practical, when she asked me to pay for the abortion."

Lee felt all of her muscles contract. "But, Sarah—"

"That's not the end of the story." Hunter blew out a stream of smoke and watched it fade into darkness. "We had a memorable fight, threats, accusations, blame-casting. At the time, I couldn't see her end of it, only the fact that she had part of me inside her that she wanted to dispose of. We parted then, both of us furious, both of us desperate enough to know we each needed time to think."

She didn't know what to say, or how to say it. "You were young," she began.

"I was twenty-four," Hunter corrected. "I'd long since stopped being a boy. I was—we were—responsible for our own actions. I didn't sleep for two days. I thought of a dozen answers and rejected them all, over and over. Only one thing stuck with me in that whole sweaty, terrified time. I wanted the child. It's not something I can explain, because I did enjoy my life, the lack of responsibilities, the possibility of becoming really successful. I simply knew I had to have the child. I called her and asked her to come back.

"We were both calmer the second time, and both more frightened than either of us had ever been in our lives. Marriage couldn't be considered, so we set it aside. She didn't want the child, so we dealt with that. I did. That was something a bit more complex to deal with. She needed freedom from the responsibility we'd made together, and she needed money. In the end, we resolved it all."

Dry-mouthed, Lee turned to him. "You paid her."

He saw, as he'd expected to see, the horror in her eyes. When he continued, his voice was calm, but it took a great deal of effort to make it so. "I paid all the medical expenses, her living expenses up until she delivered, and I gave her ten thousand dollars for my daughter."

Stunned, heartsick, Lee stared at the ground. "How could she—"

"We each wanted something. In the only way open, we gave it to each other. I've never resented that young law student for what she did. It was her choice, and she could've taken another without consulting me."

"Yes." She tried to understand, but all Lee could see was that slim, dark little girl. "She chose, but she lost."

It meant everything just to hear her say it. "Sarah's been mine, only mine, from the first moment she breathed. The woman who carried her gave me a priceless gift. I only gave her money."

"Does Sarah know?"

"Only that her mother had choices to make."

"I see." She let out a long breath. "The reason you're so careful about keeping publicity away from her is to keep speculation away."

"One of them. The other is simply that I want her to have the uncomplicated life every child's entitled to."

"You didn't have to tell me." She reached a hand for his. "I'm glad you did. It can't have been easy for you, raising a baby by yourself."

There was nothing but understanding in her eyes now. Every taut muscle in his body relaxed as if she'd stroked them. He knew now, with utter certainty, that she was what he'd been waiting for. "No, not easy, but always a pleasure." His fingers tightened on hers. "Share it with me, Lenore."

Her thoughts froze. "I don't know what you mean."

"I want you here, with me, with Sarah. I want you here with the other children we'll have together." He looked down at the ring he'd put on her hand. When his eyes came back to hers, she felt them reach inside her. "Marry me."

Marry? She could only stare at him blankly while the panic quietly built and built. "You don't—you don't know what you're asking."

"I do," he corrected, holding her hand more firmly when she tried to draw it away. "I've asked only one other woman, and that out of obligation. I'm asking you because you're the first and only woman I've ever loved. I want to share your life. I want you to share mine."

Panic steadily turned into fear. He was asking her to change everything she'd aimed for. To risk everything. "Our lives are too far apart," she managed. "I have to go back. I have my job."

"A job you know you weren't made for." Urgency slipped into his voice as he took her shoulders. "You know you were made to write about the images you have in your head, not about other people's social lives and tomorrow's trends."

"It's what I know!" Trembling, she jerked away from him. "It's what I've been working for."

"To prove a point. Damn it, Lenore, do something for yourself. For yourself."

"It is for myself," she said desperately. You love him, a voice shouted inside her. Why are you pushing away what you need, what you want? Lee shook her head, as if to block the voice out. Love wasn't enough, needs weren't enough. She knew that. She had to remember it. "You're asking me to give it all up, every hard inch I've climbed in five years. I have a life in L.A., I know who I am, where I'm going. I can't live here and risk—"

"Finding out who you really are?" he finished. He wouldn't allow despair. He barely controlled anger. "If it was only myself, I'd go anywhere you liked, live anywhere that suited you, even if I knew it was a mistake. But there's Sarah. I can't take her away from the only home she's ever known."

"You're asking for everything again." Her voice was hardly a whisper, but he'd never heard anything more clearly. "You're asking me to risk everything, and I can't. I won't."

He rose, so that shadows shifted around him. "I'm asking you to risk everything," he agreed. "Do you love me?" And by asking, he'd already risked it all.

Torn by emotions, pushed by fear, she stared at him. "Yes. Damn you, Hunter, leave me alone."

She streaked back toward the house until the darkness closed in between them.

Chapter 12

"If you're not going to break for lunch, at least take this." Bryan held out one of her inexhaustible supply of candy bars.

"I'll eat when I've finished the article." Lee kept her eyes on the typewriter and continued to pound at the keys, lightly, rhythmically.

"Lee, you've been back for two days and I haven't seen you so much as nibble on a Danish." And her photographer's eye had seen beneath the subtle use of cosmetics to the pale bruises under Lee's eyes. That must've been some interview, she thought, as the brisk, even clickity-click of the typewriter keys went on.

"Not hungry." No, she wasn't hungry any more than she was tired. She'd been working steadily on Hunter's article for the better part of forty-eight hours. It was going to be perfect, she promised herself. It was going to be polished like a fine piece of glass. And oh, God, when she finished it, *finished it*, she'd have purged her system of him.

She'd gripped that thought so tightly, it often skidded away.

If she'd stayed… If she went back…

The oath came quickly, under her breath, as her fingers faltered. Meticulously, Lee reversed the carriage to make the correction. She couldn't go back. Hadn't she made that clear to Hunter? She couldn't just toss everything over her shoulder and go. But the longer she stayed away, the larger the hole in her life became. In the life, Lee was ruthlessly reminded, that she'd so carefully carved out for herself.

So she'd work in a nervous kind of fury until the article was finished. Until, she told herself, it was all finished. Then it would be time to take the next step. When she tried to think of that next step, her mind went stunningly, desperately blank. Lee dropped her hands into her lap and stared at the paper in front of her.

Without a word, Bryan bumped the door with her hip so that it closed and muffled the noise. Dropping down into the chair across from Lee, she folded her hands and waited a beat. "Okay, now why don't you tell me the story that's not for publication?"

Lee wanted to be able to shrug and say she didn't have time to talk. She was under a deadline, after all. The article was under a deadline. But then, so was her life. Drawing a breath, she turned in her chair. She didn't want to see the neat, clever little words she'd typed. Not now.

"Bryan, if you'd taken a picture, one that required a great deal of your time and all of your skill to set up, then once you'd developed it, it had come out in a completely different way than you'd planned, what would you do?"

"I'd take a good hard look at the way it had come out," she said immediately. "There'd be a good possibility I should've planned it that way in the first place."

"But wouldn't you be tempted to go back to your original plans? After all, you'd worked very, very hard to set it up in a certain way, wanting certain specific results."

"Maybe, maybe not. It'd depend on just what I'd seen when I looked at the picture." Bryan sat back, crossing long, jeans-clad legs. "What's in your picture, Lee?"

"Hunter." Her troubled gaze shifted, and locked on Bryan's. "You know me."

"As well as you let anyone know you."

With a short laugh, Lee began to push at a paper clip on her desk. "Am I as difficult as all that?"

"Yeah." Bryan smiled a bit to soften the quick answer. "And, I've always thought, as interesting. Apparently, Hunter Brown thinks the same thing."

"He asked me to marry him." The words came out in a jolt that left both women staring.

"Marry?" Bryan leaned forward. "As in 'til death do us part'?"

"Yes."

"Oh." The word came out like a breath of air as Bryan leaned back again. "Fast work." Then she saw Lee's unhappy expression. Just because Bryan didn't smell orange blossoms when the word *marriage* came up was no reason to be flippant. "Well, how do you feel? About Hunter, I mean."

The paper clip twisted in Lee's fingers. "I'm in love with him."

"Really?" Then she smiled, because it sounded nice when said so simply. "Did all this happen in the canyon?"

"Yes." Lee's fingers moved restlessly. "Maybe it started to happen before, when we were in Flagstaff. I don't know anymore."

"Why aren't you happy?" Bryan narrowed her eyes as she did when checking the light and angle. "When the man you love, really love, wants to build a life with you, you should be ecstatic."

"How do two people build a life together when they've both already built separate ones, completely different ones?" Lee demanded. "It isn't just a matter of making more room in the closet or shifting furniture around." The end of the paper clip broke off in her fingers as she rose. "Bryan, he lives in Arizona, in the canyon. I live in L.A."

Lifting booted feet, Bryan rested them on Lee's polished desk, crossing her ankles. "You're not going to tell me it's all a matter of geography."

"It just shows how impossible it all is!" Angry, Lee whirled around. "We couldn't be more different, almost opposites. I do things step-by-step, Hunter goes in leaps and bounds. Damn it, you should see his house. It's like something out of a sophisticated fairy tale. His sister's B. B. Smithers—" Before Bryan could fully register that, Lee was blurting out, "He has a daughter."

"A daughter?" Her attention fully caught, Bryan dropped her feet again. "Hunter Brown has a child?"

Lee pressed her fingers to her eyes and waited for calm. True, it wouldn't have come out if she hadn't been so agitated, and she'd never discuss such personal agitations with anyone but Bryan, but now she had to deal with it. "Yes, a ten-year-old girl. It's important that it not be publicized."

"All right."

Lee needed no promises from Bryan. Trying to calm herself, she took a quiet breath. "She's bright, lovely and quite obviously the center of his life. I saw something in him when they were together, something incredibly beautiful. It scared the hell out of me."

"Why?"

"Bryan, he's capable of so much talent, brilliance, emotion. He's put them together to make a complete success of himself, in all ways."

"That bothers you?"

"I don't know what I'm capable of. I only know I'm afraid I'd never be able to balance it all out, make it all work."

Bryan said something short, quick and rude. "You won't marry him because you don't think you can juggle? You should know yourself better."

"I thought I did." Shaking her head, she took her seat again. "It's ridiculous, in the first place," she said more briskly. "Our lives are miles apart."

Bryan glanced out the window at the tall, sleek building that was part of Lee's view of the city. "So, he can move to L.A. and close the distance."

"He won't." Swallowing, Lee looked at the pages on her desk. The article was finished, she knew it, just as she knew that if she didn't let it go, she'd polish it to death. "He belongs there. He wants to raise his daughter there. I understand that."

"So, you move to the canyon. Great scenery."

Why did it always sound so simple, so plausible, when spoken aloud? The little trickle of fear returned, and her voice firmed. "My job's here."

"I guess it comes down to priorities, doesn't it?" Bryan knew she wasn't being sympathetic, just as she knew it wasn't sympathy that Lee needed. Because she cared a great deal, she spoke without any compassion. "You can keep your job and your apartment in L.A. and be miserable. Or you can take a few chances."

Chances. Lee ran a finger down the slick surface of her desk. But you were supposed to test the ground before you stepped forward. Even Hunter had said that. But… She looked at the mangled paper clip in the center of her spotless blotter. How long did you test it before you took the jump?

It was barely two weeks later that Lee sat in her apartment in the middle of the day. She was so rarely there during the day, during the week, that she somehow expected everything to look different. Everything looked precisely the same. Even, she was forced to admit, herself. Yet nothing was.

Quit. She tried to digest the word as she dealt with the panic she'd held off the past few days. There was a leafy, blooming African violet on the table in front of her. It was well-tended, as every area of her life had been well-tended. She'd always water it when the soil was dry and feed it when it required nourishing. As she stared at the plant, Lee knew she would never be capable of pulling it ruthlessly out by the roots. But wasn't that what she'd done to herself?

Quit, she thought again, and the word reverberated in her brain. She'd actually handed in her resignation, served her two weeks' notice and summarily turned her back on her steadily thriving career—ripped out its roots.

For what? she demanded of herself as panic trickled through. To follow some crazy dream that had planted itself in her mind years ago. To write a book that would probably never be published. To take a ridiculous risk and plunge headlong into the unknown.

Because Hunter had said she was good. Because he'd fed that dream, just as she fed the violet. More than that, Lee thought, he'd made it impossible for her to stop thinking about the "what ifs" in her life. And he was one of them. The most important one of them.

Now that the step was taken and she was here, alone in her impossibly quiet midweek, midmorning apartment, Lee wanted to run. Out there were people, noise, distractions. Here, she'd have to face those "what-ifs." Hunter would be the first.

He hadn't tried to stop her when she left the morning after he'd asked her to marry him. He'd said nothing when she'd made her goodbyes to Sarah. Nothing at all. Perhaps they'd both known that he'd said all there was to say the night before. He'd looked at her once, and she'd nearly wavered. Then Lee had climbed into the car with Bonnie, who'd driven her to the airport that was one step closer to L.A.

He hadn't phoned her since she'd returned. Had she expected him to? Lee wondered. Maybe she had, but she'd hoped he wouldn't. She didn't know how long it would take before she'd be able to hear his voice without going to pieces.

Glancing down, she stared at the twisted gold-and-silver ring on her hand. Why had she kept it? It wasn't hers. It should've been left behind. It was easy to tell herself she'd simply forgotten to take it off in the confusion, but it wasn't the truth. She'd known the ring was still on her finger as she packed, as she walked out of Hunter's house, as she stepped into the car. She just hadn't been capable of taking it off.

She needed time, and it was time, Lee realized, that she

now had. She had to prove something again, but not to her parents, not to Hunter. Now there was only herself. If she could finish the book. If she could give it her very best and really finish it…

Rising, Lee went to her desk, sat down at the typewriter and faced the fear of the blank page.

Lee had known pressure in her work on *Celebrity.* The minutes ticking away while deadlines drew closer and closer. There was the pressure of making not-so-fascinating seem fascinating, in a limited space, and of having to do it week after week. And yet, after nearly a month of being away from it, and having only herself and the story to account for, Lee had learned the full meaning of pressure. And of delight.

She hadn't believed—truly believed—that it would be possible for her to sit down, hour after hour, and finish a book she'd begun on a whim so long ago. And it was true that for the first few days she'd met with nothing but frustration and failure. There'd been a ring of terror in her head. Why had she left a job where she was respected and knowledgeable to stumble in the dark this way?

Time after time, she was tempted to push it all aside and go back, even if it would mean starting over at *Celebrity.* But each time, she could see Hunter's face—lightly mocking, challenging and somehow encouraging.

"It takes a certain amount of stamina and endurance. If you've reached your limit and want to quit..."

The answer was no, just as grimly, just as determinedly as it had been in that little tent. Perhaps she'd fail. She shut her eyes as she struggled to deal with the thought. Perhaps she'd fail miserably, but she wouldn't quit. Whatever happened, she'd made her own choice, and she'd live with it.

The longer she worked, the more of a symbol those typewritten pages became. If she could do this, and do it well, she could do anything. The rest of her life balanced on it.

By the end of the second week, Lee was so absorbed she rarely noticed the twelve-and fourteen-hour days she was putting in. She plugged in her phone machine and forgot to return the calls as often as she forgot to eat.

It was as Hunter had once said. The characters absorbed her, drove her, frustrated and delighted her. As time passed, Lee discovered she wanted to finish the story, not only for her sake but for theirs. She wanted, as she'd never wanted before, for these words to be read. The excitement of that, and the dread, kept her going.

She felt a queer little thrill when the last word was typed, a euphoria mixed with an odd depression. She'd finished. She'd poured her heart into her story. Lee wanted to celebrate. She wanted to weep. It was over. As she pressed her fingers against her tired eyes, she realized abruptly that she didn't even know what day it was.

He'd never had a book race so frantically, so quickly. Hunter could barely keep up with his own zooming thoughts. He knew why, and flowed with it because he had no choice. The main character of this story was Lenore, though her name would be changed to Jennifer. She was Lenore, physically, emotionally, from the elegantly groomed red-gold hair to the nervously bitten fingernails. It was the only way he had of keeping her.

It had cost him more than she'd ever know to let her go. When he'd watched her climb into the car, he'd told himself she wouldn't stay away. She couldn't. If he was wrong about her feelings for him, then he'd been wrong about everything in his life.

Two women had crashed into his life with importance. The first, Sarah's mother, he hadn't loved, yet she'd changed everything. After that, she'd gone away, unable to find it possible to mix her ambition with a life that included children and commitment.

Lee, he loved, and she'd changed everything again. She, too, had gone away. Would she stay away, for the same reasons? Was he fated to bind himself to women who wouldn't share the tie? He wouldn't believe it.

So he'd let her go, aches and fury under the calm. She'd be back.

But a month had passed, and she hadn't come. He wondered how long a man could live when he was starving.

Call her. Go after her. You were a fool to ever let her go. Drag her back if necessary. You need her. You need...

His thoughts ran this way like clockwork. Every day at dusk. Every day at dusk, Hunter fought the urge to follow through on them. He needed; God, he needed. But if she didn't come to him willingly, he'd never have what he needed, only the shell of it. He looked down at his naked finger. She hadn't left everything behind. It was more, much more, than a piece of metal that she'd taken with her.

He'd given her a talisman, and she'd kept it. As long as she had it, she didn't sever the bond. Hunter was a man who believed in fate, omens and magic.

"Dinner's ready." Sarah stood in the doorway, her hair pulled back in a ponytail, her narrow face streaked with a bit of flour.

He didn't want to eat. He wanted to go on writing. As

long as the story moved through him, he had a part of Lenore with him. Just as, whenever he stopped, the need to have all of her tore him apart. But Sarah smiled at him.

"Nearly ready," she amended. She came into the room, barefoot. "I made this meat loaf, but it looks more like a pancake. And the biscuits." She grinned, shrugging. "They're pretty hard, but we can put some jam or something on them." Sensing his mood, she wrapped her arms around his neck, resting her cheek against his. "I like it better when you cook."

"Who turned her nose up at the broccoli last night?"

"It looks like little trees that got sick." She wrinkled her nose, but when she drew back from him, her face was serious. "You really miss her a lot, huh?"

He could've evaded with anyone else. But this was Sarah. She was ten. She knew him inside out. "Yeah, I miss her a lot."

Thinking, Sarah fiddled with the hair that fell over his forehead. "I guess maybe you wanted her to marry you."

"She turned me down."

Her brows lowered, not so much from annoyance that anyone could say no to her father, but in concentration. Donna's father hardly had any hair at all, she thought, touching Hunter's again, and Kelly's dad's stomach bounced over his belt. Shelley's mother never got jokes. She didn't know anybody who was as neat to look at or as neat to be with as her dad. Anybody would want to marry him. When she'd been little, she'd wanted to marry him herself. But of course, she knew now that was just silly stuff.

Her brows were still drawn together when she brought her gaze to his. "I guess she didn't like me."

He heard everything just as clearly as if she'd spoken

her thoughts aloud. He was greatly touched, and not a little impressed. "Couldn't stand you."

Her eyes widened, then brightened with laughter. "Because I'm such a brat."

"Right. I can barely stand you myself."

"Well." Sarah huffed a moment. "She didn't look stupid, but I guess she is if she wouldn't marry you." She cuddled against him, and knowing it was to comfort, Hunter warmed with love. "I liked her," Sarah murmured. "She was nice, kinda quiet, but really nice when she smiled. I guess you love her."

"Yes, I do." He didn't offer her any words of reassurance—it's different from the way I love you, you'll always be my little girl. Hunter simply held her, and it was enough. "She loves me, too, but she has to make her own life."

Sarah didn't understand that, and personally thought it was foolish, but decided not to say so. "I guess I wouldn't mind if she decided to marry you after all. It might be nice to have somebody who'd be like a mother."

He lifted a brow. She never asked about her own mother, knowing with a child's intuition, he supposed, that there was nothing to ask about. "Aren't I?"

"You're pretty good," she told him graciously. "But you don't know a whole lot about lady stuff." Sarah sniffed the air, then grinned. "Meat loaf's done."

"Overdone, from the smell of it."

"Picky, picky." She jumped off his lap before he could retaliate. "I hear a car coming. You can ask them to dinner so we can get rid of all the biscuits."

He didn't want company, Hunter thought as he watched his daughter dash out of the room. An evening with Sarah was enough, then he'd go back to work. After switching off his machine, he rose to go to the door. It was probably one of her friends, who'd talked her parents into dropping by on their way home from town. He'd brush them off, as politely as he could manage, then see if anything could be done about Sarah's meat loaf.

When he opened the door, she was standing there, her hair caught in the light of a late summer's evening. He was, quite literally, knocked breathless.

"Hello, Hunter." How calm a voice could sound, Lee thought, even when a heart's hammering against ribs. "I'd've called, but your number's unlisted." When he said nothing, Lee felt her heart move from her ribs to her throat. Somehow, she managed to speak over it. "May I come in?"

Silently, he stepped back. Perhaps he was dreaming, like the character in "The Raven." All he needed was a bust of Pallas and a dying fire.

She'd used up nearly all of her courage just coming back. If he didn't speak soon, they'd end up simply staring at each other. Like a nervous speaker about to lecture on a subject she hadn't researched, Lee cleared her throat. "Hunter..."

"Hey, I think we'd better just give the biscuits to Santanas because—" Sarah stopped her headlong flight into the room. "Well, gee."

"Sarah, hello." Lee was able to smile now. The child looked so comically surprised, not cool and distant like her father.

"Hi." Sarah glanced uncertainly from one adult to the other. She supposed they were going to make a mess of things. Aunt Bonnie said that people who loved each other usually made a mess of things, for at least a little while. "Dinner's ready. I made meat loaf. It's probably not too bad."

Understanding the invitation, Lee grasped at it. At least it would give her more time before Hunter tossed her out again. "It smells wonderful."

"Okay, come on." Imperiously, Sarah held out her hand, waiting until Lee took it. "It doesn't look very good," she went on, as she led Lee into the kitchen. "But I did everything I was supposed to."

Lee looked at the flattened meat loaf and smiled. "Better than I could do."

"Really?" Sarah digested this with a nod. "Well, Dad and I take turns." And if they got married, Sarah figured, she'd only have to cook every third day. "You'd better set another place," she said lightly to her father. "The biscuits didn't work, but we've got potatoes."

The three of them sat down, very much as if it were the natural thing to do. Sarah served, carrying on a babbling conversation that alleviated the need for either adult to speak to the other. They each answered her, smiled, ate, while their thoughts were in a frenzy.

He doesn't want me anymore.

Why did she come?

He hasn't even spoken to me.

What does she want? She looks lovely. So lovely.

What can I do? He looks wonderful. So wonderful.

Sarah lifted the casserole containing the rest of the meat loaf. "I'll give this to Santanas." Like most children, she detested leftovers—unless it was spaghetti. "Dad has to do the dishes," she explained to Lee. "You can help him if you like." After she'd dumped Santanas's dinner in his bowl, she danced out of the room. "See you later."

Then they were alone, and Lee found she was gripping her hands together so tightly they were numb. Deliberately, she unlaced her fingers. He saw the ring, still on her finger, and felt something twist, loosen, then tighten again in his chest.

"You're angry," she said in that same calm, even voice. "I'm sorry, I shouldn't have come this way."

Hunter rose and began to stack dishes. "No, I'm not angry." Anger was possibly the only emotion he hadn't experienced in the last hour. "Why did you?"

"I…" Lee looked down helplessly at her hands. She should help him with the dishes, keep busy, stay natural. She didn't think her legs would hold her just yet. "I finished the book," she blurted out.

He stopped and turned. For the first time since she'd opened the door, she saw that hint of a smile around his mouth. "Congratulations."

"I wanted you to read it. I know I could've mailed it—I sent a copy on to your editor—but…" She lifted her eyes to his again. "I didn't want to mail it. I wanted to give it to you. Needed to."

Hunter put the dishes in the sink and came back to the table, but he didn't sit. He had to stand. If this was what she'd come for, all she'd come for, he wasn't certain he could face it. "You know I want to read it. I expect you to autograph the first copy for me."

She managed a smile. "I'm not as optimistic as that, but you were right. I had to finish it. I wanted to thank you for showing me." Her lips remained curved, but the smile left her eyes. "I quit my job."

He hadn't moved, but it seemed that he suddenly became very still. "Why?"

"I had to try to finish the book. For me." If only he'd touch her, just her hand, she wouldn't feel so cold. "I knew if I could do that, I could do anything. I needed to prove that to myself before I…" Lee trailed off, not able to say it all. "I've been reading your work, your earlier work as Laura Miles."

If he could just touch her… But once he did, he'd never let her go again. "Did you enjoy it?"

"Yes." There was enough lingering surprise in her voice to make him smile. "I'd never have believed there could be a similarity of styles between a romance novel and a horror story, but there was. Atmosphere, tension, emotion." Taking a deep breath, she stood so that she could face him. It was perhaps the most difficult step she'd taken so far. "You understand how a woman feels. It shows in your work."

"*Writer*'s a word without gender."

"Still, it's a rare gift, I think, for a man to be able to understand and appreciate the kinds of emotions and insecurities that go on inside a woman." Her eyes met his again, and this time held. "I'm hoping you can do the same with me."

He was looking into her again. She could feel it.

"It's more difficult when your own emotions are involved."

She gripped her fingers together, tightly. "Are they?"

He didn't touch her, not yet, but she thought she could almost feel his hand against her cheek. "Do you need me to tell you I love you?"

"Yes, I—"

"You've finished your book, quit your job. You've taken a lot of risks, Lenore." He waited. "But you've yet to put it all on the line."

Her breath trembled out. No, he'd never make things easy for her. There'd always be demands, expectations.

He'd never pamper. "You terrified me when you asked me to marry you. I thought about it a great deal, like the small child thinks about a dark closet. I don't know what's in there—it might be dream or nightmare. You understand that."

"Yes." Though it hadn't been a question. "I understand that."

She breathed a bit easier. "I used what I had in L.A. as an excuse because it was logical, but it wasn't the real reason. I was just afraid to walk into that closet."

"And are you still?"

"A little." It took more effort than she'd imagined to relax her fingers. She wondered if he knew it was the final step. She held out her hand. "But I want to try. I want to go there with you."

His fingers laced with hers, and she felt the nerves melt away. Of course he knew. "It won't be dream or nightmare, Lenore. Every minute of it will be real."

She laughed then, because his hand was in hers. "Now you're really trying to scare me." Stepping closer, she kissed him softly, until desire built to a quiet roar. It was so easy, like sliding into a warm, clear stream. "You won't scare me off," she whispered.

The arms around her were tight, but she barely noticed. "No, I won't scare you off." He breathed in the scent of her hair, wallowed in the texture of it. She'd come to him. Completely. "I won't let you go, either. I've waited too long for you to come back."

"You knew I would," she murmured.

"I had to, I'd've gone mad otherwise."

She closed her eyes, content, but with a thrill of excitement underneath. "Hunter, if Sarah doesn't, that is, if she isn't able to adjust..."

"Worried already." He drew her back. "Sarah gave me a pep talk just this evening. You do, I assume, know quite a bit about lady stuff?"

"Lady stuff?"

He drew her back just a bit farther, to look her up and down. "Every inch the lady. You'll do, Lenore, for me, and for Sarah."

"Okay." She let out a long breath, because as usual, she believed him. "I'd like to be with you when you tell her."

"Lenore." Framing her face, he kissed both cheeks, gently, with a hint of a laugh beneath. "She already knows."

A brow lifted. "Her father's daughter."

"Exactly." He grabbed her, swinging her around once in a moment of pure, irrepressible joy. "The lady's going to find it interesting living in a house with real and imaginary monsters."

"The lady can handle that," she tossed back. "And anything else you dream up."

"Is that so?" He shot her a wicked look—amusement, desire, knowledge—as he released her. "Then let's get these dishes done and I'll see what I can do."

* * * * *

Less of a Stranger

For my friend Joanne

Chapter 1

He watched her coming. Though she wore jeans and a jacket, with a concealing helmet over her head, Katch recognized her femininity. She rode a small Honda motorcycle. He drew on his thin cigar and appreciated the competent way she swung into the market's parking lot.

Settling the bike, she dismounted. She was tall, Katch noted, perhaps five feet eight, and slender. He leaned back on the soda machine and continued to watch her out of idle curiosity. Then she removed the helmet. Instantly, his curiosity was intensified. She was a stunner.

Her hair was loose and straight, swinging nearly to her shoulders, with a fringe of bangs sweeping over her forehead. It was a deep, rich brunette that showed glints of red and gold from the sun. Her face was narrow, the features sharp and distinct. He'd known models who'd starved themselves to get the angles and shadows that were in this woman's face. Her mouth, however, was full and generous.

Katch recognized the subtleties of cosmetics and knew

that none had been used to add interest to the woman's features. She didn't need them. Her eyes were large, and even with the distance of the parking lot between them, he caught the depth of dark brown. They reminded him of a colt's eyes—deep and wide and aware. Her movements were unaffected. They had an unrefined grace that was as coltish as her eyes. She was young, he decided, barely twenty. He drew on the cigar again. She was definitely a stunner.

"Hey, Megan!"

Megan turned at the call, brushing the bangs from her eyes as she moved. Seeing the Bailey twins pull to the curb in their Jeep, she smiled.

"Hi." Clipping the helmet onto a strap on her bike, Megan walked to the Jeep. She was very fond of the Bailey twins.

Like herself, they were twenty-three and had golden, beach-town complexions, but they were petite, blue-eyed and pertly blond. The long, baby-fine hair they shared had been tossed into confusion by the wind. Both pairs of blue eyes drifted past Megan to focus on the man who leaned against the soda machine. In reflex, both women straightened and tucked strands of hair behind their ears. Tacitly, they agreed their right profile was the most comely.

"We haven't seen you in a while." Teri Bailey kept one eye cocked on Katch as she spoke to Megan.

"I've been trying to get some things finished before the season starts." Megan's voice was low, with the gentle flow of coastal South Carolina. "How've you been?"

"Terrific!" Jeri answered, shifting in the driver's seat. "We've got the afternoon off. Why don't you come shopping with us?" She, too, kept Katch in her peripheral vision.

"I'd like to—" Megan was already shaking her head "—but I've got to pick up a few things here."

"Like the guy over there with terrific gray eyes?" Jeri demanded.

"What?" Megan laughed.

"And shoulders," Teri remarked.

"He hasn't taken those eyes off her, has he, Teri?" Jeri remarked. "And we spent twelve-fifty for this blouse." She fingered the thin strap of the pink camisole top which matched her twin's.

"What," Megan asked, totally bewildered, "are you talking about?"

"Behind you," Teri said with a faint inclination of her fair head. "The hunk by the soda machine. Absolutely gorgeous." But as Megan began to turn her head, Teri continued in a desperate whisper, "Don't turn around, for goodness' sake!"

"How can I see if I don't look?" Megan pointed out reasonably as she turned.

His hair was blond, not pale like the twins', but dusky and sun-streaked. It was thick and curled loosely and carelessly around his face. He was lean, and the jeans he wore were well faded from wear. His stance was negligent, completely relaxed as he leaned back against the machine and drank from a can. But his face wasn't lazy, Megan thought as he met her stare without a blink. It was sharply aware. He needed a shave, certainly, but his bone structure was superb. There was the faintest of clefts in his chin, and his mouth was long and thin.

Normally, Megan would have found the face fascinating—strongly sculpted, even handsome in a rough-and-ready fashion. But the eyes were insolent. They were gray, as the twins had stated, dark and smoky. And, Megan decided with a frown, rude. She'd seen his type before—drifters, loners, looking for the sun and some fleeting female companionship. Under her bangs, her eyebrows drew together. He was openly staring at her. As the can touched his lips, he sent Megan a slow wink.

Hearing one of the twins giggle, Megan whipped her head back around.

"He's adorable," Jeri decided.

"Don't be an idiot." Megan swung her hair back with a toss of her head. "He's typical."

The twins exchanged a look as Jeri started the Jeep's engine. "Too choosy," she stated. They gave Megan mirror smiles as they pulled away from the curb. "Bye!"

Megan wrinkled her nose at them, but waved before she turned away. Purposefully ignoring the man who loitered beside the concessions, Megan walked into the market.

She acknowledged the salute from the clerk behind the counter. Megan had grown up in Myrtle Beach. She knew all the small merchants in the five-mile radius around her grandfather's amusement park.

After choosing a basket, she began to push it down the first aisle. Just a few things, she decided, plucking a quart of milk from a shelf. She had only the saddlebags on the bike for transporting. If the truck hadn't been acting up… She let her thoughts drift away from that particular problem. Nothing could be done about it at the moment.

Megan paused in the cookie section. She'd missed lunch and the bags and boxes looked tempting. Maybe the oatmeal…

"These are better."

Megan started as a hand reached in front of her to

choose a bag of cookies promising a double dose of chocolate chips. Twisting her head, she looked up into the insolent gray eyes.

"Want the cookies?" He grinned much as he had outside.

"No," she said, giving a meaningful glance at his hand on her basket. Shrugging, he took his hand away but, to Megan's irritation, he strolled along beside her.

"What's on the list, Meg?" he asked companionably as he tore open the bag of cookies.

"I can handle it alone, thanks." She started down the next aisle, grabbing a can of tuna. He walked, Megan noted, like a gunslinger—long, lanky strides with just a hint of swagger.

"You've got a nice bike." He bit into a cookie as he strolled along beside her. "Live around here?"

Megan chose a box of tea bags. She gave it a critical glance before tossing it into the basket. "It lives with me," she told him as she moved on.

"Cute," he decided and offered her a cookie. Megan ignored him and moved down the next aisle. When she reached for a loaf of bread, however, he laid a hand on top of hers. "Whole wheat's better for you." His palm was hard and firm on the back of her hand. Megan met his eyes indignantly and tried to pull away.

"Listen, I have…"

"No rings," he commented, lacing his fingers through hers and lifting her hand for a closer study. "No entanglements. How about dinner?"

"No way." She shook her hand but found it firmly locked in his.

"Don't be unfriendly, Meg. You have fantastic eyes." He smiled into them, looking at her as though they were the only two people on earth. Someone reached around her, with an annoyed mutter, to get a loaf of rye.

"Will you go away?" she demanded in an undertone. It amazed her that his smile was having an effect on her even though she knew what was behind it. "I'll make a scene if you don't."

"That's all right," he said genially, "I don't mind scenes."

He wouldn't, she thought, eyeing him. He'd thrive on them. "Look," she began angrily. "I don't know who you are, but…"

"David Katcherton," he volunteered with another easy smile. "Katch. What time should I pick you up?"

"You're not going to pick me up," she said distinctly. "Not now, not later." Megan cast a quick look around. The market was all but empty. She couldn't cause a decent scene if she'd wanted to. "Let go of my hand," she ordered firmly.

"The Chamber of Commerce claims Myrtle Beach is a friendly town, Meg." Katch released her hand. "You're going to give them a bad name."

"And stop calling me Meg," she said furiously. "I don't know you."

She stomped off, wheeling the basket in front of her.

"You will." He made the claim quietly, but she heard him.

Their eyes met again, hers dark with temper, his assured. Turning away, she quickened her pace to the checkout counter.

"You wouldn't believe what happened at the market." Megan set the bag on the kitchen table with a thump.

Her grandfather sat at the table, on one of the four

matching maple chairs, earnestly tying a fly. He grunted in acknowledgment but didn't glance up. Wires and feathers and weights were neatly piled in front of him.

"This man," she began, pulling the bread from the top bag. "This incredibly rude man tried to pick me up. Right in the cookie section." Megan frowned as she stored tea bags in a canister. "He wanted me to go to dinner with him."

"Hmm." Her grandfather meticulously attached a yellow feather to the fly. "Have a nice time."

"Pop!" Megan shook her head in frustration, but a smile tugged at her mouth.

Timothy Miller was a small, spare man in his mid-sixties. His round, lined face was tanned, surrounded by a shock of white hair and a full beard. The beard was soft as a cloud and carefully tended. His blue eyes, unfaded by the years, were settled deeply into the folds and lines of his face. They missed little. Megan could see he was focused on his lures. That he had heard her at all was a tribute to his affection for his granddaughter.

Moving over, she dropped a kiss on the crown of his head. "Going fishing tomorrow?"

"Yessiree, bright and early." Pop counted out his assortment of lures and mentally reviewed his strategy. Fishing was a serious business. "The truck should be fixed this evening. I'll be back before supper."

Megan nodded, giving him a second kiss. He needed his fishing days. The amusement parks opened for business on weekends in the spring and fall. In the three summer months they worked seven days a week. The summer kept the town alive; it drew tourists, and tourists meant business. For one-fourth of the year, the town swelled from a population of thirteen or fourteen thousand to three hundred thousand. The bulk of those three hundred thousand people had come to the small coastal town to have fun.

To provide it, and make his living, her grandfather worked hard. He always had, Megan mused. It would have been a trial if he hadn't loved the park so much. It had been part of her life for as long as she could remember.

Megan had been barely five when she had lost her parents. Over the years, Pop had been mother, father and friend to her. And Joyland was home to her as much as the beach-side cottage they lived in. Years before, they had turned to each other in grief. Now, their love was bedrock firm. With the exclusion of her grandfather, Megan was careful with her emotions, for once involved, they were intense. When she loved, she loved totally.

"Trout would be nice," she murmured, as she gave him a last, quick hug. "We'll have to settle for tuna casserole tonight."

"Thought you were going out."

"Pop!" Megan leaned back against the stove and pushed her hair from her face with both hands. "Do you think I'd spend the evening with a man who tried to pick me up with a bag of chocolate chip cookies?" With a jerk of her wrist, she flicked on the burner under the teakettle.

"Depends on the man." She saw the twinkle in his eye as he glanced up at her. Megan knew she finally had his full attention. "What'd he look like?"

"A beach bum," she retorted, although she knew the answer wasn't precisely true. "With a bit of cowboy thrown in." She smiled then in response to Pop's grin. "Actually, he had a great face. Lean and strong, very attractive in an unscrupulous sort of way. He'd do well in bronze."

"Sounds interesting. Where'd you meet him again?"

"In the cookie section."

"And you're going to fix tuna casserole instead of having dinner out?" Pop gave a heavy sigh and shook his head. "I don't know what's the matter with this girl," he addressed a favored lure.

"He was cocky," Megan claimed and folded her arms. "And he *leered* at me. Aren't grandfathers supposed to tote shotguns around for the purpose of discouraging leerers?"

"Want to borrow one and go hunting for him?"

The shrill whistling of the kettle drowned out her response. Pop watched Megan as she rose to fix the tea.

She was a good girl, he mused. A bit too serious about things at times, but a good girl. And a beauty, too. It didn't surprise him that a stranger had tried to make a date with her. He was more surprised that it hadn't happened more often. But Megan could discourage a man without opening her mouth, he recalled. All she had to do was aim one of her "I beg your pardon" looks and most of them backed off. That seemed to be the way she wanted it.

Between the amusement park and her art, she never seemed to have time for much socializing. Or didn't make time, Pop amended thoughtfully. Still, he wasn't certain that he didn't detect more than just annoyance in her attitude toward the man in the market. Unless he missed his guess, she had been amused and perhaps a touch attracted. Because he knew his granddaughter well, he decided to let the subject ride for the time being.

"The weather's supposed to hold all weekend," he commented as he carefully placed his lures in his fishing box. "There should be a good crowd in the park. Are you going to work in the arcade?"

"Of course." Megan set two cups of tea on the table and sat again. "Have those seats been adjusted on the Ferris wheel?"

"Saw to it myself this morning." Pop blew on his tea to cool it, then sipped.

He was relaxed, Megan saw. Pop was a simple man. She'd always admired his unassuming manner, his quiet humor, his lack of pretensions. He loved to watch people enjoy. More, she added with a sigh, than he liked to charge them for doing so. Joyland never made more than a modest profit. He was, Megan concluded, a much better grandfather than businessman.

To a large extent, it was she who handled the profit-and-loss aspect of the park. Though the responsibility took time away from her art, she knew it was the park that supported them. And, more important, it was the park that Pop loved.

At the moment, the books were teetering a bit too steeply into the red for comfort. Neither of them spoke of it at any length with the other. They mentioned improvements during the busy season, talked vaguely about promoting business during the Easter break and over Memorial Day weekend.

Megan sipped at her tea and half listened to Pop's rambling about hiring summer help. She would see to it when the time came. Pop was a whiz in dealing with cranky machines and sunburned tourists, but he tended to overpay and underwork his employees. Megan was more practical. She had to be.

I'll have to work full-time myself this summer, she reflected. She thought fleetingly of the half-completed sculpture in her studio over the garage. It'll just have to wait for December, she told herself and tried not to sigh. There's no other way until things are on a more even keel again. Maybe next year…it was always next year. There were things to do, always things to do. With a small shrug, she turned back to Pop's monologue.

"So, I figure we'll get some of the usual college kids and drifters to run the rides."

"I don't imagine that'll be a problem," Megan murmured. Pop's mention of drifters had led her thoughts back to David Katcherton.

Katch, she mused, letting his face form in her mind again. Ordinarily, she'd have cast his type as a drifter, but there had been something more than that. Megan prided herself on her observations, her characterizations of people. It annoyed her that she wasn't able to make a conclusive profile on this man. It annoyed her further that she was again thinking of a silly encounter with a rude stranger.

"Want some more tea?" Pop was already making his way to the stove when Megan shook herself back.

"Ah…yeah, sure." She scolded herself for dwelling on the insignificant when there were things to do. "I guess I'd better start dinner. You'll want an early night if you're going fishing in the morning."

"That's my girl." Pop turned the flame back on under the kettle as he glanced out the window. He cast a quick look at his unsuspecting granddaughter. "I hope you've got enough for three," he said casually. "It looks like your beach-cowboy found his way to the ranch."

"What?" Megan's brows drew together as she stood up.

"A perfect description, as usual, Megan," Pop complimented her as he watched the man approach, loose-limbed with a touch of a swashbuckler, a strong, good-looking face. Pop liked his looks. He turned with a grin as Megan walked to the window to stare out. Pop suppressed a chuckle at her expression.

"It *is* him," she whispered, hardly believing her eyes as she watched Katch approach her kitchen door.

"I thought it might be," Pop said mildly.

"Of all the nerve," she muttered darkly. "Of all the *incredible* nerve!"

Chapter 2

Before her grandfather could comment, Megan took the few strides necessary to bring her to the kitchen door. She swung it open just as Katch stepped up on the stoop. There was a flicker, only a flicker, of surprise in the gray eyes.

"You have a nerve," she said coolly.

"So I've been told," he agreed easily. "You're prettier than you were an hour ago." He ran a finger down her cheek. "There's a bit of rose under the honey now. Very becoming." He traced the line of her chin before dropping his hand. "Do you live here?"

"You know very well I do," she retorted. "You followed me."

Katch grinned. "Sorry to disappoint you, Meg. Finding you here's just a bonus. I'm looking for Timothy Miller. Friend of yours?"

"He's my grandfather." She moved, almost imperceptibly, positioning herself between Katch and the doorway. "What do you want with him?"

Katch recognized the protective move, but before he could comment, Pop spoke from behind her.

"Why don't you let the man in, Megan? He can tell me himself."

"I'm basically human, Meg," Katch said quietly. The tone of his voice had her looking at him more closely.

She glanced briefly over her shoulder, then turned back to Katch. The look she gave him was a warning. Don't do anything to upset him.

She noticed something in his eyes she hadn't expected—gentleness. It was more disconcerting than his earlier arrogance. Megan backed into the kitchen, holding open the door in silent invitation.

Katch smiled at her, casually brushing a strand of hair from her cheek as he walked by and into the kitchen. Megan stood for a moment, wondering why she should be so moved by a stranger's touch.

"Mr. Miller?" She heard the unaffected friendliness in Katch's voice and glanced over as he held out a hand to her grandfather. "I'm David Katcherton."

Pop nodded in approval. "You're the fellow who called me a couple of hours ago." He shot a look past Katch's shoulder to Megan. "I see you've already met my granddaughter."

His eyes smiled in response. "Yes. Charming."

Pop chuckled and moved toward the stove. "I was just about to make some more tea. How about a cup?"

Megan noticed the faint lift of his brow. Tea, she thought, was probably not his first choice.

"That'd be nice. Thanks." He walked to the table and sat, Megan decided, as if his acquaintance were long-standing and personal. Half reluctant, half defiant, she sat next to him. Her eyes asked him questions behind Pop's back.

"Did I tell you before that you have fabulous eyes?" he murmured. Without waiting for her answer, he turned his attention to Pop's tackle box. "You've got some great lures here," he observed to Pop, picking up a bone squid, then a wood plug painted to simulate a small frog. "Do you make any of your own?"

"That's half the sport," Pop stated, bringing a fresh cup to the table. "Have you done much fishing?"

"Here and there. I'd guess you'd know the best spots along the Grand Strand."

"A few of them," Pop said modestly.

Megan scowled into her tea. Once the subject of fishing had been brought up, Pop could go on for hours. And hours.

"I thought I'd do some surf casting while I'm here," Katch mentioned offhandedly. Megan was surprised to catch a shrewdly measuring expression in his eyes.

"Well now—" Pop warmed to the theme "—I might just be able to show you a spot or two. Do you have your own gear?"

"Not with me, no."

Pop brushed this off as inconsequential. "Where are you from, Mr. Katcherton?"

"Katch," he corrected, leaning back in his chair. "California originally."

That, Megan decided, explained the beachboy look. She drank her cooling tea with a casual air while studying him over the rim.

"You're a long way from home," Pop commented. He shifted comfortably, then brought out a pipe he saved for interesting conversations. “Do you plan to be in Myrtle Beach long?”

“Depends. I’d like to talk with you about your amusement park.”

Pop puffed rapidly on his pipe while holding a match to the bowl. The tobacco caught, sending out cherry-scented smoke. “So you said on the phone. Funny, Megan and I were just talking about hiring on help for the summer. Only about six weeks before the season starts.” He puffed and let the smoke waft lazily. “Less than three until Easter. Ever worked rides or a booth?”

“No.” Katch sampled his tea.

“Well…” Pop shrugged his inexperience away. “It’s simple enough to learn. You look smart.” Again, Megan caught the flash of Katch’s grin. She set down her cup.

“We can’t pay more than minimum to a novice,” she said dampeningly.

He made her nervous, she was forced to admit. With any luck, she could discourage him from Joyland so that he’d try his luck elsewhere. But something nagged at her. He didn’t look the type to take a job running a roller coaster or hawking a pitch-and-toss for a summer. There were hints of authority in his face, touches of casual power in his stance. Yet there was something not altogether respectable in his raffish charm.

He met her stare with a complete lack of self-consciousness. “That seems reasonable. Do you work in the park, Meg?”

She bit back a retort to his familiarity. “Often,” she said succinctly.

“Megan’s got a good business head,” Pop interjected. “She keeps me straight.”

"Funny," Katch said speculatively. "Somehow I thought you might be a model. You've the face for it." There was no flirtatiousness in his tone.

"Megan's an artist," Pop said, puffing contentedly at his pipe.

"Oh?"

She watched Katch's eyes narrow and focus on her. Uncomfortable, she shifted in her chair. "We seem to be drifting away from the subject," she said crisply. "If you've come about a job—"

"No."

"But…didn't you say—"

"I don't think so," he cut her off again and added a smile. He turned to Pop now, and Megan recognized a subtle change in his manner. "I don't want a job in your park, Mr. Miller. I want to buy it."

Both men were intent on each other. Pop was surprised, unmistakably so, but there was also a look of consideration in his eyes. Neither of them noticed Megan. She stared at Katch, her face open and young, and just a little frightened. She wanted to laugh and say he was making a foolish joke, but she knew better. Katch said exactly what he meant.

She'd recognized the understated authority and power beneath the glib exterior. This was business, pure and simple. She could see it on his face. There was a flutter of panic in her stomach as she looked at her grandfather.

"Pop?" Her voice was very small, and he made no sign that he heard her.

"You're a surprise," the old man said eventually. Then he began to puff on his pipe again. "Why my park?"

"I've done some research on the amusements here." Katch shrugged off the details. "I like yours."

Pop sighed and blew smoke at the ceiling. "I can't say I'm interested in selling out, son. A man gets used to a certain way of life."

"With the offer I'm prepared to make, you might find it easy to get used to another."

Pop gave a quiet laugh. "How old are you, Katch?"

"Thirty-one."

"That's just about how long I've been in this business. How much do you know about running a park?"

"Not as much as you do." Katch grinned and leaned back again. "But I could learn fast with the right teacher."

Megan saw that her grandfather was studying Katch carefully. She felt excluded from the conversation and resented it. Her grandfather was capable of doing this very subtly. She recognized that David Katcherton had the same talent. Megan sat silently; natural courtesy forbade her interrupting private conversation.

"Why do you want to own an amusement park?" Pop asked suddenly. Megan could tell he was interested in David Katcherton. A warning bell began to ring in her head. The last thing she wanted was for her grandfather to become too involved with Katch. He was trouble, Megan was sure of it.

"It's good business," Katch answered Pop's question after a moment. "And fun." He smiled. "I like things that put fun into life."

He knows how to say the right thing, Megan acknowledged grudgingly, noting Pop's expression.

"I'd appreciate it if you'd think about it, Mr. Miller," Katch continued. "We could talk about it again in a few days."

And how to advance and retreat, she thought.

"I can't refuse to think about it," Pop agreed, but shook his head. "Still, you might take another look around. Megan and I've run Joyland for a good many years. It's home to us." He looked to his granddaughter teasingly. "Weren't you two going out to dinner?"

"No!" She flashed him a scowl.

"Exactly what I had in mind," Katch said smoothly. "Come on, Meg, I'll buy you a hamburger." As he rose, he took her hand, pulling her to her feet. Feeling her temper rise with her, Megan attempted to control it.

"I can't tell you how I hate to refuse such a charming invitation," she began.

"Then don't," Katch cut her off before turning to Pop. "Would you like to join us?"

Pop chuckled and motioned them away with the back of his hand. "Go on. I've got to get my gear together for the morning."

"Want company?"

Pop studied Katch over the bowl of his pipe. "I'm leaving at five-thirty," he said after a moment. "I have extra gear."

"I'll be here."

Megan was so astonished that she allowed Katch to lead her outside without making another protest. Pop never invited anyone along on his fishing mornings. They were his relaxation, and he enjoyed his solitude too much to share it.

"He never takes anyone with him," she murmured, thinking aloud.

"Then I'm flattered."

Megan noticed that Katch still had her hand, his fingers comfortably laced with hers.

"I'm not going out with you," she said positively and

stopped walking. "You might be able to charm Pop into taking you fishing, but—"

"So you think I'm charming?" His smile was audacious as he took her other hand.

"Not in the least," she said firmly, repressing an answering smile.

"Why won't you have dinner with me?"

"Because," she said, meeting his eyes directly, "I don't like you."

His smile broadened. "I'd like the chance to change your mind."

"You couldn't." Megan started to draw her hands away, but he tightened his fingers.

"Wanna bet?" Again, she squashed the desire to smile. "If I change your mind, you'll go to the park with me Friday night."

"And if I don't change my mind?" she asked. "What then?"

"I won't bother you anymore." He grinned, as persuasive, she noted, as he was confident.

Her brow lifted in speculation. It might, she reflected, it just might be worth it.

"All you have to do is have dinner with me tonight," Katch continued, watching Megan's face. "Just a couple of hours."

"All right," she agreed impulsively. "It's a deal." She wriggled her fingers, but he didn't release them. "We could shake on it," she said, "but you still have my hands."

"So I do," he agreed. "We'll seal it my way then."

With a quick tug, he had her colliding against his chest. She felt a strength there which wasn't apparent in the lean, somewhat lanky frame. Before she could express annoyance, his mouth had taken hers.

He was skillful and thorough. She never knew whether she had parted her lips instinctively or if he had urged her to do so with the gently probing tip of his tongue.

From the instant of contact, Megan's mind had emptied, to be filled only with thoughts she couldn't center on. Her body dominated, taking command in simple surrender. She was melted against him, aware of his chest hard against her breasts…aware of his mouth quietly savaging hers. There was nothing else. She found there was nothing to hold on to. No anchor to keep her from veering off into wild water. Megan gave a small, protesting moan and drew away.

His eyes were darker than she'd thought, and too smoky to read clearly. Why had she thought them so decipherable? Why had she thought him so manageable? Nothing was as she had thought it had been minutes before. Her breath trembled as she fought to collect herself.

"You're very warm," Katch said softly. "It's a pity you struggle so hard to be remote."

"I'm not. I don't…" Megan shook her head, wishing desperately for her heartbeat to slow.

"You are," he corrected, "and you do." Katch gave her hands a companionable squeeze before releasing one of them. The other he kept snugly in his as he turned toward his car.

Panic was welling up inside Megan, and she tried to suppress it. *You've been kissed before,* she reminded herself. This was just unexpected. It just caught you off guard. Even as the excuse ran through her mind, she knew it for a lie. She'd never been kissed like that before. And the situation was no longer under her control.

"I don't think I'll go after all," she told him in calmer tones.

Katch turned, smiling at her as he opened the car door. "A bet's a bet, Meg."

Chapter 3

Katch drove a black Porsche. Megan wasn't surprised. She wouldn't have expected him to drive anything ordinary. It wasn't difficult to deduce that David Katcherton could afford the best of everything.

He'd probably inherited his money, she decided as she settled back against the silver-gray seat cushion. He'd probably never worked a day in his life. She remembered the hard, unpampered feel of his palm. Probably a whiz at sports, she thought. Plays tennis, squash, sails his own yacht. Never does anything worthwhile. Only looks for pleasure. *And finds it,* she thought.

Megan turned to him, pushing her swinging hair back behind her shoulders. His profile was sharply attractive, with the dusky blond hair curling negligently over his ear.

"See something you like?"

Megan flushed in annoyance, aware that she'd been caught staring.

"You need a shave," she said primly.

Katch turned the rearview mirror toward him as if to check her analysis. "Guess I do." He smiled as they merged into the traffic. "On our next date I'll be sure to remember. Don't say anything," he added, feeling her stiffen at his side. "Didn't your mother ever tell you not to say anything if you couldn't say something pleasant?"

Megan stifled a retort.

Katch smiled as he merged into traffic. "How long have you lived here?"

"Always." With the windows down, Megan could hear the outdoor noises. The music from a variety of car radios competed against each other and merged into a strange sort of harmony. Megan liked the cluttered, indefinable sound. She felt herself relaxing and straightened her shoulders and faced Katch again.

"And what do you do?"

He caught the thread of disdain in the question, but merely lifted a brow. "I own things."

"Really? What sort of things?"

Katch stopped at a red light, then turned, giving her a long, direct look. "Anything I want." The light changed and he deftly slid the car into the parking lot.

"We can't go in there," Megan told him with a glance at the exclusive restaurant.

"Why not?" Katch switched off the ignition. "The food's good here."

"I know, but we're not dressed properly, and—"

"Do you like doing things properly all the time, Meg?"

The question stopped her. She searched his face carefully, wondering if he was laughing at her, and unsure of the answer.

"Tell you what." He eased himself out of the car, then

leaned back in the window. "Think about it for a few minutes. I'll be back."

Megan watched him slide through the elegant doors of the restaurant and shook her head. They'll boot him out, she thought. Still, she couldn't help admiring his confidence. There was something rather elusive about it. She crossed her arms over. "Still, I don't really *like* him," she muttered.

Fifteen minutes later, she decided she liked him even less. How impossibly rude! she fumed as she slammed out of his car. Keeping me waiting out here all this time!

She decided to find the nearest phone booth and call her grandfather to ask him to come pick her up. She searched the pockets in her jeans and her jacket. Not a dime, she thought furiously. Not one thin dime to my name. Taking a deep breath, she stared at the doors of the restaurant. She'd have to borrow change, or beg their permission to use the house phone. Anything was better than waiting in the car. Just as she pulled open the door of the restaurant, Katch strolled out.

"Thanks," he said casually and moved past her.

Megan stared after him. He was carrying the biggest picnic basket she'd ever seen. After he'd opened the trunk and settled it inside, he glanced back up at her.

"Well, come on." He slammed the lid. "I'm starving."

"What's in there?" she asked suspiciously.

"Dinner." He motioned for her to get in the car. Megan stood beside the closed door on the passenger side.

"How did you get them to do that?"

"I asked. Are you hungry?"

"Well, yes… But how—"

"Then let's go." Katch dropped into the driver's seat

and started the engine. The moment she sat beside him, he swung out of the parking lot. "Where's your favorite place?" he demanded.

"My favorite place?" she repeated dumbly.

"You can't tell me you've lived here all your life and don't have a favorite place." Katch turned the car toward the ocean. "Where is it?"

"Toward the north end of the beach," she said. "Not many people go there, except at the height of the season."

"Good. I want to be alone with you."

The simple directness had butterflies dancing in her stomach. Slowly, she turned to look at him again.

"Anything wrong with that?" The smile was back, irreverent and engaging. Megan sighed, feeling like she was just climbing the first hill of a roller coaster.

"Probably," she murmured.

The beach was deserted but for the crying gulls. She stood for a moment facing west, enjoying the rich glow of the dying sun.

"I love this time of day," she said softly. "Everything seems so still. As if the day's holding its breath." She jumped when Katch's hands came to her shoulders.

"Easy," he murmured, kneading the suddenly tense muscles as he stood behind her. He looked over her head to the sunset. "I like it just before dawn, when the birds first start to sing and the light's still soft.

"You should relax more often," he told her. He slid his fingers lazily up her neck and down again. The pleasure became less quiet and more demanding. When she would have slipped away, Katch turned her to face him.

"No," she said immediately, "don't." Megan placed both her hands on his chest. "Don't."

"All right." He relaxed his hold, but didn't release her for a moment. Then he stooped for the picnic basket and pulled out a white tablecloth saying briskly, "Besides, it's time to eat." Megan took it from him, marveling that the restaurant had given him their best linen.

"Here you go." With his head still bent over the basket, he handed her the glasses.

And they're crystal, she thought, dazed as she accepted the elegant wineglasses. There was china next, then silver.

"Why did they give you all this?"

"They were low on paper plates."

"Champagne?" She glanced at the label as he poured. "You must be crazy!"

"What's the matter?" he returned mildly. "Don't you like champagne?"

"Actually I do, though I've only had American."

"Here's to the French." Katch held out a glass to her.

Megan sipped. "It's wonderful," she said before experimenting with another sip. "But you didn't have to…" she gestured expansively.

"I decided I wasn't in the mood for a hamburger." Katch screwed the bottle down into the sand. He placed a small container on the cloth, then dived back into the basket.

"What's this?" Megan demanded as she opened it. She frowned at the shiny black mass inside. He placed toast points on a plate. "Is it…" She paused in disbelief and glanced at him. "Is this caviar?"

"Yeah. Let me have some, will you? I'm starving." Katch took it from her and spread a generous amount on a piece of toast. "Don't you want any?" he asked her as he took a bite.

"I don't know." Megan examined it critically. "I've never tasted it before."

"No?" He offered her his piece. "Taste it." When she hesitated, Katch grinned and held it closer to her mouth. "Go on, Meg, have a bite."

"It's salty," she said with surprise. She plucked the toast from his hand and took another bite. "And it's good," she decided, swallowing.

"You might've left me some," he complained when Megan finished off the toast. She laughed and, heaping caviar onto another piece, handed it to him. "I wondered how it would sound." Katch took the offering, but his attention was on Megan.

"What?" Still smiling, she licked a bit of caviar from her thumb.

"Your laugh. I wondered if it would be as appealing as your face." He took a bite now, still watching her. "It is."

Megan tried to calm her fluttering pulse. "You didn't have to feed me caviar and champagne to hear me laugh." With a casual shrug, she moved out of his reach. "I laugh quite a bit."

"Not often enough."

She looked back at him in surprise. "Why do you say that?"

"Your eyes are so serious. So's your mouth." His glance swept over her face. "Perhaps that's why I feel compelled to make you smile."

"How extraordinary." Megan sat back on her heels and stared at him. "You barely know me."

"Does it matter?"

"I always thought it should," she murmured as he reached into the hamper again. Megan watched, no longer surprised as he drew out lobster tails and fresh strawberries. She laughed again and, pushing back her hair, moved closer to him.

"Here," she said. "Let me help."

The sun sank as they ate. The moon rose. It shot a shimmering white line across the sea. Megan thought it was like a dream—the china and silver gleaming in the moonlight, the exotic tastes on her tongue, the familiar sound of surf and the stranger beside her, who was becoming less of a stranger every minute.

Already Megan knew the exact movement of his face when he smiled, the precise tonal quality of his voice. She knew the exact pattern of the curls over his ear. More than once, bewitched by moonlight and champagne, she had to restrain her fingers from reaching for them, experimenting with them.

"Aren't you going to eat any cheesecake?" Katch gestured with a forkful, then slid it into his mouth.

"I can't." Megan brought her knees up to her chest and rested her chin on them. She watched his obvious enjoyment with dessert. "How do you do it?"

"Dedication." Katch took the last bite. "I try to see every project through to the finish."

"I've never had a picnic like this," she told him with a contented sigh. Leaning back on her elbows, she stretched out her legs and looked up at the stars. "I've never tasted anything so wonderful."

"I'll give Ricardo your compliments." Katch moved to sit beside her. His eyes moved from the crown of her head down the slender arch of her neck. Her face was thrown up to the stars.

"Who's Ricardo?" she asked absently. There was no

thought of objection when Katch tucked her hair behind her ear with his fingertip.

"The chef. He loves compliments."

Megan smiled, liking the way the sound of his voice mixed with the sound of the sea. "How do you know?"

"That's how I lured him away from Chicago."

"Lured him away? What do you mean?" It took only an instant for the answer to come to her. "You own that restaurant?"

"Yes." He smiled at the incredulity in her face. "I bought it a couple of years ago."

Megan glanced at the white linen cloth scattered with fine china and heavy silver. She recalled that a little more than two years before, the restaurant had been ready to go under. The food had been overpriced and the service slack. Then it had received a face-lift. The interior had been redesigned, boasting, she was told, a mirrored ceiling. Since its reopening, it had maintained the highest of reputations in a town which prided itself on its quality and variety of restaurants.

She shifted her attention back to him. "*You* bought it?"

"That's right." Katch smiled at her. He sat Indian-style, facing her as she leaned back on her elbows. "Does that surprise you?"

Megan looked at him carefully: the careless toss of curls, the white knees of his jeans, the frayed sneakers. He was not her conception of a successful businessman. Where was the three-piece suit, the careful hairstyling? And yet… she had to admit there was something in his face.

"No," she said at length. "No, I suppose it doesn't." Megan frowned as he shifted his position. In a moment he was close, facing the sea as she did. "You bought it the same way you want to buy Joyland."

"I told you, that's what I do."

"But it's more than owning things, isn't it?" she insisted, not satisfied with his offhand answers. "It's making a success of them."

"That's the idea," he agreed. "There's a certain satisfaction in succeeding, don't you think?"

Megan sat up and turned to him. "But you can't have Joyland, it's Pop's whole life. You don't understand..."

"Maybe not," he said easily. "You can explain it to me later. Not tonight." He covered her hand with his. "This isn't a night for business."

"Katch, you have to—"

"Look at the stars, Meg," he suggested as he did so himself. "Have you ever tried to count them?"

Her eyes were irresistibly drawn upward. "When I was little. But—"

"Star counting isn't just for kids," he instructed in a voice warm and laced with humor. "Do you come here at night?"

The stars were brilliant and low over the sea. "Sometimes," she murmured. "When a project isn't going well and I need to clear my head, or just be alone."

"What sort of artist are you?" His fingers trailed over her knuckles. "Do you paint seascapes? Portraits?"

She smiled and shook her head. "No, I sculpt."

"Ah." He lifted her hand, then examined it—one side, then the other—while she watched him. "Yes, I can see that. Your hands are strong and capable." When he pressed his lips to the center of her palm, she felt the jolt shoot through her entire body.

Carefully, Megan drew her hand away; then, bringing her knees up to her chest, wrapped her arms around them. She could feel Katch smile without seeing it.

"What do you work in? Clay, wood, stone?"

"All three." Turning her head, she smiled again.

"Where did you study?"

"I took courses in college." With a shrug, she passed this off. "There hasn't been much time for it." She looked up at the sky again. "The moon's so white tonight. I like to come here when it's full like this, so that the light's silvery."

When his lips brushed her ear, she would have jerked away, but he slipped an arm around her shoulders. "Relax, Meg." His voice was a whisper at her cheek. "There's a moon and the ocean. That's all there is besides us."

With his lips tingling on her skin, she could almost believe him. Her limbs were heavy, drugged with wine and the magic of his touch. Katch trailed his mouth down to her throat so that she moaned with the leap of her pulse.

"Katch, I'd better go." He was tracing her jaw with light kisses. "Please," she said weakly.

"Later," he murmured, going back to nuzzle her ear. "Much, much later."

"No, I…" Megan turned her head, and the words died.

Her lips were no more than a breath from his. She stared at him, eyes wide and aware as he bent closer. Still his mouth didn't touch hers. It hovered, offering, promising. She moaned again, lids lowering as he teased the corners of her lips. His hands never touched her. He had moved his arm so that their only contact was his mouth and tongue on her skin and the mingling of their breath.

Megan felt her resistance peel away, layer by layer until there was only need. She forgot to question the dangers, the consequences. She could only feel. Her mouth sought his. There was no hesitation or shyness now but demand, impatient demand, as she hungered to feel what she had felt before—the delicious confusion, the dark awareness.

When he still didn't touch her, Megan slipped her arms around him. She pulled him close, enjoying his soft sound of pleasure as the kiss deepened. Still, he let her lead, touching her now, but lightly, his fingers in her hair. She could barely hear the hissing of the surf over the pounding of her heart. Finally, she drew away, pulling in a deep breath as their lips separated.

But he wouldn't let her go. "Again?" The question was quiet and seemed to shout through the still night.

Refusal trembled on Megan's tongue. She knew the ground beneath her was far from solid. His hand on the back of her neck brought her a whisper closer.

"Yes," she said, and went into his arms.

This time he was less passive. He showed her there were many ways to kiss. Short and light, long and deep. Tongue and teeth and lips could all bring pleasure. Together, they lowered themselves to the sand.

It was a rough blanket, but she felt only the excitement of his lips on her skin as they wandered to her throat. She ran her fingers through his hair. His mouth returned to hers, harder now, more insistent. She was ready for it, answering it. Craving it.

When his hand took the naked skin of her breast, she murmured in resistance. She hadn't felt him release the zipper of her jacket or the buttons of her shirt. But his hand was gentle, persuasive. He let his fingers trail over her, a whispering touch. Resistance melted into surrender, then heated into passion. It was smoldering just under her skin, threatening to explode into something out of her control. She moved under him and his hands became less gentle.

There was a hunger in the kiss now. She could taste it, a flavor sharper than any she'd known. It was more seductive than soft words or champagne, and more frightening.

"I want you." Katch spoke against her mouth, but the words were not in his easygoing tone. "I want to make love with you."

Megan felt control slipping from her grasp. Her need for him was overpowering, her appetite ravenous. She struggled to climb back to reality, to remember who they were. Names, places, responsibilities. There was more than the moon and the sea. And he was a stranger, a man she barely knew.

"No." Megan managed to free her mouth from his. She struggled to her feet. "No." The repetition was shaky. Quickly, she began to fumble with the buttons of her shirt.

Katch stood and gathered the shirttail in his hands. Surprised, Megan looked up at him. His eyes were no longer calm, but his voice was deadly so. "Why not?"

Megan swallowed. There wasn't lazy arrogance here, but a hint of ruthlessness. She had sensed it, but seeing it was much more potent. "I don't want to."

"Liar," he said simply.

"All right." She nodded, conceding his point. "I don't know you."

Katch inclined his head in agreement but tugged on the tails of her shirt to bring her closer. "You will," he assured her. He kissed her then, searingly. "But we'll wait until you do."

She fought to steady her breathing and stabilize her pulse.

"Do you think you should always get what you want?" she demanded. The defiance was back, calming her.

"Yes," he said and grinned. "Of course."

"You're going to be disappointed." She smacked his hands from her shirt and began doing the buttons. Her fingers were unfaltering. "You can't have Joyland and you can't have me. Neither of us is for sale."

The roughness with which he took her arm had her eyes flying back to his face. "I don't buy women." He was angry, his eyes dark with it. The appealing voice had hardened like flint. The artist in her was fascinated by the planes of his face, the woman was uneasy with his harsh tone. "I don't have to. We're both aware that with a bit more persuasion I'd have had you tonight."

Megan pulled out of his hold. "What happened tonight doesn't mean I find you irresistible, you know." She zipped up her jacket with one quick jerk. "I can only repeat, you can't have Joyland and you can't have me."

Katch watched her a moment as she stood in the moonlight, her back to the sea. The smile came again, slowly, arrogantly. "I'll have you both, Meg," he promised quietly. "Before the season begins."

Chapter 4

The afternoon sun poured into Megan's studio. She was oblivious to it, and to the birdsong outside the windows. Her mind was focused on the clay her hands worked with, or, more precisely, on what she saw in the partially formed mound.

She had put her current project aside, something she rarely did, to begin a new one. The new subject had haunted her throughout the night. She would exorcise David Katcherton by doing a bust of him.

Megan could see it clearly, knew precisely what she wanted to capture: strength and determination behind a surface affability.

Though she had yet to admit it, Katch had frightened her the night before. Not physically—he was too intelligent to use brute force, she acknowledged—but by the force of his personality. Angrily, she stabbed at the clay. Obviously, this was a man who got what he wanted. But she was determined that this time he would not have his way. He would soon find out that she couldn't be pushed around any more than Pop could. Slowly and meticulously, her fingers worked to mold the planes of his face. It gave her a certain satisfaction to have control over him—if only vicariously with the clay.

Almost without thinking, she shaped a careless curl over the high brow. She stepped back to survey it. Somehow, she had caught a facet of his nature. He was a rogue, she decided. The old-fashioned word suited him. She could picture him with boots and six-guns, dealing cards for stud poker in a Tucson saloon; with a saber, captaining a ship into the Barbary Coast. Her fingers absently caressed the clay curls. He would laugh in the face of the wind, take treasure and women where he found them. *Women.* Megan's thoughts zeroed in on the night before.... On the feel of his lips on hers, the touch of his hand on her skin. She could remember the texture of the sand as they had lain together, the scent and sounds of the sea. And she remembered how the moonlight had fallen on his hair, how her hands had sought it while his lips had wandered over her. How thick and soft it had felt. How...

Megan stopped, appalled. She glanced down to see her fingers in the clay replica of Katch's hair. She swore, and nearly, very nearly, reduced the clay to a formless mass. Controlling herself, she rose, backing away from the forming bust. I should never allow myself to be distracted from my work by petty annoyances, she thought. Her evening with Katch belonged in that category. Just a petty annoyancc. Not important.

But it was difficult for Megan to convince herself this was true. Both her intuition and her emotions told her that

Katch was important, far more important than a stranger should be to a sensible woman.

And I *am* sensible, she reminded herself. Taking a long breath, she moved to the basin to rinse the clay from her hands. She had to be sensible. Pop needed someone around to remind him that bills had to be paid. A smile crept across her mouth as she dried her hands. Megan thought, as she did from time to time, that she had been almost as much of a savior to her grandfather as he had been to her.

In the beginning, she'd been so young, so dependent upon him. And he hadn't let her down. Then, as she had grown older, Megan had helped by assuming the duties her grandfather had found tiresome: accounts and bank reconciliations. Often, Megan suppressed her own desires in order to fulfill what she thought of as her duty. She dealt with figures, the unromantic process of adding and subtracting. But she also dealt with the illusionary world of art. There were times, when she was deep in her work, that she forgot the rules she had set up for day-to-day living. Often she felt pulled in two directions. She had enough to think about without David Katcherton.

Why a man virtually unknown to her should so successfully upset the delicate balance of her world, she didn't know. She shook her head. Instead of dwelling on it, she decided, she would work out her frustration by finishing the bust. When it was done, perhaps she would be able to see more clearly exactly how she perceived him. She returned to her work.

The next hour passed quickly. She forgot her irritation with Katch for going fishing with her grandfather. How annoying to have seen him so eager and well rested when she had peeked through her bedroom curtain at five-thirty that morning! She'd fallen back into her rumpled bed to spend another hour staring, heavy-eyed, at the ceiling. She refused to remember how appealing his laugh had sounded in the hush of dawn.

The planes of his face were just taking shape under her hands when she heard a car drive up. Katch's laugh was followed by the more gravelly tones of her grandfather's.

Because her studio was above the garage, Megan had a bird's-eye view of the house and drive. She watched as Katch lifted their fishing cooler from the back of the pickup. A grin was on his face, but whatever he said was too low for Megan to hear. Pop threw back his head, his dramatic mane of white flying back as he roared his appreciation. He gave Katch a companionable slap on the back. Unaccountably, Megan was miffed. They seemed to be getting along entirely too well.

She continued to watch the man as they unloaded tackle boxes and gear. Katch was dressed much as he had been the day before. The pale blue T-shirt had lettering across the chest, but the words were faded and the distance was too great for Megan to read them. He wore Pop's fishing cap, another source of annoyance for Megan. She was forced to admit the two of them looked good together. There was the contrast between their ages and their builds, but both seemed to her to be extraordinarily masculine men. Their looks were neither smooth nor pampered. She became engrossed with the similarities and differences between them. When Katch looked up, spotting her at the window, Megan continued to stare down, oblivious, absorbed with what she saw in them.

Katch grinned, pushing the fishing cap back so that he had a clearer view. The window was long, the sill coming low at her knees. It had the effect of making Megan seem to be standing in a full-size picture frame. As was her habit when working, she had pulled her hair back in a ribbon. Her face seemed younger and more vulnerable, her eyes wider. The ancient shirt of Pop's she used as a smock dwarfed her.

Her eyes locked on Katch's, and for a moment she thought she saw something flash in them—something she'd seen briefly the night before in the moonlight. A response trembled along her skin. Then his grin was arrogant again, his eyes amused.

"Come on down, Meg." He gestured before he bent to lift the cooler again. "We brought you a present." He turned to carry the cooler around the side of the house.

"I'd rather have emeralds," she called back.

"Next time," Katch promised carelessly, before turning to carry the cooler around the side of the house.

She found Katch alone, setting up for the cleaning of the catch. He smiled when he saw her and set down the knife he held, then pulled her into his arms and kissed her thoroughly, to her utter astonishment. It was a kiss of casual ownership rather than passion, but it elicited a response that surprised her with its force. More than a little shaken, Megan pushed away.

"You can't just…"

"I already did," he pointed out. "You've been working," Katch stated as if the searing kiss had never taken place. "I'd like to see your studio."

It was better, Megan decided, to follow his lead and keep the conversation light. "Where's my grandfather?"

she asked as she moved to the cooler and prepared to lift the lid.

"Pop's inside stowing the gear."

Though it was the habit of everyone who knew him to refer to Timothy Miller as Pop, Megan frowned at Katch.

"You work fast, don't you?"

"Yes, I do. I like your grandfather, Meg. You of all people should understand how easy that is to do."

Megan regarded him steadily. She took a step closer, as if testing the air between them. "I don't know if I should trust you."

"You shouldn't." Katch grinned again and ran a finger down the bridge of her nose. "Not for a second." He tossed open the lid of the cooler, then gestured to the fish inside. "Hungry?"

Megan smiled, letting herself be charmed despite the warnings of her sensible self. "I wasn't. But I could be. Especially if I don't have to clean them."

"Pop told me you were squeamish."

"Oh, he *did,* did he?" Megan cast a long, baleful look over her shoulder toward the house. "What else did he tell you?"

"That you like daffodils and used to have a stuffed elephant named Henry."

Megan's mouth dropped open. "He told you that?"

"And that you watch horror movies, then sleep with the blankets over your head."

Megan narrowed her eyes as Katch's grin widened. "Excuse me," she said crossly, pushing Katch aside before racing through the kitchen door. She could hear Katch's laughter behind her.

"Pop!" She found him in the narrow room off the kitchen

where he stored his fishing paraphernalia. He gave her an affectionate smile as she stood, hands on hips, in the doorway.

"Hi, Megan. Let me tell you, that boy knows how to fish. Yessiree, he knows how to fish."

His obvious delight with Katch caused Megan to clench her teeth. "That's the best news I've had all day," she said, stepping into the room. "But exactly why did you feel it necessary to tell *that boy* that I had a stuffed elephant and slept with the covers over my head?"

Pop lifted a hand, ostensibly to scratch his head. It wasn't in time, however, to conceal the grin. Megan's brows drew together.

"Pop, really," she said in exasperation. "Must you babble about me as if I were a little girl?"

"You'll always be my little girl," he said maddeningly, and kissed her cheek. "Did you see those trout? We'll have a heck of a fish fry tonight."

"I suppose," Megan began and folded her arms, "*he's* going to eat with us."

"Well, of course." Pop blinked his eyes. "After all, Meg, he caught half the fish."

"That's just peachy."

"We thought you might whip up some of your special blueberry tarts." He smiled ingenuously.

Megan sighed, recognizing defeat.

Within minutes, Pop heard the thumping and banging of pans. He grinned, then slipped out of the room, moving noiselessly through the house and out the front door.

"Whip up some tarts," Megan muttered later as she cut shortening into the flour. *"Men."*

She was bending over to slip the pastry shells into the

oven when the screen door slammed shut behind her. Turning, she brushed at the seat of her pants and met the predictable grin.

"I've heard about your tarts," Katch commented, setting the cleaned, filleted fish on the counter. "Pop said he had a few things to see to in the garage and to call him when dinner's ready."

Megan glared through the screen door at the adjoining building. "Oh, he did, did he?" She turned back to Katch. "Well, if you think you can just sit back and be waited on, then you're in for a disappointment."

"You didn't think I'd allow you to cook my fish, did you?" he interrupted.

She stared at his unperturbed face.

"I always cook my own fish. Where's the frying pan?"

Silently, still eyeing him, Megan pointed out the cabinet. She watched as he squatted down to rummage for it.

"It's not that I don't think you're a good cook," he went on as he stood again with the cast-iron skillet in his hand. "It's that I know I am."

"Are you implying I couldn't cook those pathetic little sardines properly?"

"Let's just say I just don't like to take chances with my dinner." He began poking into cupboards. "Why don't you make a salad," he suggested mildly, "and leave the fish to me?" There was a grunt of approval as he located the cracker meal.

Megan watched him casually going through her kitchen cupboards. "Why don't you," she began, "take your trout and…"

Her suggestion was interrupted by the rude buzz of the oven timer.

"Your tarts." Katch walked to the refrigerator for eggs and milk.

With supreme effort, Megan controlled herself enough to deal with the pastry shells. Setting them on the rack to cool, she decided to create the salad of the decade. It would put his pan-fried trout to shame.

For a time there were no words. The hot oil hissed as Katch added his coated trout. Megan tore the lettuce. She sliced raw vegetables. The scent from the pan was enticing. Megan peeled a carrot and sighed. Hearing her, Katch raised a questioning eyebrow.

"You had to be good at it, didn't you?" Megan's smile was reluctant. "You had to do it right."

He shrugged, then snatched the peeled carrot from her hand. "You'd like it better if I didn't?" Katch took a bite of the carrot before Megan could retrieve it. Shaking her head, she selected another.

"It would have been more gratifying if you'd fumbled around and made a mess of things."

Katch tilted his head as he poked at the sizzling fish with a spatula. "Is that a compliment?"

Megan diced the carrot, frowning at it thoughtfully. "I don't know. It might be easier to deal with you if you didn't seem so capable."

He caught her off guard by taking her shoulders and turning her around to face him. "Is that what you want to do?" His fingers gently massaged her flesh. "Deal with me?" When she felt herself being drawn closer, she placed her hands on his chest. "Do I make you nervous?"

"No." Megan shook her head with the denial. "No, of course not." Katch only lifted a brow and drew her closer. "Yes," she admitted in a rush, and pulled away. "Yes, blast it, you do." Stalking to the refrigerator, she yanked out the blueberry filling she had prepared. "You needn't look so pleased about it," she told him, wishing she could work up the annoyance she thought she should feel.

"Several things make me nervous." Megan moved to the pastry shells and began to spoon in the filling. "Snakes, tooth decay, large unfriendly dogs." When she heard him chuckle, Megan turned her head and found herself grinning at him. "It's difficult to actively dislike you when you make me laugh."

"Do you have to actively dislike me?" Katch flipped the fish expertly and sent oil sizzling.

"That was my plan," Megan admitted. "It seemed like a good idea."

"Why don't we work on a different plan?" Katch suggested, searching through a cupboard again for a platter. "What do you like? Besides daffodils?"

"Soft ice cream," Megan responded spontaneously. "Oscar Wilde, walking barefoot."

"How about baseball?" Katch demanded.

Megan paused in the act of filling the shells. "What about it?"

"Do you like it?"

"Yes," she considered, smiling. "As a matter of fact, I do."

"I knew we had something in common." Katch grinned. He turned the flame off under the pan. "Why don't you call Pop? The fish is done."

There was something altogether too cozy about the three of them sitting around the kitchen table eating a meal each of them had a part in providing, Megan thought.

She could sense the growing affection between the two men and it worried her. She was sure that Katch was still as determined as ever to buy Joyland. Yet Pop was so obviously happy in his company. Megan decided that, while she couldn't trust Katch unreservedly, neither could she maintain her original plan. She couldn't dislike him or keep him from touching their lives. She thought it best not to dwell on precisely how he was touching hers.

"Tell you what." Pop sighed over his empty plate and leaned back in his chair. "Since the pair of you cooked dinner, I'll do the dishes." His eyes passed over Megan to Katch. "Why don't you two go for a walk? Megan likes to walk on the beach."

"Pop!"

"I know you young people like to be alone," he continued shamelessly.

Megan opened her mouth to protest, but Katch spoke first. "I'm always willing to take a walk with a beautiful woman, especially if it means getting out of KP," he said.

"You have such a gracious way of putting things," Megan began.

"Actually, I'd really like to see your studio."

"Take Katch up, Megan," Pop insisted. "I've been bragging about your pieces all day. Let him see for himself."

After a moment's hesitation, Megan decided it was simpler to agree. Certainly she didn't mind showing Katch her work. And, there was little doubt that it was safer to let him putter around her studio than to walk with him on the beach.

"All right." She rose. "I'll take you up."

As they passed through the screen door, Katch slipped his arm over her shoulders. "This is a nice place," he commented. He looked around the small trim yard lined with azalea shrubs. "Very quiet and settled."

The weight of his arm was pleasant. Megan allowed it to remain as they walked toward the garage. "I wouldn't think you'd find something quiet and settled terribly appealing."

"There's a time for porch swings and a time for roller coasters." Katch glanced down at her as she paused at the foot of the steps. "I'd think you'd know that."

"I do," she said, knowing her involvement with him was beginning to slip beyond her control. "I wasn't aware you did." Thoughtfully, Megan climbed the stairs. "It's rather a small-scale studio, I suppose, and not very impressive. It's really just a place to work where I won't disturb Pop and he won't disturb me."

Megan opened the door, flicking on the light as the sun was growing dim.

There was much less order here than she permitted herself in other areas of her life. The room was hers, personally, more exclusively than her bedroom in the house next door. There were tools—calipers, chisels, gouges, and an assortment of knives and files. There was the smock she'd carelessly thrown over a chair when Katch had called her downstairs. Future projects sat waiting inside, untouched slabs of limestone and chunks of wood. There was a precious piece of marble she hoarded like a miser. Everywhere, on shelves, tables and even the floor, were samples of her work.

Katch moved past her into the room. Strangely, Megan felt a flutter of nerves. She found herself wondering how to react if he spoke critically, or worse, offered some trite compliment. Her work was important to her and very personal. To her surprise she realized that she cared about his opinion. Quietly, she closed the door behind her, then stood with her back against it.

Katch had gone directly to a small walnut study of a young girl building a sand castle. She was particularly pleased with the piece, as she had achieved exactly the mood she had sought. There was more than youth and innocence in the child's face. The girl saw herself as the princess in the castle tower. The half-smile on her face made the onlooker believe in happy endings.

It was painstakingly detailed, the beginnings of a crenellated roof and the turrets of the castle, the slender fingers of the girl as she sculpted the sand. Her hair was long, falling over her shoulders and wisping into her face as though a breeze teased it. Megan had felt successful when the study had been complete, but now, watching Katch turn it over in his hands, his mouth oddly grave, his eyes intent, she felt a twinge of doubt.

"This is your work?" Because the silence had seemed so permanent, Megan jerked when Katch spoke.

"Well, yes." While she was still searching for something more to say, Katch turned away to prowl the room.

He picked up piece after piece, examining, saying nothing. As the silence dragged on, minute upon minute, Megan became more and more tense. If he'd just say something, she thought. She picked up the discarded smock and folded it, nervously smoothing creases as she listened to the soft sound of his tennis shoes on the wood floor.

"What are you doing here?"

She whirled, eyes wide. Whatever reaction she had expected, it certainly hadn't been anger. And there was anger on his face, a sharp, penetrating anger which caused her to grip the worn material of the smock tighter.

"I don't know what you mean." Megan's voice was calm, but her heart had begun to beat faster.

"Why are you hiding?" he demanded. "What are you afraid of?"

She shook her head in bewilderment. "I'm not hiding, Katch. You're not making any sense."

"I'm not making sense?" He took a step toward her, then stopped, turning away to pace again. She watched in fascination. "Do you think it makes sense to create things like this and lock them up in a room over a garage?" He lifted polished limestone which had been formed into a head-and-shoulders study of a man and a woman in each other's arms. "When you've been given talent like this, you have an obligation. What are you going to do, continue to stack them in here until there isn't any more room?"

His reaction had thrown Megan completely off-balance. She looked around the room. "No, I…I take pieces into an art gallery downtown now and then. They sell fairly well, especially during the season, and—"

Katch's pungent oath cut her off. Megan gave her full attention back to him. Was this furious, disapproving man the same one who had amiably prepared trout in her kitchen a short time ago?

"I don't understand why you're so mad." Annoyed with herself for nervously pleating the material of the smock, Megan tossed it down.

"Waste," he said tersely, placing the limestone back on the shelf. "Waste infuriates me." He came to her, taking her deliberately by thc shoulders. "Why haven't you done anything with your work?" His eyes were direct on hers, demanding answers, not evasions.

"It's not as simple as that," she began. "I have responsibilities."

"Your responsibilities are to yourself, to your talent."

"You make it sound as though I've done something wrong." Confused, Megan searched his face. "I've done what I know how to do. I don't understand why you're angry. There are things, like time and money, to be considered," she went on. "A business to run. And reality to face." Megan shook her head. "I can hardly cart my work to a Charleston art gallery and demand a showing."

"That would make more sense than cloistering it up here." He released her abruptly, then paced again.

He was, Megan discovered, much more volatile than her first impression had allowed. She glanced at the clay wrapped in the damp towel. Her fingertips itched to work while fresh impressions were streaming through her brain.

"When's the last time you've been to New York?" Katch demanded, facing her again. "Chicago, L.A.?"

"We can't all be globetrotters," she told him. "Some are born to other things."

He picked up the sand-castle girl again, then strode over to the limestone couple. "I want these two," he stated. "Will you sell them to me?"

They were two of her favorites, though totally opposite in tone. "Yes, I suppose. If you want them."

"I'll give you five hundred." Megan's eyes widened. "Apiece."

"Oh, no, they're not worth—"

"They're worth a lot more, I imagine." Katch lifted the limestone. "Have you got a box I can carry them in?"

"Yes, but, Katch." Megan paused and pushed the bangs from her eyes. "A thousand dollars?"

He set down both pieces and came back to her. He was still angry; she could feel it vibrating from him. "Do you think it's safer to underestimate yourself than to face up to your own worth?"

Megan started to make a furious denial, then stopped. Uncertain, she made a helpless gesture with her hands. Katch turned away again to search for a box himself. She watched him as he wrapped the sculptures in old newspapers. The frown was still on his face, the temper in his eyes.

"I'll bring you a check," he stated, and was gone without another word.

Chapter 5

There was a long, high-pitched scream. The roller coaster rumbled along the track as it whipped around another curve and tilted its passengers. Lights along the midway were twinkling, and there was noise. Such noise. There was the whirl and whine of machinery, the electronic buzz and beeps from video games, the pop of arcade rifles and the call of concessionaires.

Tinny music floated all over, but for the most part, there was the sound of people. They were laughing, calling, talking, shouting. There were smells: popcorn, peanuts, grilled hot dogs, machine oil.

Megan loaded another clip into the scaled-down rifle and handed it to a would-be Wyatt Earp. "Rabbits are five points, ducks ten, deer twenty-five and the bears fifty."

The sixteen-year-old sharpshooter aimed and managed to bag a duck and a rabbit. He chose a rubber snake as his prize, to the ensuing screams and disgust of his girl.

Shaking her head, Megan watched them walk away.

The boy slipped his arm around the girl's shoulders, then pursued the romance by dangling the snake in front of her face. He earned a quick jab in the ribs.

The crowd was thin tonight, but that was to be expected in the off-season. Particularly, Megan knew, when there were so many other parks with more rides, live entertainment and a more sophisticated selection of video games. She didn't mind the slack. Megan was preoccupied, as she had been since the evening Katch had seen her studio. In three days, she hadn't heard a word from him. At first, she had wanted badly to see him, to talk about the things he'd said to her. He had made her think, made her consider a part of herself she had ignored or submerged most of her life.

Her desire to speak with Katch had faded as the days had passed, however. After all, what right did he have to criticize her lifestyle? What right did he have to make her feel as if she'd committed a crime? He'd accused, tried and condemned her in the space of minutes. Then, he'd disappeared.

Three days, Megan mused, handing another hopeful deadeye a rifle. Three days without a word. And she'd watched for him—much to her self-disgust. She'd waited for him. As the days had passed, Megan had taken refuge in anger. Not only had he criticized and scolded her, she remembered, but he'd walked out with two of her favorite sculptures. A thousand dollars my foot, she mused, frowning fiercely as she slid a fresh clip into an empty rifle. Just talk, that's all. Talk. He does that very well. It was probably all a line, owning that restaurant. *But why?* Men like that don't need logical reasons, she decided. It's all ego.

"Men," she muttered as she handed a rifle to a new customer.

"I know what you mean, honey." The plump blond woman took the rifle from Megan with a wink.

Megan pushed her bangs back and frowned deeper. "Who needs them?" she demanded.

The woman shouldered the rifle. "We do, honey. That's the problem."

Megan let out a long sigh as the woman earned 125 points. "Nice shooting," she congratulated. "Your choice on the second row."

"Let me have the hippo, sweetie. It looks a little like my second husband."

Laughing, Megan plucked it from the shelf and handed it over. "Here you go." With another wink, the woman tucked the hippo under her arm and waddled off.

Megan settled back while two kids tried their luck. The exchange had been typical of the informality enjoyed by people in amusement parks. She smiled, feeling less grim, if not entirely mollified by the woman's remarks. But she doesn't know Katch, Megan reflected, again exchanging a rifle for a quarter. And neither, she reminded herself, do I.

Automatically, Megan made change when a dollar bill was placed on the counter. "Ten shots for a quarter," she began the spiel. "Rabbits are five, ducks ten…" Megan pushed three quarters back as she reached for a rifle. The moment the fingers pushed the change back to her, she recognized them.

"I'll take a dollar's worth," Katch told her as she looked up in surprise. He grinned, then leaned over to press a quick kiss to her lips. "For luck," he claimed when she jerked away.

Before Megan had pocketed the quarters, Katch had bull's-eyed every one of the bears.

"Wow!" The two boys standing next to Katch were suitably impressed. "Hey, mister, can you do it again?" one asked.

"Maybe." Katch turned to Megan. "Let's have a reload." Without speaking, she handed him the rifle.

"I like the perfume you're wearing," he commented as he sighed. "What is it?"

"Gun oil."

He laughed, then blasted the hapless bears one by one. The two boys gave simultaneous yelps of appreciation. A crowd began to gather.

"Hey, Megan." She glanced up to see the Bailey twins leaning over the counter. Both pairs of eyes drifted meaningfully to Katch. "Isn't he the…"

"Yes," Megan said shortly, not wanting to explain.

"Delicious," Teri decided quietly, giving Katch a flirtatious smile when he straightened.

"Mmm-hmm," Jeri agreed with a twin smile.

Katch gave them a long, appreciative look.

"Here." Megan shoved the rifle at him. "This is your last quarter."

Katch accepted the rifle. "Thanks." He hefted it again. "Going to wish me luck?"

Megan met his eyes levelly. "Why not?"

"Meg, I'm crazy about you."

She dealt with the surge his careless words brought her as he picked off his fourth set of bears. Bystanders broke into raucous applause. Katch set the rifle on the counter, then gave his full attention to Meg.

"What'd I win?"

"Anything you want."

His grin was a flash, and his eyes never left her face. She blushed instantly, hating herself. Deliberately, she stepped to the side and gestured toward the prizes.

"I'll take Henry," he told her. When she gave him a puzzled look, he pointed. "The elephant." Glancing up, Megan spotted the three-foot lavender elephant. She lifted it down from its perch. Even as she set it on the counter for him, Katch took her hands. "And you."

She made her voice prim. "Only the items on display are eligible prizes."

"I love it when you talk that way," he commented.

"Stop it!" she hissed, flushing as she heard the Bailey twins giggle.

"We had a bet, remember?" Katch smiled at her. "It's Friday night."

Megan tried to tug her hands away, but his fingers interlocked with hers. "Who says I lost the bet?" she demanded. The crowd was still milling around the stand so she spoke in an undertone, but Katch didn't bother.

"Come on, Meg, I won fair and square. You're not going to welch, are you?"

"Shh!" She glanced behind him at the curious crowd. "I never welch," she whispered furiously. "And even if I did lose, which I never said I did, I can't leave the stand. I'm sure you can find somebody else to keep you company."

"I want you."

She struggled to keep her eyes steady on his. "Well, I can't leave. Someone has to run the booth."

"Megan." One of the part-timers slipped under the counter. "Pop sent me to relieve you." He smiled innocently when she gave him a disgusted look.

"Perfect timing," she mumbled, then stripped off the change apron and stuffed it in his hands. "Thanks a lot."

"Sure, Megan."

"Hey, keep this back there for me, will you?" Katch dumped the elephant into his arms and captured Megan's hands again as she ducked under the counter. As she straightened, he tugged, tumbling her into his arms.

The kiss was long and demanding. When Katch drew her away, her arms were around his neck. She left them there, staring up into his face with eyes newly aware and darkened.

"I've wanted to do that for three days," he murmured, and rubbed her nose lightly with his.

"Why didn't you?"

He lifted a brow at that, then grinned when her blush betrayed the impetuousness of her words.

"I didn't mean that the way it sounded," Megan began, dropping her arms and trying to wriggle away.

"Yes, you did," he countered. Katch released her but dropped a friendly arm over her shoulder. "It was nice, don't spoil it." He took a sweeping glance of the park. "How about a tour?"

"I don't know why you want one. We're not selling."

"We'll see about that," he said, as maddeningly confident as ever. "But in any case, I'm interested. Do you know why people come here? To a place like this?" He gestured with his free arm to encompass the park.

"To be entertained," Megan told him as she followed the movement of his arm.

"You left out two of the most important reasons," he added. "To fantasize and to show off."

They stopped to watch a middle-aged man strip out of

his jacket and attempt to ring the bell. The hammer came down with a loud thump, but the ball rose only halfway up the pole. He rubbed his hands together and prepared to try again.

"Yes, you're right." Megan tossed her hair back with a move of her head, then smiled at Katch. "You ought to know."

He tilted his head and shot her a grin. "Want me to ring the bell?"

"Muscles don't impress me," she said firmly.

"No?" He guided her away with his arm still around her. "What does?"

"Poetry," Megan decided all at once.

"Hmm." Katch rubbed his chin and avoided a trio of teenagers. "How about a limerick? I know some great limericks."

"I bet you do." Megan shook her head. "I think I'll pass."

"Coward."

"Oh? Let's ride the roller coaster, then we'll see who's a coward."

"You're on." Taking her hand, he set off in a sprint. He stopped at the ticket booth, and gratefully she caught her breath.

I might as well face it, she reflected as she studied his face. I enjoy him. There isn't any use in pretending I don't.

"What are you thinking?" Katch demanded as he paid for their ride.

"That I could learn to like you—in three or four years. For short periods of time," she added, still smiling.

Katch took both her hands and kissed them, surprising Megan with the shock that raced up her arms. "Flatterer," he murmured, and his eyes laughed at her over their joined hands.

Distressed by the power she felt rushing through her system, Megan tried to tug her hands from his. It was imperative, for reasons only half-formed in her brain, that she keep their relationship casual.

"You have to hold my hand." Katch jerked his head toward the roller coaster. "I'm afraid of heights."

Megan laughed. She let herself forget the tempestuous instant and the hint of danger. She kept her hand in his.

Katch wasn't satisfied with only the roller coaster. He pulled Megan to ride after ride. They were scrambled on the Mind Maze, spooked in the Haunted Castle and spun lazily on the Ferris wheel.

From the top of the wheel, they watched the colored lights of the park, and the sea stretching out to the right. The wind tossed her hair into her face. Katch took it in his hand as they rose toward the top again. When he kissed her, it felt natural and right…a shared thing, a moment which belonged only to them. The noise and people below were of another world. Theirs was only the gentle movement of the wheel and the dance of the breeze. And the touch of mouth on mouth. There was no demand, only an offering of pleasure.

Megan relaxed against him, finding her head fit naturally in the curve of his shoulder. Held close beside him, she watched the world revolve. Above, the stars were scattered and few. A waning moon shifted in and out of the clouds. The air was cool with a hint of the sea. She sighed, utterly content.

"When's the last time you did this?"

"Did what?" Megan tilted her head to look at him. Their

faces were close, but she felt no danger now, only satisfaction.

"Enjoyed this park." Katch had caught the confusion on her face. "Just enjoyed it, Megan, for the fun."

"I..." The Ferris wheel slowed, then stopped. The carts rocked gently as old passengers were exchanged for new. She remembered times when she had been very young. When had they stopped? "I don't know." Megan rose when the attendant lifted the safety bar.

This time, as she walked with Katch, she looked around thoughtfully. She saw several people she knew; locals out for an evening's entertainment mixed with tourists taking a preseason vacation.

"You need to do this more often," Katch commented, steering her toward the east end of the park. "Laugh," he continued as she turned her head to him. "Unbend, relax those restrictions you put on yourself."

Megan's spine stiffened. "For somebody who barely knows me, you seem remarkably certain of what's good for me."

"It isn't difficult." He stopped at a concession wagon and ordered two ice-cream cones. "You haven't any mysteries, Meg."

"Thank you very much."

With a laugh, Katch handed her a cone. "Don't get huffy, I meant that as a compliment."

"I suppose you've known a lot of sophisticated women."

Katch smiled, then his arm came around her as they began to walk again. "There's one, her name's Jessica. She's one of the most beautiful women I know."

"Really?" Megan licked at the soft swirl of vanilla.

"That blond, classical look. You know, fair skin, finely chiseled features, blue eyes. Terrific blue eyes."

"How interesting."

"Oh, she's all of that," he continued. "And more: intelligent, a sense of humor."

"You sound very fond of her." Megan gave the ice cream her undivided attention.

"A bit more than that actually. Jessica and I lived together for a number of years." He dropped the bomb matter-of-factly. "She's married now and has a couple of kids, but we still manage to see each other now and again. Maybe she can make it down for a few days, then you can meet her."

"Oh, really!" Megan stopped, incensed. "Flaunt your relationship somewhere else. If you think I want to meet your—your…"

"Sister," Katch supplied, then crunched into his cone. "You'd like her. Your ice cream's dripping, Meg."

They walked to the entrance gates of the park.

"It's a very nice park," Katch murmured. "Small but well set up. No bored-faced attendants." He reached absently in his pocket and pulled out a slip of paper.

"I forgot to give you your check."

Megan stuffed it into her pocket without even glancing at it. Her eyes were on Katch's face. She was all too aware of the direction his thoughts had taken. "My grandfather's devoted his life to this park," she reminded him.

"So have you," Katch said.

"Why do you want to buy it?" she asked. "To make money?"

Katch was silent for a long moment. By mutual consent, they cut across the boardwalk and moved down the sloping sand toward the water. "Is that such a bad reason, Megan? Do you object to making money?"

"No, of course not. That would be ridiculous."

"I wondered if that was why you haven't done anything with your sculpting."

"No. I do what I'm capable of doing, and what I have time for. There are priorities."

"Perhaps you have them wrong." Before she could comment, he spoke again. "How would it affect the park's business if it had some updated rides and an expanded arcade?"

"We can't afford…"

"That wasn't my question." He took her by the shoulders and his eyes were serious.

"Business would improve, naturally," Megan answered. "People come here to be entertained. The more entertainment provided, the slicker, the faster the entertainment, the happier they are. And the more money they spend."

Katch nodded as he searched her face. "Those were my thoughts."

"It's academic because we simply haven't the sort of money necessary for an overhaul."

"Hmm?" Though he was looking directly at her, Megan saw that his attention had wandered. She watched it refocus.

"What are you thinking?" she demanded.

The grip on her shoulder altered to a caress. "That you're extraordinarily beautiful."

Megan pulled away. "No, you weren't."

"It's what I'm thinking now." The gleam was back in his eyes as he put his hands to her waist. "It's what I was thinking the first time I saw you."

"You're ridiculous." She made an attempt to pull away, but he caught her closer.

"I've never denied that. But you can't call me ridiculous for finding you beautiful." The wind blew her hair back, leaving her face unframed. He laid a soft, unexpected kiss on her forehead. Megan felt her knees turn to water. She placed her hands on his chest both for support and in protest. "You're an artist." He drew her fractionally closer, and his voice lowered. "You recognize beauty when you see it."

"Don't!" The protest was feeble as she made no attempt to struggle out of his gentle hold.

"Don't what? Don't kiss you?" Slowly, luxuriously, his mouth journeyed over her skin. "But I have to, Meg." His lips touched hers softly, then withdrew, and her heart seemed to stop. The flavor of his lips as they brushed against hers overwhelmed her. They tempted, then ruled. With a moan of pleasure, Megan drew him close against her.

Something seemed to explode inside her as the kiss deepened. She clung to him a moment, dazed, then terrified by the power of it. Needs, emotions and new sensations tumbled together too quickly for her to control them. As panic swamped her, Megan struggled in his arms. She would have run, blindly, without direction, but Katch took her arms and held her still.

"What is it? You're trembling." Gently, he tilted her chin until their eyes met. Hers were wide, his serious. "I didn't mean to frighten you. I'm sorry."

The gentleness was nearly her undoing. Love, so newly discovered, hammered for release. She shook her head, knowing her voice would be thick with tears if she spoke. Swallowing, Megan prayed she could steady it.

"No, it's…I have to get back. They're closing." Behind him, she could see the lights flickering off.

"Meg." The tone halted her. It was not a demand this time, but a request. "Have dinner with me."

"No—"

"I haven't even suggested an evening," he pointed out mildly. "How about Monday?"

Megan stood firm. "No."

"Please."

Her resolution dissolved on a sigh. "You don't play fair," she murmured.

"Never. How about seven?"

"No picnics on the beach," she compromised.

"We'll eat inside, I promise."

"All right, but just dinner." She stepped away from him. "Now, I have to go."

"I'll walk you back." Katch took her hand and kissed it before she could stop him. "I have to get my elephant."

Chapter 6

Megan held Katch's face in her hands. With totally focused absorption, she formed his cheekbones. She had thought when she had first begun to work on this bust that morning that it would be good therapy. To an extent, she'd been right. The hours had passed peacefully, without the restless worry of the past two nights. Her mind was centered on her work, leaving no spaces for the disturbing thoughts that had plagued her all weekend.

She opened and closed her hands slowly, using the muscles until the cramping was a dull ache. A glance at her watch told her she had worked for longer than she'd intended. Late afternoon sun poured through the windows. Critically, as she pulled on each finger to soothe it, Megan studied her work.

The model was good, she decided, with just the proper touches of roughness and intelligence she had aimed for. The mouth was strong and sensuous, the eyes perceptive and far too aware. The mobility of the face which Megan found fascinating could only be suggested. It was a face that urged one to trust against better judgment and common sense.

Narrowing her eyes, she studied the clay replica of Katch's face. There are certain men, she thought, who make a career out of women—winning them, making love to them, leaving them. There are other men who settle down and marry, raise families. How could she doubt which category Katch fell into?

Megan rose to wash her hands. Infatuation, she reflected. It's simply infatuation. He's different, and I can't deny he's exciting. I wouldn't be human if I weren't flattered that he's attracted to me. I've overreacted, that's all. She dried her hands on a towel and tried to convince herself. A person doesn't fall in love this quickly. And if they do, it's just a surface thing, nothing lasting. Megan's eyes were drawn to the clay model. Katch's smile seemed to mock all her sensible arguments. She hurled the towel to the floor.

"It can't happen this fast!" she told him furiously. "Not this way. Not to me." She swung away from his assured expression. "I won't let it."

It's only the park he wants, she reminded herself. Once he's finally convinced he can't have it, he'll go away. The ache was unexpected, and unwelcome. That's what I want, she thought. For him to go away and leave us alone. She tried not to remember the new frontiers she had glimpsed while being held in his arms.

With a brisk shake of her head, Megan pulled the tie from her hair so that it tumbled back to brush her shoulders. I'll start in wood tomorrow, she decided, and covered the clay model. Tonight, I'll simply enjoy a dinner date with an attractive man. It's that simple.

With a great deal more ease than she was feeling, Megan took off her work smock and left her studio.

"Hi, sweetheart." Pop pulled the truck into the driveway just as Megan reached the bottom step.

She noticed the weariness the moment he climbed from the cab. Knowing he hated fussing, she said nothing, but walked over and slipped an arm around his waist.

"Hi, yourself. You've been gone a long time."

"A problem or two at the park," he told her as they moved together toward the house.

That explained the weariness, Megan thought as she pushed open the back door. "What sort of problem?" Megan waited for him to settle himself at the kitchen table before she walked to the stove to brew tea.

"Repairs, Megan, just repairs. The coaster and the Octopus and a few of the smaller rides." He leaned back in his chair as Megan turned to face him.

"How bad?"

Pop sighed, knowing it was better to tell her outright than to hedge. "Ten thousand, maybe fifteen."

Megan let out a long, steady breath. "Ten thousand dollars." She ran a hand under her bangs to rub her brow. There was no purpose in asking if he was sure. If he'd had any doubt, he'd have kept the matter to himself.

"Well, we can come up with five," she began, lumping the check she had just received from Katch into their savings. "We'll have to have a more exact amount so we can decide how big a loan we'll need."

"Banks take a dim view of lending great lumps of money to people my age," Pop murmured.

Because she saw he was tired and discouraged, she spoke briskly. "Don't be silly." She walked back to the stove to set on the kettle. "In any case, they'd be lending it to the park, wouldn't they?" She tried not to think of tight money and high interest rates.

"I'll go see a few people tomorrow," he promised, reaching for his pipe as if to indicate their business talk was over. "You're having dinner with Katch tonight?"

"Yes." Megan took out cups and saucers.

"Fine young man." He puffed pleasantly on his pipe. "I like him. Has style."

"He has style all right," she grumbled as the kettle began to sing. Carefully, she poured boiling water into cups.

"Knows how to fish," Pop pointed out.

"Which, of course, makes him a paragon of virtue."

"Well, it doesn't make me think any less of him." He spoke genially, smiling into Megan's face. "I couldn't help noticing the two of you on the wheel the other night. You looked real pretty together."

"Pop, really." Feeling her cheeks warm, Megan walked back to fiddle with the dishes in the sink.

"You seemed to like him well enough then," he pointed out before he tested his tea. "I didn't notice any objections when he kissed you." Pop sipped, enjoying. "In fact, you seemed to like it."

"Pop!" Megan turned back, astonished.

"Now, Meg, I wasn't spying," he said soothingly, and coughed to mask a chuckle. "You were right out in public, you know. I'd wager a lot of people noticed. Like I said, you looked real pretty together."

Megan came back to sit at the table without any idea of what she should say. "It was just a kiss," she managed at length. "It didn't mean anything."

Pop nodded twice and drank his tea.

"It didn't," Megan insisted.

He gave her one of his angelic smiles. "But you do like him, don't you?"

Megan dropped her eyes. "Sometimes," she murmured. "Sometimes I do."

Pop covered her hand with his and waited until she looked at him again. "Caring for someone is the easiest thing in the world if you let it be."

"I hardly know him," she said quickly.

"I trust him," Pop said simply.

Megan searched his face. "Why?"

After a shrug, Pop drew on his pipe again. "A feeling I have, a look in his eyes. In a people business like mine, you get to be a good judge of character. He has integrity. He wants his way, all right, but he doesn't cheat. That's important."

Megan sat silently for a moment, not touching her cooling tea. "He wants the park," she said quietly.

Pop looked at her through a nimbus of pipe smoke. "Yes, I know. He said so up front. He doesn't sneak around either." Pop's expression softened a bit as he looked into Megan's eyes. "Things don't always stay the same in life, Megan. That's what makes it work."

"I don't know what you mean. Do you…are you thinking of selling him the park?"

Pop heard the underlying hint of panic and patted her hand again. "Let's not worry about that now. The first problem is getting the rides repaired for the Easter break.

Why don't you wear the yellow dress I like tonight, Meg? The one with the little jacket. It makes me think of spring."

Megan considered questioning him further, then subsided. There was no harder nut to crack than her grandfather when he had made up his mind to close a subject. "All right. I think I'll go up and have a bath."

"Megan." She turned at the door and looked back at him. "Enjoy yourself. Sometimes it's best to roll with the punches."

When she walked away, he looked at the empty doorway and thoughtfully stroked his beard.

An hour later, Megan looked at herself in the yellow dress. The shade hinted at apricot and warmed against her skin. The lines were simple, suiting her willow-slim figure and height. Without the jacket, her arms and shoulders were bare but for wispy straps. She ran a brush through her hair in long, steady strokes. The tiny gold hoops in her ears were her only jewelry.

"Hey, Megan!"

The brush paused in midair as she watched her own eyes widen in the mirror. He wasn't really standing outside shouting for her!

"Meg!"

Shaking her head in disbelief, Megan went to the window. Katch stood two stories down. He lifted a hand in salute when she appeared in the window.

"What are you doing?" she demanded.

"Open the screen."

"Why?"

"Open it," he repeated.

"If you expect me to jump, you can forget it." Out of curiosity, she leaned out the window.

"Catch!"

Her reflexes responded before she could think. Megan reached for the bundle he tossed up to her, and found her hands full of daffodils. She buried her face in the bouquet.

"They're beautiful." Her eyes smiled over the blooms and down at him. "Thank you."

"You're welcome," he returned. "Are you coming down?"

"Yes." She tossed her hair behind her shoulder. "Yes, yes, in a minute."

Katch drove quickly and competently, but not toward Restaurant Row as Megan had anticipated. He turned toward the ocean and headed north. She relaxed, enjoying the quieting light of dusk and his effortless driving.

She recognized the area. The houses there were larger, more elaborate than those in and on the very outskirts of town. There were tall hedges to assure privacy both from other houses and the public beaches. There were neatly trimmed lawns, willows, blossoming crepe myrtle, and asphalt drives. Katch pulled into one set well away from the other homes and bordered by purplish shrubbery.

The house was small by the neighborhood standards, and done in the weathered wood Megan invariably found attractive. It was a split-level building, with an observation deck crowning the upper story.

"What's this?" she asked, liking the house immediately.

"This is where I live." Katch leaned across her to unlatch her door, then slid out his own side.

"You live here?"

Katch smiled at the surprised doubt in her voice. "I have to live somewhere, Meg."

She wandered farther along the stone path that led to

the house. "I suppose I really didn't think about you buying a house here. It suggests roots."

"I have them," he told her. "I just transplant them easily."

She looked at the house, the widespread yard. "You've picked the perfect spot."

Katch took her hand, interlocking fingers. "Come inside," he invited.

"When did you buy this?" she asked as they climbed the front steps.

"Oh, a few months ago when I came through. I moved in last week and haven't had a lot of time to look for furniture." The key shot into the lock. "I've picked up a few things here and there, and had others sent down from my apartment in New York."

It was scantily furnished, but with style. There was a low, sectional sofa in biscuit with a hodgepodge of colored pillows and a wicker throne chair coupled with a large hanging ivy in a pottery dish. A pair of étagères in brass and glass held a collection of shells; on the oak planked floor lay a large sisal rug.

The room was open, with stairs to the right leading to the second level, and a stone fireplace on the left wall. The quick survey showed Megan he had not placed her sculptures in the main room. She wondered fleetingly what he had done with them.

"It's wonderful, Katch." She wandered to a window. The lawn sloped downward and ended in tall hedges that gave the house comfortable privacy. "Can you see the ocean from the top level?"

When he didn't answer, she turned back to him. Her smile faded against the intensity of his gaze. Her heart beat faster. This was the part of him she had to fear, not the amiable gallant who had tossed her daffodils.

She tilted her head back, afraid, but wanting to meet him equally. He brought his hands to her face, and she felt the hardness of his palms on her skin. He brushed her hair back from her face as he brought her closer. He lowered his mouth, pausing only briefly before it claimed hers, as if to ascertain the need mirrored in her eyes. The kiss was instantly deep, instantly seeking.

She had been a fool—a fool to believe she could talk herself out of being in love with him. A fool to think that reason had anything to do with the heart.

When Katch drew her away, Megan pressed her cheek against his chest, letting her arms wind their way around his waist. His hesitation was almost too brief to measure before he gathered her close. She felt his lips in her hair and sighed from the sheer joy of it. His heartbeat was quick and steady in her ear.

"Did you say something?" he murmured.

"Hmm? When?"

"Before." His fingers came up to massage the back of her neck. Megan shivered with pleasure as she tried to remember the world before she had been in his arms.

"I think I asked if I could see the ocean from the top level."

"Yes." Again he took his hands to her face to tilt it back for one long, searing kiss. "You can."

"Will you show me?"

The grip on her skin tightened and her eyes closed in anticipation of the next kiss. But he drew her away until only their hands were touching. "After dinner."

Megan, content with looking at him, smiled. "Are we eating here?"

"I hate restaurants," Katch said, leading her toward the kitchen.

"An odd sentiment from a man who owns one."

"Let's say there are times when I prefer more intimate surroundings."

"I see." He pushed open the door to the kitchen and Megan glanced around at efficiency in wood and stainless steel. "And who's doing the cooking this time?"

"We are," he said easily, and grinned at her. "How do you like your steak?"

There was a rich, red wine to accompany the meal they ate at a smoked-glass table. A dozen candles flickered on a sideboard behind them, held in small brass holders. Megan's mood was as mellow as the wine that waltzed in her head. The man across from her held her in the palm of his hand. When she rose to stack the dishes, he took her hand. "Not now. There's a moon tonight."

Without hesitation, she went with him.

They climbed the stairs together, wide, uncarpeted stairs which were split into two sections by a landing. He led her through the main bedroom, a room dominated by a large bed with brass head-and footboards. There were long glass doors which led to a walkway. From there, stairs ascended to the observation deck.

Megan could hear the breakers before she moved to the rail. Beyond the hedgerow, the surf was turbulent. White water frothed against the dark. The moon's light was thin, but was aided by the power of uncountable stars.

She took a long breath and leaned on the rail. "It's lovely here. I never tire of looking at the ocean." There was a click from his lighter, then tobacco mixed pleasantly with the scent of the sea.

"Do you ever think about traveling?"

Megan moved her shoulders, a sudden, restless gesture. "Of course, sometimes. It isn't possible right now."

Katch drew on the thin cigar. "Where would you go?"

"Where would I go?" she repeated.

"Yes, where would you go if you could?" The smoke from his cigar wafted upward and vanished. "Pretend, Meg. You like to pretend, don't you?"

She closed her eyes a moment, letting the wine swim with her thoughts. "New Orleans," she murmured. "I've always wanted to see New Orleans. And Paris. When I was young I used to dream about studying in Paris like the great artists." She opened her eyes again. "You've been there, I suppose. To New Orleans and to Paris?"

"Yes, I've been there."

"What are they like?"

Katch traced the line of her jaw with a fingertip before answering. "New Orleans smells of the river and swelters in the summer. There's music at all hours from open night-clubs and street musicians. It moves constantly, like New York, but at a more civilized pace."

"And Paris?" Megan insisted, wanting to see her wishes through his eyes. "Tell me about Paris."

"It's ancient and elegant, like a grand old woman. It's not very clean, but it never seems to matter. It's best in the spring; nothing smells like Paris in the spring. I'd like to take you there." Unexpectedly he took her hair in his hand. His eyes were intense again and direct on hers. "I'd like to see the emotions you control break loose. You'd never restrict them in Paris."

"I don't do that." Something more than wine began to swim in her head.

He tossed the cigar over the rail, then his free hand came to her waist to press her body against his. "Don't you?" There was a hint of impatience in his voice as he began to slide the jacket from her shoulders. "You've passion, but you bank it down. It escapes into your work, but even that's kept closed up in a studio. When I kiss you, I can taste it struggling to the surface."

He freed her arms from the confines of the jacket and laid it over the rail. Slowly, deliberately, he ran his fingers over the naked skin, feeling the warmth of response. "One day it's going to break loose. I intend to be there when it does."

Katch pushed the straps from her shoulders and replaced them with his lips. Megan made no protest as the kisses trailed to her throat. His tongue played lightly with the pulse as his hand came up to cup her breast. But when his mouth came to hers, the gentleness fled, and with it her passivity. Hunger incited hunger.

When he nipped her bottom lip, she gasped with pleasure. His tongue was avid, searching while his hands began a quest of their own. He slipped the bodice of her dress to her waist, murmuring with approval as he found her naked breasts taut with desire. Megan allowed him his freedom, riding on the crest of the wave that rose inside her. She had no knowledge to guide her, no experience. Desire ruled and instinct followed.

She trailed her fingers along the back of his neck, kneading the warm skin, thrilling to the response she felt to her touch. Here was a power she had never explored. She slipped her hands under the back of his sweater. Their journey was slow, exploring. She felt the muscles of his shoulders tense as her hands played over them.

The quality of the kiss changed from demanding to urgent. His passion swamped her, mixing with her own until the combined power was more than she could bear. The ache came from nowhere and spread through her with impossible rapidity. She hurt for him. Desire was a pain as sharp as it was irresistible. In surrender, in anticipation, Megan swayed against him.

"Katch." Her voice was husky. "I want to stay with you tonight."

She was crushed against him for a moment, held so tightly, so strongly, there was no room for breath. Then, slowly, she felt him loosen his hold. Taking her by the shoulders, Katch looked down at her, his eyes dark, spearing into hers. Her breath was uneven; shivers raced along her skin. Slowly, with hands that barely touched her skin, he slipped her dress back into place.

"I'll take you home now."

The shock of rejection struck her like a blow. Her mouth trembled open, then shut again. Quickly, fighting against the tears that were pressing for release, she fumbled for her jacket.

"Meg." He reached out to touch her shoulders, but she backed away.

"No. No, don't touch me." The tears were thickening her voice. She swallowed. "I won't be patted on the head. It appears I misunderstood."

"You didn't misunderstand anything," he tossed back. "And don't cry, damn it."

"I have no intention of crying," she said. "I'd like to go

home." The hurt was in her eyes, shimmering behind the tears she denied.

"We'll talk." Katch took her hand, but she jerked it away.

"Oh, no. No, we won't." Megan straightened her shoulders and looked at him squarely. "We had dinner—things got a bit beyond what they should have. It's as simple as that, and it's over."

"It's not simple or over, Meg." Katch took another long look into her eyes. "But we'll drop it for now."

Megan turned away and walked back down the stairs.

Chapter 7

Amusement parks lose their mystique in the light of day. Dirt, scratched paint and dents show up. What is shiny and bright under artificial light is ordinary in the sunshine. Only the very young or the very young hearted can believe in magic when faced with reality.

Megan knew her grandfather was perennially young. She loved him for it. Fondly, she watched him supervising repairs on the Haunted Castle. His ghosts, she thought with a smile, are important to him. She walked beside the track, avoiding her own ghost along the way. It had been ten days since Pop had told her of the repair problems. Ten days since she had seen Katch. Megan pushed thoughts of him from her mind and concentrated on her own reality—her grandfather and their park. She was old enough to know what was real and what was fantasy.

"Hi," she called out from behind him. "How are things going?"

Pop turned at the sound of her voice, and his grin was

expansive. “Just fine, Megan.” The sound of repairs echoed around his words. “Quicker than I thought they would. We’ll be rolling before the Easter rush.” He swung an arm around her shoulder and squeezed. “The smaller rides are already back in order. How about you?”

She made no objection when he began to steer her outside. The noise made it difficult to hear. “What about me?” she replied. The sudden flash of sunlight made her blink. The spring day had all the heat of midsummer.

“You’ve that unhappy look in your eyes. Have had, for more than a week.” Pop rubbed his palm against her shoulder as if to warm her despite the strength of the sun. “You know you don’t hide things from me, Megan. I know you too well.”

She was silent a moment, wanting to choose her words carefully. “I wasn’t trying to hide anything, Pop.” Megan shrugged, turning to watch the crew working on the roller coaster. “It’s just not important enough to talk about, that’s all. How long before the coaster’s fixed?”

“Important enough to make you unhappy,” he countered, ignoring her evasion. “That’s plenty important to me. You haven’t gotten too old to talk to me about your problems now, have you?”

She turned dark apologetic eyes on him. “Oh no, Pop, I can always talk to you.”

“Well,” he said simply, “I’m listening.”

“I made a mistake, that’s all.” She shook her head and would have walked closer to inspect the work crew had he not held her to him with a firm hand.

“Megan.” Pop placed both hands on her shoulders and looked into her eyes. As they were nearly the same height, their eyes were level. "I'm going to ask you straight," he continued. "Are you in love with him?"

"No," she denied quickly.

Pop raised an eyebrow. "I didn't have to mention any names, I see."

Megan paused a moment. She had forgotten how shrewd her grandfather could be. "I thought I was," she said more carefully. "I was wrong."

"Then why are you so unhappy?"

"Pop, please." She tried to back away, but again his broad hands held her steady.

"You've always given me straight answers, Meg, even when I've had to drag them out of you."

She sighed, knowing evasions and half-truths were useless when he was in this mood. "All right. Yes, I'm in love with him, but it doesn't matter."

"Not a very bright statement from a bright girl like you," he said with a gentle hint of disapproval. Megan shrugged. "Why don't you explain why being in love doesn't matter," he invited.

"Well, it certainly doesn't work if you're not loved back," Megan murmured.

"Who says you're not?" Pop wanted to know. His voice was so indignant, she felt some of the ache subside.

"Pop." Her expression softened. "Just because you love me doesn't mean everyone else does."

"What makes you so sure he doesn't?" her grandfather argued. "Did you ask him?"

"No!" Megan was so astonished, she nearly laughed at the thought.

"Why not? Things are simpler that way."

Megan took a deep breath, hoping to make him understand. "David Katcherton isn't a man who falls in love with a woman, not seriously. And certainly not with someone like me." The broad gesture she made was an attempt to enhance an explanation she knew was far from adequate. "He's been to Paris, he lives in New York. He has a sister named Jessica."

"That clears things up," Pop agreed, and Megan made a quick sound of frustration.

"I've never been anywhere." She dragged a hand through her hair. "In the summer I see millions, literally millions of people, but they're all transient. I don't know who they are. The only people I really know are ones who live right here. The farthest I've been away from the beach is Charleston."

Pop brushed a hand over her hair to smooth it. "I've kept you too close," he murmured. "I always told myself there'd be other times."

"Oh no, Pop, I didn't mean it that way." She threw her arms around him, burying her face in his shoulder. "I didn't mean to sound that way. I love you, I love it here. I wouldn't change anything. That was hateful of me."

He laughed and patted her back. The subtle scent of her perfume reminded him forcefully that she was no longer a girl but a woman. The years had been incredibly quick. "You've never done a hateful thing in your life. We both know you've wanted to see a bit of the world, and I know you've stuck close to keep an eye on me. Oh yes," he said, anticipating her objection. "And I was selfish enough to let you."

"You've never done anything selfish," she retorted and drew away. "I only meant that Katch and I have so little common ground. He's bound to see things differently than I do. I'm out of my depth with him."

"You're a strong swimmer, as I recall." Pop shook his head at her expression and sighed. "All right, we'll let it lie awhile. You're also stubborn."

"Adamant," she corrected, smiling again. "It's a nicer word."

"Just a fancy way of saying pigheaded," Pop said bluntly, but his eyes smiled back at her. "Why aren't you back in your studio instead of hanging around an amusement park in the middle of the day?"

"It wasn't going very well," she confessed, thinking of the half-carved face that haunted her. "Besides, I've always had a thing for amusement parks." She tucked her arm in his as they began to walk again.

"Well, this one'll be in apple-pie order in another week," Pop said, looking around in satisfaction. "With luck, we'll have a good season and be able to pay back a healthy chunk of that ten thousand."

"Maybe the bank will send us some customers so they'll get their money faster," Megan suggested, half listening to the sound of hammer against wood as they drew closer to the roller coaster.

"Oh, I didn't get the money from the bank, I got it from—" Pop cut himself off abruptly. With a cough and a wheeze, he bent down to tie his shoe.

"You didn't get the money from the bank?" Megan frowned at the snowy white head in puzzlement. "Well, where in the world did you get it then?"

His answer was an unintelligible grunt.

"You don't know anybody with that kind of money," she began with a half-smile. "Where..." The smile flew away. "No. No, you didn't." Even as she denied it, Megan knew it had to be the truth. "You didn't get it from him?"

"Oh now, Megan, you weren't to know." Distress showed in his eyes and seemed to weaken his voice. "He especially didn't want you to know."

"Why?" she demanded. "Why did you do it?"

"It just sort of happened, Meg." Pop reached out to pat her hand in his old, soothing fashion. "He was here, I was telling him about the repairs and getting a loan, and he offered. It seemed like the perfect solution." He fiddled with his shoestrings. "Banks poke around and take all that time for paperwork, and he isn't charging me nearly as much interest. I thought you'd be happy about that…" He trailed off.

"Is everything in writing?" she asked, deadly calm.

"Of course." Pop assumed a vaguely injured air. "Katch said it didn't matter, but I know how fussy you are, so I had papers drawn up, nice and legal."

"Didn't matter," she repeated softly. "And what did you use as collateral?"

"The park, naturally."

"Naturally," she repeated. Fury bubbled in the single word. "I bet he loved that."

"Now, don't you worry, Megan. Everything's coming along just fine. The repairs are going well, and we'll be opening right on schedule. Besides," he added with a sigh, "you weren't even supposed to know. Katch wanted it that way."

"Oh, I'm sure he did," she said bitterly. "I'm sure he did."

Turning, she darted away. Pop watched her streak out of sight, then hauled himself to his feet. She had the devil's own temper when she cut loose, that girl. Brushing his hands together, he grinned. That, he decided, pleased with his own maneuvering, should stir up something.

* * *

Megan brought the bike to a halt at the crest of Katch's drive, then killed the engine. She took off her helmet and clipped it on the seat. He was not, she determined, going to get away with it.

Cutting across the lawn, she marched to the front door. The knock was closer to a pound but still brought no response. Megan stuffed her hands into her pockets and scowled. Her bike sat behind his black Porsche. Ignoring amenities, she tried the knob. When it turned, she didn't hesitate. She opened the door and walked inside.

The house was quiet. Instinct told her immediately that no one was inside. Still, she walked through the living room looking for signs of him.

A watch, wafer-thin and gold, was tossed on the glass shelves of the étagère. A Nikon camera sat on the coffee table, its back open and empty of film. A pair of disreputable tennis shoes was half under the couch. A volume of John Cheever lay beside them.

Abruptly, she realized what she had done. She'd intruded where she had no right. She was both uncomfortable and fascinated. An ashtray held the short stub of a thin cigar. After a brief struggle with her conscience, she walked toward the kitchen. She wasn't prying, she told herself, only making certain he wasn't home. After all, his car was here and the door had been unlocked.

There was a cup in the sink and a half pot of cold coffee on the stove. He had spilled some on the counter and neglected to wipe it up. Megan curtailed the instinctive move to reach for a dish towel. As she turned to leave, a low mechanical hum from outside caught her attention. She walked to the window and saw him.

He was coming from the south side of the lawn, striding behind a power mower. He was naked to the waist, with jeans low and snug at his hips. He was tanned, a deep honey gold that glistened now with the effort of manual labor. She admired the play of muscles rippling down his arms and across his back.

Stepping back from the window with a jerk, she stormed through the side kitchen door and raced across the lawn.

The flurry of movement and a flash of crimson caught his eye. Katch glanced over as Megan moved toward him in a red tailored shirt and white jeans. Squinting against the sun, he wiped the back of his hand across his brow. He reached down and shut off the mower as she came to him.

"Hello, Meg," he said lightly, but his eyes weren't as casual.

"You have nerve, Katcherton," she began. "But even I didn't think you'd take advantage of a trusting old man."

He lifted a brow and leaned against the mower's handle. "Once more," he requested, "with clarity."

"You're the type who has to poke your fingers into other people's business," she continued. "You just had to be at the park, you just had to make a magnanimous offer with your tidy little pile of money."

"Ah, a glimmer of light." He stretched his back. "I didn't think you'd be thrilled the money came from me. It seems I was right."

"You knew I'd never allow it," she declared.

"I don't believe I considered that." He leaned on the mower again, but there was nothing restful in the gesture. "You don't run Pop's life from what I've seen, Meg, and you certainly don't run mine."

She did her best to keep her tone even. "I have a great

deal of interest in the park and everything that pertains to it."

"Fine, then you should be pleased that you have the money for the repairs quickly, and at a low rate of interest." His tone was cool and businesslike.

"Why?" she demanded. "Why did you lend us the money?"

"I don't," Katch said after a long, silent moment, "owe you any explanation."

"Then I'll give you one," Megan tossed back. There was passion in her voice. "You saw an opportunity and grabbed it. I suppose that's what people do in your sort of world. Take, without the least thought of the people involved."

"Perhaps I'm confused." His eyes were slate, opaque and unreadable. His voice matched them. "I was under the impression that I gave something."

"*Lent* something," Megan corrected. "With the park as collateral."

"If that's your problem, take it up with your grandfather." Katch bent down, reaching for the cord to restart the mower.

"You had no right to take advantage of him. He trusts everyone."

Katch released the cord again with a snap. "A shame it's not an inherited quality."

"I've no reason to trust you."

"And every reason, it appears, to mistrust me since the first moment." His eyes had narrowed as if in speculation. "Is it just me or a general antipathy to men?"

She refused to dignify the question with an answer. "You want the park," she began.

"Yes, and I made that clear from the beginning." Katch shoved the mower aside so that there was no obstacle between them. "I still intend to have it, but I don't need to be devious to get it. I still intend to have you." She stepped back but he was too quick. His fingers curled tightly around her upper arm. "Maybe I made a mistake by letting you go the other night."

"You didn't want me. It's just a game."

"Didn't want you?" She made another quick attempt to pull away and failed. "No, that's right, I didn't want you." He pulled her against him and her mouth was crushed and conquered. Her mind whirled with the shock of it. "I don't want you now." Before she could speak, his mouth savaged hers again. There was a taste of brutality he had never shown her. "Like I haven't wanted you for days." He pulled her to the ground.

"No," she said, frightened, "don't." But his lips were silencing hers again.

There was none of the teasing persuasion he had shown her before, no light arrogance. These were primordial demands, eliciting primordial responses from her. He would take what he wanted, his way. He plundered, dragging her with him as he raced for more. Then his lips left hers, journeying to her throat before traveling downward. Megan felt she was suffocating, suffused with heat. Her breath caught in her lungs, emerging in quick gasps or moans. His fingers ran a bruising trail over her quivering flesh. He ran his thumb over the point of her breast, back and forth, until she was beyond fear, beyond thought. His mouth came back to hers, fever hot, desperate. She murmured mindlessly, clinging to him as her body shuddered with waves of need.

Katch lifted his head, and his breath was warm and erratic on her face. Megan's lids fluttered open, revealing eyes dazed with passion, heavy with desire. Silently, she trembled. If words had been hers, she would have told him that she loved him. There was no pride in her, no shame, only soaring need and a love that was painful in its strength.

"This isn't the place for you." His voice was rough as he rolled over on his back. They lay there a moment, side by side, without touching. "And this isn't the way."

Her mind was fogged, and her blood surging. "Katch," Megan managed his name and struggled to sit up. His eyes lingered on her form, then slid up slowly to brood on her face. It was flushed and aware. She wanted to touch him but was afraid.

For a moment their eyes met. "Did I hurt you?"

She shook her head in denial. Her body ached with longing.

"Go home then." He rose, giving her a last, brief glance. "Before I do." He turned and left her.

Megan heard the slam of the kitchen door.

Chapter 8

It was difficult for Megan to cope with the two-week influx of tourists and sun seekers. They came, as they did every Easter, in droves. It was a preview of what the summer would hold. They came to bake on the beach and impress those left at home with a spring tan. They came to be battered and bounced around by the waves. They came to have fun. And what better place to find it than on white sand beaches or in an ocean with a gentle undertow and cresting waves? They came to laugh and sought their entertainment on spiraling water slides, in noisy arcades or crowded amusement parks.

For the first time in her life, Megan found herself resenting the intrusion. She wanted the quiet, the solitude that went with a resort town in its off-season. She wanted to be alone, to work, to heal. It seemed her art was the only thing she could turn to for true comfort. She was unwilling to speak of her feelings to her grandfather. There was still too much to be sorted out in her own mind. Knowing her, and her need for privacy, Pop didn't question.

The hours she spent at the park were passed mechanically. The faces she saw were all strangers. Megan resented it. She resented their enjoyment when her own life was in such turmoil. She found solace in her studio. If the light in her studio burned long past midnight, she never noticed the time. Her energy was boundless, a nervous, trembling energy that kept her going.

It was afternoon at the amusement park. At the kiddie cars Megan was taking tickets and doing her best to keep the more aggressive youngsters from trampling others. Each time the fire engines, race cars, police cruisers and ambulances were loaded, she pushed the lever which sent the caravan around in its clanging, roaring circle. Children grinned fiercely and gripped steering wheels.

One toddler rode as fire chief with eyes wide with stunned pleasure. Even though she'd been on duty nearly four hours, Megan smiled.

"Excuse me." Megan glanced over at the voice, prepared to answer a parental question. The woman was an exquisite blonde, with a mane of hair tied back from a delicately molded face. "You're Megan, aren't you? Megan Miller?"

"Yes. May I help you?"

"I'm Jessica Delaney."

Megan wondered that she hadn't seen it instantly. "Katch's sister."

"Yes." Jessica smiled. "How clever of you—but Katch told me you were. There is a family resemblance, of course, but so few people notice it unless we're standing together."

Megan's artist eyes could see the similar bone structure

beneath the surface differences. Jessica's eyes were blue, as Katch had said, and the brows above them more delicate than his, but there were the same thick lashes and long lids.

"I'm glad to meet you." Megan reached for something to say. "Are you visiting Katch?" She didn't look like a woman who would patronize amusement parks, more likely country clubs or theaters.

"For a day or so." Jessica gestured to the adjoining ride where children flew miniature piper cubs in the inevitable circle. "My family's with me. Rob, my husband." Megan smiled at a tall man with a straight shock of dark hair and an attractive, angular face. "And my girls, Erin and Laura." She nodded to the two caramel-haired girls of approximately four and six riding double in a plane.

"They're beautiful."

"We like them," Jessica said comfortably. "Katch didn't know where I might find you in the park, but he described you very accurately."

"Is he here?" Megan asked, trying without much success to sound offhanded even as her eyes scanned the crowd.

"No, he had some business to attend to."

The timer rang, signaling the ride's end. "Excuse me a moment," Megan murmured. Grateful for the interruption, she supervised the unloading and loading of children. It gave her the time she needed to steady herself. Her two final customers were Katch's nieces. Erin, the elder, smiled at her with eyes the identical shade of her uncle's.

"I'm driving," she said positively as her sister settled beside her. "She only rides."

"I do not." Laura gripped the twin steering wheel passionately.

"It runs in the family," Jessica stated from behind her.

"Stubbornness." Megan hooked the last safety belt and returned to the controls. "You've probably noticed it."

Megan smiled at her. "Yes, once or twice." The lights and noise spun and circled behind her.

"I know you're busy," Jessica stated, glancing at the packed vehicles.

Megan gave a small shrug as she followed her gaze. "It's mostly a matter of making certain everyone stays strapped in and no one's unhappy."

"My little angels," Jessica said, "will insist on dashing off to the next adventure the moment the ride's over." She paused. "Could we talk after you're finished here?"

Megan frowned. "Well, yes, I suppose…I'm due relief in an hour."

"Wonderful." Jessica's smile was as charming as her brother's. "I'd like to go to your studio, if that suits you. I could meet you in an hour and a half."

"At my studio?"

"Wonderful!" Jessica said again and patted Megan's hand. "Katch gave me directions."

The timer rang again, recalling Megan to duty. As she started yet another round of junior rides she wondered why Jessica had insisted on a date in her studio.

With a furrowed brow, Megan studied herself in the bedroom mirror. Would a man who admired Jessica's soft, delicate beauty be attracted to someone who seemed to be all planes and angles? Megan shrugged her shoulders as if it didn't matter. She twirled the stem of the brush idly between her fingers. She supposed that he, like the majority of people who came here, was looking for some passing entertainment

"You are," she said softly to the woman in the glass, "such a fool." She closed her eyes, not wanting to see the reflected accusation. Because you can't let go, her mind continued ruthlessly. Because it doesn't really matter to you why he wanted you with him, just that he wanted you. And you wish, you wish with all your heart that he still did.

She shook her head, disturbing the work she had done with the brush. It was time to stop thinking of it. Jessica Delaney would be arriving any moment.

Why? Megan set down her brush and frowned into middle distance. Why was she coming? What could she possibly want? Megan still had no sensible answer. I haven't heard from Katch in two weeks, she reflected. Why should his sister suddenly want to see me?

The sound of a car pulling into the drive below interrupted her thoughts. Megan walked to the window in time to see Jessica get out of Katch's Porsche.

Megan reached the back stoop before Jessica, as she had been taking a long, leisurely look at the yard. "Hello." Megan felt awkward and rustic. She hesitated briefly before stepping away from the door.

"What a lovely place." Jessica's smile was so like Katch's that Megan's heart lurched. "How I wish my azaleas looked like yours."

"Pop—my grandfather babies them."

"Yes." The blue eyes were warm and personal. "I've heard wonderful things about your grandfather. I'd love to meet him."

"He's still at the park." Her sense of awkwardness was fading. Charm definitely ran in the Katcherton family. "Would you like some coffee? Tea?"

"Maybe later. Let's go up to the studio, shall we?"

"If you don't mind my asking, Mrs. Delaney—"

"Jessica," she interrupted cheerfully and began to climb the open back stairs.

"Jessica," Megan agreed, "how did you know I had a studio, and that it was over the garage?"

"Oh, Katch told me," Jessica said breezily. "He tells me a great many things." She stood to the side of the door and waited for Megan to open it. "I'm very anxious to see your work. I dabble in oil from time to time."

"Do you?" Jessica's interest now made more sense. Artistic kinship.

"Badly, I'm afraid, which is a constant source of frustration to me." Again the Katcherton smile bloomed on her face.

Megan's reaction was unexpectedly sharp and swift. She fumbled for the doorknob. "I've never had much luck on canvas," she said quickly. She needed words, lots of words to cover what she feared was much too noticeable. "Nothing seems to come out the way I intend," she continued as they entered the studio. "It's maddening not to be able to express yourself properly. I do some airbrushing during the summer rush, but…"

Jessica wasn't listening. She moved around the room much the same way her brother had—intently, gracefully, silently. She fingered a piece here, lifted a piece there. Once, she studied a small ivory unicorn for so long, Megan fidgeted with nerves.

What was she doing? she wondered. *And why?*

Sunlight stippled the floor. Dust motes danced in the early evening light. Too late, Megan recalled the bust of Katch. One slanted beam of sun fell on it, highlighting the planes the chisel had already defined. Though it was still rough hewn and far from finished, it was unmistakably Katch. Feeling foolish, Megan walked over to stand in front of it, hoping to conceal it from Jessica's view.

"Katch was right," Jessica murmured. She still held the unicorn, stroking it with her fingertips. "He invariably is. Normally that annoys me to distraction, but not this time." The resemblance to Katch was startling now. Megan's fingers itched to make a quick sketch even as she tried to follow the twisting roads in Jessica's conversation.

"Right about what?"

"Your extraordinary talent."

"What?" Meg's eyes widened.

"Katch told me your work was remarkable," she went on, giving the unicorn a final study before setting it down. "I agreed when I received the two pieces he sent up to me, but they were only two, after all." She picked up a chisel and tapped it absently against her palm while her eyes continued to wander. "This is astonishing."

"He sent you the sculptures he bought from me?"

"Yes, a few weeks ago. I was very impressed." Jessica set down the chisel with a clatter and moved to a nearly completed study in limestone of a woman rising from the sea. It was the piece Megan had been working on before she had set it aside to begin Katch's bust. "This is fabulous!" Jessica declared. "I'm going to have to have it as well as the unicorn. The response to the two pieces Katch sent me has been very favorable."

"I don't understand what you're talking about." Try as she might, Megan couldn't keep up with Jessica's conversation. "Whose response?"

"My clients'," said Jessica. "At my gallery in New York."

She gave Megan a brilliant smile. "Didn't I tell you I run my own gallery?"

"No," Megan answered. "No, you didn't."

"I suppose I thought Katch did. I'd better start at the beginning then."

"I'd really appreciate it if you would," Megan told her, and waited until she had settled herself in the small wooden chair beside her.

"Katch sent me two of your pieces a few weeks ago," Jessica began briskly. "He wanted a professional opinion. I may only be able to dabble in oil, but I know art." She spoke with a confidence that Megan recognized. "Since I knew I'd never make it as a working artist, I put all the years of study to good use. I opened a gallery in Manhattan. *Jessica's.* Over the past six years, I've developed a rather nice clientele." She smiled. "So naturally, when my wandering brother saw your work, he sent it off to me. He always has his instincts verified by an expert, then plunges along his own way notwithstanding." She sighed indulgently. "I happen to know he was advised against building that hospital in Central Africa last year but he did it anyway. He does what he wants to."

"Hospital." Megan barely made the jump to Jessica's new train of thought.

"Yes, a children's hospital. He has a soft spot for kids." Jessica tried to speak teasingly, but the love came through. "He did some astonishing things for orphaned refugees after Vietnam. And there was the really fabulous little park he built in New South Wales."

Megan sat dumbly. Could they possibly be speaking about the same David Katcherton? Was this the man who had brashly approached her in the local market?

She remembered with uncomfortable clarity that she had accused him of trying to cheat her grandfather. She had told herself that he was an opportunist, a man spoiled by wealth and good looks. She'd tried to tell herself he was irresponsible, undependable, a man in search of his own pleasure.

"I didn't know," she murmured. "I didn't know anything about it."

"Oh, Katch keeps a low profile when he chooses," Jessica told her. "And he chooses to have no publicity when he's doing that sort of thing. He has incredible energy and outrageous self-confidence, but he's also very warm." Her gaze slipped beyond Megan's shoulder. "But then, you appear to know him well."

For a moment, Megan regarded Jessica blankly. Then she twisted her head and saw Katch's bust. In her confusion, she had forgotten her desire to conceal it. Slowly, she turned her head back, trying to keep her voice and face passive.

"No. No, really I don't think I know him at all. He has a fascinating face. I couldn't resist sculpt-ing it."

She noted a glint of understanding in Jessica's eyes. "He's a fascinating man," Jessica murmured.

Megan's gaze faltered.

"I'm sorry," Jessica said immediately. "I've intruded, a bad habit of mine. We won't talk about Katch. Let's talk about your showing."

Megan lifted her eyes again. "My what?"

"Your showing," Jessica repeated, dashing swiftly up a new path. "When do you think you'll have enough pieces ready? You certainly have a tremendous start here, and

Katch mentioned something about a gallery in town having some of your pieces. I think we can shoot for the fall."

"Please, Jessica, I don't know what you're talking about." A note of panic slipped into Megan's voice. It was faint, almost buried, but Jessica detected it. She reached over and took both of Megan's hands. The grip was surprisingly firm.

"Megan, you have something special, something powerful. It's time to share it." She rose then, urging Megan up with her. "Let's have that coffee now, shall we? And we'll talk about it."

An hour later, Megan sat alone in the kitchen. Darkness was encroaching, but she didn't rise from the table to switch on the light. Two cups sat, her own half-filled with now cold coffee, Jessica's empty but for dregs. She tried to take her mind methodically over what had happened in the last sixty minutes.

A showing at Jessica's, an art gallery in Manhattan. New York. A public show. Of her work.

It didn't happen, she thought. I imagined it. Then she looked down at the empty cup across from her. The air still smelled faintly of Jessica's light, sophisticated scent.

Half-dazed, Megan took both cups to the sink and automatically began rinsing them. How did she talk me into it? she wondered. I was agreeing to dates and details before I had agreed to do the showing. Does anyone ever say no to a Katcherton? She sighed and looked down at her wet hands. I have to call him. The knowledge increased the sense of panic. *I have to.*

Carefully, she placed the washed cups and saucers in the drainboard. I have to thank him. Nerves fluttered in her throat, but she made a pretense, for herself, of casually drying her damp hands on the hips of her jeans. She walked to the wall phone beside the stove.

"It's simple," she whispered, then bit her lip. She cleared her throat. "All I have to do is thank him, that's all. It'll only take a minute." Megan reached for the phone, then drew her hand away. Her mind raced on with her heartbeat.

She lifted the receiver. She knew the number. Hadn't she started to dial it a dozen times during the past two weeks? She took a long breath before pushing the first digit. It would take five minutes, and then, in all probability, she'd have no reason to contact him again. It would be better if they erased the remnants of their last meeting. It would be easier if their relationship ended on a calmer, more civilized note. Megan pressed the last button and waited for the click of connection, the whisper of transmitters and the ring.

It took four rings—four long, endless rings before he picked up the phone.

"Katch." His name was barely audible. She closed her eyes.

"Meg?"

"Yes, I…" She fought herself to speak. "I hope I'm not calling you at a bad time." How trite, she thought desperately. How ordinary.

"Are you all right?" There was concern in the question.

"Yes, yes, of course." Her mind fretted for the simple, casual words she had planned to speak. "Katch, I wanted to talk to you. Your sister was here—"

"I know, she got back a few minutes ago." There was a trace of impatience in his tone. "Is anything wrong?"

"No, nothing's wrong." Her voice refused to level. Megan searched for a quick way to end the conversation.

"Are you alone?"

"Yes, I…"

"I'll be there in ten minutes."

"No." Megan ran a frustrated hand through her hair. "No, please—"

"Ten minutes," he repeated and broke the connection.

Chapter 9

Megan stared at the dead receiver for several silent moments. How had she, in a few uncompleted sentences, managed to make such a mess of things? She didn't want him to come. She never wanted to see him again. *That is a lie.*

Carefully, Megan replaced the receiver. I do want to see him, she admitted, have wanted to see him for days. It's just that I'm afraid to see him. Turning, she gazed blindly around the kitchen. The room was almost in complete darkness now. The table and chairs were dark shadows. She walked to the switch, avoiding obstacles with the knowledge of years. The room flooded with brightness. That's better, she thought, more secure in the artificial light. Coffee, she decided, needing something, anything, to occupy her hands. I'll make fresh coffee.

Megan went to the percolator and began a step-by-step preparation, but her nerves continued to jump. In a few moments, she hoped, she'd be calm again. When he arrived, she would say what she needed to say, and then they would part.

The phone rang, and she jolted, juggling the cup she held and nearly dropping it. Chiding herself, Megan set it down and answered the call.

"Hello, Megan." Pop's voice crackled jovially across the wire.

"Pop…are you still at the park?" What time is it? she wondered distractedly and glanced down at her watch.

"That's why I called. George stopped by. We're going to have dinner in town. I didn't want you to worry."

"I won't." She smiled as the band of tension around her head loosened. "I suppose you and George have a lot of fish stories to exchange."

"His have gotten bigger since he retired," Pop claimed. "Hey, why don't you run into town, sweetheart? We'll treat you."

"You two just want an audience," she accused and her smile deepened with Pop's chuckle. "But I'll pass tonight, thanks. As I recall, there's some leftover spaghetti in the fridge."

"I'll bring you back dessert." It was an old custom. For as long as Megan could remember, if Pop had dinner without her, he'd bring her back some treat. "What do you want?"

"Rainbow sherbet," she decided instantly. "Have a good time."

"I will, darling. Don't work too late."

As she hung up the phone, Megan asked herself why she hadn't told her grandfather of Katch's impending visit. Why hadn't she mentioned Jessica or the incredible plans that had been made? It has to wait until we can talk, she told herself. Really talk. It's the only way I'll be certain how he really feels—and how everything will affect him.

It's probably a bad idea. Megan began to fret, pushing a hand through her hair in agitation. It's a crazy idea. How can I go to New York and—

Her thoughts were interrupted by the glaring sweep of headlights against the kitchen window. She struggled to compose herself, going deliberately to the cupboard to close it before heading to the screen door.

Katch stepped onto the stoop as she reached for the handle. For a moment, in silence, they studied each other through the mesh. She heard the soft flutter of moths' wings on the outside light.

Finally he turned the knob and opened the door. After he had shut it quietly behind him, he reached up to touch her cheek. His hand lingered there while his eyes traveled her face.

"You sounded upset."

Megan moistened her lips. "No, no, I'm fine." She stepped back so that his palm no longer touched her skin. Slowly, his eyes on hers, Katch lowered his hand. "I'm sorry I bothered you—"

"Megan, stop it." His voice was quiet and controlled. Her eyes came back to his, a little puzzled, a little desperate. "Stop backing away from me. Stop apologizing."

Her hands fluttered once before she could control the movement. "I'm making coffee," she began. "It should be ready in a minute." She would have turned to arrange the cups and saucers, but he took her arm.

"I didn't come for coffee." His hand slid down until it encircled her wrist. Her pulse vibrated against his fingers.

"Katch, please, don't make this difficult."

Something flared in his eyes while she watched. Then it was gone, and her hand was released. "I'm sorry. I've had some difficulty the past couple of weeks dealing with what happened the last time I saw you." He noted the color that shot into her cheeks, but she kept her eyes steady. He slipped his hands into his pockets. "Megan, I'd like to make it up to you."

Megan shook her head, disturbed by the gentleness in his voice, and turned to the coffeepot.

"Don't you want to forgive me?"

The question had her turning back, her eyes darkened with distressed confusion. "No…that is, yes, of course."

"Of course you don't want to forgive me?" There was a faint glimmer of a smile in his eyes and the charm was around his mouth. She could feel herself sinking.

"Yes, of course I forgive you," she corrected and this time did turn to the coffee. "It's forgotten." He laid his hands on her shoulders, and she jumped.

"Is it?" Katch turned her until they were again face-to-face. The glimpse of humor in his eyes was gone. "You can't seem to abide my touching you. I don't much like thinking I frighten you."

She made a conscious effort to relax under his hands. "You don't frighten me, Katch," Megan murmured. "You confuse me. Constantly."

She watched his brow lift in consideration. "I don't have any intention of confusing you. I am sorry, Megan."

"Yes." She smiled, recognizing the simple sincerity. "I know you are."

He drew her closer. "Can we kiss and make up then?"

Megan started to protest, but his mouth was already on hers, light and gentle. Her heart began to hammer in her throat. He made no attempt to deepen the kiss. His hands were easy on her shoulders. Against all the warnings of her mind, she relaxed against him, inviting him to take whatever he chose. But he took no more.

Katch drew her away, waiting until her heavy lids fluttered open before he touched her hair. Without speaking, he turned and paced to the window. Megan struggled to fill the new gap.

"I wanted to talk to you about your sister." She busied her hands with the now noisy percolator. "Or, more accurately, about what Jessica came to see me about."

Katch turned his head, watching her pour the coffee into the waiting cups. He walked to the refrigerator and took out the milk.

"All right." Standing beside her now, he poured milk into one cup and, at her nod, into the second.

"Why didn't you tell me you were sending my work to your sister?"

"I thought it best to wait until I had her opinion." Katch sat beside Megan and cradled the cup in both hands. "I trust her.… And I thought you'd trust her opinion more than mine. Are you going to do the showing? Jessica and I didn't have time to talk before you called."

She shifted in her chair, studied her coffee, then looked directly at him. "She's very persuasive. I was agreeing before I realized it."

"Good," Katch said simply and drank.

"I want to thank you," Meg continued in a stronger voice, "for arranging things."

"I didn't arrange anything," he responded. "Jessica makes her own decisions, personal and professional. I simply sent her your sculptures for an opinion."

"Then I'll thank you for that, for making a move I might never have made for the hundreds of reasons which occurred to me five minutes after she'd left."

Katch shrugged. "All right, if you're determined to be grateful."

"I am," she said. "And I'm scared," she continued, "really terrified at the thought of putting my work on public display." Megan let out a shaky breath at the admission. "I may despise you when all this is over and art critics stomp all over my ego, so you'd better take the gratitude now."

Katch crossed to her, and her heart lifted dizzily, so sure was she that he would take her into his arms. He merely stroked her cheek with the back of his hand. "When you're a smashing success, you can give it to me again." He smiled at her, and the world snapped into sharp focus. Until that moment, she hadn't realized how dull everything had been without him.

"I'm so glad you came," she whispered and, unable to resist, slipped her arms around him, pressing her face into his shoulder. After a moment, he rested his hands lightly at her waist. "I'm sorry for the things I said…about the loan. I didn't mean any of it really, but I say horrible things when I lose my temper."

"Is this your turn to be penitent?"

He made her laugh. "Yes." She smiled and tilted back her head. Her arms stayed around him. He kissed her and drew away. Reluctantly, she let him slip out of her arms. Then he stood silently, staring down at her.

"What are you doing?" she asked with a quick, self-conscious smile.

"Memorizing your face. Have you eaten?"

She shook her head, wondering why it should come as a

surprise that he continued to baffle her. "No, I was going to heat up some leftovers."

"Unacceptable. Want a pizza?"

"*Mmm,* I'd love it, but you have company."

"Jessica and Rob took the kids to play miniature golf. I won't be missed." Katch held out his hands. "Come on."

His eyes were smiling, and her heart was lost. "Oh wait," she began even as she put her hand into his. Quickly, Megan scrawled a message on the chalkboard by the screen door.

OUT WITH KATCH

It was enough.

Chapter 10

Katch drove along Ocean Boulevard so they could creep along in the traffic filled with tourists and beachers. Car radios were turned up high and windows rolled down low. Laughter and music poured out everywhere. The lights from a twin Ferris wheel glittered red and blue in the distance. People sat out on their hotel balconies, with colorful beach towels flapping over the railings, as they watched the sluggish flow of cars and pedestrians. To the left, there were glimpses of the sea in between buildings.

Sleepily content after pizza and Chianti, Megan snuggled deeper into the soft leather seat. "Things'll quiet down after this weekend," she commented. "Until Memorial Day."

"Do you ever feel as though you're being invaded?" Katch asked her with a gesture at the clogged traffic.

"I like the crowds," she said immediately, then laughed. "And I like the winter when the beaches are deserted. I suppose there's something about the honky-tonk that appeals to me, especially since I know I'm going to have a few isolated months in the winter."

"That's your time," Katch murmured, glancing back at her. "The time you give yourself for sculpting."

She shrugged, a bit uncomfortable with the intense look. "I do some in the summer, too—when I can. Time's something I forgot when Jessica was talking about a showing and making all those plans..." Megan trailed off, frowning. "I don't know how I can possibly get things ready."

"Not backing out, are you?"

"No, but—" The look in his eyes had her swallowing excuses. "No," she said more firmly. "I'm not backing out."

"What're you working on now?"

"I, ah..." Megan looked fixedly out the window, thinking of the half-formed bust of Katch's head. "It's just..." She shrugged and began to fiddle with the dial of the radio. "It's just a wood carving."

"Of what?"

Megan made a few inarticulate mumbles until Katch turned to grin at her. "A pirate," she decided as the light from a street lamp slanted over his face, throwing it into planes and shadows. "It's the head of a pirate."

His brow lifted at the sudden, narrow-eyed concentration with which she was studying him. "I'd like to see it."

"It's not finished," she said quickly. "I've barely got the clay model done. In any case, I might have to put it off if I'm going to get the rest of my pieces organized for your sister."

"Meg, why don't you stop worrying and just enjoy it?"

Confused, she shook her head and stared at him. "Enjoy it?"

"The show," he said, ruffling her hair.

"Oh, yes." She fought to get her thoughts back into some kind of order. "I will…after it's over," she added with a smile. "Do you think you'll be in New York, then?"

As the rhythm of the traffic picked up, he shifted into third. "I'm considering it."

"I'd like you to be there if you could arrange it." When he laughed, shaking his head, she continued, "It's just that I'm going to need all the friendly faces I can get."

"You're not going to need anything but your sculptures," Katch corrected, but the amusement was still in his eyes. "Don't you think I'd want to be around the night of your opening so that I can brag I discovered you?"

"Let's just hope we both don't live to regret it," Megan muttered, but he only laughed again. "You just can't consider the possibility that you might have made a mistake," she accused testily.

"You can't consider the possibility that you might be successful," he countered.

Megan opened her mouth, then shut it again. "Well," she said after a moment, "we're both right." Waiting until they were stopped in traffic again, Megan touched his shoulder. "Katch?"

"Hmm?"

"Why did you build a hospital in Central Africa?"

He turned to her then, a faint frown between his brows. "It was needed," he said simply.

"Just that?" she persisted, though she could see he wasn't pleased with her question. "I mean, Jessica said you were advised against it, and—"

"As it happens, I have a comfortable amount of money." He cut her off with an annoyed movement of his shoulder. "I do what I choose with it." Seeing her expression, Katch shook his head. "There are things I want to do, that's all. Don't canonize me, Meg."

She relaxed again and found herself brushing at the curls over his ear. "I wouldn't dream of it." He'd rather be thought of as eccentric than benevolent, she mused. And how much simpler it was to love him, knowing that one small secret. "You're much easier to like than I thought you'd be when you made a nuisance of yourself in the market."

"I tried to tell you," he pointed out. "You were too busy pretending you weren't interested."

"I wasn't interested," Megan insisted, "in the least." He turned to grin at her and she found herself laughing. "Well, not very much anyway." When he swung the car onto a side street, she looked back at him in question. "What are you doing?"

"Let's go out on the boardwalk." Expertly, he slid the Porsche into a parking space. "Maybe I'll buy you a souvenir." He was already out of the car—primed, impatient.

"Oh, I love rash promises," Megan crowed as she joined him.

"I said maybe."

"I didn't hear that part. And," she added as she laced her fingers with his, "I want something extravagant."

"Such as?" They jaywalked, maneuvering around stopped cars.

"I'll know when I see it."

The boardwalk was crowded, full of people and light and noise. The breeze off the ocean carried the scent of salt to compete with the aroma of grilling meat from concessions. Instead of going into one of the little shops, Katch pulled Megan into an arcade.

"Big talk about presents and no delivery," Megan said in disgust as Katch exchanged bills for tokens.

"It's early yet. Here." He poured a few tokens into her hand. "Why don't you try your luck at saving the galaxy from invaders?"

With a smirk, Megan chose a machine, then slipped two tokens into the slot. "I'll go first." Pressing the start button, she took the control stick in hand and began systematically to vaporize the enemy. Brows knit, she swung her ship right and left while the machine exploded with color and noise with each hit. Amused, Katch dipped his hands into his pockets and watched her face. It was a more interesting show than the sophisticated graphics.

She chewed her bottom lip while maneuvering into position, narrowing her eyes when a laser blast headed her way. Her breath hissed through her teeth at a narrow escape. But all the while, her face held that composed, almost serious expression that was so much a part of her. Fighting gamely to avoid being blown up in cross fire, Megan's ship at last succumbed.

"Well," Katch murmured, glancing at her score as she wiped her hands on the back of her jeans. "You're pretty good."

"You have to be," Megan returned soberly, "when you're the planet's last hope."

With a chuckle, he nudged her out of the way and took the control.

Megan acknowledged his skill as Katch began to blast away the invaders with as much regularity as she had, and a bit more dash. He likes to take chances, she mused as he narrowly missed being blown apart by laser fire in order to zap three ships in quick succession. As his score mounted, she stepped a bit closer to watch his technique.

At the brush of her arm against his, Megan noticed a quick, almost imperceptible break in his rhythm. Now, that was interesting, she reflected. Feeling an irrepressible surge of mischief, she edged slightly closer. There was another brief fluctuation in his timing. Softly, she touched her lips to his shoulder, then smiled up into his face. She heard rather than saw the explosion that marked his ship's untimely end.

Katch wasn't looking at the screen either, but at her. She saw something flash into his eyes—something hot, barely suppressed, before his hand released the control to dive into her hair.

"Cheat," he murmured.

For a moment, Megan forgot the cacophony of sound, forgot the crowds of people that milled around them. She was lost somewhere in those smoky gray eyes and her own giddy sense of power.

"Cheat?" she repeated, and her lips stayed slightly parted. "I don't know what you mean."

The hand on her hair tightened. He was struggling, she realized, surprised and excited. "I think you do," Katch said quietly. "And I think I'm going to have to be very careful now that you know just what you can do to me."

"Katch." Her gaze lowered to his mouth as the longings built. "Maybe I don't want you to be careful anymore."

Slowly, his hand slid out of her hair, over her cheek, then dropped. "All the more reason I have to be," he muttered. "Come on." He took her arm and propelled her away from the machine. "Let's play something else."

Megan flowed with his mood, content just to be with him. They pumped tokens into machines and competed fiercely—as much with each other as with the computers. Megan felt the same lighthearted ease with him that she'd experienced that night at the carnival. Spending time with him was much like a trip on one of the wild, breathless rides at the park. Quick curves, fast hills, unexpected starts and stops. No one liked the windy power of a roller coaster better than Megan.

Hands on hips, she stood back as he consistently won coupons at Skee Ball. She watched another click off on the already lengthy strip as he tossed the ball neatly into the center hole.

"Don't you ever lose?" she demanded.

Katch tossed the next ball for another forty points. "I try not to make a habit of it. Wanna toss the last two?"

"No." She brushed imaginary lint from her shirt. "You're having such a good time showing off."

With a laugh, Katch dumped the last two balls for ninety points, then leaned over to tear off his stream of coupons. "Just for that, I might not turn these in for your souvenir."

"These?" Megan gave the ream of thin cardboard an arched-brow look. "You were supposed to *buy* me a souvenir."

"I did." He grinned, rolling them up. "Indirectly." Slipping an arm companionably around her shoulder, he walked to the center counter where prizes were displayed. "Let's see…I've got two dozen. How about one of those six-function penknives?"

"Just who's this souvenir for?" Megan asked dryly as she scanned the shelves. "I like that little silk rose." She tapped the glass counter to indicate a small lapel pin. "I have all the tools I need," she added with an impish grin.

"Okay." Katch nodded to the woman behind the counter, then tore off all but four of the tickets. "That leaves us these. Ah…" With a quick scan of the shelves, he pointed. "That."

Thoughtfully, Megan studied the tiny shell figure the woman lifted down. It seemed to be a cross between a duck and a penguin. "What're you going to do with that?"

"Give it to you." Katch handed over the rest of the tickets. "I'm a very generous man."

"I'm overwhelmed," she murmured. Megan turned it over in the palm of her hand as Katch pinned the rose to the collar of her shirt. "But what is it?"

"It's a mallard." Draping his arm over her shoulder again, he led her out of the arcade. "I'm surprised at your attitude. I figured, as an artist, you'd recognize its aesthetic value."

"Hmm." Megan took another study, then slipped it into her pocket. "Well, I do recognize a certain winsome charm. And," she added, rising on her toes to kiss his cheek, "it was sweet of you to spend all your winnings on me."

Smiling, Katch ran a finger down her nose. "Is a kiss on the cheek the best you can do?"

"For a shell penguin it is."

"It's a mallard," he reminded her.

"Whatever." Laughing, Megan slipped an arm around his waist as they crossed the boardwalk and walked down the slope to the beach.

The moon was only a thin slice of white, but the stars were brilliant and mirrored in the water. There was a quiet swish of waves flowing and ebbing over the sand. Lovers walked here and there, arm in arm, talking quietly or not speaking at all. Children dashed along with flashlights bobbing, searching the sand and the surf for treasures.

Bending, Megan slipped out of her shoes and rolled up the hem of her jeans. In silent agreement, Katch followed suit. The water lapped cool over their ankles as they began to walk north, until the laughter and music from the boardwalk was only a background echo.

"Your sister's lovely," Megan said at length. "Just as you said."

"Jessica was always a beauty," he agreed absently. "A little hardheaded, but always a beauty."

"I saw your nieces at the park." Megan lifted her head so that the ocean breeze caught at her hair. "They had chocolate all over their faces."

"Typical." He laughed, running a hand up and down her arm as they walked. Megan felt the blood begin to hum beneath her flesh. "Before they left tonight, they were out digging for worms. I've been drafted to take them fishing tomorrow."

"You like children."

He twisted his head to glance down at her, but Megan was looking out to sea. "Yes. They're a constant adventure, aren't they?"

"I see so many of them in the park every summer, yet they never cease to amaze me." She turned back then with her slow, serious smile hovering on her lips. "And I see a fair number of harassed or long-suffering parents."

"When did you lose yours?"

He saw the flicker of surprise in her eyes before she looked down the stretch of beach again. "I was five."

"It's difficult for you to remember them."

"Yes. I have some vague memories—impressions really, I suppose. Pop has pictures, of course. When I see them, it always surprises me how young they were."

"It must have been hard on you," Katch murmured. "Growing up without them."

The gentleness in his voice had her turning back to him. They'd walked far down the beach so that the only light now came from the stars. His eyes caught the glitter of reflection as they held hers. "It would have been," Megan told him, "without Pop. He did much more than fill in." She stopped to take a step farther into the surf. The water frothed and bubbled over her skin. "One of my best memories is of him struggling to iron this pink organdy party dress. I was eight or nine, I think." With a shake of her head, she laughed and kicked the water. "I can still see him."

Katch's arms came around her waist, drawing her back against him. "So can I."

"He was standing there, struggling with frills and flounces—and swearing like a sailor because he didn't know I was there. I still love him for that," she murmured. "For just that."

Katch brushed his lips over the top of her hair. "And I imagine you told him not long afterward that you didn't care much for party dresses."

Surprised, Megan turned around. "How did you know that?"

"I know you." Slowly, he traced the shape of her face with his fingertip.

Frowning, she looked beyond his shoulder. "Am I so simple?"

"No." With his fingertip still on her jaw, he turned her face back to his. "You might say I've made a study of you."

She felt her blood begin to churn. "Why?"

Katch shook his head and combed his fingers through her hair. "No questions tonight," he said quietly. "I don't have the answers yet."

"No questions," she agreed, then rose on her toes to meet his mouth with hers.

It was a soft, exploring kiss—a kiss of renewal. Megan could taste the gentleness. For the moment, he seemed to prize her, to find her precious and rare. He held her lightly, as though she would break at the slightest pressure. Her lips parted, and it was she who entered his mouth first, teasing his tongue with hers. His sound of pleasure warmed her. The water swayed, soft and cool, on her calves.

She ran her hands up his back, letting her strong, artist's fingers trail under his hair to caress the nape of his neck. There was tension there, and she murmured against his lips as if to soothe it. Megan felt both his resistance and the tightening of his fingers against her skin. Her body pressed more demandingly into his.

Passion began to smolder quietly. Megan knew she was drawing it from him without his complete consent. The wonder of her own power struck her like a flash. He was holding back, letting her set the pace, but she could feel the near-violence of need in him. It tempted her. She wanted to undermine his control as he had undermined hers. She wanted to make him need as blindly as she needed. It wasn't possible to make him love her, but she could make him want. If it was all she could have from him, then she would be satisfied with his desire.

Megan felt his control slipping. His arms tightened

around her, drawing her close so they were silhouetted as one. The kiss grew harder, more urgent. He lifted a hand to her hair, gripping it, pulling her head back as if now he would take command. There was fire now, burning brightly. Heat rose in her, smoking through her blood. She caught his bottom lip between her teeth and heard his quiet moan. Abruptly, he drew her away.

"Meg."

She waited, having no idea what she wanted him to say. Her head was tossed back, her face open to his, her hair free to the breeze. She felt incredibly strong. His eyes were nearly black, searching her face deeply. She could feel his breath feather, warm and uneven, on her lips.

"Meg." He repeated her name, bringing his hands back to her shoulders slowly. "I have to go now."

Daring more than she would have believed possible, Megan pressed her lips to his again. Hers were soft and hungry and drew instant response from him. "Is that what you want?" she murmured. "Do you want to leave me now?"

His fingers tightened on her arms convulsively, then he pulled her away again. "You know the answer to that," he said roughly. "What are you trying to do, make me crazy?"

"Maybe." Desire still churned in her. It smoldered in her eyes as they met his. "Maybe I am."

He caught her against him, close and tight. She could feel the furious race of his heart against hers. His control, she knew, balanced on a razor's edge. Their lips were only a whisper apart.

"There'll be a time," he said softly, "I swear it, when it'll just be you and me. Next time, the very next time, Meg. Remember it."

It took no effort to keep her eyes level with his. The power was still flowing through her. “Is that a warning?”

“Yes,” he told her. “That’s just what it is.”

Chapter 11

It took two more days for Megan to finish the bust of Katch. She tried, when it was time, to divorce herself from emotion and judge it objectively.

She'd been right to choose wood. It was warmer than stone. With her tongue caught between her teeth, she searched for flaws in her workmanship. Megan knew without conceit it was one of her better pieces. Perhaps the best.

The face wasn't stylishly handsome, but strong and compelling. Humor was expressed in the tilt of the brows and mouth. She ran her fingertips over his lips. An incredibly expressive mouth, she mused, remembering the taste and texture. I know just how it looks when he's amused or angry or aroused. And his eyes. Hers drifted up to linger. I know how they look, how they change shades and expression with a mood. Light for pleasure, turning smoky in anger, darker in passion.

I know his face as well as my own…but I still don't

know his mind. That's still a stranger. With a sigh she folded her arms on the table and lowered her chin to them.

Would he ever permit me to know him? she wondered. Tenderly, she touched a lock of the disordered hair. Jessica knows him, probably better than anyone else. If he loved someone…

What would happen if I drew up the courage to tell him that I love him? What would happen if I simply walked up to him and said *I love you?* Demanding nothing, expecting nothing. Doesn't he perhaps have the right to know? Isn't love too special, too rare to be closed up? Then Megan imagined his eyes with pity in them.

"I couldn't bear it," she murmured, lowering her forehead to Katch's wooden one. "I just couldn't bear it." A knock interrupted her soul-searching. Quickly, Megan composed her features and swiveled in her chair. "Come in."

Her grandfather entered, his fishing cap perched jauntily on his mane of white hair. "How do you feel about fresh fish for supper?" His grin told her that his early morning expedition had been a success. Megan cocked her head.

"I could probably choke down a few bites." She smiled, pleased to see his eyes sparkling and color in his cheeks. She sprang up and wound her arms around his neck as she had done as a child. "Oh, I love you, Pop!"

"Well, well." He patted her hair, both surprised and pleased. "I love you too, Megan. I guess I should bring you home trout more often."

She lifted her face from the warm curve of his neck and smiled at him. "It doesn't take much to make me happy."

His eyes sobered as he tucked her hair behind her ear. "No…. It never has." His wide, blunt hand touched her cheek. "You've given me so much pleasure over the years, Megan, so much joy. I'm going to miss you when you're in New York."

"Oh, Pop." She buried her face again and clung. "It'll only be for a month or two, then I'll be home." She could smell the cherry-flavored scent of the tobacco he carried in his breast pocket. "You could even come with me—the season'll be over."

"Meg." He stopped her rambling and drew her up so that their eyes met. "This is a start for you. Don't put restrictions on it."

Shaking her head, Megan rose to pace nervously. "I'm not. I don't know what you mean…."

"You're going to make something of yourself, something important. You have talent." Pop glanced around the room at her work until his eyes rested on the bust of Katch. "You've got a life to start. I want you to go after it at full speed."

"You make it sound as if I'm not coming home." Megan turned and, seeing where his eyes rested, clasped her hands together. "I've just finished that." She moistened her lips and struggled to keep her voice casual. "It's rather good, don't you think?"

"Yes, I think it's very good." He looked at her then. "Sit down, Megan, I need to talk to you."

She recognized the tone and tensed. Without a word, she obeyed, going to the chair across from him. Pop waited until she was settled, then studied her face carefully.

"Awhile back," he began, "I told you things change. Most of your life, it's been just the two of us. We needed each other, depended on each other. We had the park to keep a roof over our heads and to give us something to work for." His tone softened. "There hasn't been one minute in the eighteen years I've had you with me that you've been a burden. You've kept me young. I've watched you through all the stages of growing up, and each time, you've made me more proud of you. It's time for the next change."

Because her throat was dry as dust, Megan swallowed. "I don't understand what you're trying to tell me."

"It's time you moved out into the world, Megan, time I let you." Pop reached in the pocket of his shirt and took out carefully folded papers. After spreading them out, he handed them to Megan.

She hesitated before accepting them, her eyes clinging to his. The instant she saw the papers, she knew what they were. But when she read, she read each sentence, each word, until the finish. "So," she said, dry-eyed, dry-voiced. "You've sold it to him."

"When I sign the papers," Pop told her, "and you witness it." He saw the look of devastation in her eyes. "Megan, hear me out. I've given this a lot of thought." Pop took the papers and set them on the table, then gripped her hands. "Katch isn't the first to approach me about selling, and this isn't the first time I've considered it. Everything didn't fit the way I wanted before—this time it does."

"What fits?" she demanded, feeling her eyes fill.

"It's the right man, Meg, the right time." He soothed her hands, hating to watch her distress. "I knew it when all those repairs fell on me. I'm ready to let it go, to let someone younger take over so I can go fishing. That's what I want now, Megan, a boat and a rod. And he's the man I want taking over." He paused, fumbling in his pocket for a handkerchief to wipe his eyes. "I told you I trusted him and that still holds. Managing the park for Katch won't keep me from my fishing, and I'll have the stimulation without the headaches. And you," he continued, brushing tears from her cheeks, "you need to cut the strings. You can't do what you're meant to do if you're struggling to balance books and make payroll."

"If it's what you want," Megan began, but Pop cut her off.

"No, it has to be what you want. That's why the last lines are still blank." He looked at her with his deep-set eyes sober and quiet. "I won't sign it, Megan, unless you agree. It has to be what's best for both of us."

Megan stood again, and he released her hands to let her walk to the window. At the moment, she was unable to understand her own feelings. She knew agreeing to do a show in New York was a giant step away from the life she had led. And the park was a major part of that life. She knew in order to pursue her own career, she couldn't continue to tie herself to the business end of Joyland.

The park had been security—her responsibility, her second home—as the man behind her had been both mother and father to her. She remembered the look of weariness on his face when he had come to tell her that the park needed money. Megan knew the hours and endless demands that summer would bring.

He was entitled to live his winter years as he chose, she decided. With less worry, less responsibility. He was entitled to fish, and to sleep late and putter around his azaleas. What right did she have to deny him that because she was afraid to cut the last tie with her childhood? He was right, it was time for the change.

Slowly, she walked to her workbox and searched out a

pen. Going to Pop, Megan held it out to him. "Sign it. We'll have champagne with the trout."

Pop took the pen, but kept his eyes on her. "Are you sure, Meg?"

She nodded, as sure for him as she was uncertain for herself. "Positive." She smiled and watched the answering light in his eyes before he bent over the paper.

He signed his name with a flourish, then passed her the pen so that she could witness his signature. Megan wrote her name in clear, distinct letters, not allowing her hand to tremble.

"I suppose I should call Katch," Pop mused, sighing as though a weight had been lifted. "Or take the papers to him."

"I'll take them." Carefully, Megan folded them again. "I'd like to talk to him."

"That's a good idea. Take the pickup," he suggested as she headed for the door. "It looks like rain."

Megan was calm by the time she reached Katch's house. The papers were tucked securely in the back pocket of her cutoffs. She pulled the truck behind his car and climbed out.

The air was deadly still and heavy, nearly shimmering with restrained rain. The clouds overhead were black and bulging with it. She walked to the front door and knocked as she had many days before. As before, there was no answer. She walked back down the steps and skirted the house.

There was no sign of him in the yard, no sound but the voice of the sea muffled by the tall hedges. He'd planted a willow, a young, slender one near the slope which led to the beach. The earth was still dark around it, freshly turned. Unable to resist, Megan walked to it, wanting to touch the tender young leaves. It was no taller than she, but she knew one day it would be magnificent…sweeping, graceful, a haven of shade in the summer. Instinct made her continue down the slope to the beach.

Hands in his pockets, he stood, watching the swiftly incoming tide. As if sensing her, he turned.

"I was standing here thinking of you," he said. "Did I wish you here?"

She took the papers and held them out to him. "It's yours," she told him calmly. "Just as you wanted."

He didn't even glance down at the papers, but she saw the shift of expression in his eyes. "I'd like to talk to you, Meg. Let's go inside."

"No." She stepped back to emphasize her refusal. "There really isn't anything more to say."

"That might be true for you, but I have a great deal to say. And you're going to listen." Impatience intruded into his tone. Megan heard it as she felt the sudden gust of wind which broke the calm.

"I don't want to listen to you, Katch. This is what Pop wants, too." She thrust the papers into his hands as the first spear of lightning split the sky. "Take them, will you?"

"Megan, wait." He grabbed her arm as she turned to go. The thunder all but drowned out his words.

"I will not wait!" she tossed back, jerking her arm free. "And stop grabbing me. You have what you wanted—you don't need me anymore."

Katch swore, thrust the papers in his pocket and caught her again before she'd taken three steps. He whirled her back around. "You're not that big an idiot."

"Don't tell me how big an idiot I am." She tried to shake herself loose.

"We have to talk. I have things to say to you. It's important." A gust of wind whipped violently across Megan's face.

"Don't you understand a simple no?" she shouted at him, her voice competing with pounding surf and rising wind. She struggled against his hold. "I don't want to talk. I don't want to hear what you have to say. I don't *care* about what you have to say."

The rain burst from the clouds and poured over them. Instantly, they were drenched.

"Tough," he retorted, every bit as angry as she. "Because you're going to hear it. Now, let's go inside."

He started to pull her across the sand, but she swung violently away and freed herself. Rain gushed down in torrents, sheeting around them. "No!" she shouted. "I won't go inside with you."

"Oh, yes, you will," he corrected.

"What are you going to do?" she demanded. "Drag me by the hair?"

"Don't tempt me." Katch took her hand again only to have her pull away. "All right," he said. "Enough." In a swift move that caught her off guard, he swept her up into his arms.

"Put me down." Megan wriggled and kicked, blind with fury. He ignored her, dealing with her struggles by shifting her closer and climbing the slope without any apparent effort. Lightning and thunder warred around them. "Oh, I hate you!" she claimed as he walked briskly across the lawn.

"Good. That's a start." Katch pushed open the door with

his hip, then continued through the kitchen and into the living room. A trail of rain streamed behind them. Without ceremony, he dumped her on the sofa. “Sit still,” he ordered before she could regain her breath, “and just be quiet a minute.” He walked to the hearth. Taking a long match, he set fire to the paper waiting beneath kindling and logs. Dry wood crackled and caught almost instantly.

Regaining her breath, Megan rose and bounded for the door. Katch stopped her before her fingers touched the knob. He held her by the shoulders with her back to the door. “I warn you, Meg, my tolerance is at a very low ebb. Don’t push me.”

“You don’t frighten me,” she told him, impatiently flipping her dripping hair from her eyes.

“I’m not trying to frighten you. I’m trying to reason with you. But you’re too stubborn to shut up and listen.”

Her eyes widened with fresh fury. “Don’t you talk to me that way! I don’t have to take that.”

“Yes, you do.” Deftly, he reached in her right front pocket and pulled out the truck keys. “As long as I have these.”

“I can walk,” she tossed back as he pocketed them himself.

“In this rain?”

Megan hugged her arms as she began to shiver. “Let me have my keys.”

Instead of answering, he pulled her across the room in front of the fire. “You’re freezing. You’ll have to get out of those wet clothes.”

“I will not. You’re crazy if you think I’m going to take off my clothes in your house.”

“Suit yourself.” He stripped off his own sopping T-shirt

and tossed it angrily aside. "You're the most hardheaded, single-minded, stubborn woman I know."

"Thanks." Barely, Megan controlled the urge to sneeze. "Is that all you wanted to say?"

"No." He walked to the fire again. "That's just the beginning—there's a lot more. Sit down."

"Then maybe I'll have my say first." Chills were running over her skin, and she struggled not to tremble. "I was wrong about you in a lot of ways. You're not lazy or careless or glory-seeking. And you were certainly honest with me." She wiped water from her eyes, a mixture of rain and tears. "You told me up front that you intended to have the park, and it seems perhaps for the best. What happened between then and now is my fault for being foolish enough to let you get to me." Megan swallowed, wanting to salvage a little pride. "But then you're a difficult man to ignore. Now you have what you wanted, and it's over and done."

"I only have part of what I wanted." Katch came to her and gathered her streaming hair in his hand. "Only part, Meg."

She looked at him, too tired to argue. "Can't you just let me be?" she asked.

"Let you be? Do you know how many times I've walked that beach at three in the morning because wanting you kept me awake and aching? Do you know how hard it was for me to let you go every time I had you in my arms?" The fingers in her hair tightened, pulled her closer.

Her eyes were huge now while chills shivered over her skin. *What was he saying?* She couldn't risk asking, couldn't risk wondering. Abruptly, he cursed her and dragged her into his arms.

Thin wet clothes were no barrier to his hands. He molded

her breasts even while his mouth ravished hers. She made no protest when he lowered her to the floor, as his fingers worked desperately at the buttons of her blouse. Her chilled wet skin turned to fire under his fingertips. His mouth was hungry, hot as it roamed to her throat and downward.

There was only the crackle of wood and the splash of rain on the windows to mix with their breathing. A log shifted in the grate.

Megan heard him take a long, deep breath. "I'm sorry. I wanted to talk—there are things I need to tell you. But I need you. I've kept it pent up a long time."

Need. Her mind centered on the word. Need was infinitely different from want. Need was more personal—still apart from love—but she let her heart grip the word.

"It's all right." Megan started to sit up, but he leaned over her. Sparks flicked inside her at the touch of naked flesh to naked flesh. "Katch…"

"Please, Meg. Listen to me."

She searched his face, noting the uncharacteristically grave eyes and mouth. Whatever he had to say was important to him. "All right," she said, quieter now, ready. "I'll listen."

"When I first saw you, the first minute, I wanted you. You know that." His voice was low, but without its usual calm. Something boiled just under the surface. "The first night we were together, you intrigued me as much as you attracted me. I thought it would be a simple matter to have you…a casual, pleasant affair for a few weeks."

"I know," she spoke softly, trying not to be wounded by the truth.

"No—shh." He lay a finger over her lips a moment. "You don't know. It stopped being simple almost immediately. When I had you here for dinner, and you asked to stay…" He paused, brushing wet strands of hair from her cheeks. "I couldn't let you, and I wasn't completely sure why. I wanted you—wanted you more than any woman I'd ever touched, any woman I'd ever dreamed about—but I couldn't take you."

"Katch…" Megan shook her head, not certain she was strong enough to hear the words.

"Please." She had closed her eyes, and Katch waited until she opened them again before he continued. "I tried to stay away from you, Meg. I tried to convince myself I was imagining what was happening to me. Then you were charging across the lawn, looking outraged and so beautiful I couldn't think of anything. Just looking at you took my breath away." While she lay motionless, he lifted her hand and pressed it to his lips. The gesture moved her unbearably.

"Don't," she murmured. "Please."

Katch stared into her eyes for a long moment, then released her hand. "I wanted you," he went on in a voice more calm than his eyes. "Needed you, was furious with you because of it." He rested his forehead on hers and shut his eyes. "I never wanted to hurt you, Meg—to frighten you."

Megan lay still, aware of the turmoil in him. Firelight played over the skin on his arms and back.

"It seemed impossible that I could be so involved I couldn't pull away," he continued. "But you were so tangled up in my thoughts, so wound up in my dreams. There wasn't any escape. The other night, after I'd taken you home, I finally admitted to myself I didn't want an escape. Not this time. Not from you." He lifted his head and looked down at her again. "I have something for you, but first I want you to know I'd decided against buying the park until your grandfather came to me last night. I didn't want that between us, but it was what he wanted. What he thought was best for you and for himself. But if it hurts you, I'll tear the papers up."

"No." Megan gave a weary sigh. "I know it's best. It's just like losing someone you love. Even when you know it's the best thing, it still hurts." The outburst seemed to have driven out the fears and the pain. "Please, I don't want you to apologize. I was wrong, coming here this way, shouting at you. Pop has every right to sell the park, and you have every right to buy it." She sighed, wanting explanations over. "I suppose I felt betrayed somehow and didn't want to think it all through."

"And now?"

"And now I'm ashamed of myself for acting like a fool." She managed a weak smile. "I'd like to get up and go home. Pop'll be worried."

"Not just yet." When Katch leaned back on his heels to take something from his pocket, Megan sat up, pushing her wet, tangled hair behind her. He held a box, small and thin. Briefly, he hesitated before offering it to her. Puzzled, both by the gift and by the tension she felt emanating from him, Megan opened it. Her breath caught.

It was a dark, smoky green emerald, square cut and exquisite in its simplicity. Stunned, Megan stared at it, then at Katch. She shook her head wordlessly.

"Katch." Megan shook her head again. "I don't understand…I can't accept this."

"Don't say no, Meg." Katch closed his hand over hers. "I don't handle rejection well." The words were light, but she recognized, and was puzzled by, the strain in the tone. A thought trembled in her brain, and her heart leaped with it.

She tried to be calm and keep her eyes steady on his. "I don't know what you're asking me."

His fingers tightened on hers. "Marry me. I love you."

Emotions ran riot through her. He must be joking, she thought quickly, though no hint of amusement showed in his eyes. His face was so serious, she reflected, and the words so simple. Where were the carelessly witty phrases, the glib charm? Shaken, Megan rose with the box held tightly in her hand. She needed to think.

Marriage. Never had she expected him to ask her to share a lifetime. What would life be like with him? *Like the roller coaster.* She knew it instantly. It would be a fast, furious ride, full of unexpected curves and indescribable thrills. And quiet moments too, she reflected. Precious, solitary moments which would make each new twist and turn more exciting.

Perhaps he had asked her this way, so simply, without any of the frills he could so easily provide because he was as vulnerable as she. What a thought that was! She lifted her fingers to her temple. David Katcherton vulnerable. And yet…Megan remembered what she had seen in his eyes.

I love you. The three simple words, words spoken every day by people everywhere, had changed her life forever. Megan turned, then walking back, knelt beside him. Her eyes were as grave, as searching as his. She held the box out, then spoke quickly as she saw the flicker of desperation.

"It belongs on the third finger of my left hand."

Then she was caught against him, her mouth silenced

bruisingly. "Oh, Meg," he murmured her name as he rained kisses on her face. "I thought you were turning me down."

"How could I?" She wound her arms around his neck and tried to stop his roaming mouth with her own. "I love you, Katch." The words were against his lips. "Desperately, completely. I'd prepared myself for a slow death when you were ready to walk away."

"No one's going to walk away now." They lay on the floor again, and he buried his face in her rain-scented hair. "We'll go to New Orleans. A quick honeymoon before you have to come back and work on the show. In the spring, we'll go to Paris." He lifted his face and looked down on her. "I've thought about you and me in Paris, making love. I want to see your face in the morning when the light's soft."

She touched his cheek. "Soon," she whispered. "Marry me soon. I want to be with you."

He picked up the box that had fallen beside them. Drawing out the ring, he slipped it on her finger. Then, gripping her hand with his, he looked down at her.

"Consider it binding, Meg," he told her huskily. "You can't get away now."

"I'm not going anywhere." She lifted her mouth to meet his kiss.

Epilogue

Nervously, Megan twisted the emerald on her finger and tried to drink the champagne Jessica had pushed into her hand. She felt as though the smile had frozen onto her face. People, she thought. She'd never expected so many people. What was she doing, standing in a Manhattan gallery pretending she was an artist? What she wanted to do was creep into the back room and be very, very sick.

"Here now, Meg." Pop strolled over beside her, looking oddly distinguished in his best—and only—black suit. "You should try one of these—tasty little things." He held out a canapé.

"No." Megan felt her stomach roll and shook her head. "No, thanks. I'm so glad you flew up for the weekend."

"Think I'd miss my granddaughter's big night?" He ate the canapé and grinned. "How about this turnout?"

"I feel like an impostor," Megan murmured, smiling gamely as a man in a flowing cape moved past her to study one of her marble pieces.

"Never seen you look prettier." Pop plucked at the sleeve of her dress, a swirl of watercolored silk. "'Cept maybe at your wedding."

"I wasn't nearly as scared then." She made a quick scan of the crowd and found only strangers. "Where's Katch?"

"Last time I saw him he was cornered by a couple of ritzy-looking people. Didn't I hear Jessica say you were supposed to mingle?"

"Yes." Megan made a small, frustrated sound. "I don't think I can move."

"Now, Meg, I've never known you to be chicken-hearted."

With her mouth half-opened in protest, she watched him walk away. *Chicken-hearted,* she repeated silently. Straightening her shoulders, she drank some champagne. All right then, she decided, she wouldn't stand there cowering in the corner. If she was going to be shot down, she'd face it head on. Moving slowly, and with determined confidence, Megan walked toward the buffet.

"You're the artist, aren't you?"

Megan turned to face a striking old woman in diamonds and black silk. "Yes," she said with a fractional lift of her chin. "I am."

"Hmmm." The woman took Megan in with a long, sweeping glance. "I noticed the study of the girl with the sand castle isn't for sale."

"No, it's my husband's." After two months, the words still brought the familiar warmth to her blood. *Katch, my husband.* Megan's eyes darted around the room to find him.

"A pity," the woman in black commented.

"I beg your pardon?"

"I said it's a pity—I wanted it."

"You—" Stunned, Megan stared at her. "You wanted it?"

"I've purchased 'The Lovers,'" she went on as Megan only gaped. "An excellent piece, but I want to commission you to do another sand castle. I'll contact you through Jessica."

"Yes, of course." *Commission?* Megan thought numbly as she automatically offered her hand. "Thank you," she added as the woman swept away.

"Miriam Tailor Marcus," a voice whispered beside her ear. "A tough nut to crack."

Megan half turned and grabbed Katch's arm. "Katch, that woman, she—"

"Miriam Tailor Marcus," he repeated and bent down to kiss her astonished mouth. "And I heard. I've just been modestly accepting compliments on my contribution to the art world." He touched the rim of his glass to hers. "Congratulations, love."

"They like my work?" she whispered.

"If you hadn't been so busy trying to be invisible, you'd know you're a smashing success. Walk around with me," he told her as he took her hand. "And look at all the little blue dots under your sculptures that mean SOLD."

"They're buying?" Megan gave a wondering laugh as she spotted sale after sale. "They're really buying them?"

"Jessica's frantically trying to keep up. Three people've tried to buy the alabaster piece she bought from you herself—at twice what you charged her. And if you don't talk to a couple of the art critics soon, she's going to go crazy."

"I can't believe it."

"Believe it." He brought Megan's hand to his lips. "I'm very proud of you, Meg."

Tears welled up, threatening to brim over. "I have to get out of here for a minute," she whispered. "Please."

Without a word, Katch maneuvered his way through the crowd, taking Megan into the storage room and shutting the door behind them.

"This is silly," she said immediately as the tears rolled freely down her cheeks. "I'm an idiot. I have everything I've ever dreamed of and I'm crying in the back room. I'd have handled failure better than this."

"Megan." With a soft laugh, he gathered her close. "I love you."

"It doesn't seem real," she said with a quaver in her voice. "Not just the showing…it's everything. I see your ring on my finger and I keep wondering when I'm going to wake up. I can't believe that—"

His mouth silenced her. With a low, melting sigh, she dissolved against him. Even after all the days of her marriage, and all the intimate nights, he could still turn her to putty with only his mouth. The tears vanished as her blood began to swim. Pulling him closer, she let her hands run up the sides of his face and into his hair.

"It's real," he murmured against her mouth. "Believe it." Tilting his head, he changed the angle of the kiss and took her deeper. "It's real every night when you're in my arms, and every morning when you wake there." Katch drew her away slowly, then kissed both her damp cheeks until her lashes fluttered up. "Tonight," he said with a smile, "I'm going to make love to the newest star in the New York art world. And when she's still riding high over the reviews in the morning papers, I'm going to make love to her all over again."

"How soon can we slip away?"

Laughing, he caught her close for a hard kiss. "Don't tempt me. Jessica'd skin us both if we didn't stay until the gallery closes tonight. Now, fix your face and go bask in the admiration for a while. It's good for the soul."

"Katch." Megan stopped him before he could open the door. "There's one piece I didn't put out tonight."

Curious, he lifted a brow. "Oh?"

"Yes, well…" A faint color rose to her cheeks. "I was afraid things might not go well, and I thought I could handle the criticism. But this piece—I knew I couldn't bear to have anyone say it was a poor attempt or amateurish."

Puzzled, he slipped his hands into his pockets. "Have I seen it?"

"No." She shook her head, tossing her bangs out of her eyes. "I'd wanted to give it to you as a wedding present, but everything happened so fast and it wasn't finished. After all," she added with a grin, "we were only engaged for three days."

"Two days longer than if you'd agreed to fly to Vegas," he pointed out. "All in all, I was very patient."

"Be that as it may, I didn't have time until later to finish it. Then I was so nervous about the showing that I couldn't give it to you." She took a deep breath. "I'd like you to have it now, tonight, while I'm feeling—really feeling like an artist."

"Is it here?"

Turning around, Megan reached up on the shelf where the bust was carefully covered in cloth. Wordlessly, she handed it to him. Katch removed the cloth, then stared down into his own face.

Megan had polished the wood very lightly, wanting it to carry that not-quite-civilized aura she perceived in the model. It had his cockiness, his confidence and the warmth the artist had sensed in him before the woman had. He stared at it for so long, she felt the nerves begin to play in her stomach again. Then he looked up, eyes dark, intense.

"Meg."

"I don't want to put it out on display," she said hurriedly. "It's too personal to me. There were times," she began as she took the bust from him and ran a thumb down a cheekbone, "when I was working on the clay model, that I wanted to smash it." With a half-laugh, she set it down on a small table. "I couldn't. When I started it, I told myself the only reason I kept thinking about you was because you had the sort of face I'd like to sculpt." She lifted her eyes then to find his fixed on hers. "I fell in love with you sitting in my studio, while my hands were forming your face." Stepping forward, Megan lifted her hands and traced her fingers over the planes and bones under his flesh. "I thought I couldn't love you more than I did then. I was wrong."

"Meg." Katch brought his hands to hers, pressing her palms to his lips. "You leave me speechless."

"Just love me."

"Always."

"That just might be long enough." Megan sighed as she rested her head against his shoulder. "And I think I'll be able to handle success knowing it."

Katch slipped an arm around her waist as he opened the door. "Let's go have some more champagne. It's a night for celebrations."

* * * * *

Nora Roberts
Unfinished Business

Nora Roberts
Mind Over Matter

Nora Roberts
Best Laid Plans

Nora Roberts
Summer with You

Nora Roberts
Lessons Learned

Nora Roberts
Snow is Falling

Nora Roberts
Loving Jack

Introducing Cordina's Royal Family...

450 million of her books in print worldwide

www.millsandboon.co.uk

CORDINAS